THE EPI
by And

THE EPIPHANY CLUB

First edition. September 4, 2018.

Written by Andrew Knighton.

Book 1: Guns and Guano

Prologue: Paris in the Spring

Dirk Dynamo sat outside a small café, watching the people of Paris go by. He didn't usually let himself sit idle like this. Life was short, and his time could be better spent improving himself. But he had to admit that, when he was forced to wait, there was a certain pleasure to these peaceful moments. Sure, the crowds might conceal men who wanted him dead. And sure, he was scanning them for signs of trouble, not simply letting the moment wash over him. But still, it was the most relaxed he'd been all week.

He smiled as a waitress appeared and refilled his cup. Coffee had been a rare treat during the Civil War, so now he made the most of it whenever he could. Just because he still wore his old blue trousers didn't mean he had to live like a soldier.

"Thank you, ma'am." He pulled a couple of coins from the leather jacket on the back of his chair. The waitress's eyes widened as she saw what the coat concealed. The custom-built Gravemaker was a hefty revolver by anyone's standards, powerful enough to stop a charging bison and worth many times more than Dirk's well worn clothes. But if it shocked the girl then she didn't show it.

"Can I get you anything else, monsieur?" She smiled at Dirk and tucked back a strand of hair, her gaze flitting across his muscular body.

"No thank you, ma'am," he replied. There was a time and place for chatting up waitresses, and this wasn't it.

As if on queue, Sir Timothy Blaze-Simms emerged from the crowd, clutching a briefcase to his narrow chest. He peered around him through wire-rimmed spectacles, as if this were some strange new world and not the familiar rendezvous they had agreed the day before.

Dirk leaned back, hand inching towards his holster. If their opponents were going to make a move, then it would come now.

"What ho, Dynamo!" Blaze-Simms sank into a wrought-iron seat.

"Tim," Dirk said with a nod. "You oversleep?"

"I'm afraid so," Blaze-Simms replied. "Am I terribly late?"

"You're buttoned up wrong."

The Englishman looked down at a tailcoat whose buttons were all through the wrong holes.

"I say, good spot." He put the case down and started redressing himself. "Was I followed?"

Dirk nodded again, still watching the crowd. Four men had appeared discreetly around the street, all wearing nondescript grey suits. Theirs was the stillness not of calm but of expectation, their expressions as flat and dull as a thousand other hired thugs the world over. And just like a thousand hired thugs the world over, Dirk was going to have to deal with them.

"Same guys who were tailing us last night." Dirk recognised one from the hotel lobby, another from the restaurant, a third from the street outside the museum. Of course, they were missing the four he'd tracked back to a cheap boarding house, and who were probably still struggling to escape their bonds.

"So what now?" Blaze-Simms nibbled at a croissant, dropping flakes of pastry down himself.

"Now they pounce."

"What makes you say that?"

"They change shifts every four hours. By now, these folks have realised that they ain't gonna be relieved."

A shot rang out, raising dust from the ground by Dirk's boot. The morning crowd turned into a whirl of screaming faces and running bodies, as innocent Parisians fled the sound of violence. Walking sticks and parasols were abandoned by their owners in the rush to get away. By the time the crowd cleared, all four grey-suited men had revolvers in their hands, the barrels pointing straight at Dirk.

Instinct took over and Dirk reached for his revolver. But that wasn't the plan.

He eased his hand back around and layed it flat on the table, ignoring the tension that hummed through his body.

"The Dane says hello," one of the men called out. "And that you won't be leaving Paris with those blueprints."

"Oh bother." Blaze-Simms put down his half-eaten croissant.

"You got the Gauss Generator?" Dirk murmured.

Blaze-Simms flung his case onto the table and flipped the lid. There was a high-pitched hum, followed a split second later by the sharp retort of gunshots. Suddenly the table was surrounded by bullets, hanging motionless in a crackling halo of light.

Dirk stared at the sparks dancing in the air. Whatever his faults, Blaze-Simms never failed to impress.

"Better act quickly," the Englishman said. "I don't know how long it can-"

Dirk vaulted the table and slammed into the first gunman with both feet. As they crashed to the ground he rolled and rose into a punch, knocking out the next guy.

A hail of cutlery flew from the café, tinkling like a wind-chime factory in a hurricane. As it hit the glowing web around Blaze-Simms it stopped, sparks crackling from each knife and fork as they hung vibrating in the air. The inventor gulped as smoke trickled from his case.

Dirk caught the second attacker's gun as it fell and swept a third man's legs out with a low kick. Still turning, he flung the pistol into the face of the last gunman. There was a crunch and the man sank to the ground, blood spurting from the ruin of his nose.

A halo of metal hung in the air, from butter knives to loose change to the thick disc of a manhole cover, all suspended in the glowing corona of the magnetic field. A steel bollard shook loose of its base and shot across the pavement trailing sparks. The aura flashed as it hit, then vanished. Cutlery clattered onto the cobbles and the bollard landed with a clang.

The case on the table burst into flames.

Dirk strolled back to the café, casually kicking one of the goons as he passed. He sat back down next to Blaze-Simms, who was beating out the fire with a copy of the Times.

"Mademoiselle?" Dirk said, waving over the nervous-looking waitress. "More coffee please, and some water for the fire."

Chapter 1: A Night at the Club

To the untrained observer, Manchester might look like nothing more than a mass of factories and tenements, a place of bustle, noise, and smoke. Here were the pounding pistons of British industry and the seething masses who operated them. Its grand public buildings, which gave such pride to the civic leaders, were surrounded by slums and draped in the constant pall of smog. No city had better embraced the soot-stained labour of the Victorian age.

But down one inconspicuous street, past the grimy bricks of the city centre, was a door to a very different world. Clean, sturdy and unremarkable, the door sat in a frame of smartly cut but unadorned stone. The boot scraper was worn and the bell pull forgettable. Only the finest architect would, after careful perusal, realise how deliberately mundane it all was.

Behind that door lay one of the most prestigious gentlemen's clubs in the country. Its well-stocked bar and brightly lit games room played host to many of the finest scholars and adventurers in the whole British Empire. On this particular Tuesday in April, it also held Dirk Dynamo.

The library of the Epiphany Club was long and narrow, with walkways accessing the higher shelves. Beneath them, piles of papers were scattered across desks, the Club's scholarly members having abandoned their research for tea. Thick velvet drapes creating a shroud of darkness at one end of the room, protecting the unique collection from the ageing effects of sunlight. Some of these books had survived centuries of use, and one of the Club's tasks was to preserve them for centuries more.

At the other end of the library, Dirk sat by a crackling fire. Its glow played across a Persian rug and the gilded chair he sat in, his wide shadow dancing by the flickering of the flames. A book on Russian history lay open in his lap, and he read it with interest while weight-lifting a bust of Julius Caesar.

The door creaked open and Professor Barrow entered, beaming at Dirk from behind his half-moon glasses. The Club's president was pushing seventy but healthily rotund, remnants of grey hair fringing the shining dome of his head. He smiled the smile of a well-travelled uncle, a smile that said he had seen many things but could think of none he would rather see than you.

Behind him came Blaze-Simms, his eyes never rising from the notebook in which he was scribbling away with a well-chewed stub of pencil.

Dirk set aside Caesar and the history of the Tsars, then rose to his feet.

"Professor Barrow," he said. "Good to see you, sir."

"And you, Mr Dynamo." The professor shook his hand. "It has been far too long."

"Dirk!" Blaze-Simms exclaimed, looking up in surprise. "How marvellous!"

"Tim," the American replied. "Ain't seen you since Paris. How you doin'?"

"Remarkably well. Yesterday, I developed a machine that uses electrical resistance to fill canapés. And the day before that, I was working on a new gun that I think..."

"Perhaps you could tell us about it later, Sir Timothy?" Barrow rested a hand gently but firmly on Blaze-Simms's shoulder. "Once we're done with this other business."

A figure in a black tailcoat and white gloves emerged from the shadows.

"Ah, Phillips," the Professor said. "Could you please fetch us some tea?"

"Very good, sir," the butler replied, gliding out of the room.

Barrow lowered himself with a creak into a chair.

"Damn things must be getting old," he said, glaring at the furniture.

"You said something about business?" Dynamo picked up the bust and flexing his arm once more. Some folks considered it obsessive, but he'd take every chance he could to better himself.

"Mm?" Barrow blinked uncertainly over the top of his glasses. "Oh, yes, the mission. Well, it's a treasure hunt, really. The committee decided to use you two again, after your success in Paris. If the Dane had got hold of the Blensberg Blueprints, no safe in the continent would have been, well, safe. But thanks to you, our mysterious friend is empty-handed again."

"We still don't know who he is?" Dirk asked.

"I'm afraid not. He's been playing his games for almost twenty years, stealing treasures and inventions from under our noses. But whether he's a collector or just a career criminal, we still have nothing on him but a codename."

The Professor sat scowling into the depths of the library, lost in his memories.

"So where are we off to this time?" Dirk asked. He was keen to get going on whatever the Club had to offer. This was a great place to learn, but he got itchy sitting around for too long.

"Mm?" Barrow wiggled a finger in his ear, then peered at Dirk across his glasses. "Sorry, something in the way. What were you saying, my boy?"

"I said, where are we going?"

"There's no need to shout. I'm not deaf, you know. In fact, these keen senses saw me through a number of scrapes when I was your age. I remember this one time in Egypt..."

And so began a rambling tale of desert adventure, filled with camels, pyramids, and a woman named Heidi who seemed to have been more than an assistant. There were cursed artefacts, daring chases and at least one ghost.

Dirk sat back with a grin and listened as the story unfolded. Barrow was always entertaining, even if his recollections became implausible with each passing year. They sounded like a jumble of half-remembered youth and fragments of dime-store novels. If even half of it was true, the professor had seen some damn strange things in his time.

Phillips reappeared, emerging from the shadows of the doorway, a laden tea-tray balanced on one hand. He leaned over and whispered in Barrow's ear.

"Oh, excellent," the professor said. "Bring her in."

Phillips vanished once more.

"The last of our little party is here," Barrow explained

The library door swung open, silhouetting a petite female figure.

The men rose in welcome as Barrow ushered her into the room. She was elegantly dressed in deep blues, her dark curls gathered above the nape of her neck.

"Sir Timothy Blaze-Simms, Mr Dirk Dynamo, might I introduce Mrs Isabelle McNair."

"Good to meet you, ma'am," Dirk said, offering his hand and his most welcoming smile.

"Mr Dynamo." She returned Dirk's firm handshake, brown eyes locked on his. "Surely that isn't a real surname, even in America?"

Dirk stood gaping, stuck for what to say. Somewhere inside him, the kid who had laboured in a dark Kentucky mine longed to have his story told. But that wasn't a story that Dirk often shared.

"I'm sorry." Even Isabelle McNair's frown was charming, without the stiff demeanour so many society ladies wore. "I was just teasing."

"No need to apologise." Dirk realised that her hand was still in his. He let it go. "And no, it ain't a real name, but it's the one I go by."

Blaze-Simms lowered his head and raised her delicately gloved fingers to his lips.

"Enchanted," he murmured.

"And they say chivalry is dead." She smiled warmly. "Professor, so good of you to invite me here. This place is an absolute delight."

"Do take a seat," Barrow said, sitting back down. "Now, where was I?"

"Egypt?" Dirk suggested, lowering himself into a chair.

"Archaeology?" Blaze-Simms enquired, leading Mrs. McNair to the sofa.

"Sugar?" she asked, reaching forwards to pour the tea.

"What? No, no, that's not the point at all." Barrow pulled a notebook from his pocket, mumbling to himself as he flicked through. The cheap, wrinkled pages were a perfect match for his age-rumpled skin. "Ah, yes." He looked up and smiled. "A mission most suited to our present setting. Gentlemen, Mrs McNair, I want you to find the lost Library of Alexandria."

Dirk and Timothy exchanged glances, wondering who should bring the old man back to reality. The Great Library was every scholar's dream, a home of texts from all over the ancient Mediterranean, many of them since lost to time. Works by the greatest minds of the classic world had filled its shelves. But it had been destroyed in the days of the Roman Empire, leaving only ashes and dreams of what might have been.

"That's an awful nice scheme, Professor," Dirk began, "but ain't there, well..."

"...practical difficulties," Timothy offered. "It has been lost for a terribly long time."

"And there might not be much to find, seein' as how it was burnt down."

"Perhaps some nice foundations, somewhere under the sand..."

They drifted into awkward silence, hiding behind their tea cups.

"Honestly, professor, you are awful." Mrs McNair helped herself to a macaroon. "Leaving these poor gentlemen dangling while you giggle to yourself. What would Mrs Barrow say?"

"She would say they shouldn't treat me as if I'm senile." The professor rose and approached one of the nearby shelves with slow, deliberate steps. He pulled down a small, leather-bound volume with a faded spine, returned to his seat and opened the book on the table by the tea-tray. The paper was dry and brittle, cracking at the edges, the print heavy and old-fashioned. The pages were too small for the cover in which they had been rebound, and which was itself now worn with age.

"Plutarch's 'Parallel Lives'," Barrow explained. "An alternative edition, lost until two years ago. Dicky Torrington-Smythe found it in the collection of a Scottish earl, while looking for old Shakespeare folios. He's determined to crack the bard's code before that Donnelly chap."

He turned a few pages, nodding and smiling to himself.

"The bard is always such a pleasure to read," he said. "Such verve, such poetry."

His smile widened as he scanned the ancient tome.

"You were sayin' something about Plutarch?" Dirk asked, eager to get them back to the point.

"What? Oh, yes." Professor Barrow looked up. "This volume contains an early edition of 'Pericles', but also some Plutarch. Most importantly for us, it contains his account of Caesar's burning of Alexandria. There's a section that isn't in the common text."

Dirk leaned forward. The print was archaic, the text certainly not English. He thought he could make out half the letters, but looking for familiar words mired him in confusion, a mass of lines dancing out of focus across the page. Timothy nodded and made soft, appreciative noises next to him, reminding Dirk of how much smarter the rest of the Club were compared with him.

"Someone gimme a clue here," he said. "What does any of it mean?"

"Short version," Timothy said, "all the books thought lost in the fire were carted off into the desert, hidden away in case of future danger. The chap who did it was a scholar, and he didn't trust the political types not to wreck everything again. So he kept the new location secret, only sharing it with other learned men. Men such as Plutarch."

"This tells us where to find it?"

A thrill ran through Dirk. The Library of Alexandria, its contents untouched for centuries. The untapped knowledge of antiquity's greatest minds, preserved somewhere beneath Egypt's shifting sands, and he would be there when it was revealed. Even after all these years of studying and listening to men like the Professor, some folks still treated him like an ignorant miner's son. That would change if he learned things no-one else on earth knew.

"Not exactly." Blaze-Simms took the book and flicked eagerly through. "Plutarch shared the scholar's concerns, so didn't write down the location. But there is a commentary at the back by an Arab scholar, ninth century I think. He claims that the location was encrypted on three stone tablets, in case it should be forgotten, but that..."

A hint of noise made Dirk look around, expecting to see Phillips approaching with fresh tea. No-one was there, but a movement caught his eye, a shifting of the darkness at the back of the room.

He stared at the shadows. Was it a rat? Maybe a loose page falling from a shelf?

"...third tablet was found in the Seine, according to this thirteenth century report, and handed to the royal family..." The professor had more books open and was expounding with the energy of a man half his age.

Another movement, in the recesses around a ceiling beam. A flutter of black, maybe the wing of a bat that had taken shelter here while it waited for night.

"...then there's this Venetian chronicle," Isabelle said, "which indicates the second was taken along the silk road..."

Dirk took a step away from the table, and another, watching the shadows that shifted with his viewpoint, watching more closely for those that didn't.

"...which was where Mrs. McNair found it earlier this year..."

There. A deeper shadow, like a black stain. And another, on the opposite side of the room, drifting towards them. The shadow of a man.

Dirk opened his mouth to raise the alarm.

Something flickered in the darkness. A bright, glittering point came hurtling towards him.

He flung himself aside.

Three razor-edged disks thudded into the armchair behind him.

Mrs McNair shouted as black-clad figures dropped soundlessly from the rafters, long straight blades extended. Dirk intercepted one, ducking beneath a sword and punching his opponent in the gut. He grabbed the man's weapon even before he fell, and rose to block the next blow. Steel clanged against steel.

As the attackers advanced, Mrs McNair picked up a poker to parry their blows. She ushered the professor out into the hallway, backing up after him with her weapon raised. Three assailants followed them from the room.

Blaze-Simms was fending off an attacker with a bust of Shakespeare. He blocked and lunged with a fencer's grace, but the statue gave him no reach. Slowly but surely, he was being worn down.

Dirk's opponent was fast and agile, attacks coming so quickly he barely had time to think, let alone take the offensive. He backed towards the fire, pulling an armchair between them. But the attacker somersaulted over it, blade extended.

Moving with frantic speed, Dirk parried one blow after another, sparks flashing from the oil-darkened blades. He knew he was out-matched. He could shoot pretty well and brawl with the best of them, but fencing wasn't his style.

In desperation, he flung his sword at his opponent's face. As the man batted it aside, Dirk leapt, slamming into him. They crashed to the ground, Dirk wrapping one arm around the black-clad figure while punching him. Fists beat hard against Dirk's back and he knew there'd be hell to pay. But he kept up the pressure, and at last his opponent fell limp.

"I say!" Blaze-Simms exclaimed, slithers of marble bard flying from the last attacker's blade.

Dirk hauled himself upright, strode over, and tapped the black-clad figure on the shoulder. As he turned, Dirk punched him straight in the face. He slumped to the ground.

"Jolly good show." Blaze-Simms dropped the remains of the statue and scooped up two abandoned blades. Passing one to Dirk, he nodded towards the door. "Shall we?"

Sounds of violence echoed down the hall. Dirk and Blaze-Simms dashed towards them, past maps and murals, stags' heads and statues, the souvenirs of the club's long and adventurous history.

They burst through the games room door and straight into a shower of white sparks. In the centre of the room, the hilt of an oriental sword protruded from an automated billiards table. Steam spewed and balls careened wildly as the table's broken workings ground against the embedded blade.

On the far side of the room, a black-clad attacker stood over the unconscious Professor Barrow. His blade menaced the unarmed club members in the opposite doorway, while one of his colleagues fought bare-handed against Lord Roger Harcourt-Phipps. In a corner, Isabelle McNair was backing away from the final assailant.

"The stone," Isabelle's attacker said. "Give it to us."

Dirk leapt feet first across the table, kicking Harcourt-Phipps's opponent before crashing into the man by the door. The club members cheered as the black-clad figure hit the ground, sword sliding away across polished floorboards.

The final attacker grabbed Mrs McNair and raised a sword to her throat.

"Don't move." The voice from beneath the black cloth was soft as silk.

Everybody froze.

"Drop your swords."

"There's really no need," Mrs McNair said. "I have this under control."

"Drop your swords!" the attacker said again.

Dirk and Blaze-Simms obeyed, their weapons clanging as they hit the floorboards.

The figure moved towards the corridor, dragging Mrs McNair with him. His movements were slow and steady, his eyes watchful behind the mask. Despite her situation, Mrs McNair was equally calm, treating the room to a relaxed smile.

"How do you intend to get me out of here?" she asked. "I won't come quietly."

"I will knock you out." He raised his sword, pommel above her head.

Mrs McNair twisted from his grip and pushed him back into the corridor.

"Now!" she snapped.

There was a clang. The attacker staggered, but before the others could act he shook himself, turned, and raced away down the corridor.

Phillips stood in the doorway, gazing sadly at a head-shaped dent in his tea-tray.

"Thank you, Phillips." Mrs McNair smiled. "I knew I could count on you."

"I do apologise, sir," the butler said as Dirk stared down the empty corridor. "Household silverware is never as effective as a good cosh."

"Don't worry." Dirk grinned. "A cosh ain't flat enough to serve sandwiches. And we got most of..."

His mouth hung open as he looked back into the room. The black-clad bodies were gone, and with them any chance to question their attackers. Whoever they had been, whatever their reasons for attacking the club, they'd gotten clean away.

#

The library was more brightly lit than before, the fire stoked high, gas lamps banishing every last shadow. A thorough search of the club had found no lingering intruders, but no-one was taking chances. Dirk sat with a fire iron in his lap, his gaze roaming the room for any lingering threats. Last time, he'd left things too long before raising the alarm. He wouldn't make that mistake again.

Professor Barrow clutched a cold, damp cloth to the back of his head.

"The Epiphany Club hasn't been infiltrated in over sixty years," he said. "I suppose it is to our credit that, when it happened, it was ninjas."

Seeing Dirk's blank face he continued. "Japanese assassins. Reputedly among the deadliest warriors on earth."

He took a sip of tea and looked at Blaze-Simms, who was squinting through a magnifying glass at a stone tablet.

It was about a foot long and half that wide, covered in letters that Dirk could make no sense of.

"What do make you of it, my boy?" Barrow asked.

"It's part of a set of directions." Blaze-Simms didn't look up, but pulled a notebook from his pocket and started scribbling with a stub of pencil. "Early Arabic, which fits. Not a lot of sense in itself, but if we can find the others..."

"This is one of those stones to lead us to the library?" Dirk asked.

"That's right." Mrs McNair sipped her tea, a spark of excitement in her eyes. "Imagine it. All that knowledge, lost to humanity for centuries, and it could be ours. It's enough to give one quite a thrill, isn't it?"

"Where'd you get it from, Mrs McNair?" Dirk said.

"Please, we've fought ninjas together, you can call me Isabelle." She set her cup aside. "My husband inherited the stone from another missionary. A man named Davidson who had bought it from a Cairo junk dealer. Apparently it came there by way of the Orient, although more than that I don't know. The Reverend Davidson was an enthusiastic antiquarian, but not always very thorough."

"No hope of findin' the other two in his collection, huh?"

"I'm afraid not. But I've been looking into this for the past year, and I have a lead on the next one. Supposedly lost in a shipwreck off an obscure African island, and lying at the bottom of the ocean. The island's a British colony, but the Governor has a reputation for liking the quiet life, and has blocked archaeological expeditions in the past. That means I need help from a private organisation, one that can help me retrieve the stone quietly."

"And quickly." Barrow looked at them all with great seriousness. "If word has got out about something this valuable, then you can be sure that the Dane will be looking to get his larcenous hands on it."

"What makes you think anyone else knows about this?" Blaze-Simms looked up from his scribblings.

"Because the day we brought this stone to the Club, someone attacked us." Barrow frowned into his tea. "It can be no coincidence. Knowledge is worth more than gold, and some people will kill for tin."

Dirk grinned. Lost treasures, unknown enemies, forgotten islands, adventures across land and sea - now they were talking his language. And at the end of it all, intellectual wealth beyond imagining.

He reached out for a tea-cup and raised it in a toast. "Great Library, here we come."

Chapter 2: Welcome to Hakon

The pier was made of salvaged planks bleached by the tropical sun. It creaked beneath Dirk's feet as he stepped from the St Mary's gangplank, leaving behind the comfortable shade of the yacht. They seemed to have sailed into the ghost of an inlet, pale sand stretching back to white cliffs, topped off by a lighthouse. The scrubby bushes at the base of the cliffs were the sickly yellow of old sheets.

A procession emerged out of this ethereal scene - half a dozen men dressed only in trousers and shoes, none shorter than six feet tall, their skin a deep brown. They prowled along the pier, sticks swinging loose and ready in their hands, muscular chests shining in the tropical heat.

Dirk turned to face them, his hand settling on the butt of his Gravemaker pistol. The only sounds were the caw of gulls and the pad of their footfalls. He tensed, ready to draw.

Was it his imagination, or did one of the men roll his eyes at the sight?

A dozen feet away the men stopped and split into two columns, standing solemnly at the sides of the pier. Another figure strode through the gap.

"I say, are you Mister Dynamo?"

The man was short and rotund, immaculately dressed in a linen suit and Panama hat. Pink cheeked and freckled, his ginger moustache wriggled into a welcoming smile.

"Reginald Cullen, Her Majesty's Governor of Hakon."

He switched his ivory handled stick to his left hand and reached out with the right, delivering a hearty handshake.

"Dirk Dynamo. Pleased to meet you." Dirk turned to gesture at the figure now descending from the boat. "This is Timothy Blaze-Simms. Tim, this is Governor Cullen."

"A pleasure to meet you, sir." Blaze-Simms set aside a box of instruments and shook hands.

"The pleasure's all mine, Sir Timothy. Might I ask how your brother is doing?"

"Arthur? He's very well. Just back from a posting in India."

"We were in the second team at Eton together, don't you know."

"I say, how splendid! You'll have to tell me the truth behind Arty's tales of sporting glory."

Dirk coughed and gestured again towards the plank.

"And this is-" he began.

"Mrs McNair!" Cullen exclaimed. "What an unexpected pleasure."

"Reginald." Isabelle smiled and offered her hand. "How sweet of you to meet us."

She hooked one arm through that of the Governor and began strolling towards the shore, blue skirts swirling, chattering about shared friends and acquaintances. Blaze-Simms ambled behind, joining in with the gossip and laughter, leaving Dirk with the silent islanders.

"Guess I'd better get the bags."

Cullen's entourage were ahead of him, picking up the luggage he'd fetched off the boat. Dirk tried to grab a couple of bags, to stop this turning into the old familiar pattern of black men labouring in the service of whites. But the bags had all been taken up.

"Let me get some of those," he said.

One of the men gave him a serious look and shook his head.

"No, sir," he said. "That's our job."

#

A buggy was waiting at the shore, drawn by a pair of chalk-white horses. A young woman sat in the coachman's place, her yellow robes providing a bright contrast with her skin. She cracked the reins and they shot off, over the beach and up a track running diagonally across the cliff-face. Gulls scattered as they passed, soaring and croaking to each other, returning to their perches once the buggy had passed.

"The rocks themselves aren't white, of course." Cullen clutched his hat as they sped around a tight corner. "It's the gulls that do it. Only a little of their leavings sticks to the steep cliffs here on Hakon. But Kerelm, the next island over, is absolutely thick in the stuff. Some of our chaps spend months over there, mining for British Guano Incorporated."

"So the whole island's covered in..." Just in time, Dirk remembered there were ladies present.

"Absolutely. Wonderful stuff, it's reviving the local economy. Where there's muck there's gold, as Braithwaite keeps saying."

"There's gold in the gull goo?"

"Not literally, old chap." Cullen smiled the cosy smile of a man repeating an old joke. "But there's a huge market for it as a fertiliser, and even in experimental explosives. They make a fortune selling it back home. Some say the African stuff isn't as good as the Chilean birds produce, but Braithwaite – he's British Guano's chap out here – he says that's poppycock. And isn't it far more patriotic to buy British?"

White coated rocks glared at them from all around. It seemed incredible to Dirk that something so common could really be worth so much.

"How do you know it works?" he asked.

"Because of this..."

They crested the rise and a blaze of greenery opened up before them. Groves of oranges and mangoes. Fields of beans and golden grain. Acre after acre of farmland carved from the thin soil of a rocky land. And beyond that, lush jungle, swaying up the side of the island's mountain heart.

Dark faces looked up from the fields as the buggy rattled past. The labourers' clothes were worn but not ragged, the mark of poor but careful people. A few smiled and waved at the travellers. Blaze-Simms waved back with his top hat, grinning and gazing around.

Dirk shifted uncomfortably in his seat. Just like back home, slavery might be gone but racial divisions remained. He'd taken up arms to make men free, but freedom alone was never enough.

"What sort of crop rotations do you use?" Blaze-Simms asked excitedly.

"Rather outside my area of expertise, I'm afraid." Cullen scratched his head. "You can ask one of the estate managers at the reception this evening."

"There's to be a party?" Isabelle smiled. "How splendid."

#

Gravel crunched beneath their feet as they stepped from the buggy onto the driveway of the governor's mansion. The main building was three storeys of white-washed wood, with servants' quarters and kitchens sprawling off the back. Framed by the jungle and a mountain beyond, it seemed a lone artefact of humanity amid nature's vast expanse. Balconies and wide windows looked out through open storm shutters across flowering gardens and a croquet lawn whose restrained greenery was in marked contrast to the wild jungle canopy.

Dirk strode up creaking steps onto a sheltered porch. A servant in a tailcoat opened double doors, allowing them into an entrance hall that could have held a regiment. The space was bright and airy, lit by wide windows and a glass ceiling high above. To the left of the door hung an oil painting of a French country scene, trees and walkers fanning out along a still river. On a pedestal to the right stood a curious sculpture, a metal man twelve inches high, oblong face gazed disdainfully from beneath a wide hat, cold fingers clutching crude steel swords.

"I say, this is rather splendid." Timothy had stopped before the statue, head darting from side to side as he took in its every angle. "Dahomeyan?"

"That's right," Cullen said. "Many of the locals have ties with the kingdom, and I like to think that I've built a good working relationship. King Glele sent that piece as a gift last summer. Apparently it's some sort of war god. They built him to celebrate a victory over their neighbours."

"Aren't the Dahomey absolutely beastly to people they defeat?" There was a hint of shock in Isabelle's voice.

"I'm afraid they all are on the mainland." Cullen played thoughtfully with the tip of his moustache. "Dahomey, Oyo, Sokoto, all these little African kingdoms with their pot-bellied tyrants and their bloodthirsty goons. But I rather feel that, if we are to bring civilisation to these poor people, that can be done better with an open ear and a whispered word than by shouting at them every time they fight. The white man's burden is a heavy one, but we must bear it with grace."

Dirk gritted his teeth. He had to remember, these were old ways of thinking, habits it took men a long time to break. Passing judgement wouldn't help them get the governor's help.

With a sudden hiss the statue turned, raising its arms. Steam erupted from beneath its hat as it leaped from the pedestal and marched toward Isabelle. Dirk moved to intercept, but Isabelle had the situation under control. She flung her shawl across the machine, grabbed the ends, and scooped it up in a tangle of cloth. Miniature blades protruded through town cotton, but the arms were pinned tight and the legs waggled ineffectually in the air.

Dirk stood, holding out his jacket to do, and realised he was completely redundant.

"Much as I appreciate the gesture," Isabelle said, "I don't need rescuing from toy soldiers."

Heat rose in Dirk's cheeks.

"I just figured-" His mumbled words were cut short by a final spray of steam. The statue fell still.

"Dash it all." Cullen peered at the metal man. "That was meant to be a surprise for the party. You haven't bent the arms, have you?"

"I'm sure it will be fine," Isabelle said, returning the statue to its pedestal

They followed the governor towards the stairs. Other works of art lined the hall, some European, some local. The perfectly polished floor reflected doorways as dark pools on its gleaming surface.

The room smelled of stale cigar smoke and expensive perfume, the scents of petty power. Dirk half-expected his feet to shoot out beneath him on the mirror-smooth boards. This building was a statement, not a home.

"I say," Blaze-Simms exclaimed as they were led up to their rooms. "Isn't this whole place marvellous?"

Dirk glanced back down the stairs at the native servants dragging their baggage into the hall.

"Yep," he said bitterly, "it's real special."

#

Night was falling when Dirk returned to the hall, suited and booted, ready to face the evening reception. For such an isolated island, Hakon had a surprising number of foreign guests.

"Tis the guano that does it." George Braithwaite, a tall Yorkshireman with a beard like a bramble, knocked his wine back before continuing. "All sorts of folks want in these days. We even sell to the French."

A tray appeared at Braithwaite's shoulder, supported by a straight-laced servant in bowtie and tails. Being waited on like this was something Dirk had never got a liking for. It felt doubly awkward when the servants were the only black faces in the room.

"Ta." The British Guano manager switched glasses and continued. "Yon fellow in the yellow jacket, he's from some fancy French farming consortium. Those great muscle-bound fellows are meant to be his secretaries, but if they take minutes I'm the Queen of Sheba. The little fellow in the robes is Chinese, of course. Don't trust 'im myself, shifty eyes, but his missus is pretty as a picture. Then there's Simpson..."

Dirk nodded and smiled as Braithwaite gave a verbal tour of the room, picking over the dregs of each guest's habits and reputation. He seemed to have picked Dirk out as a kindred spirit, a good sort to keep company with.

While Braithwaite talked, Dirk took the time to absorb his surroundings. Upwards of seventy guests were milling around the hall, a half dozen native waiters drifting between them with placid assurance. He noticed the Chinese woman watching Blaze-Simms, then hastily looking away when she caught Dirk's eye.

The room was lit by scores of candles, fixed to brackets on the walls or reaching up from iron stands in the centre of the room. Sculptures threw long shadows across the floor, their edges blurring with the flicker of flames. Beside Dirk, the silhouette of the warrior statue stretched across the threshold, his blades guarding against intruders from the outer dark. The doors had been fastened wide, allowing fresh night air into the house. The scent of jungle flowers and the chirp of crickets flooded in, the African wild mingling with the bustle, chatter and clinking glasses of a very European evening's entertainment.

Undercover work was always tense, and undercover work was what this boiled down to. Isabelle had insisted that they maintain the image of tourists, just curious about this out-of-the-way island. Blend in. Keep people happy. Look for any clues about where the wreck might be. Dirk had done his share of undercover work for the Pinkerton Agency both during and after the war. But that had mostly been on the streets and carrying a gun. A mansion and a champagne glass were a very different matter.

"Cracking canapes," Blaze-Simms said, wandering up with Isabelle on his arm. He brushed absently at the crumbs on his lapel, then reached out a hand to Braithwaite. "Sir Timothy Blaze-Simms, at your service."

"Pleased to meet you. I'm George Braithwaite."

"And this is Mrs Isabelle McNair."

"Think we've met," Braithwaite said. "Some London do."

"The African Importers' Ball." Isabelle beamed, and Braithwaite came as close to cheerful as he'd looked all evening. "Perhaps we could find some champagne and you could finish telling me about puffin guano."

She took his arm and sailed off into the crowd, red velvet skirts swirling, nodding and smiling as he enthused at her about the merits of exotic bird waste.

Dirk breathed a sigh of relief. A man could only take so much gossip and guano.

"Come on," Blaze-Simms said, snatching a glass of wine from a passing waiter. "I'm sure it's not that bad."

Dirk shifted uncomfortably in his dinner suit. He'd never enjoyed dressing up smart, not even when it was an army uniform. He didn't own a black tie outfit, and wouldn't have brought it if he did. The servants had found an old suit that just about fit him, but the shoes pinched his feet, and he didn't dare breathe deeply for fear of bursting buttons across the room.

Blaze-Simms, on the other hand, looked at home in both clothes and surroundings. His suit fitted him like skin and there were enough people in any conversation to hide his occasional mental absences.

"I'll say this for Cullen," Blaze-Simms said, sipping his drink. "He doesn't let a remote posting get in the way of a party."

Dirk nodded. He didn't know much about parties, but this one seemed to be a success. A selection of wines and spirits were circulating the room in elegant glasses, accompanied by small pastries in the French style. The waiters, all locals, wore immaculate black tie, not a bead of perspiration showing on their straight faces. They stepped anonymously through the room, taking orders and collecting glasses. The host also roamed the floor, making introductions, cracking jokes, finding the connections necessary to spark conversations. Ever present at his shoulder, striking in a yellow and blue dress of African design, was the woman who had driven the cart earlier, staring at the world with a sternness that would have taken the jollity out of any lesser man.

"Ain't that a funny thing though?" Dirk said. "Such a sociable guy, working out here, miles from society."

It was hard not to like the governor, despite some of the things he said. He was so cheerful, so eager to please. That attitude seemed out of place on an isolated island with all the worst trappings of colonialism. Unless it was all a cover, and Dirk just couldn't admit that anyone would smile while oppressing his fellow man.

"Comes with the career." Timothy waved a hand, absently sloshing white wine over his sleeve. "Chap does a year or two in some quaint backwater, shows he can take the responsibility, gets moved on to somewhere a bit more civilised."

"Listen to Cullen talk." Dirk noticed the unease lying behind his own words. "He's been here more than a year or two."

"Maybe he likes the place."

"Maybe he likes the women."

"I say, Dynamo, there's no call for that sort of..."

"Relax. I'm messing with you." Dirk turned and guided his colleague to one of the governor's objets d'art, a painting of tangled pink and brown bodies against a background of swirling blue and grey. "I've been staring at this thing half the damn evening, trying to fathom it out. What do you make of it?"

"I suspect it is the work of a local artist." Blaze-Simms peered at the painting. "Note the distinctive proportions of the figures and the formalised facial expressions. The abstracted scene indicates the influence of French impressionist work, an attempt to use foreign methods to depict native experiences, encapsulating the moment of exposure to the alien. Note the intertwining of African and European bodies, reflecting the coming together of the fates of two continents."

"I note that the white guys are on top."

"Oh yes, so they are."

Blaze-Simms's casual tone showed how little Dirk's point had sunk in. Folks like Blaze-Simms were so used to the top of the tree that they never thought about what lay amid the roots.

"What do you make of that thing down the bottom?" Dirk asked.

"Very dynamic brushwork. Probably a burnt umber pigment."

"What does it represent?" Dirk had once read a teaching manual. It said folks learnt more by drawing their own conclusions. Moments like this made him doubt it, but he soldiered on.

"Oh, well, it's rather angular, lots of straight lines, so something man made. Brown could be soil or wood, probably the latter, and the background colours fit a maritime context, which combined with the curved lower lines implies a boat or ship. The lines become disjointed in the centre, as by some sort of rupture – clearly the ship is broken."

"Which would make this a painting of...?"

"A shipwreck, of course."

There was a pause, Blaze-Simms smiling indulgently. Then his jaw dropped and his eyebrows shot up.

"You think it's the wreck our stone was lost in?"

"Well, it doesn't have a label saying '1733' or 'lost treasure here', but how many wrecks do you reckon there have been around these parts?"

"Let's find out."

Cullen was talking with the Chinaman, his lively demeanour restrained to suit his guest. The governor's amazon companion stood motionless opposite the Chinaman's diminutive wife, their eyes locked, frozen glares filling the air between them.

Dirk waited for Cullen to excuse himself, then waved him over.

"Gentlemen! I trust you're enjoying our little soirée?" Cullen's face was lit by a jovial grin.

"Splendid."

"Mighty fine, thank you."

"I don't believe I made proper introductions earlier." Cullen turned to his female companion. "Sir Timothy Blaze-Simms, Mr Dirk Dynamo, this is Bekoe-Kumi of the ahosi."

"Pleased to meet you, ma'am," Dirk said.

"Delighted," Blaze-Simms added.

Bekoe-Kumi nodded silently. In a place like this, Dirk could understand anyone getting a little reserved.

"Tell me, is ahosi your tribe?" Timothy flashed his most winning smile, to no response. "I don't believe I've heard the term before."

"It means that I am a bride of the King of Dahomey," Bekoe-Kumi replied.

"Gosh, royalty eh?" Blaze-Simms raised his eyebrows. "Does the king have many wives?"

"Enough to crush the Yoruba and send them whimpering like dogs."

"Must make family parties terribly crowded."

If Bekoe-Kumi was royalty then she'd be comfortable in high society. Her stiffness probably reflected a different feeling from Dirk's discomfort, a disdain for others he had seen far too often in his life.

"Governor Cullen," Dirk said. "Could you tell me about this painting?"

"Of course, old chap." Cullen turned with a smile toward the picture. "It was painted by Felipe, one of the local lads. Frightfully pleasant young man from a good churchgoing family. Our minister, back when we had one, encouraged him to take an interest in culture. Turned out he was rather gifted. He's even had some sales in the more excitable European galleries."

"And this painting?" Dirk asked.

"Based on a local legend. A slave ship went down outside the bay, near Reinhart's Spur, sometime in the 1730s I believe. All aboard were lost, terrible tragedy, but of course that whole period was pretty ghastly. Fellows dragged off in chains, worked to the bone in plantations in the Americas. Thank God even your lot have stopped that business now."

"Every nation has its shame," Dirk replied.

Down memory's long trail he saw soldiers in grey marched toward him as he stood, hands bloody, in the thin blue line. He remembered a summer's day on a small, round hill, the crackle of gunfire and wet thud of bayonets into flesh, the ache of his arms and the sudden flash of pain. He tilted his head to one side, felt damaged muscles twinge.

"The locals have rather clung onto the story of this sinking," Cullen continued. "They believe that the spirits of the slaves, still shackled to the ship as it went down, were unable to leave this world. They haunt the vessel, trapped in the suffering and fear that were their lot in life and death. So powerful is their loss that they draw others to them, the ghosts of drowned slaves from all over the Atlantic. Men, women and children, victims of that terrible trade. Those who died trying to escape. Others who were thrown overboard for expediency's sake. Now they supposedly gather at our wreck, a sort of alumni reunion for the departed, rattling their ethereal chains and talking about the bad old days."

"I say," Blaze-Simms said, "that sounds rather like-"

"Fine story, governor," Dirk interjected. He shouldn't let Blaze-Simms get carried away when other folks were after the same treasure as them. "I bet this island has plenty more like it."

"Oh yes," Cullen said. "They say it was first settled by a man named Nahweni, who arrived by accident after getting drunk on fermented mango juice and falling asleep on his raft. He woke up just down the coast from here, on the beach now known as Coconut Cove. Of course, he couldn't settle the place alone..."

Cullen started into an account of the island's early history, prior to its days as a slave staging post. It was a rich mix of the deeply implausible and the all too likely, mingling tales of talking animals and angry hills with those of petty tyrants and unfaithful husbands. Before he reached the arrival of Europeans, he was interrupted by an eager young man who wanted to know about the next day's hunting. The two of them headed off to one side, leaving Bekoe-Kumi to entertain the governor's guests.

"You bring much baggage," she said sternly.

"Mostly scientific equipment," Blaze-Simms said. "I promised a chap at the Royal Society that I'd take some weather recordings and soil samples. And then there's the diving clobber, that's most of the heavy stuff."

"You go diving?" Her stare was like her body, fierce and unwavering.

"Oh yes, of course," Blaze-Simms said before Dirk could stop him.

"You stay away from the wreck."

So much for secrecy. Dirk let out a sigh, then looked around for a waiter who might fetch him a drink..

"Oh, I'm not worried about ghost stories," Blaze-Simms said, smiling. "This is the age of science, I consider myself very safe from the unprovable."

Bekoe-Kumi stepped closer. "I am not asking. I am telling."

"What?" Blaze-Simms blinked.

"The wreck is a special place. If you go there people will be angry." She flexed the muscles of her well-formed arms. "I will be angry."

Blaze-Simms backed away, bumping up against a wall. "Well, I'm sure we can..."

"You do not want me angry."

They were so close now that their faces almost touched. She took the glass from his hand, squeezing it between finger and thumb. It frosted with cracks, then exploded, showering them both in flashing points of crystallised light. Other guests made a great show of not staring, even as their glances flicked toward the confrontation.

Enough was enough. Dirk hadn't wanted to argue with his hosts, but there was a limit.

"No need for things to get unpleasant," he said, stepping between Bekoe-Kumi and Blaze-Simms. "We ain't here to make trouble for anyone, are we Tim?"

"On no," Blaze-Simms said. "We just want to-"

"We just want to take in the sights," Dirk said. "Then we'll be on our way."

He snatched an empty tray from a passing waiter, bent it casually in half and held up the twisted results in front of Bekoe-Kumi.

"No need for trouble," he said.

She fixed Dirk with a dark stare, then turned on her heel and strode away.

"What a strange girl." Blaze-Simms said. He frowned at the broken glass, then brightened, turning to Dirk with a grin. "Good thing it was such awful wine. Do you fancy a brandy?"

Chapter 3: Honoured Guests

Fresh night air greeted Dirk as he slipped unseen onto the veranda. For all his bulk, he'd gotten good at getting in and out of places unnoticed, making the most of distractions and darkened doorways. Plenty of villains had learned the hard way that Dirk Dynamo was more than just muscle for hire.

With a sense of relief, he strolled away from the light and chatter, meandering along the front of the house. He struck a match against the wall and lit a cigar, closing his eyes to relish the moment. He could hear the buzz of insects and the cry of a wounded beast in the jungle, but the only company close enough to impose its presence was the guests' horses, most still in harness to their carriages, stamping their feet and snorting to each other on the drive.

The horses, like their owners, had a party laid on for them, with water troughs and feed bags all around. They chomped and slurped and sniffed at each other while the drivers smoked and played cards.

Still relishing the rich taste of tobacco, Dirk stepped off the veranda and down onto the gravel, approaching the nearest horse with an outstretched hand. Her nostrils fluttered and she nuzzled up against his palm, whiskers tickling his hand as she sought a sugar lump that wasn't there.

"Sorry, ma'am." Dirk patted her head and stroked the rough hair of her mane. "Maybe next time."

After the bustle of the party, the horse was soothing company. The openness of an animal's motives made a nice change from people's schemes and subtleties, while the rise and fall of her warm flank beneath his hand brought back happy memories. He thought of the western plains at night, the same stars shining on them as looked down on him now. Nothing but a man and his mount, in a world of potential stretching to the horizon.

Dirk left his new friend and carried on around the side of the building, happily puffing away at his cigar. The shoes still pinched, but at least he could loosen his collar now and let the bow tie hang free. He started going over the things he'd been told about the governor's art, repeating everything three times, fixing facts to memory. Some folks, like Blaze-Simms, could just hear a thing and comprehend it, but it didn't come so easy to Dirk. He had to work to make himself even half as smart as his friend.

The drive swept around to the back of the mansion's main building. The pole star hung low over a wide dusty yard. Beyond it, a barn-like building was connected to the residence by the servants' quarters. The bottom floor looked to be stables, dark and empty. Above that, light crept through the cracks in two storeys of shuttered windows, narrow beams stabbing across rough timber walls. Faint rumbling and clacking sounds drifted into the night.

Glancing up, Dirk noticed that there were no lit windows on this side of the house. In fact, barely any windows at all. Something here wasn't quite right. And why were the stables empty while the horses were kept out on the drive?

Dropping his cigar, he ground the butt beneath his heel. Habit took hold as he started taking soft steps, reducing the crunch of his feet on gravel. Sticking to the deep shadows of the house he sidled around the yard, past the noise and smells spilling from the kitchen doorway, along the wall of the servants' quarters and up to a small door in the side of the barn.

He tried the latch but the door had been barred from the inside. The same with all the other doors of the barn, except those leading into the dead end of the stables. But a row of windows was open on the top floor, letting acrid smells and wafts of steam out into the night.

It seemed like someone wanted to hide what was going on here, and that just made him more curious.

Dirk glanced around. No-one was nearby. He took two sharp steps and sprang upwards, grasping the ledge of a window. Arms straining, he hauled himself upwards, levering his elbows onto the narrow ledge. He shifted all his weight onto one arm, swaying pendulum-like, his feet scraping against the wall below. The other arm shot up, grabbing the top of the window frame. He swung and, with a heave and a grunt, flung himself through the open gap of the window.

Dirk landed in a crouch and paused, gazing into the shadows that surrounded him. His eyes quickly adjusted to the deeper dark out of moonlight's reach, revealing a large room, hollow as a warehouse, filled with the angular shadows of crates and strange machines. Voices filtered through from the floor above, backed by a rumble of machinery. The room smelt dusty, but it was a sharp dust that burned at the senses.

Curiosity was turning into suspicion. This all seemed very industrial, more like a factory than a governor's mansion.

Hitching up the leg of his pants, Dirk pulled a sturdy knife from the sheath strapped to his ankle. It was a moment's work to slide the blade beneath the lid of one of the crates and crack it open. He scooped up a heap of powder and held it close to his face. Not all explosives smelled the same, but he knew the odours that went into them. He wasn't going to try lighting a match around this stuff.

Replacing the lid, he hammered the nails back in with his knife. Then he put another, smaller crate on top and climbed up to peer through a hole in the floorboards above.

The view wasn't great, but there was enough light for Dirk to make out pistons hammering back and forth. He glimpsed a barrel as someone rolled it across the hole and heard people talking in a language he didn't know. With his hand against the boards, he could feel the machines shaking the floor.

There was a hell of a lot more going on in Hakon than just plantations and a shipwreck.

Taking care not to make any noise, Dirk climbed down and put the crates back where he'd found them. Splinters of light emerged around a doorway at the end of the room. He crept forward and pressed his eye against the crack.

A short, round woman stood in a stairwell, lit by gas lamps that burned with a green corona. She wore a servant's dress of plain brown cotton a shade lighter than her skin, her hair bundled in a yellow scarf. She tapped impatiently against the wall with fingers stained chalky white.

There was a clatter of footsteps on the stairs and Cullen rose into view, ginger moustache twitching as he huffed and puffed.

"Sorry, Omalara, sorry," he muttered, leaning forward to catch his breath. "Had trouble getting away. That McNair woman was following me all over the place. Can't decide if she's a charming conversationalist or just damned nosey."

The woman folded her arms and fixed him with a stare.

"Omalara said no good would come of this," she said. "But would you listen to her? No. You got to have your white man guests and your big party. Now the vats going wild with only Omalara and her daughter to fix them, 'cause you got her boys dressed up and serving drinks."

"It is important that we keep up appearances." Cullen's expression was that of a naughty schoolboy, making excuses for talking in the back of class. "I know you don't like it, but if something is wrong, if suspicions are roused, everything we've built could come tumbling down."

"If something is wrong?" Her glare could have withered the strongest of men, and Cullen was no Hercules. "Like maybe you have a party like you never done before."

"I've never had such prestigious guests at the mansion before. The Blaze-Simms name alone is enough to open doors, and the Epiphany Club have a certain bohemian glamour among the adventurous sorts. Etiquette dictates..."

"Etiquette don't dictate round here, boy. That English talk."

"And this is an English colony. If word of what we are doing gets back to the Colonial Office then they'll send soldiers to prove that the sharp way."

Cullen stopped his rising voice and slapped a shocked hand over his mouth. Silence reigned for a long minute.

"You right," Omalara said at last. "And it better to give your white folks some distraction, so they don't go poking where they shouldn't. You keep them distracted, take them hunting, away from house and farms. Give me time to think."

"Of course." Cullen stooped and kissed the serving woman's hand before retreating down the stairs.

Omalara turned. For a moment, her eyes seemed to pierce the door and fix on Dirk. He tensed, certain despite all evidence that he was found out. His body strained, ready to flee the intensity of her gaze.

Omalara stepped towards him, one hand stretched out. She grabbed the bannister and walked past, up the stairs to the right of the door. Footfalls padded up and away, leaving Dirk watching an empty stairwell, breathing a deep sigh of relief.

#

He found Blaze-Simms in the trophy room, beneath the glassy gaze of a dozen stuffed animals. A cluster of party-goers were crowded around, watching as he constructed a steam engine from an oil lamp, half a bottle of claret, and a napkin.

"But what is its purpose?" Cullen's oriental guest was peering at the starched, folded cloth spinning above the open neck of the bottle.

"To power factories." Blaze-Simms waved his hands around excitedly. "By connecting such a turbine to a drive shaft, one can more efficiently transform the chemical energy of coal or wood into the kinetic energy required by modern industry."

"You power your factories with napkins?" The guest looked even more confused.

"Gosh no, even the finest starch wouldn't stop them flopping when enlarged to an efficient scale. One would use steel instead."

With a flourish, Blaze-Simms set a folded napkin on top of the bottle, drawing applause as it started to spin, moving faster and faster in the hot air.

"Factories use this now, yes?" A French lilt inflected the question. A pale man in a yellow jacket peered up at Blaze-Simms whilst pointing at the improvised engine.

"The principles are the same, but a blade of this design would increase productivity by thirty to forty percent." Blaze-Simms grabbed a bottle from a passing waiter, tipped its contents into the Frenchman's glass, and knocked the bottom out with a sharp tap on the table. "If I introduce an extra funnel, and a suitable source of smoke, you will be able to witness the critical difference in air flows..."

Oblivious to the broken glass now littering the table and the nervous looks of his audience, Blaze-Simms began rebuilding his device, constantly talking about its design. The Frenchman and the Chinaman remained among the attentive crowd, while the former's bodyguards and the latter's wife stood quietly by, their faces the blank slates of the professionally patient. When the bodyguards looked around at all it was to watch Blaze-Simms's antics, a hint of a sneer on their lips.

Sidling out of the trophy room and into the main hall, Dirk let his body drift through the buzz of laughter and perfume while his mind lingered on what he had seen in the out-building. It should have pleased him to see an African servant giving orders to an upper class Englishman like Cullen. In a just world, such reversals would happen all the time. But in his gut he felt a deep sense of unease. There was a contradiction between what he'd seen there and what was happening out here in the party. He was a guest in a house of lies, surrounded by deception and distraction. That sort of situation seldom ended well.

He watched the household servants as they wandered the hall. They were all native men, dressed in jackets and bow ties. They followed the rules a servant should, formal in manner, silent until questioned, polite in speech and style. They acted promptly on every request, arriving with new drinks before guests even realised that their glasses were empty. It was a book perfect rendition of good service.

But not life perfect. Real servants, worn into instinct over the years, held themselves differently. They stood straight like these men, but it was a straightness of formality, where this was pride. And a servant's eyes, an honest servant's eyes, did not dart around as these did. A servant used the corners of his vision, catching every movement without shifting his gaze, holding only those details required by his role. These servants scoured the room, watching guests when they weren't looking, soaking up the events around them. They knew not to catch a guest's gaze, but they didn't know not to gaze at all.

Unease growing inside him, Dirk edged away from the servants, trying to watch without being watched. Was it his imagination or were more eyes on him? More gazes swiftly shifting when he looked their way?

Someone grabbed at his elbow. He spun around, twisting his arm free and gripping his assailant's wrist.

"Why, Mr Dynamo, I didn't know you cared." Isabelle smiled sweetly up at him. "But I'm afraid this hand is reserved for Mr McNair."

"Sorry, ma'am." Dirk released his grip and returned her smile. "You startled me, that's all."

"I quite understand. I must be a hideous sight, looming out of the darkness of a party."

"I didn't mean..."

"I'm teasing, Mr Dynamo. Are all Americans so literal-minded?"

"America's a big place, ma'am. I wouldn't care to speak for all my countrymen. But most folks I know back home are straight shooters, except for politicians and Pinkertons, and neither of them are trusted much."

"You don't dabble in politics yourself?"

"No, ma'am." Dirk hesitated. He knew some folks considered this a sensitive subject, and that his own opinions weren't those of the British upper class. "I read about it a bit, mostly your European thinkers like Mr Marx. But it's no business for a man of spirit."

"And being a Pinkerton is?" She smiled playfully.

"Well, that's another matter. I've done my share of spying and prying, some of it on my nation's dime, some not. But we all do things we ain't proud of from time to time."

"How very true." Isabelle was solemn for a moment. Then she seemed to remember herself, glancing around with a smile. "Of course an Englishman takes pride in everything he does, and occasionally the things he doesn't. When one defines civilisation, it is very easy to always be right."

Dirk grinned, caught out by quietly mocking tone as much as by her words.

They strolled through the throng, her arm now linked through his as she nodded and smiled to the people they passed. Dirk guided her away from the servants and found himself once more heading for the open front door.

One of the servants walked parallel to them along the side of the room, dispensing drinks from his heavily laden tray, replacing them with empty glasses. His face was familiar, one of the men who'd fetched their bags from the dock.

"Apparently his name is Gu," Isabelle said, leaning close to Dirk.

"Did he tell you that?"

"No, silly, Bekoe-Kumi did. She knows all about him."

"Close, are they?" Dirk was amazed that Isabelle had got so much out of the Dahomey woman.

"I suppose that would be one way to put it. She worships him."

Dirk raised an eyebrow in surprise.

"Passionate girl," he said.

"It's in the nature of the ahosi."

"Not like English women, huh?"

"That's a little unfair. We are as dedicated to our Lord as the next nation of housewives, even if we only have the one god."

"God?"

"Gu deals with war, apparently. But then, so must any god of Englishmen."

Dirk turned to look in confusion at Isabelle. She was gazing at the statue by the door, its swords moving up and down to the entertainment of the guests.

"This is Gu?" he asked, pointing at the figure.

"Have you listened to a word I've said?"

Dirk glanced once more at the servant, now disappearing towards the back of the room.

"Seems not." Dirk's shoes creaked as he shifted uncomfortably on the spot. "You noticed anything odd about this place?"

"Apart from the servants?"

"You noticed too, huh?"

"Never under-estimate a woman, Mr Dynamo." Isabelle frowned at him. "Especially not where the running of a household is concerned. Of course I noticed the servants, but there are other things too. The library is at the rear of the house, facing north, meaning it gets less light than the guest rooms, which are all at the front. Hardly conducive to reading, or to sleep, even if they given the library any windows."

"Could just be poor design."

"I doubt it. Reginald's father was an architect, he would notice details like that." She looked thoughtfully around the room. "Shall we have a little wander, see what else we might see?"

They strolled back through the party, Isabelle drifting between conversations while Dirk stood awkwardly at her side, a knight in dress tails on the arm of a picture-book princess. Most of the guests were British, and she knew them all by reputation if not personally. Conversation flowed around her like a spring breeze, leaves of laughter dancing on the wind. She brought out the best in those around her – fascinating anecdotes, rapier wit, gems of obscure and intriguing knowledge.

"What do you want from life?" she asked during one of their brief moments alone.

"The usual stuff." Dirk shrugged sheepishly.

"And what's the usual stuff?"

"To be better. To be smarter."

"I'm really not sure that's the usual stuff." She laughed, and Dirk felt his face redden.

"What about you?" he asked, looking for a distraction.

"What do I want?" She seemed surprised by the question.

"Uhuh."

"I want to decide my own fate." Her voice had gone quiet, and she looked the closest he'd seen her to timid. "I don't believe that's too much to ask."

"Damn straight." Dirk nodded. "Where I come from, it's every man's right to do that."

"Well. Quite." She raised an eyebrow and looked up at him, searching his face. Whatever she was after, she didn't seem to find it. Her usual tone returned, and she whisked him off once more into the crowds, to Dirk's confusion and disappointment.

Even with Isabelle's civilising touch, the party was entering its final phase, a long drawn-out death by denial. The older guests were growing red-faced and wobbly, fat merchants groping inappropriately for their long-suffering wives. The young had reached the drinking from bottles stage, casting aside the safest social convention in slender hopes of starting a wild time. A tired and tipsy young woman was being whisked around the centre of the room by a dandy, dancing to the music in their own minds. Around the edges the foreign visitors stood uncertain, watching the English at their most uncharacteristically riotous.

"Don't these folks ever give up?" Dirk stepped out of the waltzing couple's path.

"Freeport doesn't have much of a social scene," Isabelle said. "They're making hay while Cullen's sun shines."

"Freeport?" Dirk had heard the name mentioned, but that was as far as his knowledge went.

"The main town and harbour." Isabelle smiled and nodded her head to a passer by. "It's on the far side of the island from where we docked."

"I wondered why we didn't see more of these folks earlier."

"It seemed wise to keep our boat away from the rest. We don't want people asking about Timothy's diving devices or watching us trawl for treasure."

Dirk nodded. "So now we've got a hint of the wreck, what's our next move?"

"A quick one, if possible. First thing tomorrow let's-"

The rapping of wood on wood sounded behind them. Dirk turned to see Cullen standing on the stairs, knocking his walking stick against the banister.

"Your attention please!" he called to the crowd. A hush fell across the room, interspersed with drunken giggling. "It is my pleasure to announce a hunt tomorrow, meeting here at ten for a jaunt into the jungle."

Applause broke out, raucous and relieved. With something else to look forward to, the party could finally finish.

Cullen held up a hand for silence.

"It is my further pleasure to invite one of our honoured guests, a renowned master of tracking and trapping, to lead us in the chase. Mr Dynamo, would you be willing to lead the hunt?"

All eyes turned on Dirk. He looked to Isabelle, uncertain whether to accept. What would help them blend in best, saying yes or no? He didn't want to draw attention if he didn't have to.

She gave the faintest of nods.

"Sure thing, Mr Cullen." Dirk grinned a predator's grin. If he was going hunting he might as well enjoy it. "I'm always up for a little sport."

"First thing tomorrow, huh?" he whispered to Isabelle as applause filled the hall.

She smiled up at him, a glint in her eyes. "What's a day's delay, compared with seeing a renowned master at work?"

Chapter 4: The Hunt

Years of disciplined living had given Dirk habits that no fancy party could break. As dawn rose in glory over the jungle of Hakon, he was up and exercising on the governor's lawn, running laps and heaving rocks among the croquet hoops. On the veranda, Gibbon's Decline and Fall of the Roman Empire waited for him to pause and catch breath.

The servants were up early too. A gang came around the side of the house, chattering and laughing, spades and picks over their shoulders. Young and old, they walked bare-chested and bare-foot in the fresh morning air, relishing the sun's rays and the gentle breeze blowing off the sea. As they noticed Dirk, their stances stiffened and they walked past in silence, heads bowed.

"Morning," Dirk called out.

They nodded silent responses and disappeared down the gravel path.

"What ho!" Timothy Blaze-Simms wandered out of the house, bottle in one hand, glass in the other, bow-tie dangling free around his neck.

"Up already?" Dirk asked, pausing in his labours.

"Not so much 'already' as 'still'." Timothy blinked at the bright outdoor light and took a sip of champagne.

"You remember there's a hunt this morning?" Dirk asked.

"Oh yes." Blaze-Simms flung himself down on a lawn-side bench, head at one end, feet sticking off the other.

"Don't worry about me. I can go days without sleep, when the whim seizes me."

Dirk looked around. With no-one else nearby, this would be the perfect chance to catch up on what they had seen.

"Listen, there's something odd going on here." He stepped closer to his friend, lowering his voice to a whisper. "You notice the servants last night?"

A gentle snore was the only reply.

#

By the time the household had risen and breakfasted, the hunting party was beginning to assemble. Arriving alone or in small groups, two dozen of the island's more prominent inhabitants galloped up the driveway, gravel crunching beneath their horses' hooves, calling out excitedly to each other. The British were kitted out in a strange mix of formal jackets and large guns, looking like an emergency militia raised to defend the home counties. They were in festive spirits, Braithwaite laughing and joking as he sipped sherry brought out by the servants. The whole tone was bewildering, like no kind of hunt Dirk had ever been part of - more carnival than expedition into the wilds.

The French visitor, a businessman named Regis Marat, was trying to join in the jollity, but he responded blankly to the jokes and was clearly unimpressed with the sherry. His hulking "secretaries" seemed happy playing with their guns, though the looks they sometimes gave Dirk were downright hostile. He wondered if he'd done something to of-fend them, or if they just got riled when they weren't the toughest guys in town.

Isabelle emerged from the house and joined Dirk on the veranda. She was wearing jodhpurs and a jacket, and held a riding crop.

"Ready for that little sport you mentioned?" She smiled and tucked a strand of hair behind her ear.

Dirk paused before replying, grinding a cigarillo out beneath his boot.

"Pardon my French, but why are we even going on this damn hunt?" he asked. "We've got work to do."

"Firstly, Mr Dynamo, French is a language of sophistication and elegance." Isabelle tapped the riding crop against her empty palm. "The idea that it epitomises crudity reflects a level of prejudice most unbecoming of a citizen of the land of the free.

"Secondly, our host has invited us on this hunt. Given that he has extended us such hospitality, it would be most impolite not to attend. Such niceties may have no value in New York or the mining outposts of the Black Hills, but in British territories they are as oil to the social machine, ensuring its smooth and peaceful running.

"Thirdly, in case you have forgotten, you are leading the hunt. It can hardly happen without you."

"That's me told." Dirk scowled.

"Please don't mope." Isabelle shook her head. "One would think your mother never had to tell you off."

"She didn't get much of a chance." He'd barely been old enough to understand what was happening at the funeral, but some things left such a deep memory that they were never lost.

"I'm so sorry." Isabelle hung her head. "I didn't know. That was thoughtless of me."

"It happens." Dirk took a deep breath. "I should get ready to ride."

"Of course."

Isabelle went to join Cullen and Bekoe-Kumi, who were examining horses brought around from behind the house. Dirk wondered where the animals lived, because they sure hadn't been in the stables.

"Action time!" A breezy Blaze-Simms strode out onto the gravel, freshly groomed and sporting a clean jacket, a long paper-wrapped package over his shoulder and a smaller one in his hand.

"How are you even moving?" Dirk asked.

"Pluck of the English," Timothy replied. "Besides, I couldn't miss this. You know they hardly ever hunt around here? This is a real occasion."

He sprang into the saddle of a nearby horse, settling the large package in front of him.

"What is that thing?" Dirk asked.

"Wait and see," Timothy said. "I think you're going to like this one."

#

As the first hour of riding slid by, Dirk came to understand why the local residents didn't hunt often. Hakon was the biggest of a cluster of guano islands, big enough to have a jungle and its own small mountain, but not to support the big game for which Africa was famed. In its place, Cullen had developed something of a bastard sport, combining fox-hunt-style chasing with the odd bit of bird shooting. A pack of enthusiastic but ill-trained hounds scampered around the hunters, dashing off whenever they caught a scent. Sometimes they scared up parakeets, giving the party's guns a target. More often they came back carrying a snake or vole, or were found barking at the heels of a nervous field hand.

Blaze-Simms's smaller package contained a device he called the Automated Aerial Beater. He unwrapped it as they rode, revealing a brass box half a foot across with a sack hanging from the top. With a flourish he lit a gas nozzle and the sack inflated, turning the device into a miniature airship. It sailed up above the jungle, then began to shake as its mechanisms rattled, scaring birds up out of the trees.

Dirk applauded enthusiastically along with the rest of the hunting party. It was an ingenious device, and he could see that it might have uses beyond sport. But just as the hunters were readying their guns, flames sprang up the side of the inflated sack. There was a whoosh, a dull thud, and the balloon exploded. The Automated Aerial Beater crashed onto the path, scattering gears and chunks of brass casing.

Blaze-Simms sighed, and Dirk shared his disappointment. It was a shame when smart ideas didn't work out.

Many in the party found the whole thing hysterical, creating a pantomime atmosphere of inane banter and running jokes, to the evident bemusement of the oriental trader and his wife. They rode at the back of the group, whispering to each other and exchanging occasional comments with a disappointed-looking Blaze-Simms, who sat stroking his remaining package and gazing into the distance.

Dirk, stuck at the head of the hunt and determined to make use of the time, turned his attention away from the dogs and onto quizzing Cullen.

"Where do the rest of your guests live?" He gestured back at the hunting party. By now he'd heard a whole history of the island's uses and ownership, but nothing that threw light on the strange things he had seen.

"Mostly in Freeport." Cullen shifted his rifle across his lap. "It used to be the slave depot, when this place lived off the Atlantic trade. The cages and cells are gone, thank God, but the docks still work. There are offices for the guano companies, warehouses and suchlike, and a hotel for visitors.

"Nobody but me lives here full time. They stop by to check on operations for a month or two, then move on. Braithwaite's as close as I have to a permanent neighbour, and even he's never stayed more than a summer. In fact, you've come at the perfect time. Late spring is usually when we're busiest, and the nearest to a social season that we can scrape together. Leave it four weeks and you'll find me alone with the birds and the servants."

That cast a different light on the conversations Dirk had overheard. The governor was clearly excited at the thought of having a social season. His claim to Omalara that he felt obliged to throw the party was just an excuse.

"I say, good shot!" Cullen exclaimed.

A brightly coloured bird tumbled out of the air, to wild applause and some bickering over who'd hit it. A servant followed the dogs to retrieve this rare prize. To Dirk, it seemed pathetic, a death that wouldn't feed anyone or keep them safe. This wasn't his sort of hunt.

As they rode into the denser jungle, the tone changed. Hushed by the lush beauty of their surroundings, even the English members of the party were reduced to whispers.

For such a small island, Hakon had an amazing abundance of wildlife. Spirals of bright red leaves hung next to bursts of blue and yellow flowers. The hunters pointed in wonder at a rainbow hued blossom, only to see it spread its wings and flap away. Tree-frogs swam in the rain-filled cups of upturned leaves while bees buzzed from bloom to bloom, to be caught in the snapping jaws of a Venus flytrap. Somewhere in the warm green depths, a stream babbled its Edenic tune. Every space seemed swollen to bursting with life, the plants larger and more luscious even than those Dirk had seen in the Amazon.

He paused to look at one of the carnivorous plants, letting the rest of the party drift past. Bekoe-Kumi and Braithwaite took the lead, their shifting gazes those of true hunters, not the horse and hounds set who followed behind. It was a side of the gruff guano merchant that Dirk hadn't expected, but entirely in keeping with his companion's demeanour. Bekoe-Kumi was every inch the warrior, riding high in the saddle, always ready for action.

The oriental couple were at the back of the pack, riding with a stiff formality that accentuated their evident discomfort. They reminded Dirk of folks he'd seen driving the railways across the great west - both the Chinese labourers, dignified despite their sweat and dirt, and the white investors riding uneasily past half-laid tracks, trying to fathom the things they had funded.

The couple bowed slightly as he approached, not much more than a nod of the head. Dirk nodded back and tried to engage them in a conversation about the surrounding plants. There was so much to see, it seemed like the perfect chance to draw them out, to learn a little about what had brought them here. The man responded, but briefly and with a stiffness that matched his posture. Like his wife, he kept scanning the jungle, not frantically but persistently, constantly absorbing his surroundings.

Dirk was about to give up on the conversation when Isabelle joined them. Her bow was deeper than those greeting her, and this seemed to please the Chinaman. To Dirk she appeared to be talking about the same things he had, pointing out the same sights and sounds, making the same queries about these strangers' lives. And yet the tone was lighter, livelier. Where he had laboured to get a response, she drew them easily into quiet chatter about the jungle, the hunt, even themselves.

His name was Hasegawa Minoru, hers Miura Noriko. Dirk was surprised that, as what seemed to be a married couple, they didn't share a name or two, but he guessed that was an eastern thing. Like Braithwaite, Hasegawa Minoru had come to Hakon for the guano. He planned on exporting it to places Dirk had never heard of, but all of which held acquaintances of Isabelle. As business talk it sounded plausible, and Dirk figured that his unease at the situation cam from his own lack of grace. His contributions were blunt and stumbling, while Isabelle responded with ease to their enquiries and showed curiosity about things they said. Dirk made a mental note to ask her later about oriental customs, as she seemed to know how to set these folks at ease.

The dogs were yapping up ahead. Horses jerked to a halt, whinnying and pawing the ground. Excusing himself, Dirk rode to the head of the hunt. His horse snorted and he had to work the spurs to keep her moving, past the others and into a clearing.

What he saw there was like a butcher's board, strewn with entrails and spattered a raw, dripping red. Glistening strings of guts trembled beneath the paws of the dogs, who scampered around yipping gleefully for their masters. Dirk swung down from the saddle and approached one of the larger heaps. With the tip of his old Bowie knife he prodded carefully through the pieces, studying splintered bones and shredded skin. He'd seen this sort of carnage on a battlefield, but here there were no sword strokes or bullet holes, only the smells of blood and ruptured bowels.

Blaze-Simms jumped from his horse and approached the bloody remains, Braithwaite and Bekoe-Kumi close behind.

"Good heavens, what is it?" Blaze-Simms asked.

"Looks like it was a mule." Braithwaite peered at a piece of fur. "Locals let them graze free when they're not in use, so that they don't need so much feeding. A few of the older ones even live in the wild, wandering around like they own the place."

"The poor blighter's been absolutely shredded." Timothy looked appalled. "Mostly by claws, by the looks of it, but there are teeth marks too."

"Whatever killed it wasn't hungry." Braithwaite pointed at a long string of innards stretching towards the treeline. "There's nowt missing but a few shreds of hide."

"What about the heart?" A glimmer of excitement appeared in Blaze-Simms's eyes. "Perhaps this was a ritual."

"That's over there." Braithwaite pointed to a small, grisly heap. "Under the stomach."

"Oh yes."

Dirk followed the grisly trail out of the clearing. The guts reached their end not far into the treeline, but a set of bloody paw-prints continued west through the jungle.

Braithwaite came up behind Dirk, stroking his beard as he gazed at the tracks.

"Looks to me like 'twas a bear." The Yorkshireman knelt down, dabbed at one of the prints, his finger coming away sticky with half-dried blood. "'Bout an hour ago."

"Many bears around here, Mr Braithwaite?" Dirk reckoned he could make a good guess. This sort of jungle wasn't normally bear country.

"No lad." Braithwaite shook his head thoughtfully. "And bears don't attack mules, neither."

"That's what I figured."

A suspicion was settling over Dirk. He didn't have enough details to fit it all together yet, but this jungle seemed as stilted and exaggerated as life in the governor's mansion. Everything about it, every plant and animal, made sense as part of a jungle or a forest. Just not all together, and not with such success on such a tiny spot of land. If this was about guano, then it was mighty powerful guano.

They walked back to the clearing, where Blaze-Simms was excitedly unwrapping his paper parcel.

"What the hell is that?" Dirk asked.

Timothy was holding something almost like a hunting rifle. Unlike a rifle, the stock was a mass of brass tubes and funnels, and the barrel consisted of three spiralling lengths of pipe.

"It's a new gun I've been working on," he explained, pumping a handle on the side. "It's steam powered, but without the need for fire. You see, there's a radium chamber here, next to the water tank, and by a series of swift mechanical compressions one can squeeze enough power from the radium to evaporate a brief but intense burst of steam. This drives a set of magnetised pellets up the barrel, and their spin around each other helps retain accuracy. It has quite a punch, and can fire an incredible distance, in theory."

"In theory?" Dirk eyed the contraption warily. He remembered how, in theory, Blaze-Simms's automated serving table had brought swift service and perfect drinks for the Epiphany Club. In practice it had brought two fires, one explosion and the infamous Champagne Tsunami.

"This is the first chance I've had to fire it." Blaze-Simms beamed with pride. "I look forward to testing its range."

"Lad," Braithwaite interjected, "in this jungle, nothing's got a range of more than a hundred yards. On account of that's how far you can see."

"Oh." Blaze-Simms slumped, then brightened. "Maybe if we flush out more birds? No cover in the sky."

"We've got more to worry about than birds." Dirk vaulted into the saddle. "Come on, the trail's fresh. Let's do some proper hunting at last."

#

Now that they had the bear's trail, following it was easy. With or without blood, it left hefty prints as it passed, crushing the undergrowth in its wake.

The tone of the trip had changed. The horses had been spooked by the butchery in the clearing, and so had their riders. Many of the party were chattering about the prospect of a real kill, but it was a quieter chatter than before, all boisterousness drained away, and Cullen himself looked nervous despite Bekoe-Kumi's presence at his side. Monsieur Marat was talking with Timothy, who was taking a screw-driver to the barrel of his gun. Dirk still took the lead, but Braithwaite rode up front with him now, alert in the saddle.

"You seem to know a lot about animals and their insides, Mr Braithwaite," Dirk said.

"Aye, well, I've been quartermaster in some pretty queer corners of the Empire." Braithwaite grinned broadly beneath his beard. "When you might have to skin and butcher a camel on five minutes notice, you start taking an interest in what's inside. When I got home I joined one of them scientific clubs, learned some anatomy, zoology and such. Reckon I know my way around most of the animal kingdom by now."

"So how do you reckon a bear ended up here?"

"Probably Cullen." Braithwaite glanced back at the ambassador. "He's pulled some funny stunts in his time. Shipping in strange plants and animals or bits of exotic machinery, whatever takes his fancy. There's at least three half-assembled breweries lurking around his place, and the parts for a decent pipe organ. We had a wild lion 'til some poor bugger got his arm ripped off collecting its dung. Have you seen the ostrich pen? I like guano as much as the next man, more than my wife thinks I should, but you wouldn't catch me keeping those buggers if their shit were made of gold."

"So he got a bear for the dung?"

"That or the hunting. You don't get much excitement around here if you don't make it yourself."

Dirk shook his head. Cullen seemed a pretty sane guy, as Englishmen went. Now he was starting to sound like a crazy old uncle or some inbred Prussian aristocrat, lurching from one obsession to the next. How did that fit with what he'd seen the other night? The whole of Hakon was crowded with oddities. Logic said there had to be a pattern, so what was it?

A distraction was what it was. Not the thing they'd come here for, and certainly not what he should think about now.

"Another thing." Braithwaite kept his voice low. "Have you seen the size of the plants around here?"

Something stirred in the bushes up ahead.

Dirk straightened, watching warily, and pulled out the hunting rifle holstered at his horse's side. It was a fancy breach loader, with a long polished barrel and carved hardwood stock. Pretty but unwieldy and without much stopping power. Against a bear in the jungle, Dirk wished he'd brought his Gravemaker. It might not have the range, but it had brought down bison, a rhino, and even giant rats.

A branch swung up. These was a flash of brown fur. Dirk snapped the rifle up and fired.

The gunshot cracked like thunder through the jungle, waves of noise sending birds flying from their roosts. A pack of monkeys swung away in howling terror. A small body fell through the leaves, a half-eaten banana tumbling from its hand, and Dirk felt a pang of guilt.

Then there was a roar.

He turned to see the bear burst out of the greenery. It appeared behind Hasegawa Minoru, a bloodstained whirlwind of hungry muscle and razor edges. The Chinaman raised his hands as if he hoped to wave it away.

Claws bared, the beast leapt.

Chapter 5: Scars

It wasn't just a roar. It was the ancestor of all roars, hurtling out of the primal past, clawing ragged across the mind. Deep inside Dirk's unconscious a small, frightened fragment of his animal ancestry trembled and cowered.

The bear charged in heavy bounds, dirt flying as its paws tore the ground. Mouth gaping wide, blood drooling from its jaws, it leapt at Hasegawa Minoru.

Minoru ducked and twisted, rolling out of the saddle. One hand shot up, brushing against the bear as it hurtled over him. Minoru's horse, momentarily frozen in panic, now bolted into the trees. The oriental, one hand grabbing at a stirrup, was dragged away through the leaf-mould, his wife galloping after him.

The rest of the horses whinnied and scattered, fleeing the stinking mass of fur and muscles in their midst. Most of their riders went with them, hanging on for dear life.

Dirk fought to keep his steed under control, the gun tumbling from his hand as he was thrown about. Blaze-Simms, already on the floor, fumbled for his experimental rifle. The only ones controlling of their horses were Isabelle and Braithwaite.

Isabelle fired her rifle straight into the body of the onrushing bear. The bullets didn't even slow the beast. As her horse reared up in panic the bear gutted it with a swipe of one massive paw. Dropping the rifle, Isabelle leaped for an overhanging branch and scrambled into the safety of the treetops.

Its stablemate's evisceration was too much for Braithwaite's horse. Even as the Yorkshireman brought his gun around, the animal whinnied in terror and galloped into the trees, taking him cursing and swearing with it.

Cullen had been flung from the saddle. He lay groaning at the base of a tree, blood seeping from a gash in his forehead. His eyes flickered on the edge of consciousness.

The bear prowled towards him, eyes glittering, breathing the salt smell of the injured man. Its breath came in rasping growls.

Dirk leapt to the ground, reaching for his boot-knife even as he landed. The bear ignored him as he stalked towards it. In the background, Blaze-Simms was furiously pumping a lever on his gun.

Bekoe-Kumi appeared between Cullen and the bear, a machete in her hand. She slashed at the bear's claw, knocking it aside but not drawing blood. The bear roared and swung at her with both arms. She ducked too late and with a dreadful crunch was thrown to the floor, her arm twisted unnaturally beneath her.

The bear sniffed the air and turned back towards the bleeding Cullen, eyes gleaming with the madness of fixation. It paused for a moment over the injured governor, watching as he turned his head with broken, twitching movements. It snorted and raised a paw, sunlight glinting off claws as it prepared to strike.

Dirk leapt.

Fur filled his senses as he landed on the bear's back - the smell of it, the sight of it, the coarse strands of it between his fingers. He grabbed with one hand and pulled hard.

Bellowing, the beast swung its head, even as his knife hit its shoulder. He plunged the blade through layers of tough, writhing muscle, the edge scraping against bone. The bear howled as he pulled the blade free and drove it in again - once, twice, three times, blood flying.

Twisting its head around, the bear snapped at Dirk with jaws like a steel trap. Rattlesnake fast, he jerked his arm back. The knife, slippery with blood, slid from his grasp.

The beast reared up on its hind legs, almost throwing him. In desperation he swung one arm around its neck, and then the other, gripping his own wrists and tugging hard against its throat. The creature wheezed and staggered, one fore-leg hanging blood-soaked and useless, the other trying to swat the giant fly clinging to its back.

Triumph rose up within Dirk. But it was knocked from him, and his breath with it, as he was slammed against the trunk of a tree. The bear leaned back, crushing him between its weight and the towering palm. Squeezing as hard as he could at the beast's neck, he tried to strangle it before it could suffocate him. Man and bear grunted in unison as they threw the last of their strength into the fight. But try as he might, Dirk couldn't breathe. Black spots danced across his vision. His ears filled with a roaring that wasn't all bear. Head spinning, he felt his grip loosening, his muscles falling limp as his eyelids drooped and he sank back into...

Whump!

Something spattered across his face, strangely comforting in its soft warmth. The pressure on his body lessened and then disappeared as the bear slumped to the ground, and Dirk with it.

A glorious rush of air flooded his lungs. Though his head still ached, the black spots had vanished, and the roaring with them. Staggering to his feet, he looked down in bewilderment at the headless bear.

"Did you see!" Blaze-Simms appeared at his shoulder, a grin splitting his face. Green smoke drifted from the barrel of his rifle. "And look there!"

The tree against which Dirk had been pressed now featured a hole half an inch across, smoothly bored all the way through. It was spattered with brain.

Dirk ran a finger down his face. It came away unpleasantly sticky.

"You shot right by my head." He didn't like feeling angry. Loss of self-control was never good. But right now, the feeling was hard to resist.

"That's right!" Blaze-Simms waved his gun. "Splendidly accurate, isn't it?"

"You shot right by my head." Dirk fought to keep his voice calm. "Not knowing how accurate your gun would be. Or how destructive. Or a hell of a lot else about how it would work."

"And it worked out splendidly." Blaze-Simms's good cheer seemed to seep away. "I say, is something the matter?"

"You could have blown my head off, you goddamn lunatic!" Dirk bellowed. He took a deep, panting breath. That hadn't been the right thing to do, but he felt a whole lot better.

"I'm so sorry." Blaze-Simms looked crestfallen. "I didn't think..."

"I know, Tim." Calmer now, and feeling a little guilty for the upset he'd caused, Dirk patted his friend on the shoulder. "You never do. But it worked out in the end."

"It did rather, didn't it?" Blaze-Simms's brow furrowed. "I really am sorry, old chap. Are you frightfully peeved?"

"I'll get over it." Dirk shook his head. It was hard to stay mad at someone like Timothy Blaze-Simms. There was too much of the charming, innocent child about the guy - not an ounce of ill intention, and every desire to do better, however hard he sometimes failed. "This critter seem odd to you?"

He prodded at the bear with his riding boot.

Timothy scratched his head in thought, all signs of distress gone as curiosity took over. "It's a bear on a tropical island. That's odd. And it is unusually large, even for a bear..."

Dirk pointed at the spot where his knife had gone in. Exposed muscles still twitched and writhed, severed ends flailing about like blood-engorged worms. Both men knelt and touched the bear's back.

"Damn thing's squirming like a sack full of snakes." Dirk raised an eyebrow. "What do you reckon is causing that?"

Blaze-Simms shrugged. "A number of conjectures spring to mind, but I think dissection is the way to..."

Cullen groaned as Bekoe-Kumi tried to lift him with her good arm. Timothy continued talking, caught up in his thoughts about the bear. Not for the first time, Dirk decided to just leave him to it.

At Dirk's approach Bekoe-Kumi reluctantly stepped aside, letting him pick up the injured governor.

"C'mon." Dirk easily lifted Cullen, cradling him like a baby. "Lets go get some help. The scientist and the grizzly are gonna be a while."

As he spoke, Isabelle dropped from a tree, landing gracefully beside him.

"Would you like some company?" She picked up her rifle and checked the chamber of the gun.

"You up to protecting him if anything else comes around?" Dirk nodded toward Blaze-Simms.

"I may have the body of a weak and feeble woman." Isabelle took an ammunition belt from the saddle of her dead horse and wrapped it around her waste. "But I have twenty-five rounds and a good eye for details. We will be fine."

#

The hunting party had scattered and the horses with them. Dirk couldn't blame the beasts, or even their riders. That bear would have given a rhinoceros a heart attack. There was no good reason for innocent animals or their soft living owners to stay and get themselves mauled.

That created a problem for those they had left behind. Miles from the mansion, without help or horses, and with a man badly in need of medical care, they were reduced to marching through the jungle, heading as quickly as they could toward the nearest settlement. Fortunately for Dirk, Bekoe-Kumi knew the island, and she knew the quickest route to help. Unfortunately, that meant an hour of dense undergrowth, boiling heat and swarming mosquitoes.

The journey gave him a chance to walk off his anger at Blaze-Simms. He mutter darkly about lunatic inventors, venting his frustration as he stamped through the undergrowth. Strange looks from Bekoe-Kumi didn't bother him, and soon he was more worried about Blaze-Simms's safety than about his idiocy. He was glad that Isabelle and her gun were with the inventor in case more trouble turned up. At the very least, she would make him see a threat before it was breathing down his neck.

At last they emerged from the jungle on a valley side, looking down across fields of vegetables to the small port below. A couple of locals, bare to the waist and sweating in the midday sun, were busy planting yams in soil grey with guano. Seeing Dirk's burden, one of them ran for help. The other led them down the track into town.

Freeport was a colonial town in the traditional style, not planned and built by design but laid down over years like silt in a river. A seafront hotel sat amid a thick crust of warehouses. Behind them, a drift of makeshift workshops and shanty cottages sprawled out to fields and jungle. The settlement didn't so much end as fade away, becoming one with the undergrowth up the valley side.

Cullen was a dead weight in Dirk's arms. The governor's breath was irregular, broken by coughing spasms. His eyes had rolled back in his head, white orbs showing beneath flickering eyelids. Arms and legs hung limp and useless as a new-born baby. His pants were damp as a baby's too, but at least they didn't smell so bad.

Dirk hated that the most. The moment when the scent of blood was overwhelmed by the stench of loosened bowels, and you tried not to show the guy you knew he was dying. He'd been through it on a cold night on the plains, while the footfalls of braves whispered out of the darkness, and three times in one day on that shot-blasted hillside north of Washington.

Shifting Cullen in his arms, he tried to keep this sack of fragile humanity from slipping through his grasp. Normally he'd have had no problem, but normally he hadn't been wrestling a bear. His arms ached and his bruised chest sang with pain where the governor pressed against it.

Four men in patched trousers, their flesh worn but their stance proud, rushed out to meet him. They slid Cullen onto a stretcher, stained canvas sinking beneath his weight, and lifted him to their shoulders. Relieved of his burden but still concerned for his unconscious host, Dirk followed them.

The buildings reminded Dirk of towns on the western frontier, places with names like Hanging Rock, Deadwood, and Tombstone. The closer they got to the heart of the place, to the space where outsiders might go, the grander the fronts of the buildings became, while what lay behind remained as cheap and shabby as ever. But the air stayed clear, even for a coastal town, without the sewage smell of civilisation. The care these folks took over their home seemed at odds with the rickety state of the buildings. Dirk figured that care could only do so much.

The marketplace was bright with yellow ears of corn and the red-green skin of mangoes. Dirk stared at the crops, huge and healthy at the wrong time of year. No-one else seemed amazed at the sight, so he set the observation aside and moved on.

"You like what you see?" Bekoe-Kumi asked. The look she gave him was half challenge, half judgement.

"Ain't too different from where I grew up," Dirk said. "A lot of folks scraping by on not very much."

"Maybe I misjudged you, American," she said.

"Kind of you to say so."

"Only maybe."

Around the edges of the market, old women sat on worn carpets. Heaps of battered tools, driftwood furniture and threadbare sheets were spread out in front of them, detritus lost or abandoned by passing ships and privileged visitors. Too old to work the fields, these women sifted through what others threw away, mended it and bartered it for food.

Many of the market stalls were sheltered by awnings rigged out of sheets and canes. The stretcher bearers stopped in front of the sturdiest shelter, walled on three sides with thick blue wool that blocked out the sunlight, creating a pool of darkness amid the market's bright bustle. They lowered Cullen to the ground and stood back.

A hand reached out of the darkness, brown skin spotted white and purple with chemical stains. Bleached finger tips brushed Cullen's face and he murmured, turning unconsciously to the hand for comfort.

"Omalara told him be careful in the jungle, but he don't listen."

A face emerged, disembodied against the darkness, round features topped with a yellow headscarf. A face Dirk had seen once before, conspiring with Cullen in the back passages of the governor's mansion. Eyes of sparkling darkness passed over Bekoe-Kumi and locked onto Dirk. He felt a chill. Whatever was happening here, he was one step closer to the heart of it.

"What happened?" she asked, and as an afterthought, "Sir?"

Omalara listened to Dirk calmly describing the bear attack, while her hands danced over Cullen's body. He'd given dozens of reports on acts of violence in the past, whether on the battlefield or while investigating a crime. It wasn't hard to stay matter-of-fact.

She asked questions about the way Cullen fell, the angle he'd lain at, how long since the attack. Hands like leather raised a damp cloth to the governor's brow, mopping away sweat and blood with maternal tenderness. She pulled back a flickering eyelid to peer at the pupil beneath, prodded swiftly and expertly at his wounds, turned the angle of his shoulders so that he settled back and the rasping of his breath eased. Then she disappeared again into the darkness, emerging with pestle and mortar and a palm-frond basket of dried herbs.

"Omalara'll tend to Mister Governor's wounds," she said, dropping leaves and seeds into the bowel. A fresh, sweet scent rose as she pounded them. "Ubu Peter, he show you the town while you wait, sir. Make sure you not missing your tourist time."

One of the stretcher bearers stepped forward and nodded to Dirk. He was younger than the others, shaved bald on top, with a body like a Greek statue. There was nothing Dirk could do for Cullen, so he let himself be led away between the market stalls.

They walked towards the docks, a small cloud of children flurrying like dust in their wake, pointing in open curiosity at the large, blood-stained white man.

"Stop your rudeness." Ubu Peter frowned at the children. "That any way to treat the governor's guest?"

They backed away but kept giggling, just outside of Ubu Peter's reach.

"I'm sorry for their rudeness," he said to Dirk. "Not many white men come to our market, or to town on foot."

"Don't worry." Dirk was struck by Ubu Peter's very English way of talking, so different from the other voices here. Once again, his curiosity was piqued, but he was learning not to be too direct with these folks. "I ain't gonna get offended at a bunch of kids starin' at the stranger. It ain't like there's a whole lot else going on around here, right?"

Ubu Peter's eyes narrowed in a moment of suspicion, giving Dirk all the confirmation he needed. If this guy knew that his question was loaded then the island's secret went beyond the governor and the old lady.

"I grew up in a place like this." Dirk touched his injured shoulder. It hurt like hell, but he hadn't wanted to distract Omalara from the governor. He kept on walking, talking so as to stop himself gritting his teeth. "It's the sort of place folks in the States call a one horse town. 'Cept around here it's more of a one town island. Not much excitement for a youngster."

Ubu Peter's expression softened and he smiled, the expression almost patronising. "We keep them busy. Hakon has its own excitements."

He pointed towards the near end of the docks, where a weathered heap of skulls stood - an aging, bleached pile like a morbid pyramid. As they came close, Dirk saw that they were all human, a hundred mementoes of the long dead, some fractured or pierced, those at the bottom of the heap mottled with lichen.

"That is how things used to be." Ubu Peter looked solemn. "The strong crushed the weak, the powerful the powerless. Traders at the top, beating the slaves, keeping them in place. Then the strong slaves below them, keeping the weak in line for their masters and themselves. On down through layers of pain, to the children snatched from the African coast and dragged through here for sale. At every level, 'examples' were made. Some were more guilty than others, but in a time like that, no-one stays innocent for long."

"And now?"

"What do you think, Mr Dynamo?"

Dirk hadn't given his name since he came to town. No matter what novelty he had for the children, Ubu Peter had known he was coming.

They strolled along the docks, his guide pointing out what passed for the sights of Freeport, mostly the warehouses and ships of guano companies. As they were walking, a barge drifted into the bay and bumped up against one of the ships, a cloud of grey dust rising from both. Men scrambled over the smaller vessel, cloths over their mouths, skin mottled white by their cargo. They filled buckets with guano, white men on the deck above hauling the precious waste into their hold for its journey to Europe.

"How are things for the black man in America?" Ubu Peter watched his countrymen shovel the same shit that smeared their skin. "Are they free, like us?"

"Damn straight they are." The tone of the question put Dirk on edge, as if a doctor were prodding at a painful wound. "Plenty of good men died making sure it happened."

"So now, for you, slavery is fixed?"

"Unless I got two more scars and five less buddies for nothing, hell yes it's fixed."

Ubu Peter had that look on his face again, the soft, secret smile that unsettled and infuriated Dirk, making him want to shake the man and find out what the hell he was missing. But this was his host in a foreign town, not some stranger in a bar, so he kept his cool and kept walking, trying to fathom it in his mind.

Something about the island, its people, its history, maybe something about Dirk himself, it amused Ubu Peter. Did he think this place was somehow superior? Because Dirk didn't see much to be superior about. Maybe it was the sort of twisted superiority he'd seen in Confederate officers at the end of the war, the inner victory of knowing you were right even when the world had gone so very wrong.

With slavery at the front of his mind, he looked again around the bay, seeing details he hadn't noticed before. Rusted remnants of chains embedded in the hotel walls. The ghosts of signs showing through faded whitewash, advertising the strength and health of their wares.

"This place was pretty big in the trade, huh?" he asked.

"It was a no-place." There was a sorrow beneath Ubu Peter's words. "Not truly Africa, nor England, nor the promised hell of the Americas. A place where slavers and merchants could do business without needing to dirty their feet on a foreign land."

The ships, like the buildings, told part of the story. Dirk had seen their like off the coast of Florida and Louisiana, old hulks whose creaking timbers that once carried poor wretches across the Atlantic. With that realisation, he saw the port through Ubu Peter's eyes, still full of oppressed blacks, their fates tied to the tools of the slave trade, and to the white men who dictated to them from the faded grandeur of the hotel. Dirk's America might have moved on, but this place was still living its history.

Had America really moved on? Dirk found that he couldn't bring himself to face that question, so instead he turned to the business that had brought him here.

"Didn't a slave ship sink somewhere around this bay?" He lit a cigarillo, offered another to his guide.

"No, thank you." Ubu Peter waved away the offer and pointed past the southern headland. "Around the coast there are two tall rocks standing out of the sea. The captain of that ship was young, the pilot foolish. They tried to sail between those pillars, showing off their skill. But there are other rocks too, hidden below the water."

"Any survivors?"

"The crew." There was bitterness in the words.

Their route was taking them away from the docks now, back towards the market. Dirk pictured every person they passed in chains, trapped in a hold fast filling with water as their captors left them to die. The thought made him shudder, but at least now he knew where he needed to go.

"You know if anyone's ever been out to the wreck?" he asked.

"No!" Ubu Peter looked shocked. "It is a bad place, haunted by the spirits of the ones who died. Those waters are death."

Important as it was to respect his host, Dirk didn't hold with talk of spirits or of God. His was the rational mind of the modern age, and he hated to hear smart folks slip into superstition. But before he could assemble an answer in his head, they reached Omalara's tent and the rising sound of Cullen's voice.

"...was meant to be in a cage for experiments, not roaming the jungle."

"You asked for hunt, we gave you hunt."

"With the greatest of respect, I wanted a couple of colourful... Oh, Dynamo, you're back!"

Stooping to peer inside, Dirk nodded to Cullen and the two women tending to him - loyal Bekoe-Kumi, looking at the patient in concern, and elderly Omalara, whose voice he'd just heard. He wished he'd had the chance to listen to more of their conversation, hinting as it did at yet more secrets. If he hadn't been with Ubu Peter he might have stayed out of sight and listened, but there was no point skulking when you'd already been spotted.

Ubu Peter watched him with a piercing gaze, while Dirk tried to act nonchalant.

"I hear I have you to thank for saving my life." Cullen shifted himself up on his elbows, against the protests of Omalara and Bekoe-Kumi. His shirt had been cut away, his head and chest swathed in bandages and sharp smelling poultices.

"Tim did his share too." Dirk tried not to think about how close that had come to killing him.

"And where is Sir Timothy now?" Cullen's ingratiating smile gave way to a wince.

"Probably back at your mansion, playin' with the kill." Dirk could picture staff rushing from the grand house, intent on helping the injured from the hunting party, only to find Blaze-Simms digging around in a heap of guts. He hoped they'd have the sense to drag both the Englishman and the bear home. "We should head back too, let them know you're OK."

Cullen paused long enough for Omalara to give an almost imperceptible nod.

"You're right," he said. "After all, it's nearly time for tea."

#

The mirror above Dirk's dresser had an ornate frame of gilt fruit and leaves. Like other decorations in the mansion, it looked like the handywork of someone who knew Europe and its culture second-hand. The leaves were a strange mix of oak and jungle fronds, the clustered fruits mangoes and blackberries. In its mismatched flora, it achieved an exoticism and travelled diversity that at once exceeded and undermined the world-spanning grandeur of its glittering antecedents.

In the centre of this magnificence Dirk saw himself, dirty and battered. He fumbled with worn fingers at the buttons of his stained shirt, revealing a chest so bruised it was more blue than pink, crushed the colour of ripe berries by the bear.

Wincing at every movement, he hung his shirt over the back of a chair next to his holstered Gravemaker. Tomorrow it was coming with him. It didn't matter if they were shopping for coconuts, he wasn't going anywhere without the pistol.

Not that his plans for tomorrow involved much time on the island. He'd talked with Blaze-Simms and Isabelle since getting back to the house, and they'd settled on a plan. Blaze-Simms had been excited about the bear, its body distorted by some compound that stimulated muscle growth. He'd wanted to go hunting again, to see if he could find more critters like it. But when Dirk told him what he'd learned, that excitement turned towards the wreck instead. He started talking about ocean currents, underwater archaeology, and his new diving kit, before drifting off into sketching fresh ideas in his notepad.

Tomorrow was a day for treasure hunting.

Night drifted in through an open window, a medley of cricket song and bat cries. The warm scents of the day faded from the air as jungle flowers closed up against the darkness, leaving the freshness of leaves and lawn, undercut and an inescapable hint of ageing bird shit.

Dirk settled on the edge of the bed, carefully stitching up a tear in his shirt. He'd had a hell of a time getting needle and thread. The servants had fallen over themselves to fix the shirt for him, and he'd had to shout to get what he wanted. He'd been patching his same three shirts for years, he didn't need someone else doing it now.

The shouting had thrown him. Hearing his voice echoing back across the kitchen, like some lazy aristocrat screaming the servants into line. It was no way to treat anyone, never mind real workers. But he'd felt so frustrated. The feeling had been building for a while, at least since the bear. He'd just been so damned stupid, letting it trap him against the tree, grating him on the bark like a giant pink fruit. He should have jumped clear and grabbed a weapon, or scrambled up and gone for the eyes. Instead, Blaze-Simms had had to rescue him from his own screw-up. Next time, he'd know better. Next time he'd...

A shout pierced the stillness of night. Not pausing to think, Dirk rushed onto the landing, listening as another yell tore the air. It was coming from Isabelle's room.

He grabbed the handle and turned, but it was locked. He rattled it up and down, hoping that the door had just gotten jammed.

"Mrs McNair?" He hammered at the door. "Mrs McNair? You need help?"

The only answer was another drawn-out scream.

Chapter 6: Runners Under Starlight

The door crashed open beneath Dirk's shoulder, pain flaring from his injury. Isabelle stood in her night-dress by a four-poster bed, pointing a pistol at the floor-length window. Her mouth hung wide as she drew breath for another cry for help.

Dirk crossed to the window in four swift strides and gazed out into darkness.

"What happened?" he asked.

"There was a face." Isabelle steadied herself on one of the bedposts. "It appeared out of nowhere, just staring at me through the window."

"What did he look like?" He couldn't see anything out there in the dark.

"Black, with pale eyes." There was something in Isabelle's face that Dirk couldn't quite read, as focused on him as on the intruder.

Blaze-Simms dashed through the door, tie hanging loose, walking stick raised for action. A lead ran from there to the box hanging in his other hand. He saw Dirk, stern and bare-chested, and stopped.

"I say, what's going on?" A gear fell from the gadget, started rolling across the floor, and then changed direction, heading straight toward the lowered walking stick.

"One of the servants, maybe?" Dirk ignored him, still focused on Isabelle.

"Not that sort of black." She shook her head. "Pitch black."

Dirk pushed the window open and stepped out onto a balcony. No-one was there. He peered over the edge and across the balconies to left and right, but saw nothing unusual. Across the grounds, a couple of figures were heading off the lawn and into the jungle. Could it have been one of them?

He spun around, ready to dash back through the house.

Caught by the light shining out of Isabelle's room, a shadow clung to the wall. A frozen pool of midnight black, staring down at him through a pale slit around a pair of twinkling eyes.

"Holy..." Dirk reached beneath his left arm, finding neither holster nor gun. "Damn."

The black figure skittered across the wall, human in shape but spider-like in agility, then dropped into the darkness around the base of the mansion. Cursing again, Dirk vaulted over the rail. He landed with a thump on the veranda roof, which sagged beneath him. Feet sliding, he tumbled over the edge and onto the gravel drive. His arm stung where he'd scraped it on the rough boards.

Leaping to his feet, Dirk glanced around. A deeper darkness, almost invisible under starlight, was rushing across the night-blackened lawn. He dashed after it, over the rough crunch of gravel and then the soft spring of well-manicured grass, heading into the jungle.

The darkness was deeper beneath the trees, grey patches of starlit ground broken by tall palms. Dirk halted, peering through the foliage. Fronds swayed in the night wind, the lungs of the jungle lifting as it breathed. He crept forward, straining to hear anything other than the rasp of crickets. A snapping twig made him jump, only to realise that the sound had come from beneath his feet. Shifting deeper into the shadows, he skulked like a predator through the foliage, looking for any clue that his prey had passed.

Something hissed through the air. Dirk dived, landing in a heap of rotting leaves. A glistening disk buried itself in the tree behind him. He scrambled for cover, more razor-edged circles spinning into the ground where he had been.

"Dynamo!" Blaze-Simms's voice cut through the night. "I say, Dynamo, are you in there?"

The Englishman was silhouetted against a break in the tree-line, his experimental rifle pointing into the deeper darkness.

"Dynamo?" he called out again.

Dirk leapt, grappling Blaze-Simms to the ground as something hissed past their heads. The gun went off with a loud whump and a crack of bullets hitting tree-trunks. Then silence.

"What was that?" Blaze-Simms whispered.

"Shuriken," Dirk replied.

"Any more to come?" Blaze-Simms was wriggling beneath him, trying to peer out. "I left my Nocturnal Visual Stimulator back in Manchester."

"Your what?"

"Night vision hat."

"Oh." Dirk shook his head. Blaze-Simms had brought his clockwork sheet straightener and a miniature steam turbine, but not a night vision hat. They needed to talk later about priorities.

He grabbed a branch and waved it above his head. Nothing moved. A cricket, silenced by the sounds of violence, recommenced its rasping song.

"Reckon that's it." Dirk's relief didn't quite chase away the tension.

"Do you think I bagged the blighter?" There was an eagerness in Blaze-Simms's voice.

"We'd have heard the body fall. Reckon he's made his escape."

"Shame."

Dirk lay listening. There wasn't the faintest footfall or rustle of foliage.

"Dirk, old chap?"

"Yeah?"

"Would you mind moving? The gun's pressing somewhere rather delicate."

Warily, Dirk rose to his feet, turning his head as he listened to the noises of the night. Their attacker walked as silent as a ghost, but that didn't mean there weren't any clues. The jungle was alive with nature, the rattling of insects, the shriek of bats, the rustle of leaves where other things stalked. But it was quieter in one direction than others, as if its inhabitants were hiding from an unfamiliar and menacing beast.

"This way," Dirk whispered.

The jungle floor was soft beneath his bare feet, a mulch of moss and rotting leaves. Fronds brushed his skin, sensation heightened by the still darkness.

Creeping through the jungle with Blaze-Simms was like attending a funeral with a small, well-intentioned child. He tried hard to blend in, but he didn't quite get it, and he couldn't help but make some noise. If the tables had been turned, if they'd been the ones trying to evade the ninja's pursuit, Dirk might as well have lain down on the ground and bared his neck for the blade. But a predator could afford to be less subtle than its prey.

With no sounds to lead him, Dirk instead stalked a trail of silence. Part of the jungle was quieter than the rest, as if the animals and birds had been scared away. Flanked by the slow sway of trees dancing in the warm Atlantic wind, he advanced through that silent space.

Insects chased each other through the night and Dirk felt the prickle of tiny legs against his bare chest. For all that he swatted away, more kept coming, colonising his skin with suckered feet and probing tongues.

Their path took them away from the house for an hour or more, until the texture of the night changed again. Up ahead, the silence they had been pursuing was replaced by a murmur of humanity, rising in volume as they approached. Fragments of amber light flickered between the trees, accompanied by voices arguing in the local dialect.

They crept closer to the noise, Dirk keeping tree trunks between them and the source of the light. At last they found themselves peering through a fat, rubber-leafed bush at the source of the noise.

A bonfire cast a warm glow across a wide clearing. Dozens of locals sat cross-legged around it, listening to two of their number argue. Dirk recognised the statuesque form of Ubu Peter, his guide from earlier in the day, gesticulating wildly as he made his points. Across from him was a younger, leaner man who rubbed his head in exasperation as he spoke. At first they seemed wild and furious. But after a few minutes Dirk saw a rhythm to the back and forth, a pattern like an old familiar dance. One man offered a swift stab of query, the other a lengthy, audience-pleasing response, and then the roles reversed, the questioner now the questioned, his focus not on reasoning with his opponent but on swaying the crowd, who were clearly enjoying the spectacle, signalling approval or approbation with the movement of their heads. Every so often they pounded the ground in applause.

Whatever Dirk had expected to find out here, this wasn't it, but it could provide answers to some of the questions bothering him.

"I say," Timothy whispered, "I haven't seen such a jolly debate since Eton."

There were several familiar faces in the crowd, mostly servants from the party, more relaxed now without tailcoats and bow ties.

Across the clearing, Dirk saw a shadow shift, the silhouette of a tree trunk blowing the opposite way from its neighbours. The ninja was also watching their hosts at play.

The discussion ended amid much applause. Ubu Peter bowed to his opponent, who raised his hands in surrender.

Spectators offered handshakes, slaps on the back, and earnest praise as the two men sat down among them.

Another figure raised a withered arm, and silence fell.

"Friends, you all practised your good arguing." Omalara was the first speaker to use English. She leaned on a younger woman for support. "Done your rhetoric like the lesson plan says, even though we out of the big house on account of our guests. And now's time for English lesson. Ain't in the plan, Omalara knows, but we got our public face here, and he don't talk our tongue good as we talk his. So you listen to him first, then you show how well you learn."

Omalara turned to her left and Governor Cullen stepped into the firelight, his usually smiling face crumpled into a frown beneath a swathe of bandages. Bekoe-Kumi stood beside him, a muscular pillar of support, and Cullen leaned towards her with an easy intimacy. When he stumbled and grabbed her bandaged arm she didn't flinch, but looked at him with concern. They made a strange pair, a heavily bandaged white man publicly supported by an African woman. Their audience did not seem to mind, smiling warmly at them both.

"Friends." Cullen's British voice sounded harsh compared with the other voices. "Honoured council. Thank you for taking the time to listen to your humble servant.

"We face a difficult decision. As you know, we currently have three guests staying at the mansion. Whether they came to investigate our situation, the wreck off Reinhart's Spur, or something else entirely I don't know, but they are looking our way now. Through an act of foolishness earlier today, we have let them get hold of the body of the bear."

"Act of foolishness?" The man who had debated with Ubu Peter rose. "You the one who took them hunting."

"Well you're the one who let that blasted experiment out, Felipe." Cullen's face crumpled in fury. "You could have picked any animal in the enclosures, but no, you had to pick the most malformed, over-developed specimen in the whole growth project."

"You just angry 'cause you was too slow to get outta the way." Felipe grinned with cruel amusement.

"Too slow? That thing's a monster!"

"Monster you helped make. Jus' like all th'other craziness."

"The difference being, I've kept our guests away from the other craziness." Cullen waved a finger at him, like a teacher telling off a rowdy pupil. "They have not been near the laboratory, the pens, even the palm groves. The closest they had been to seeing our super-guano was riding past a few half-grown fields. Then you went and let the bear out!"

"Hush now." Ubu Peter was on his feet, a placating presence between Felipe and Cullen. "Friend Felipe, friend Reginald, be calm. So they've seen the bear. What does it matter? What we have here is not about those things. We can explain them away, be rid of them if need be. We will still have what we are about. Our way of life is secure."

Dirk sat back in the bushes, putting the pieces together in his mind. This island was no mere colony, with a governing elite oppressing the working masses. Instead, the people were working together, with Cullen just one man among equals. Together, they were learning rhetoric, English, and who knew what else, sharpening their skills to build a stronger society. They were experimenting with guano, growing strange animals and plants, finding ways to better feed themselves. It was the sort of world he dreamed of, one emerging from the horrors of the past to forge something smarter and more equal. And it was happening in secret, beneath the noses of the British.

"It's not that simple." Cullen shook his head. "Blaze-Simms is a noted scientist. Dynamo's a private investigator. McNair is famed for her shrewdness. They won't stop with the bear, they'll want to know what's behind it. We have enough trouble hiding our way of life from Braithwaite and his colleagues. How do you think the government will react when word gets out? An enclave of African socialists, growing strong on wild science and British commerce. We'll be overrun with redcoats before you can say Bonaparte. Our dreams will become a damp squib in the footnotes of history, all for the sake of that blasted bear."

Agitated voices filled the clearing. People shouted and waved sticks.

Dirk reached again for the gun that wasn't there, while he scanned the jungle for any sign of guards. He didn't want to be these people's enemy, but that was how they saw him. If someone stumbled across him and Blaze-Simms now they were as good as dead.

"Quiet." Ubu Peter raised his hands and the commotion died away. "You have been our cunning and cover before, Reginald. How do we avoid this?"

Cullen looked around the circle. Some of his audience eyed him with respect, others with wariness. What none of them showed was the deference due a colonial governor.

"Explain the situation." His look was defiant. "Dynamo's a radical, the others seem reasonable, we might-"

His words were lost amid a rising wave of outrage. Dirk suffered the terrible sinking feeling of watching an opportunity slip out of his grasp. These folks were too scared for their way of life to risk trusting him. Given their history, he couldn't blame them.

Omalara raised a hand and silence fell again across the clearing.

"This island is governed by reason, not braying jackals." She glared around her. "You listen to Omalara, and you listen to friend Reginald. Then you want to disagree, you do it like civilised men.

"So, who gonna be a civilised man?"

Hope stirred in Dirk's heart. Maybe reason would prevail.

Felipe stepped forward.

"Those people get back to England, who knows what they do." His expression was one of deadly calm. "Maybe they keep quiet and we keep safe. Maybe they run tell the government, who send soldiers to put us in our place. Maybe they go tell the guano men, and they come steal what we been learning. Or maybe a hundred other things, none of them good.

"But it is not just about that. They came for the wreck. You think they go home without seeing that? These are white men. They will not listen when we say no."

There were murmurs of outrage around the circle, the audience's faces creasing into frowns. This was how mobs started, and three adventurers couldn't do much against a whole crowd.

"We could at least try," Cullen said. "Ask them not to disturb the wreck. Explain our situation. They might not just keep quiet. They might be of help. Imagine how useful it would be to have friends in the outside world."

For a moment longer Dirk's hope lived, but then he saw Felipe's face.

"We got friends in the outside world." Felipe pointed at Bekoe-Kumi, who stiffened but stood silent. "You forget you own friends from Dahomey? You don' mean friends of th'island, you mean friends in Europe."

"Well, yes, alright," Cullen blustered. "And is that bad?"

"Is Europe bad?" Felipe held up his hands, wrists together as if bound in manacles. "Remember the chains of our ancestors! Remember why the wreck is sacred!"

"That's not what I..." Cullen clutched his head. "I just mean that..."

"We know what you mean. You mean it different now you people in danger."

"I don't..." Even by the warm glow of the fire, Cullen looked pale and worn. He shook his head as if fending off invisible flies. A bandage came loose, trailing down his face.

"We understand." Ubu Peter again stepped forward, hands spread wide, gesturing for calm. "It would be sad to hurt these people who have done us no harm. They do not seem cruel or wicked. One of them saved your life. But Felipe is right. They are not likely to listen to us. They will go to the wreck and disturb the spirits of the lost. If they go home they will tell the English what they have seen here. For the good of the island, they cannot leave."

"How are you going to stop them?" From somewhere inside, Cullen found one last burst of strength, trembling with pain and passion as he spoke. "Steal their boat? They'll get passage on a guano ship. Persuade them to live in Hakon? These people have jobs, families, friends, they won't want to stay on this god-forsaken cluster of rocks. Maybe lock them up in the cellar? I don't believe that you can bear to see other people in chains."

"For your sake we will talk to them first, governor." Ubu Peter emphasised that final word, a brutal reminder of who Cullen was meant to be. "But if that does not work, you know what we must do."

He turned solemnly to speak to the whole gathered group.

"For all our sakes, these people will die."

Chapter 7: The World Turns

Dirk burst through Isabelle's door for the second time that night

"Mr Dynamo," she exclaimed. "It would be polite to knock."

Dirk opened the curtains and peered out onto the balcony, checking for any sign of intruders, ninja or otherwise. Intruders other than himself, he thought after a moment. He saw nothing but his own ghostly reflection and the swaying jungle.

"Pardon me, ma'am," he said, "but something's come up."

He closed the curtains and turned to face Isabelle. She sat up in bed, a lamp burning on her nightstand, a French novel open on her lap. Her night-dress revealed pale, slender arms. She raised one eyebrow, fingers drumming on the cover of the book. No doubting it, Mrs McNair was damned pleasing on the eye, even dressed in bedsheets and disapproval. In fact, a guilty corner of Dirk's brain figured that school-ma'am sternness was probably part of the appeal.

That and the pistol sticking out from under the book.

"I see you haven't had time to dress," she said.

Dirk looked down and remembered, for the first time since the clearing, that he was naked from the waist up. Imminent danger was briefly forgotten as he stood, mouth flapping like a guppy, trying to recall what he'd meant to say.

Then Blaze-Simms stumbled through the door, panting for breath, and reality rushed in with him.

#

"But what about the ninja?"

Isabelle snapped the lid of her travel case shut. She was dressed now, having disappeared behind a screen while Dirk and Blaze-Simms told their story. Knowing she might be naked behind there had left Dirk stumbling over words, leaving Blaze-Simms to fill the gaps. To Dirk, class meant status and struggle. To his friend it was about poise under social pressure, even with a naked lady just out of view.

"Don't suppose you've got anythin' in dark grey?" Dirk asked. "Blends in better."

"I am a noble daughter of England, not a footpad." Clad in black from hairpins to boot-heels, Mrs McNair was as well dressed for night-time escapades as a lady of leisure could be. "There are certain places to which fashion will not go, and dark grey, apparently like the Americas, is one of them."

"Just askin'." Dirk didn't care for patriotism any more than he did for fashion, yet her comment had cut him.

"As was I, so please tell me about the ninja."

"Lost track of him while we were watching the debate." Dirk peered once more through the window. "Reckon he'll catch up with us later. Right now, I'm more worried about our hosts."

All was quiet out front of the governor's mansion. Of course, it would be. Everything that mattered happened around back or in the jungle, out of sight and out of mind.

"How long d'you need to pack, Tim?" Dynamo asked.

"Gosh, I'm not really sure," Blaze-Simms replied. "There are usually servants for that sort of thing. Twenty minutes, perhaps?"

"You've got five."

Timothy scurried away down the corridor.

"Someone's comin'." Dirk dimmed the light and pointed out across the lawn. Two horses were approaching, shadow creatures silhouetted against the pale, starlit drive. On one, a rider sat tall in the saddle. Reins trailed back to the other horse, whose rider might as well have been a sack of guano, hunched limp and useless across the beast's neck.

"Who is it?" Isabelle stood beside him, gazing out.

"Reckon the front one's that Dahomeyan gal," Dirk said. "Other could be Omalara or Cullen, or just a bundle of blankets for all I can tell."

She leaned forward to peer past a partition in the window panes.

"It's Reginald," she said. "Look, that's the shoulders of a man in a suit."

Dirk nodded. There was a sharpness to the edges of the shadow, the distinct lines that separated a well-dressed European from the shapes of nature.

Isabelle was close now. He could smell her body beneath her lavender scent. Her eyes were wide in the soft glow of the lamp.

"Don't you need to pack?" she asked.

"I'm always ready to go." He felt proud, then instantly foolish, scrabbling to explain himself. "Comes from livin' so long on the road."

"You're going like this?" Her hand hovered over his chest. He could feel the air curling around her fingertips.

"How long d'you think it takes me to throw clothes on and off?"

"I'm afraid I couldn't say."

Her breath brushed his skin, sending a shiver through him despite the tropical heat. He shouldn't be thinking like this about a married woman, but those thoughts kept him from backing away.

"Shouldn't you be going?" Her words were no more than a whisper. "You only gave Timothy five minutes."

"That's five Blaze-Simms minutes. If he gets distracted, it'll be dawn before he knows time's up."

"So we're..."

But mention of Blaze-Simms had broken the spell, letting Dirk escape his treacherous thoughts.

"I'll grab my boots." He took a step back. "Be ready to go."

Two minutes later, Dirk was on the landing - booted, shirted and dragging Blaze-Simms from his room. A pile of bags weighed down the Englishman, clothes, papers, and esoteric equipment bursting from every seam, his experimental gun hanging from his shoulder.

"What state's the boat in?"

Dirk grabbed the largest of the cases. His own luggage consisted of a single carpet bag and a shoulder holster. He'd experienced Blaze-Simms's travelling style before, weighed down by everything from callipers to spare cravats, and exasperating as it was, there was no point arguing about it. If push really came to shove, he trusted Blaze-Simms to cut to what was vital. It wasn't like he couldn't afford new luggage.

"The old girl's ready to go whenever we are." Blaze-Simms wriggled a kit bag up onto his shoulder, freeing a hand for his walking stick. "There are plenty of preserved supplies, my dodecahedric evaporator can desalinate water for us, and there was never a chance to unload the diving kit."

Isabelle emerged from her room. Dirk had been ready to do the chivalrous thing and take her cases, but she seemed to be coping fine. Certainly better than Blaze-Simms.

"We grab a buggy and head straight for the boat." Dirk shifted his bags, getting a better balance. "Dawn can't be far off. We get round to Reinhart's Spur, do the dive, and get out to sea before anyone catches us."

The others nodded.

"But before we do that," he said, "I want a word with Cullen."

A door creaked open in the hallway below. Without a word, all three of them set their bags down and reached for their weapons.

Dirk slid along the wall, cloaked in shadows until he reached the balcony overlooking the hall. Candles fluttered, making the shadow of the Dahomeyan statue dance, its sword rising and falling above the front door.

Bekoe-Kumi stepped across the threshold, Cullen held in her arms. She strode through the room, casually kicking the door shut behind her, and disappeared beneath the stairs. Another door slammed and Dirk relaxed.

He turned to Blaze-Simms.

"You fetch the buggy and get her loaded up. Mrs Mc-Nair, you're with me."

#

The servants' quarters smelled of work. The smoke and spices of the kitchen. The damp sheets and detergent of the laundry. The polish, flour and sawdust of the storeroom. They smelled like diligence and round-the-clock labour.

But at three in the morning they were silent. No clatter of pans. No sloshing of buckets. No thump of boxes and sacks. Just tidy rooms off a long, empty passage, Dirk and Isabelle's footfalls whispering across the floor.

Near the far end, a door hung open. Light fell in a bright block across the darkened corridor, and the crackle of a fire crept out beneath a murmur of conversation - one voice weak, another whispering.

Dirk rounded the doorway and looked into the servants' dining room. Unlike the other rooms at the back of the house this one had windows, though they were shuttered against the night. A fire was lit in the grate, casting a rich glow as it heated a pan of water.

A table ran down the centre of the room, a space of rest for those who kept the governor's house running. In most households, this would have been the one sanctuary of the servants, a place for them to share their food and thoughts in the few moments when they were allowed to rest. Dirk wondered how long it had been since that was true here, what sort of lives had been lived in this kitchen instead. Had it been a place of joy and laughter? Had the staff simply left it empty, returning to their own homes instead?

Cullen slouched at the table, looking very comfortable for a gentleman in the servants' quarters. Not that there were servants here. Most of them, Dirk was sure, were out in the jungle, continuing the council on which he and Blaze-Simms had spied. Only regal Bekoe-Kumi was present, bathing the governor's wounds. She lingered about the task, the fingers of her free hand entwined with Cullen's, heedless of the bandage in which her shoulder was wrapped. It was such a tender moment, Dirk was loath to break it.

Cullen saved him from that choice.

"What can I do for you, Mr Dynamo?" The governor's voice was weary. He seemed unable to look Dirk in the eye.

Bekoe-Kumi rose, her face hardening, her body tightening. She pulled a poker from the fire and stood between the two men, a guardian angel with a sword of red hot iron.

"You can give me some straight answers." Dirk took a step forward.

"I'm afraid I don't understand, old chap." Cullen had more spirit than Dirk had realised. Even injured and exhausted he put on a good front.

"Don't be a fool, Reginald." Isabelle's skirts brushed against Dirk as she walked past him into the room. "We've only been here two days and already your charade is falling apart. You can't keep up the pretence any longer."

"Can't I?" Cullen laughed. "How is Mr McNair? Will we be seeing him soon? Will anyone?"

Dirk wondered what he meant, but now wasn't the time to ask.

"You're right, this is about me." Isabelle rolled her eyes. "Not your African lover and her alchemist friends."

"You think you're better than me?" Bekoe-Kumi leaned forwards, her stare like a drill boring into Isabelle's brain. "Of course you do. You are white."

The look Isabelle returned was softer but just as strong, one that over-whelmed with sympathy instead of piercing to the soul.

"I don't think that I'm better." She stood steady as the stones beneath their feet. "We are both women. We have both found strength despite the injustices brought by men." An intensity took hold of her voice. "But I have struggled all my life to get to where I am now. I have never let a man stand in my way once my course is set, and I am damned if I will let you."

The air was taut as a palm tree straining in a hurricane, a fraction of pressure away from snapping.

"I am of the ahosi," Bekoe-Kumi said. "The brides of the King of Dahomey. Do you know what that means?"

"Means the king's a pretty liberal guy." Dirk stepped between the two women. He was too world-weary to enjoy a cat-fight, even if he'd fancied Isabelle's chances. "And you're well trained in crown wearing and whatever else kings like."

Bekoe-Kumi narrowed her eyes. There was a squeal of brutalised metal as she pressed the poker point-first against the floor and it buckled under her strength. She drop it, and it hit the ground with a clang.

Dirk rolled his shoulders and raised his fists.

"It's not that sort of marriage," Isabelle said. "The ahosi are the king's fighting elite, the marriage ceremonial. King Glele once told me that to be ahosi means to be more than a warrior. It means to march without rest, to fight without mercy, to stand when around you is nothing but fire, and then to carry the injured men home."

Suddenly it all made sense. Bekoe-Kumi's muscled arms, her peerless fighting stance, the perfect indifference with which she watched them. Dirk listened to the half hoop of metal that had once been the poker, rocking back and forth on the cracked granite floor.

"It's always an honour to meet someone who strives to be the best," he said. "And after this past week, there ain't a part of me that doesn't hurt, even before we've started fighting. But I'm an American, and you know what that means? It means not to giving a crap about any of that."

"You come to our land and tell us you will do whatever you want, that you don't care what it means to us?" Bekoe-Kumi glared at him. "Felipe is right. There is only one way to stop the white man."

She snatched a knife from the table. It glistened in the firelight, a deadly point of steel driven by perfectly toned muscles.

Twisting on the spot, Dirk let the strike slide past. He brought his fist down where she should have been, hitting only empty space. Bekoe-Kumi slashed out with the knife and Dirk dived clear, rolling across the floor, grabbing the pot from the fire, and turning as he came to his feet. Pan and knife clanged against each other. Boiling water steamed across the stones.

"Stop!" Cullen dragged himself to his feet, hunched over the table like a man twice his age. "If we stoop to their level what does that make us?"

His eyes sparkled with unshed tears.

"I will not listen to the orders of a white man," Bekoe-Kumi snarled.

"Then listen to the plea of a man who loves you." Cullen's voice cracked and tears ran down his cheeks. "After everything I've lost, I can't stand to see you hurt too."

The fierce lines of Bekoe-Kumi's face soften. At last she stepped back, lowered the knife onto the table, and went to Cullen. With her help, he sank back into his seat. But her eyes never left Dirk. Her expression was that of a prize fighter, ready to spring into action at the ringing of the bell.

Silhouetted against the firelight, Cullen waved Dirk and Isabelle into a pair of rough seats. He pulled cigars from his pocket and passed one to Dirk, setting the seal on their truce. Their faces were briefly lit by the phosphorescent flare of a match.

Both men breathed deep lungfuls of rich smoke as they settled in front of the roaring fire. Dirk was reminded of a time he'd shared a peace pipe with plains Indians. Tobacco, it seemed, was the great healer.

"I was sent here as a punishment." Cullen took a drag on his cigar, gazing up into the blue skies of memory. "You might not think it to look at me, but I've always been something of a rebel. My father was stationed in Paris in the forties, and I was there during the revolution of forty-eight. The atmosphere that year was electrifying. All the way from Brazil to Poland, people were rising up to change the world. I was young and naive, caught up in the romance of revolutions. Even as so many were thwarted, I still believed.

"I kept believing, even as I went through Eton and Oxford, then took up a place in the diplomatic service. But my superiors eventually realised that my views were out of step. They didn't want to make a fuss - no-one ever does, and father was well respected. So instead of firing me they sent me to the most obscure posting they could find. After all, what harm could a socialist do in Hakon?"

He chuckled, then took another drag on his cigar.

"It took me a while, after I got here, to realise anything was odd. There hadn't been a governor for a good five years, and there was a lot to get into order. They hadn't given me a secretary or an estate manager so I had to do it all myself. Relationships with the guano companies, visits to our neighbours, even adjusting to the climate. I didn't bother about the background stuff - the farmers, the dock crews, the household staff. I didn't have to. There were no problems."

He faltered, touching his bandaged head with a grimace.

Bekoe-Kumi reached out a hand. As their fingers met, his confidence returned.

"Everything worked so damned smoothly." His eyes followed the smoke trailing from his cigar. "I never thought about what kept it all ticking. Then one day I got up, and

I did all the things one does of a morning – get dressed, eat breakfast, take a little stroll around the grounds. Everything looked well, the chaps were at their work, the house and gardens were in order.

"Then I noticed this little old lady watching me. I was filled with the queerest sensation of deja vu. My imagination ran wild, wondering if she was a witch casting her hex on me. Finally I realised the truth of it, that I had simply been doing the same thing, day after day, for three months. Clothes laid out by my bed, breakfast on schedule, servants in the grounds on my walk, and her there, every day, watching me.

That was when I knew that something wasn't right. The estate was running like clockwork, and I wasn't lifting a finger to make it happen. Someone was in control, and that someone wasn't me.

"The next day I woke up early, my guts churning with tension. I was going to confront them, whoever they were. I'd be out on the lawn when that creepy old lady arrived and I'd demand some answers. I put on my most official suit, imagining how shocked she'd look when she turned up to spy on me and I was there first. I strode down the stairs, puffed up with my own smartness.

"And there she was in the hallway, waiting for me.

"That day I heard the truth."

The words poured from Cullen like a confession. The more he talked the more he sat up straight, as if a weight had been lifted from him.

He talked about the real life of the island, as shown to him by Omalara. A secret commune working and studying together, hidden in plain sight. Government by a council for all the islanders, inspired by the Dahomeyan Great Council. A government more radically egalitarian than even young Cullen had dreamed of. A society kept free from the white man in the only way it could be - by being invisible to him.

The locals acted like good servants while Europeans were - bowing and scraping, working the land, keeping talkative children away from visitors. The white man's indifference to native Africans became an asset, visiting merchants happy to pay them no attention as long as the guano flowed. But out of sight, hidden in their homes or in the depths of the jungle, they were their own masters - literate, democratic, self-supporting, independent of the white man and his reluctantly dispersed wealth. Theirs was a soft revolution, unknown and unopposed.

Suddenly, Cullen was faced with a chance to see his ideals succeed. His posting to Hakon was a dead-end promotion. Curious Cullen with his radical views had been put out to pasture before he was far past thirty. But his containment had become an opportunity. He could support these people. He could help change this small corner of the world.

So an alliance was born. Cullen became the public face of the island society, fending off awkward questions and sharing profits from the guano trade. He stopped talking about socialism and started playing the traditional diplomat. He opened up the governor's mansion as a secret school-house and shared home. He bought in books on science and engineering, the latest agricultural tools, all manner of modern machinery.

Soon the island wasn't just a social experiment, it was a scientific one too. In laboratories above the stables, the best and brightest set to work. Their ancestors had made dozens of different preparations from the guano, and now they took that further. They created super-fertilisers and growth serums, letting them grow enough crops to become self-sufficient. They created new chemicals, including explosives to defend themselves and fuel for machines like the warrior statue. The progress they achieved made them hungry for more.

"Is that what happened to the bear?" Dirk asked. "One of those compounds?"

Cullen nodded. "I imported animals to experiment on, to see the full effects of the chemicals. Some results were amazing, some horrifying, most short-lived. None were meant to get loose."

"Might I ask where you fit in?" Isabelle was looking at Bekoe-Kumi, who had remained silent throughout the story.

"Dahomey trades with Hakon," Bekoe-Kumi said. "The king knows something of the truth. There is... unity of purpose, if not of ways. I was sent as an emissary. Perhaps that is still my place. Perhaps not."

She looked at Cullen, then down at her hands, folded in her lap.

A long silence followed. The tension that came from holding in a secret had drained out of Cullen and he sat crumpled in his seat, Bekoe-Kumi waiting patiently on his next words. The others were lost in their own thoughts, trying to process what they'd heard.

Dirk was awash with admiration. These people had thrown off their shackles not through violence but through learning and progress. It was a magnificent achievement, especially given the challenges facing them. Could he stay and join their struggle, take the chance to better himself while improving the lives around him? Was this his chance to change the world?

One glance at Isabelle reminded him of what else was at stake. Not just this one community, but lost knowledge that could benefit all of humanity.

"We don't have to tell anyone," Dirk said at last. "We're here to fetch something from the wreck. You folks let us do that, we can leave you in peace, pretend all we saw was sand and sea."

To his relief, Isabelle was nodding agreement.

But Cullen wasn't.

"I'm afraid it's not that easy." The governor's face was filled with sadness. "The wreck is a symbol of what this island was, of what it has become. And it's a graveyard, filled with the victims of a most abhorrent trade. Even if I thought you should be allowed to go there, the others wouldn't let you. Please, before you come to any more harm, just go home."

"I'm sure we can win your friends around." Isabelle rose from her seat. "Mr Dynamo, we have a tablet to find. Shall we?"

As they stepped through the door, Dirk looked back one last time. Bekoe-Kumi was holding Reginald Cullen close, cradling him against a world of pain and disappointment. She held him gently, stroking his hair and whispering words of comfort. But the gaze she fixed on Dirk was one of hate.

#

Blaze-Simms tugged on the horse's reins, bringing the buggy to a halt. Dirk dropped their bags onto the sand and leapt out after them, turning to offer Isabelle a hand. Ignoring the gesture, she jumped down beside him.

Dawn was approaching, the sky a washed-out grey, starting to glow with excitement at the glory to come. The pier was a pale path across a darkly rippling sea, their boat a vague silhouette in the pre-dawn light. Dirk listened to the lapping of waves, the thud of the yacht against its moorings, the creak of something shifting on the boards.

There were other noises too. Small, subtle noises like people made when they were trying not to be seen.

"We ain't the first ones here." He stepped onto the dock and the others followed, leaving the bags where they lay.

"Hello?" Isabelle called out. "Who's there?"

A match flared, then another, and another, lighting tar-cloth torches down the length of the pier. Beneath them stood a dozen men, Ubu Peter and Felipe among them, all carrying rifles. At Ubu Peter's feet stood the statue that had guarded the entrance to the governor's mansion. Its blades twitched and steam trickled from its head.

"Where are you going at this time of night?" Ubu Peter asked.

"Where d'you think?" Dirk kept his hands lowered. They'd reasoned with Cullen, maybe they could reason with these folks too.

"Tell me." Ubu Peter's face was still as a mask.

"The wreck." These were good people. Dirk didn't want to fight them, but he didn't want to deceive either.

"No." Ubu Peter hefted a pick. "It is the only peace those spirits will ever have, and it is staying that way."

"But it's terribly important," Blaze-Simms blurted out. "There's a clue to the Great Library. No-one's been there in centuries. We'll find learning that was thought lost forever. This is your chance to be part of-"

"We will not let you near the ship." Ubu Peter trembled with barely-contained rage.

"You're an intelligent man," Isabelle said. "Think about the bigger picture."

"What picture is that?" He was snarling now, unable to hold back his anger. "The picture where white devils come out of Europe, tell men what to do, drag them half way around the world to die in sweat and chains? Where they make colonies and laws, so that the land is not their own? That picture is big enough. Maybe too big."

"We can share what we gather." She held her hands wide, the very image of a peace-maker. "Imagine what your people can achieve with knowledge that has been lost for centuries."

"We have enough of your knowledge. We do not need to sacrifice our independence to have more."

"But your whole society is based on our learning!" Blaze-Simms was red-faced with frustration. "Reading, writing, masonry, crop rotations, the laboratory in the barn, would you have any of that without us?"

"You think we are such savages that we would be homeless, hungry and illiterate without you?" Ubu Peter clenched his fists. "You think only a white man could learn to use bird shit? Yes, we have learned from you. Why shouldn't we, when African labour made your lives of learning possible? But now we are finding ways to learn for ourselves."

Blaze-Simms spluttered, dumbfounded.

"We can all learn from each other." Isabelle's tone was honeyed. "Surely you and Cullen have shown that. Why waste the opportunity?"

Ubu Peter stood silent a long moment. His companions shifted impatiently, twisting guns in their hands.

"Even if I agreed with you," he said, "even if I thought your reasons were good, even if I thought that this was something more than hollow words, still I could not let you go on.

"This is not about learning. It is not about the advancement of civilisation. It is about power. It is about white men who come into our world and think they can do as they please.

"To you, maybe learning is most important. Maybe what lies in that wreck is the most precious thing in the world, against which all else pales into insignificance. But to us the wreck is something else. It is a grave. It is a shrine. It is a home to hundreds, thousands, millions who will never return to the light of day. You may not believe that, but we do not believe in the sanctity of your learning."

As he spoke, his eyes roamed across Dirk and his companions, holding each of their gazes in turn. He never faltered, never blinked.

"To the white slavers, our ancestors were nothing but machines, to be worked until they broke beyond repair. To their families, they were people to be loved or hated, cherished or ignored. The white man's view triumphed because he had the power, not because he was right.

"You assume because you are white, your view will triumph now. We cannot let this happen. If we let you win, we let the white man continue to hold sway. Our small island of hope is too precious to surrender like that, no matter what you will learn. We will have lost, because we will not have decided our own fate.

"On such moments the world turns. You will not touch the wreck."

Chapter 8: To the Sea

It wasn't the first time Dirk had faced a firing line, and though he didn't fear death, he regretted bringing it upon his friends. Even the rattle of one of Blaze-Simms's contraptions sounded melancholy to his ears.

"Sorry for getting you into this." Dirk looked at Isabelle, who glared back at him.

"Do you know how patronising you sound?" She shook her head. "I'm the one who led you to this island. If I'm about to die, at least I will have made my own fate."

"I just meant-"

There was a click of guns being cocked.

"Well, I'm still sorry," Dirk said.

"No need for that yet." As Blaze-Simms spoke, there was a whirring sound.

Turning, Dirk saw a shimmering in the air. It expanded out from the Englishman's walking stick, forming a halo around them.

"Go on, fire!" Blaze-Simms exclaimed.

The natives looked at each other in confusion, except for Felipe. His eyes narrowed, there was a roar, and smoke belched from his gun.

The air rippled and a bullet clicked against the walking stick. More guns fired, and a moment later a dozen bullets were attached to Blaze-Simms's device.

"Mark Two Gauss Generator!" He grinned. "More portable than the one that burned out in Paris, but it only diverts light missiles."

"Looks good to me." Dirk stretched his aching arms, ready to fight. One hand went for his pistol before he realised that the generator made that useless too.

The locals had abandoned their guns, picking up shovels and picks from a pile on the pier.

The statue rushed forward, a foot-tall embodiment of the god of war. Its cold steel and slashing blades charged straight at Dirk.

He pulled his leg back and kicked with all his might, hitting the body of the statue. His toes slammed against a solid mass of metal, the pain almost making him scream, but it was worth it. The statue went flying, dropping into the sea with a splash and a hiss.

"Listen." Dirk limped toward the locals. "I hear why the wreck's important to you, but the world moves on. You can't keep us here forever, so let us onto our boat."

Yelling with rage, Felipe lunged to the attack.

Dirk ducked as Felipe swung a shovel at his head. Reaching out, he grabbed the handle, tugging his assailant onto his upraised knee. Felipe grunted and curled in upon himself. Without pausing, Dirk shoved him back into one of his comrades and turned the shovel on them, hitting both men with one swipe. One slumped to the deck. The other, reeling and clutching his face, stumbled off the pier with a splash.

A shout of panic made Dirk turn. Blaze-Simms was waving his walking stick wildly through the air. Its tip was glowing like the heart of a fire and smoke poured out around the handle.

With a flick of the wrist, Blaze-Simms flung the device away. It land on the sand, which started to melt around it. There was a crack like thunder and the stick exploded in a shower of shrapnel.

Ubu Peter advanced on Dirk, pick in hand.

"We could have worked together." Dirk hefted the shovel.

"I have seen what white men mean by working together," Ubu Peter said. "It is not good enough."

Torchlight sparkled on the tip of the pick as he swung it up and over. Dirk parried with the shovel, caught the pick on the blade, and brought both tools down. They hit the ground with a crack, the pick head burying itself in the pier. Before Ubu Peter could tug it free, Dirk darted forward, both fists swinging.

Abandoning the weapon, Ubu Peter raised his hands. Dodged and diving, he blocked Dirk's blows while trying to get his own through. Aiming high then low, lashing out as often as he blocked, he forced Dirk to slow his assault.

They swayed on their feet, eyeing each other like rival lions, ready to pounce at the first sign of weakness.

Dirk feinted left then jumped right, reaching for the abandoned shovel. But Ubu Peter saw it coming. His kicked Dirk in the forearm, stunning his nerves and sending the shovel spinning into the water.

Numbness seized Dirk's injured arm, the fingers frozen in place. Ubu Peter kicked out again, and Dirk jumped clear just in time, feeling the breeze of the blow's passage. His opponent was gaining momentum, shifting nimbly on his feet, pressing Dirk back with a series of swift strikes. He wobbled as his heel reached the edge of the pier. Nowhere left to go.

Taking a deep breath, Dirk leapt forward. He ignored the pain of blows battering his head and shoulders, focused on slamming his whole body against his opponent. They grabbed each other as they fell, rolling across the planks, both trying to end up on top. After a few dizzying turns Dirk found himself pinned, left arm trapped as Ubu Peter punched him repeatedly in the face.

Focusing all his will on his right shoulder, Dirk heaved his numb arm up and around, smashing it wildly against his opponent's head. Ubu Peter sagged, his gaze became unfocused, and Dirk seized his moment. With a grunt he hurled Ubu Peter to the floor.

The African looked up, his eyes unfocused, as Dirk hauled himself onto his knees and raised his fist.

"I'm sorry," Dirk said.

Then he delivered the knock-out blow.

Staggering to his feet, Dirk looked around. Several of their attackers were down but three remained, pressing Isabelle and Blaze-Simms back toward land. Blaze-Simms had his fists up Queensberry style and was fending off most of the attacks, but half his face was red and blood trickled from one hand. Isabelle, her skirts torn, waved a broken spade handle with exaggerated menace.

Life was returning to Dirk's right arm. Stalking forwards, he grabbed an opponent with each hand and slammed their heads together with a resounding thud. The third man turned with a start, only for Isabelle to smash the splintered handle against the back of his head. His eyes rolled and he slumped next to his allies.

"I see you're handy with a cudgel," Dirk said, smiling at Isabelle. "Good to know an English education ain't just manners."

One of his teeth felt loose. He turned and spat, trying to get the taste of blood out of his mouth.

"Mr Dynamo." Isabelle frowned at the sight. "Being assailed by ruffians is no excuse for behaving like one." She flung her improvised weapon into the water and nodded toward the boat. "Shall we?"

As Dirk went to fetch their bags, Blaze-Simms stared in disappointment at the charred remains of his portable Gauss Generator.

"I suppose I'd better not build that again," he said sadly. Then his face brightened. "Oh well, there's always something new."

#

Dawn cast a rosy glow across taut sails as they scudded out of the harbour. Trapped inside the diving suit, Dirk watched tiny waves ripple the clear blue waters and listened to his own breathing. He could do nothing else while Blaze-Simms fussed around him, tightening straps and testing seals.

The suit was a strange, bulbous thing, made of curved metal plates edged with rubber. The shoulders didn't fit quite right, causing the helmet to slip back and press against Dirk's face. His view was restricted to what he could see through a pair of thick glass lenses, and his own breath echoed eerily around him.

"Don't you Brits know anything about comfort?" Dirk's voice sounded hollow, trapped in the echo chamber of the helmet.

"Actually, a lot of the features are American," Blaze-Simms said, his voice muffled through the suit. "Your Commodore Maury left some notes with the Club while he was in England. Loose ideas for oceanographic devices. I've made them real."

Blaze-Simms waved a belt in front of the helmet's distorting window.

"A couple of extras, just in case." He held up a series of sheathed objects, explaining each one as he attached it to the belt. "Collapsing spade, in case the tablet's buried.

"Miniature harpoon gun, radium powered to shoot underwater. Should be handy if you meet sharks."

"Am I likely to meet sharks?" Dirk asked in alarm.

"You never know." Blaze-Simms shrugged and held up the next object. "Bowie knife, in case the harpoon fails.

"Underwater flares, magnesium and phosphorus compound with a jet funnel base. Pull the tab and release. They'll self-propel to the surface as they burn.

"Hatchet, for cutting into the wreck.

"Emergency air. Twist the tube and two compounds combine, reacting to provide oxygen through this hole for about three minutes. I'm rather pleased with that one. Took me hours to get the mix right."

Blaze-Simms reached around Dirk, clipping the belt into place. Last of all he attached an empty oil-skin bag.

"For the tablet."

Dirk clumped to the back of the yacht, the weight of the suit threatening to over-balance him at any moment. Chains clattered as Blaze-Simms readied the winch.

The harness tightened, lifting him off his feet and out over the water. Cut off from the world around him, he couldn't hear the passing seagulls or feel the wind that filled their wings. He was the epitome of humanity, cut off from nature by the products of progress. Man, perfected and alone.

He caught a glimpse of Isabelle waving and wishing him good luck. He smiled back, then remembered that she couldn't see his face, closed in by this cage of glass and brass. Instead, he raised a hand in salute.

The chain rattled, and he dropped into the ocean's embrace.

#

It wasn't like any kind of diving Dirk had done before. Instead of holding his breath, he had air piped down to him, flowing over his face from the tube above. He had to fight against the urge to swim, letting his weight carry him lower as the chain unwound above him. He could push himself forward a little but even that was hard work, his arms ungainly in the padded layers of the suit, his legs little more than dead weight.

He shifted his shoulders, straining to move the helmet for a better view. Sunlight, warped by the waves above, created a glowing web on the sea floor, a net through which fish happily swam. It fell across low ridges of sand that rose and fell with the waves.

As he settled on the bottom, sand spurted beneath his feet, a brief murky cloud that scattered the nearby fishes. As it fell away, he found that he could see for only fifty yards in any direction before the world faded to a blue-green haze.

Dirk trudged forwards, his legs slowed by the water and the weight of the suit. One step, two, three, gaining as much momentum as he could, sand rising behind him then settling to obliterate his footfalls. He leaned forwards, instinctively shifting towards a diver's stance. The weight of the helmet almost tipped him over. He had to stand back upright or risk falling face down on the sea floor.

Ahead, the silvery bodies of fish shimmered in the broken light as they fed on tumbling green balls of weed, darting away at Dirk's approach. They would dash out of reach, pause to watch him, then dash off again. The moved as they lived, brief and fast, rushing from one moment to another then waiting on the tide. Larger shoals swirled above and around, their many individual movements becoming a single shimmering pattern, an undersea dance whose meaning and purpose eluded Dirk.

For all the life and movement, Dirk found himself enclosed in eerie silence, the only sound his own breath making hollow circuits of the helmet.

A shape loomed out of the green gloom. Three long, straight fingers reaching towards the bright surface and sky. Beneath them two dark mounds, separated by a jagged line of sea. The wreck.

Dirk's spirits soared as he strode towards the wreck. Soon he'd hold the second piece of the puzzle in his hands, two thirds of the way to unlocking the lost secrets of Alexandria. He thrilled at the thought of what they might find. Forgotten philosophical insights of Plato and Socrates. Histories of nations now lost to memory. Designs of devices that had sat for centuries waiting to be built. The wisdom of the ancients, ready to shed light on the modern world. And he would be one of the first to read it. His head would cradle knowledge absent from the lofty spires of Oxford and Paris. He would show them that anyone could bring insight to the world, even a grubby kid from a Kentucky mining town.

No wobbly tooth could bring down his spirits now.

A shoal of fish swimming ahead of him suddenly froze. Their unity shattered as they turned and darted away from the wreck, dragging other fish in their wake. Dirk found himself alone, the only movement a few strands of weed swaying in the current.

A shadow shifted in the darkness of the wreck.

Dirk's throat tightened as he remembered Blaze-Simms's talk of sharks. He imagined them appearing at the edge of his vision, teeth flashing as they went for his throat. His movements horribly slow in the water, he reached for the harpoon gun.

Another shape moved at the far end of the wreck. And another. And another. Easing out of the shelter of the ruined ship, they slid across the sand - dark, indistinct forms, growing in number as they flowed out of portholes and across the deck. A shoal of shadows, ragged at their edges as if the current were snatching them away. There were no fins, no legs, but as they grew closer Dirk made out glittering eyes and pale mouths, drawn back in expressions of anguish. Faces not of sharks but of human beings. Men, women, children, all dangling with ghostly chains.

Angry hisses grew to a discordant wail as the spirits closed in. The sound became a fearsome shriek that rang around his helmet and made his head spin.

He raised the gun, aimed it at the nearest shadow, and fired. Bubbles burst forth. His arm jolted back. The harpoon shot through the shadow without even slowing.

The creature expanded, flowing into the others. They became a mass of swirling chains and blurred faces, a whirl of pure rage that closed over Dirk, blocking his vision and plunging him into icy darkness.

Chapter 9: Dangers of the Deep

Dirk's heart was the world and the world was void - icy dark and without hope.

In that world there was nothing but a heartbeat, a funereal rhythm slowing towards its end. What else could there ever be?

Dirk sank through the void, his mind tracing faces against the black. Terrible faces, sharing with him their agony and grief. Faces shrouded in chains and pain, swallowed by the dreadful deep. They were his only companions and he followed them down.

The beat grew slower, his mind duller, his body accepting the inevitability of death. Al that existed was the shadows, the drifting spirits sucking him down into their depths. The lost ones. The ones Ubu Peter had tried to save him from, or tried to save from him.

Ubu Peter.

The name became a face in his memory.

Became a body.

Became a moment of action, bodies grappling on the docks.

Became a whole scene, a tangle of motive and emotion, of protecting his friends and seeking something beyond himself, beyond the swirling faces, beyond the icy reach of death.

Purpose flooded back into Dirk's mind. He was not the darkness that surrounded him. He would not be ruled by it.

But still the gloom pressed against him, a swirl of shapes so black that they blurred into one, blotting out everything beyond them. Dirk took a step forward, and another, and another, but still they surrounded him, following him along the ocean floor, keeping him constantly surrounded. He tried to brush them away but the ghostly shapes flowed through his fingers with the current. They weren't going anywhere.

Feeling was returning to his mind but not to his body. His legs and arms grew numb as the spirits sucked the warmth away. He couldn't feel his feet, could barely move his fingers. Stumbling, he fell with terrible slowness to the ocean floor. If only it wasn't so damn dark.

He fumbled at his belt, trying to work out what he could use. The harpoon gun was no good. He couldn't slice ghosts up with a knife or a hatchet. So many blades and nothing to stick them into.

Then he touched something cylindrical.

Numb fingers fumbled to unhook the tube. He fought back the terror whose tendrils were snaking into his mind. His left hand would barely obey his commands. He couldn't feel his legs.

Finally unhooking the tube, he rolled onto his back. The fingers of his distant hand closed slowly, achingly, a metal tab.

The flare burst into life, spraying Dirk with bright white light. The ghosts screeched and scattered, fading as they fled, their shadow bodies dissolving in the harsh magnesium glare.

Feeling flooded back into Dirk's hands. The feeling was pain. Seeing the suit's gauntlets begin to glow he let the flare go, trailing pearlescent bubbles as it raced like a shooting star towards the surface of the sea.

The warm ocean currents flowed around Dirk, thawing his body and soothing his hands. He twisted around, rising on one knee. Sand rose in a cloud around his legs as he dragged himself upright and set off again towards the wreck.

#

Inside the wreck, broken planks cast jagged shadows across the sand. Dirk approached them warily, watching for any sign of movement, any hint that the spirits remained.

A century and more of drifting currents had buried the base of the ship and speckled her sides with sea-life. Clumps of weed hung between patches of barnacles. Brightly coloured fish flitted through the weeds, while anemones stretched for prey just out of reach. A crab scuttled out of the shattered stern, tapped an experimental claw against Dirk's boot, and thought better of it, disappearing back into the shelter of the wreck.

Dirk walked towards the back of the ship, each step a study in slow motion. He pushed harder, trying to force the pace against the overwhelming weight of water. It wasn't that he minded going slow, some goals needed a little patience. But enforced slowness was frustrating.

The ocean changed for no man. For all his straining he moved no quicker, and trying to just made him more annoyed. The helmet didn't help. He wanted to glance around, to scan the wreckage for any sign of the tablet, to look out for returning shadows. But his view was constricted to the glass panel at the front, and he had to turn his whole body to look around. It was like being a toddler, unable to move faster than a waddle or see anything above his own height.

He turned left as fast as he could, then back to the right, the side of his face pressing on the glass as he struggled against the suit. All he could see were splintered planks and seaweed. He didn't even know what he was looking for. Would the tablet be in a chest? Lying loose? Buried five feet beneath the drifting sand? It could be anywhere in this wreck, or nowhere.

Stopping for a moment, he took a deep breath, reining in his emotions. The air was thick with sweat and the scent of rubber seals, but a pipe to the surface kept it breathable. He closed his eyes and let the staleness pass over him. He focused on the rhythm of his breath, a technique he'd learned on a visit to Tibet. Just using it reminded him of the Brothers of Sleeplessness, their saffron robes and wrinkled smiles. He let that memory go too, let all memory and mindfulness leave him, until there was only his breath.

In and out.

In and out.

In and out.

He opened his eyes and waited, still in body and mind, taking in every detail of his surroundings. Then slowly, he turned on the spot. Instead of frantically hunting out his prey, this time he gazed ahead, letting the details wash over him. The drifting sand, the rippling weeds, the intricate pattern of interlaced timbers. As he accepted the patterns of the world around him, other details stood out. The scuttling of a crab. The shimmer of a fish. The sharp angles of an iron-bound box, protruding from the sand.

Of all the things he'd seen, the box looked most likely to hold something of value. It seemed a good place to start.

There was a handle on the end of the box, as rusted as the other fittings but solid enough to grip. Dirk took hold of it and heaved, a cloud of sand rising around him as he drew the box from its resting place.

As the cloud settled he knelt down next to the box. It was a foot across and deep, by two wide. Knocking on the top and the front he felt no give - the wood was still solid. There was an iron clasp on the front, its padlock rusted into place. Dirk took the knife from his belt, slid the tip between the clasp and the wood. Pressing against the pommel, he managed to get the blade beneath half the clasp, then pressed his foot against the box and heaved. For a long moment he thought it wouldn't give, that the nails so firmly rusted into the wood that they wouldn't part. Then something shifted, the knife slid sharply down, and the whole clasp fell to the sea floor.

Dirk lifted the lid and laughed. The front of the chest had been so solid, it never occurred to him to check all the way around. But the back was completely gone, probably smashed out during the wreck. The box itself was empty.

The sand where the box had been buried was still loose. Dirk stabbed at it with his knife, probing the soft ground. On the fourth go he met resistance. Setting the knife aside he dug with his hands, sand sliding back almost as fast as he could shovel it away.

A nearby shoal of fish scattered and darted into the distance.

Down in the hole, his fingers brushed against something solid. Something hard and square edged. He wormed them around in the sand until he had a grip on the end of the object, then pulled it clear.

The cloudy water swirled at the edge of his restricted vision. He ignored it, focusing on the task in hand.

The sand settled, revealing a lump of stone. A tablet, just like the one he'd seen at the Epiphany Club. The next step on the road to the Great Library.

This time his laughter was joyful, not self-mocking, as he slid the stone into the bag on his belt. It wouldn't be fun, walking with that banging at his thigh, but once he was clear of the wreck all he needed was to tug on the chain and Blaze-Simms would haul him back to the surface.

He turned to face the open sea.

Two feet away, staring right at him, was a shark.

Dirk grabbed his harpoon gun, raised it and pulled the trigger.

The radium chamber glowed and shot a string of bubbles from the empty barrel. He hadn't reloaded since the ghosts.

The shark lunged, a mass of razor teeth and hunger. It slammed into Dirk, throwing him against the wall of the wreck.

Dirk fumbled at his belt where the knife should have been. He cursed his own stupidity. He'd got so damned excited digging up the box that he'd left the knife on the floor.

The shark lunged again. Dirk dodged as best he could, twisting right and down, away from the attack. Teeth snagged at his leg, not reaching the flesh but snagging on one of the metal plates, tearing the rubber seal that joined it to the suit. Water poured in.

Dirk grabbed the torn seal, trying to stem the leak. If he couldn't stop it, the suit would flood and he'd be drowning in moments. With his other hand he grabbed the hatchet from his belt. He'd struggle to fight hunched over like this, but it was better than nothing.

The shark flashed towards him again. Dirk waited until the moment before it struck, water rising past his thigh and down the other leg, then lashed out with the hatchet.

The timing was perfect. The flat of the axe slammed against the creature's nose, turning it from its attack. Before it had time to recover, he swung again, burying the blade in the flesh behind its right eye. Blood turned the water red.

The shark jerked, wrenching the axe from Dirk's hand. It turned, one fin twitching, blood streaming from its head as it lined up for another attack.

The water was up to his waist inside the suit. There'd be no more dodging.

Flicking its tail, the shark opened its mouth wide, its movements sluggish but its teeth still deadly points.

Dirk clenched his fist. If that was all he had then that was what he would use.

The shark gave one last twitch and fell still, blood streaming into the water.

Dirk sighed in relief and almost choked on the water rising past his neck. Saved from being shark-food only to drown. He could almost taste the bitterness of that.

Then he remembered the other piece of equipment Blaze-Simms had given him.

He grabbed the tube from his belt, but he couldn't get it to his face. The damn suit was in the way.

Who the hell came up with emergency oxygen you couldn't use?

He fumbled at the fastenings around the helmet, but they were too small to work with his hands enclosed in the suit.

Each step forward was a greater struggle than the last, weighed down with a suit full of water and no air. How long without breath now? Half a minute? A minute?

He sank to his knees by the box, grabbed the Bowie knife, and slid the blade between the plates across his chest. With a great wrench he prised them apart, the rubber seal splitting from the point of the knife. He tore one clear, then the other.

Thoughts became blurred. His chest strained as if against a great weight.

He freed his right arm from the suit, let the metal limb drop to the ground. He was dizzy, the knife trembling in his hands, dangerously close to his flesh as he pressed at another plate.

The blade stopped, stuck in a shoulder seal. He wrenched at it once, twice, the knife still stuck, the plates not parting.

In desperation, he punched at the knife. It spiralled away, becoming lost in a stand of seaweed.

Behind it, the shoulder plate popped free and the left arm fell from the suit.

With the last of his strength, Dirk lifted the helmet from his head. He grabbed the emergency breathing cylinder, twisted the tube, and pressed the opening to his lips. Sweet, merciful air rushed into his lungs.

#

The ocean parted and Dirk burst into the open air. He took a long breath, and another, filling his lungs with the joy of fresh oxygen. The emergency air had been enough to get him to the surface, just, but it couldn't compare to the real thing.

Lying back, he floated on the surface of the sea, letting his aching muscles rest. He relished the breeze brushing his skin, the sun warming his body, the waves lapping against him.

But the weight of the tablet was dragging him back down. He couldn't lie here forever. Spying the yacht a few hundred yards away, he rolled onto his front and swam towards his friends.

A rope ladder hung from the back of the boat, trailing down into the water. Dirk grabbed the rungs and climbed. At last he grasped the edge of the deck and hauled himself up, flopping down on the warm wood. He sprawled there, eyes closed, letting the exhaustion of two long days drip away with the salt water.

But rest was for the weak when there were better things to do. Dirk grabbed the bag at his side, rolled over and looked up.

Straight into the barrel of a gun.

Chapter 10: Two Down

A fist like a cured ham clutched the revolver, the grip dwarfed by sausage fingers.

"Up." The man's pale skin was reddened by the sun and peeling at the tips of his ears. Sunlight flashed off the tip of the barrel as he gestured for Dirk to rise.

Blaze-Simms lay on the far side of the deck, a bruise on his forehead. Isabelle nestled his head on her knee. She managed a smile for Dirk, then went back to frowning at a second thug leaning by the wheel.

Dirk stood, water dribbling from his saturated clothes.

Both of the brutish figures were dressed in badly cut suits, the jackets loose enough to have concealed their guns. Even with an extra day's sunburn, the "secretaries" of Cullen's French guest were easily recognisable. They looked like they'd been carved out of beef and left to stew in the sun. Guns suited them like a bow tie suited a chimp.

"Drop it." The man gestured at Dirk's sack. From him, even a French accent sounded inelegant.

The guy was standing too close for his own good. From here Dirk could swing the bag around, smack the gun clear and be on him before he even took a shot. Even tired, wet and aching, it would be easy.

The problem was the other guy, out of reach and aiming for Isabelle and Blaze-Simms. Dirk could guard himself with the first thug's body, but that wouldn't help the others. There'd be a messy few seconds, and it would be over for his opponents. But it might be over for his friends too.

Dirk dropped the bag.

"Kick it to me." The thug eyed the bag eagerly.

"It's a lump of stone." Dirk had dealt with some stupid people, but this one was real special. "That ain't gonna work."

The thugs exchanged words in French, the brief sentences of slow men debating obvious issues.

Now that he had time to look around, Dirk saw a rowboat tied against the yacht, knocking on the side as waves pulled it away and back again. It was easy to see how they'd gotten aboard without Blaze-Simms noticing. Caught up in testing his diving gear, the world around him would have just disappeared. But Isabelle...

The thug in front of Dirk stepped aside and gestured him towards the other captives.

"How are you doing?" Dirk asked, settling down beside Isabelle.

"Better than poor Timothy."

Blaze-Simms's eyes were closed, his breathing shallow. Dirk felt his pulse.

"He's been worse." Dirk could remember at least three times that fit the bill, and only one had been Blaze-Simms's own doing.

"Is that meant to be reassuring?" Isabelle asked.

"It's meant to be true."

The thugs stood together as one of them pulled the tablet from the bag. He peered at it, made a comment in French, and thrust it at his companion. They both laughed.

"Maybe they've cracked the code already," Dirk said. "Or maybe it was a fart joke. Hard to tell."

"Really, Mr Dynamo." Isabelle raised an eyebrow. "If you can't say anything polite, you can at least say something useful."

"Alright. How long do you reckon it would take to get from our pier to Freeport, and then to row out here?"

"That would depend on whether you had horses. Why?"

"'Cause I think I just heard oars."

Their captors turned back towards them. Dirk found himself staring down the barrel of not one but two pistols. They were ugly devices, the product of some cut-rate Prussian workshop, barely functional and utterly charmless.

"It is almost over, Monsieur Dynamo," one of the men said. "For you and for your little friend."

He slowly thumbed the hammer of his gun, letting it click back one notch at a time.

Behind him, hands appeared on the ship's railing, then arms, and then bruised, muscular bodies.

"Why are you here?" Dirk asked, playing for time. He didn't think the natives meant him and his companions much good, but if they were creeping up on the Frenchmen then they weren't on their side either. Maybe any white folks out by the wreck were fair game. Maybe there had been some other trouble. All that mattered for now was that his enemies were divided.

"Why do you think?" The English speaker waved the tablet. "You think you are the only ones looking for this?"

Ubu Peter and Felipe slid over the rail, knives gripped between their teeth, pistols holstered at their sides. Sunlight gleamed off wicked blades and angry eyes.

"But who sent you?" Dirk asked

"The Dane, of course!" The thug's expression was one of pig-faced malice. "Who else ever stands in your-"

The deck creaked beneath Ubu Peter. The Frenchman turned in alarm, gun raised.

Not pausing to draw his own pistol, Felipe leapt onto the other Frenchman's back. Clamping one arm around his opponent's throat, he swung a knife at his chest. The Frenchman blocked the blow with his arm, cloth ripping as his sleeve caught on the blade. With his other arm he flailed above his shoulder, trying to point his gun in Felipe's face.

Ubu Peter ducked beneath the other Frenchman's gun and lunged at his side. The African's knife sank six inches through fat and muscle, but the Frenchman snarled and batted him aside.

Dirk sprang from the deck, channelling all his strength down a line that ended in his fist. The stabbed Frenchman knocked down Ubu Peter, only to stagger back as Dirk hit him in the face.

A gun roared, its single shot like a thunderclap across the still sea. The other two combatants stumbled apart, the Frenchman clutching his powder-burned ear, Felipe clutching his blood-streaked face.

All five of them stood for a moment, staring at each other in confusion.

Then someone moved to attack, someone moved to intercept, and they all got tangled together in a muddled melee. They rolled back and forth, fists flying, feet flailing, guns drawn just long enough to be knocked out of hands. The boat rocked to the rhythm of violence.

Dirk took an elbow to the guts and a face full of fingers. His foot hit something that gave with a satisfying crunch. Sliding on a patch of blood, he turned the movement into a lunge and sent one of the Frenchmen spinning towards the bow. Before the man could regain his balance, Dirk rushed after him, slamming into his chest and launching him over the rail. The man had less than a second to cry out before he hit the ocean and disappeared with a splash.

Turning, Dirk saw Felipe darting toward him, knife outstretched. He twisted clear of the lunge, then ducked as Felipe swung the blade at neck height. The point glistened menacingly in the sunlight.

Rising behind the strike, Dirk grabbed Felipe's arm and flung him over his shoulder. With a splash, Felipe followed the Frenchman into the sea.

Something hit Dirk like a steam train. Black spots danced across his vision, obscuring his view of the remaining Frenchman's fist. Pain roared through his face as another punch knocked his head back on his shoulders. He tried to duck, and took a blow to the side of the head. His attacker's idiot grin, like a pig rammed hard against a wall, filled his vision. The world tasted of blood and sounded like all the bells in New York ringing just for him.

This time the darkness was warm and inviting, creeping in from the corners of his mind. He struggled to keep consciousness from slipping away, while that flat, bestial face blotted out the sky.

The Frenchman raised his fist, roaring with laughter. Then suddenly he slumped, face falling, grip loosening, body sliding to the floor.

Dirk blinked back darkness and pushed himself to his feet, using the rail for support. Ubu Peter faced him, looking nearly as bad as Dirk felt. He clutched an oar, its broken end lying beneath the Frenchman's head.

"Guess I owe you," Dirk mumbled through fat lips, wobbling as he raised his hands in defence.

"You desecrated the wreck." Rage blazed in Ubu Peter's eyes. "You stole from the graves of our fallen. Felipe is right. There is only one way to stop you."

He hefted the oar ready to swing. Dirk wondered how long he could stay afloat in his present condition. Assuming he was even conscious when he hit the water. Damn stupid way to die.

They were interrupted by the small, sharp click of a gun being cocked.

"Enough." Isabelle stood in the middle of the deck, clutching one of the Frenchmen's ugly guns. It looked absurdly large in her hands, like she was a farmgirl playing with her Pa's tools. But her stance made clear that she knew what she was doing.

Ubu Peter dropped the oar and squared his shoulders, standing proud despite his blood and bruises.

"Are you going to drop me in the water, too?" he asked. "Maybe knock me out first, to make sure I sink?"

Dirk shook his head.

"Take your boat." He nudged the fallen Frenchman with his foot. "Hell, take theirs if you want. We've got no use for either."

"We came to stop you leaving." Ubu Peter looked at each of them in turn. "To kill you if we could. Why let me go?"

"I understand your anger." Dirk took a deep breath. He ached all over and was too damn tired for a long debate. "I know what it's like for your life to be in the hands of folks who don't give a damn. I know what it's like to lose good people and to see their memory dishonoured. But to me, the dead are just bones, and what matters here is what we can learn for the living.

"I don't agree with what you wanted, but that doesn't mean I don't understand. Now we've done what we came for, and soon we'll be too far away for you to do us any harm. The least we can do is not cause any more grief."

"You will tell others what you've seen here." Ubu Peter's tone was one of resignation, matching the slump of his shoulders.

"Me?" Dirk shrugged. "Probably not. Him..." He gestured towards Blaze-Simms. "Discretion ain't his strong suit. But attention ain't either, so who knows."

"I..." Ubu Peter paused at the rail.

"Just go. I'm too damn tired to care, whatever it is."

The African nodded and disappeared over the side. Moments later, oars splashed in the water, then were joined by voices as Ubu Peter helped Felipe into the boat. The sounds faded as they sculled back towards the island. Overhead, gulls soared on the wind off the ocean, hundreds of them flocking above the white-stained cliffs.

Dirk leaned against the rail and closed his eyes, sensing all the aches and pains that riddled his body. There was a salt taste on his tongue and a distant ringing in one ear. It was years since he'd been so tired and battered, and he'd been having more fun that time around.

Cold and heavy, the tablet lay abandoned in the middle of the deck. He picked it up and peered at it. One face was inscribed with elaborate lettering. Its edges had been smoothed by decades of ocean currents but the letters were still legible. Meaningless to him, just a jumble of foreign characters, but someone at the Club would be able to crack the code.

After all this, it had better be worth the reading.

Isabelle lowered the gun as she came to his side, staring at the tablet.

"Two down..." she said.

"You couldn't have stepped in sooner?" Dirk asked. He spat out a mouthful of blood.

Isabelle frowned.

"I'm sorry, not my finest moment." She looked over at Blaze-Simms, still stretched unconscious on the deck. "We should get moving, before anybody else comes our way. Can you while the helm while I see to Timothy?"

The doubtful look she gave Dirk made up his mind for him.

"Guess I'm gonna have to," he said.

Dirk dumped the unconscious Frenchman into a rowboat bobbing at their side. He cast it off, not wishing the guy a safe voyage, and set to raising the anchor. Beautiful as Hakon was, inspiring as its people were, he felt glad to be getting out of there. Ninjas, bears, gangsters, locals - there were only so many random attacks one man could take. He needed time to rest, and to work out who was behind some of this.

A few minutes later he was at the wheel, sun beating down on his back, breeze brushing his wounds as it filled the sail. They sailed north, leaving behind the ghosts of a cruel trade and the scars it left in its wake. Back to England and the search for the next tablet.

The sun was shining. They had what they'd come for. At last, Dirk smiled. It was turning into a mighty fine day.

Book 2: Suits and Sewers

Chapter 1: What Makes the Man

Bright summer sunshine blazed in through the tailor's front window. Dirk Dynamo sat with his feet up by the window, reading a book on sharks. Having nearly been eaten by one in the Hakon expedition, he wanted to know what he was facing next time. It was that or face the nonsense of fashion going on around him.

"Are you sure we can't do something for your friend, Sir Timothy?" Pietro Gellanti, the shop's owner, looked with disdain at Dirk's faded black trousers and frayed shirt. "These are production line clothes of the most monstrous sort. No shape to them at all, baggy in all the wrong places. And the repairs..."

He reached out toward Dirk's frequently repaired sleeve, but Dirk batted the hand away.

"You got a problem with my handiwork?" He glared at the tailor.

"Sewing is hardly the work of a gentleman." Gellanti waved his scissors. "And this is certainly not the work of a professional."

"These clothes have seen me through more scrapes than you've had pinpricks." Dirk turned back to his book. It was good that the guy took pride in his skills, but that didn't give him the right to mock another man's handiwork. "I ain't givin' up on 'em now."

The tailor tutted but turned away.

"And you, Sir Timothy." He shook his head. "What have you been doing to this jacket?"

Sir Timothy Blaze-Simms looked down, eyes wide behind his spectacles. Fitters - the sons in Gellanti and Sons - paused to look at him across oak tables scattered with lengths of cloth.

"But this one doesn't even have any holes." He brushed at the green cotton. "And hardly any stains."

"Does your father do such things to my clothes?" Gellanti sighed and extended his tape measure. "Does your brother?"

"I suppose not." Blaze-Simms shrugged. "It looks all right to me though."

"All right?" Pietro waved his chalk wildly and looked to one of his fitters for support. "All right, he says, in a coat that suffers a hundred creases. All right, with a frayed cuff and mis-matched trousers. And as for the cravat..."

"It was a gift from Mater." Blaze-Simms smiled. "I think she found it in Italy."

"In that case, we shall find something to match."

Gellanti grabbed a swatch book and began flicking through, glancing up to oversee his team as they launched themselves upon Blaze-Simms, waving tape measures and taking notes in a leather-bound ledger.

At least now they were making progress. Dirk hadn't wanted to take this break in London, not while they were still hunting the tablets that would lead them to the lost Great Library. With two out of three in their possession, and both a gang of ninjas and the Dane's criminal network racing them for the third, he hated to waste time shopping. But Isabelle McNair, owner of the first tablet, wanted to do research before they went after the French tablet. And there was no denying that Blaze-Simms went through clothes like most folks got through hot meals. Those were the hazards of having expensive tastes and a carefree nature.

Now that his initial resentment had passed, Dirk realised there was something in what Gellanti had said. Sure, Dirk had been repairing his own clothes his whole life, but he didn't have much skill at it. He put his book down and got ready to learn from these folks.

Most of the tables were piled high with pyramids of fabric. More filled the deep shelves towards the back of the long, low ceilinged room. The place would have been dark and dismal if not for the ornate dress mirrors that caught the light and scattered it back, picking out rolls of silk and satin, cotton and wool, in hundreds of colours and shades. The palette was that of a refined and genteel painter, rather than a draftsman of cheap, eye-catching spectacle. There were reds, blues, greens, even the odd yellow, but they were pastel pale or deep and rich, never bright.

The fitters tutted some more as they draped samples of cloth across Blaze-Simms's chest and he looked at his reflection in the mirrors.

"You should have brought Mrs McNair," Dirk said. "This kind of fuss seems more her than me."

"I thought you might learn something interesting." Blaze-Simms turned to the fitters. "That with the green, perhaps?"

"Like how to blow ten times a steer-hand's wage on one suit? No thanks."

"More like how to dress for society. Tailoring is a fine art, evolved from bare necessity into a thing of beauty. It marks out the civilised man, who takes some trouble over his appearance, from the burly savage of ancient times in his rough furs and sandals. It shows how far we've come."

"We've come four streets over from ragged kids begging in the gutter, while bankers walk by with their noses in the air. That the sort of refinement you're after?"

"Is it any different from spending money on art, opera or academia?" Blaze-Simms lifted his arms to let Gellanti measure his chest. "You value those, but are they any deeper a part of our culture than clothing? At least suits are worn regularly."

Frowning, Dirk swung his legs around and sat up straight. He'd heard these arguments rehearsed enough times, but he'd never gotten into them with his friend. The Epiphany Club brought folks together for learning, not to debate politics.

"Those things are about learning," he said. "About making yourself better."

"I'm told that clothes also make the man."

"No, the man makes himself. Clothes just show how privileged he is."

"Have you been talking with that chap from the British Museum again?"

"Hell yes. And let me tell you, when the proletariat start to listen to him, there ain't gonna be fancy tailors for some and ragged trousers for the rest."

There was an awkward silence, broken by the snip of Gellanti's scissors. Dust motes swirled through the air as the cutter flung precisely shaped pieces of cloth to the fitters, who in turn pinned them together around Blaze-Simms. Dirk opened his book and started reading again, closing his eyes from time to time to test what he had learned.

"I'm meeting up with Isabelle for tea after this," Blaze-Simms said at last. "It should be a jolly afternoon, if you'd like to join us."

"I dunno." In that moment, the thought of high tea with a couple of aristocrats felt like class treachery to Dirk. But the chance to see Isabelle McNair was appealing. "Jolly ain't what I had planned."

"Apparently she's found new evidence to where the last tablet is." Blaze-Simms obediently turned for the tailor. "Isn't that splendid?"

"As long as there are no ghosts this time."

Dirk looked down at the book in his hands, lent to him by Professor Barrow. It was interesting, and he was learning new things. But so were hundreds of other people, reading the other copies sold across the country, even the world. Hundreds more had already read it, Barrow included. The idea of finding the Great Library of Alexandria, of reading books no-one else had in a thousand years, that had a whole other level of appeal. Dirk knew he'd hate himself if he missed out on that.

"Alright," he said. "I'll come along for a bit. But you two start yappin' on about garden parties or fashion, and I'm headin' off to find my man at the museum, tablet or no tablet.'

Blaze-Simms smiled at him in the mirror, then paused, his face overtaken by the distant expression that said inspiration had struck.

"You know, it's a funny thing about that tablet..." he said.

A shadow rushed across the window. Alarmed by the sudden movement, Dirk spun out of his seat, just as the glass shattered in a spray of sunlit shards. He raised his arms to protect his face.

A black shape slammed into him, hurling him back onto a pile of silk linings. The attacker rolled across Dirk, knocking the remaining breath from his body, then lifted him effortlessly into the air, flinging him against the far wall.

Concussed and out of breath, Dirk felt the world spin around him. He wanted to close his eyes and rest, but the black-clad figure was flying towards him again, blade outstretched. Just in time, he ducked left. Plaster dust sprayed from the wall, the blackness thudding home hard enough to send shockwaves into the floorboards. Dirk lashed out, his fist just missing the attacker as they leapt over a pile of blue and green wool weaves.

Shaking the confusion from his head, he staggered to his feet. Half a dozen black-clad people were in the room, circling its occupants with the deadly grace of expert combatants. Not a single patch of skin showed through their sinister garb, even their eyes concealed behind shrouds of gauze. Two of them were closing in on Dirk, racing along a workbench in a running crouch. Near the window, three were trying to surround Blaze-Simms, who was wielding a measuring stick like a thick striped rapier. The last attacker had Gellanti pinned against the back wall, two of his fitters already unconscious at his feet and the last disappearing out of the back door.

"Ninjas." Dirk muttered the word like a curse. It was Hakon all over again - what the hell did these folks want?

The nearest one leapt from the workbench, leg outstretched. Sidestepping groggily, Dirk felt air brush his face as the ninja sailed past. A pair of shuriken hissed by his ear as he lunged.

Trying just hard enough to be convincing, Dirk grabbed with both hands at the black-clad body. The ninja ducked between his arms, straight into his rising foot. There was a crunch, the ninja's head snapped back, and he crashed against the nearby shelves, glass jars full of buttons smashing down around him.

More shuriken sailed over Dirk's bobbing head as he turned to face the second ninja. The man stood atop a worktable, arms spread wide, one leg raised like a ballerina. Leaping into the air he spiralled around in a high kick. Dirk ducked, only for the ninja to twist in midair and slam a knee into his back. Pain jolted through Dirk, distracting him long enough for the ninja to dart away.

Still reeling, Dirk dived for shelter beneath the table as he scrambled for some sort of weapon. His gun was concealed in the jacket draped across the window seat, past half a dozen black-clad assassins, and he cursed himself angrily for not keeping it with him. The only objects within reach were bundles of tweed and velvet. So as a loud footfall sounded on the tabletop above him, he used the only hard object to hand. With a grunt he rose to his feet, slamming the table upwards. There was a crunch of ninja against ceiling, and a black-clad body tumbled limply to the floor.

Two more ninjas were closing in on Dirk, stepping over the unconscious tailors. Shuriken flashed alarmingly through the air. Dirk blocked them with the table, razor-sharp steel burying itself in the oak with a thud.

Muscles straining, he heaved the trestle at his assailants. They dodged easily, leaping aside on legs like coiled springs, one bounding over the flying furniture and straight at Dirk's head. Rather than dodge, Dirk leapt into the blow, colliding with the ninja before he could bring his foot round for a kick. They crashed to the ground, the ninja scrabbling to get out from beneath Dirk, who grabbed a handful of loose black robe and swung him around into the descending blade of the other ninja. There was a wet hiss and Dirk found himself holding two halves of a black-clad body, guts pouring across his feet. He and the sword-wielding assassin stood staring at each other, and Dirk could see by the man's posture that he too was shocked. Before he had time to recover, Dirk raised his foot sharply into the man's groin, and he crumpled over with a sigh.

Silence descended upon the room. Pietro Gellanti and his assistants lay sprawled amid heaps of unfurled cloth and broken shelves, as did the ninjas Dirk had dealt with. The faces of curious passers-by peered in through the shattered remains of the window.

There was no sign of Timothy Blaze-Simms.

Chapter 2: London Rooftops

Dirk stood on the sun-warmed pavement outside Gellanti and Sons, failing to calm old Pietro. The tailor kept bending to pick at the shards of glass glittering gem-like across the cobbles, frantically trying to do something with the shattered glory of his shop. One hand tugged at his hair, turning it from slicked-down elegance to a tangled briar-like mass.

None of it helped calm Dirk's own agitation. His heart was still racing from the fight, his back ached where he'd been hit, and his friend was missing, presumably kidnapped. He could have done without taking responsibility for these folks, but someone had to.

Inevitably the fuss had drawn a crowd, the usual London mix of gawpers, shouters and opportunistic pickpockets. A few had tried to approach the shop, but gave up when they found their way blocked by six feet of scowling American. After that they'd kept their distance, still shouting and pointing, just far enough away that Dirk would have to leave the shop unguarded if he wanted to go and make them shut up.

The injured fitters sat against the shop, legs splayed out in front of them, leaning on each other as they nursed their bruised heads. Playing to the crowd, they wailed about ruined silks and how people all in black obviously had no taste. Dirk shook his head. Anyone who cared this much about the look of cloth deserved a beat-down. It was almost enough to make him side with the ninjas.

A disturbance rippled through the centre of the crowd, stern voices and outraged jostling accompanying the movement. The babble of voices rose as the disturbance approached Dirk, then subsided as the missing fitter pushed his way into the open, jabbering away to the policemen who followed in his wake.

There were three bobbies, led by a short sergeant with a face like a prune. Striding up to Dirk, he fixed him with a gaze that fell just short of glaring.

"What have we here, then?" he asked, not pausing for an answer. "Care to explain what a ruffian in fixed-up hand-me-downs is doing in a gentleman's outfitters? Or should I save us both the trouble and slap you straight into irons?"

Reaching into his jacket, Dirk handed him a card. At the top his name was embossed copper-plate lettering. Beneath that was the seal and address of the Epiphany Club. He'd never liked introducing himself with these things. Far too fancy, and too much like employing status to get his way. But it had its uses.

The sergeant sighed as he read the card, breath rustling his neat moustache.

"I see, sir. One of those... gentlemen, are we?" He pocketed the card with exaggerated care. "Perhaps you'd like to explain what's going on here, sir. Because right now I can't shift the ignorant notion that there's been a brawl between a jumped-up explorer and a bunch of over-paid tailors."

"Bet you don't get many offers of promotion, huh?" Dirk grinned despite his weariness. In a country full of subservient bowing and scraping, it was nice to meet a man who didn't 'know his place'.

"No sir." The sergeant pulled a notepad from his pocket. "But despite my sunny and deferential disposition I've yet to be fired."

"I guess a competent policeman's a rare and valuable commodity."

"Almost as valuable as a useful American, in my experience." The sergeant opened the notebook and set pen to paper. "Now, about this fight...?"

"We were attacked by ninjas."

A look of incredulity crossed the sergeant's face. Spectators moved closer, whether drawn by Dirk's words or the expression on the sergeant's face.

"Ninjas, sir?" The sergeant wrote something in his book.

"Oriental assassins. Japanese guys in black robes."

"And did anyone outside the shop see them, sir?"

"Don't think so."

"And why is that, sir?"

"They're kinda sneaky."

"They burst into this shop, smashed the windows and assaulted the staff sneakily?" If the sergeant had raised his eyebrow any further it would have disappeared beneath his hairline.

"They got a lot less sneaky once they were inside." Dirk ran a hand through his hair. This was starting to get awkward. He knew he hadn't done anything wrong, but with his head still fuzzy from the fight it was hard to get that across.

"Why did they do this, sir?"

"I don't know." Dirk pointed back into the shop, where he'd left at least one unconscious ninja. "Maybe you could ask them."

"There's no need to get agitated, sir."

"Enough with the 'sir's already. Can you just go in there and do some policing, leave me to catch my breath?"

"Leave a suspect unattended." The sergeant made another note. "That seems unlikely, s-"

"Mr Dynamo!" The crowd parted, willingly this time, and Isabelle McNair appeared, sheltered beneath a lace-trimmed parasol. She strolled up with a smile, for all the world like a guest at a garden party.

"I don't believe we've met." With her usual effortless grace, Isabelle held out a gloved hand to the sergeant. "I'm Isabelle McNair, and you would be Sergeant...?"

"Simpkins." The policeman paused a moment before shaking her hand. "Sergeant Simpkins."

"A pleasure to meet you, sergeant. I see you've arrived just in time." She twirled the parasol and turned towards the shop. "This must be your crime scene. Tell me what you've found so far."

Simpkins followed in her wake, drawn along by a combination of charm and polite insistence. He answered questions about the crime based on the evidence in the shop, answers which came down to 'there was a fight', so far as Dirk could tell. He didn't get why Isabelle didn't just ask him. He could have given better answers, and saved her all the pointless side questions about the sergeant's job, family, and who cared what else.

But then, maybe those sorts of questions were why Isabelle was good with people, while Dirk just got by.

At least now the policeman was gone, and Dirk wasn't going to draw his attention again. He didn't want to explain to some stranger that he, Isabelle and Blaze-Simms were on the trail of the lost Library of Alexandria, not when other people were on the same trail. And without explaining that he could hardly explain his suspicion that the ninjas were after the Library too. Sometimes it was best to plead the fifth, or better yet avoid facing questions at all.

After setting the police to dispersing the crowd, Isabelle turned her attention to Pietro Gellanti. Taking the old man by the arm she led him back into the front of his shop and, brushing aside more broken glass, settled him down in an easy chair. A couple of stern words with the fitters got them up off the pavement and making tea for their stunned employer.

Finally, she returned to Dirk.

"Mr Dynamo, it really is lovely to see you." Isabelle smiled. "How have you been?"

"Not bad, ma'am." Dirk smiled back. How else could anyone respond to Isabelle McNair? "Reading books, fighting ninjas, that kinda thing."

Hearing his own words he cringed inside. He felt like a schoolboy, showing off to impress.

"How splendid." If Isabelle noticed that he was flustered then she didn't show it. "Is Sir Timothy on his way here? I was meant to meet him."

"You think I'd be here on my own?" Dirk jerked his head toward the fancy shop front. "Ninjas took him."

Isabelle's face tightened in vexation.

"Oh dear, how unfortunate."

She peered around the shop's interior, taking in the red stain and spilt guts that were all that remained of the ninjas. The fallen had disappeared before they could be taken captive, just as in the attack on the Epiphany Club.

"Where did they go?" she asked.

Dirk shrugged. "Same place they went when we met them in Manchester and Hakon. Far enough away to avoid us."

"We shall see about that."

A fruit stall was parked on the opposite side of the street. Isabelle strolled up to it, smiled, picked up some apples and began chatting with the stallholder. He bobbed his head excitedly and pointed in the direction of Holborn. After a few more minutes' conversation he patted Isabelle on the arm, smiling and refusing to take payment as she pulled out her purse. With a gracious bow of her head she turned and walked back to Dirk.

"He saw them moving across the rooftops," she explained. "His son used to be a chimney sweep, and so he is in the habit of looking upwards."

Dirk looked again, saw the way the guy's silvery head tipped back between serving customers, peering up at the pigeons and chimney pots. He hadn't noticed that, might never have done. It seemed there were things he could learn from Isabelle.

"Guess we're goin' that way then," he said.

"Do you have your gun on you, Mr Dynamo?" Isabelle was peering into her bag.

"Right here, ma'am." Dirk proudly patted a bulge in his jacket.

"Marvellous. One of these days, I hope to see you use it."

#

Dirk knew how to track. He'd made a career or two of it, chasing different sorts of prey. From gators in the bayou to yetis in the Himalayas, from Indians on the great plains to runaway husbands in the windy streets of Chicago. Any trail, any time, he could turn his nose to it.

Yet still, faced with the sprawling, seething mass of London, he was mighty glad to have Isabelle McNair's help.

To Dirk, London was like an ant-hill, teaming with life at its most chaotic. Folks bustled this way and that, jostling past each other, shouting and glaring. Unlike ants, theirs was a motion of conflict, tempers fraying as one man's path blocked another or they fought for space at a crowded street stall. The English reputation for deference showed just how small and detached a group of Englishmen most foreigners met. Tracking in a London crowd was the urban equivalent of working through a cactus grove. Slow, frustrating and prickly.

Fortunately he had Isabelle. She could feel the rhythm of the city. The bustle and flow of horses, carts, pedestrians. The strolling gentlemen, shopkeepers selling their wares, whores and pickpockets lurking on corners. She could read these crowds like a penny dreadful. Leading him effortlessly through the milling masses, she always went with the flow because she always found a flow going the way she wanted. There was no need to scour the rooftops for tracks or ask half the crowd if they'd seen anything. At every junction, every alley mouth or choice of paths, she zeroed straight in on the right person, the one looking up and paying attention. She said things to make them like her, maybe even love her a little, and moved on with clear clues as to where the ninjas had gone.

They took a long, looping route out of the centre and into north London as their quarry, a good half hour ahead, tried to throw off any potential pursuit. They passed libraries and learned societies back to back with broken down tenements where ignorance was king. After all, this was the capital city of the world.

At last they found themselves in Camden, close to the bustling locks. Soot from the railway terminals lay like a shadow over the whole area. Isabelle returned from talking with a dock hand and nodded towards a warehouse, a square, almost featureless building of soot-stained wood.

"They went in there," Isabelle said. "Slipped in through a window near the roof."

Dirk looked at Isabelle in her fashionable dress and carefully coiffured hair, lace-fringed bag in one hand and parasol in the other.

"You wait here." He didn't want to risk her getting hurt, any more than he wanted a society lady slowing him down. "I won't be long."

"I have every faith in your abilities, Mr Dynamo." She pulled a small-calibre revolver from her bag. "But I think you might benefit from a little support."

Dirk raised an eyebrow at the sight of the tiny gun. "What you gonna do with that, tickle them to death?"

"You'd be surprised." She looked him straight in the eye, a challenge and a warning against further argument. "Timothy has made me some rather splendid special rounds."

"And when all three of them run out?" Dirk had never been much for warnings, or for backing down from challenges.

She flicked her wrist and the outside of the parasol fell away. Sunlight glittered off the blade of a foil.

Dirk blinked in surprise, glanced around as a couple of passing labourers pointed their way.

"Shall we?" A superior smile played across Isabelle's ruby lips.

Dirk hefted his revolver.

"Let's do it."

The warehouse door gave way to Dirk's boot, letting them into a space of towering shadows. Heaps of bales and boxes rose around them, a self-contained city built of goods from all over the British Empire. It smelt of sawdust, coffee and cinnamon. Light crept in through windows near the ceiling, illuminating the tops of the stacks, but only a faint greyness was able to penetrate the aisles in between.

They stepped forward into the gloom, guns raised, Dirk taking the lead. A distant murmur of noise filtered in from the street, so faint that the squeaking of mice could be heard rising through it, the patter of tiny paws as the rodents raided sacks of dried food. Somewhere above them a cat growled and pounced, only to screech in fury as its prey scampered away.

A muffled yell punctured the air. Dirk headed towards the noise as another yell bounced between the crates, and another - the sound of Blaze-Simms in pain.

Dirk pressed himself through the narrow gap between two heaps of wool. He found his way by touch, prodding ahead with his foot, testing for corners of stacks with his free hand. He could barely see his own arm, but ahead an orange glow pierced the gloom. He headed towards it, pausing as he reached the edge of the shadows to see what lay ahead.

There was an open space at the centre of the warehouse, too far from the windows for any natural light. Oil lamps had been set on the floor around its edges, illuminating a scene of cruelty.

Blaze-Simms sat in the centre of the space, tied to a sturdy wooden chair. His face was a mass of bruises, blood trickling from between his lips. His left sleeve had been torn away and a series of narrow slashes cut into his arm, blood oozing from the wounds and dripping onto the floor.

Around him stood three black-clad figures, oriental swords protruding from their belts. One of them was cleaning a knife on Blaze-Simms's missing shirt sleeve. A fourth was disappearing between the stacks, darting confidently into the darkness.

Blaze-Simms groaned and looked up at his captors.

"Water?" he asked, his voice wobbling with pain.

One of the ninjas picked up a jug and held it just out of reach, tipping its contents away in a steady stream.

"Find what we want, you go," another ninja said. "Get all water you want."

Rage boiled Dirk's blood. He had seen more than enough. Gun raised, he emerged from the stacks, Isabelle with him. The ninjas turned in surprise, reaching by reflex for their blades.

Dirk didn't give them a chance. His Gravemaker roared, spitting hot lead at the nearest ninja. The man was thrown back against the bales, leaving a bloody smear as he sagged to the ground.

Isabelle snapped off two quick shots. The small bullets barely gave her target pause as he lunged towards her. Then there was a thud and his wounds burst open, showering Isabelle in gore and leaving him in pieces on the floor.

Dirk fired again. The remaining ninja staggered backwards, clutching at his wounded shoulder. A lantern skittered away, knocked by his flailing foot, leaving a trail of oil across the floor. Silent despite his injury, he dashed off between the crates.

Dirk hitched up the leg of his pants and pulled a bowie knife from its sheath. With one tug he sliced through the ropes binding Blaze-Simms.

"Frightfully good of you, old chap," Timothy said through gritted teeth as Dirk knelt to cut the bonds around his legs.

A soft sound emerged from nearby, like falling sheets.

"Gentlemen..." Isabelle was looking over Blaze-Simms's shoulder. A sheet of flame had sprung up between the packing crates, barring the way they had come. Adjacent boxes were smouldering and smoking.

"What the...?" Dirk looked around in alarm.

"The oil." Isabelle pointed to the broken lamp.

"We'd better get moving, then." Blaze-Simms wobbled to his feet, then slumped back into the chair. "Oh dear, it seems my legs have gone to sleep."

He leaned over, frantically trying to rub some life into his numb limbs, as a shadowy figure appeared behind him.

"Thought we'd got rid of you boys." Dirk raised his pistol at the approaching ninja, aimed and pulled the trigger. With a click, the hammer fell on an empty chamber.

The ninja leapt. A gleaming blade hurtled through the air, followed by a hiss of steel on silk. With a thud, the black-clad figure collapsed on the floor, Isabelle's sword protruding from his chest.

"Damn," Dirk whispered, impressed. "That's some fancy sword-work."

Blaze-Simms just stared, slack-jawed.

"No time to dawdle, Timothy." Isabelle placed a foot on the black-clad body and wrenched her blade free.

Rising more steadily this time, Blaze-Simms looked around at the encroaching flames.

"Which way?" he asked, glancing at the fire now blocking the exit.

"Guess we'll have to go around." Dirk strode into the narrow passages between heaped wares, heading to the wall and then turned south, towards where they had come in. But within moments their way was once more blocked, this time by a dead end of heavy pine crates.

Smoke billowed upwards as they rushed towards the rear of the warehouse, hunting for another exit. It swirled around them in growing clouds, scouring Dirk's throat, making his breath rasp and his lungs heave.

The whole place was burning now, rafters creaking as the roof pressed down on weakened supports. One gave way, crashing into a mound of crates. Dirk dived out of the way as a flaming roof-beam smashed into the floor where he had stood. Blaze-Simms wasn't so fast. Another beam slammed against the side of his head and he crumpled to the ground, the smouldering timber landing on him.

Isabelle rushed over and grabbed one end of the beam lying across his chest.

"Ready?" she asked.

Dirk nodded, grabbing the other end.

"Now."

They heaved, Dirk taking most of the strain, and flung the beam aside.

"He's still breathing." Isabelle leaned over and shook Blaze-Simms. His head flopped back and forth like a rag doll but he didn't stir. Alarm gripped Dirk. His friend had never been all that tough. This didn't look good.

Closing in from every direction, the flames danced across crates and packing bales, scorching the floor and warping the ceiling. Soot swirled in the restless air. Sweat seeped from Dirk's pores and in a moment was gone. He coughed as smoke smothered his senses and clawed at his throat.

"C'mon," he said, "let's get out of here."

There wasn't much of Blaze-Simms to weigh anyone down, not by the standards of a grown man, so it was no effort for Dirk to sling him over his shoulder. There was no door in sight, but to the left, between close piles of burning cloth, was a window. Breaking into a sprint, he dashed toward it, heat scorching the hairs from his arms. He dodged a burning barrel as it fell, leaped over another and stepped up onto a third, flames lapping round his shins as he launched himself at the window.

The glass gave way with a crash and a shock of cool air. Glittering points flew in every direction as he slammed into the pavement, just managing to retain his balance. He put Blaze-Simms down and turned in time to catch Isabelle as she hurtled head-first through the shattered window. She looked dazedly up at him and, reaching out, plucked a shard of glass from his cheek. Blood dripped from its tip.

Dirk shrugged, barely even feeling the wound. "Could have been worse."

With a crash like August thunder, the warehouse fell into blazing ruin.

Lowering Isabelle to the ground, Dirk took a deep breath of clean, smoke-free air and tried not to think about how close they'd come to death. A crowd was gathering around the warehouse, some of them rushing back and forth with buckets of water, trying to stop the fire spreading to neighbouring buildings. Others pointed and stared, either at the conflagration itself or at Dirk and his companions. An elderly lady had crouched down next to Blaze-Simms and was wafting smelling salts under his nose. His eyelids fluttered and then shot open.

"Dynamo!" He sat bolt upright. "The ninjas!"

"It's alright." Dirk helped him to his feet. "We got 'em. You're safe now."

"No, you don't understand." Blaze-Simms glanced around in agitation, one eye bloodshot and the other disappearing into bruised, swollen flesh. "They only wanted me for information, and I've never been terribly good with torture. They know exactly where they're going, and we have to stop them."

"Where are they going?" Dirk reached inside his jacket, feeling for bullets with which to reload his gun.

"To get the stone from Hakon."

"We've got it somewhere safe, right?" After all the trouble he'd gone through for the second clue to the Great Library, Dirk assumed it was locked up tight in a safe.

"I've been working on the inscriptions." Blaze-Simms looked down at his feet. "It's out in the open, at my flat."

Chapter 3: Chinese Tea

When Dirk had first met Blaze-Simms, the Englishman had a valet, the sort of live-in servant as essential to the British upper classes as teacups and country estates. But that poor valet had been the last one to serve Sir Timothy. After Jackson was nearly killed by an exploding hatbox, the fourth manservant in a row to suffer injuries around the experiment-littered apartment, good help became hard to come by. Careful negotiation between Blaze-Simms's father and a service agency resulted in regular visits from a tolerant cook, as well as the capital's most highly paid and most nervous looking cleaner. But for most of the day, the apartment was empty, and normally that was for the best.

Cautiously, Dirk nudged the door open with the tip of his boot, gun raised before him. When nothing moved, he stepped inside.

Blaze-Simms's home was furnished in the orderly style favoured by army officers and English public schools. The walls were crowded with shelves, drawers and cupboards, many of them labelled and all of them full. Half a dozen identical chairs and a dining table all matched the nearby sideboard. It would have been a picture of smart living, if not for the mess.

The apartment looked like it had been hit by a hurricane or an over-enthusiastic burglar. Books and papers were thrown wildly across the floor, chemical equipment scattered in pieces beneath the window. Chairs were toppled, ornaments discarded, drawers and cupboards hanging open, their contents spilling out.

"I'm so sorry, Timothy." Isabelle followed Dirk inside and drew aside the half-open curtain, letting more light fall across the disorder. "What a mess they've made. Is there anything we can do to help?"

"What?" Blaze-Simms looked up from a pile of papers. "Oh, you could check if the ninjas have been here. The tablet was on a shelf in the bathroom."

"Check if they've..." Isabelle raised an eyebrow.

"Not been to the lair of the genius before, huh?" Dirk grinned. "Lady comes in to clean up once a week, courtesy of Ma and Pa Blaze-Simms. Two days later, it's always the same. This mess just means he's been inventing a steam powered Punch and Judy show."

"Actually, it was a chemical formula for super-refined coal." Blaze-Simms waved his papers like a defence lawyer wielding exhibit A. "But I'm starting to think it won't work."

He pulled a pencil from his pocket and began scribbling.

"Not now, Timothy." Isabelle laid a hand on his arm. "The tablet?"

"Bathroom." Blaze-Simms waved distractedly toward a doorway at the far side of the room.

"Why?" Exasperation seeped through the word.

"To read in the bath, of course."

Dirk stepped carefully around a stack of old periodicals and a bowl that had clearly been bubbling over for hours. Beneath it, a paraffin burner attached to a system of rubber pipes was merrily blazing away. The carpet near the bowl was sticky under foot and the contents smelt like they could melt steel. Beyond it, the bathroom door lay ajar.

The bathroom was small but extremely modern, with a plumbed bath and white tiled walls. It contained the usual tools of cleanliness – soap, towels, razor. But there were other touches that were distinctly Blaze-Simms. A shaving brush on a mechanical arm with a pipe to squirt foam between the bristles. A thermometer on the side of the bath connected through gears and fan-belts to the taps. Wax pencils scattered around the floor and equations idly scrawled across the walls in moments of inspiration.

Next to the mirror were two shelves. One was loaded with bottles, jars and spare gears. The other was empty.

Dirk knew Blaze-Simms's mind well enough to know what that meant. If something fascinated him, as this stone tablet rightly did, then he'd keep it somewhere easily to hand. Still, Dirk rummaged through the rest of the bathroom, just in case the priceless artefact was hidden beneath an old towel.

"No good," he said as he returned to the dining room. "They beat us to it."

Isabelle had somehow found a clean cloth and bowl of water and was trying to tend to Blaze-Simms's wounds, not an easy task when he was darting back and forth, amending a sprawl of notes across the table cloth. His face looked less swollen than it had done, and his hair was only lightly singed.

"So what now?" she asked, gently pushing Blaze-Simms back into a seat. "We can't let them get away with this."

Dirk scratched his chin, fingers rasping over stubble. They could try finding the ninjas the same way they'd done before, asking folks in the street, trailing them from one sighting to the next. But the ninjas had more of a lead than before, and Blaze-Simms's street was pretty much just apartments. No tradesmen or stallholders lingered around here to provide easy witnesses.

Maybe they could follow the trail the old-fashioned way, looking for tracks in the dirt. Except that these streets would be full of footprints, burying the ones they were after. And even in London, with its clouds of soot and choking smogs, there wasn't much on the rooftops to leave footprints in.

If there was no trail to follow, then they'd have to start from scratch. For all its cosmopolitan nature, London wasn't exactly crawling with deadly, black-clad orientals. They should stand out, wherever they were. Poke the right pool of shadow and they'd come scuttling out. The problem was working out where to prod.

"Remember the Skelmersdale theft?" Dirk asked.

"Of course!" Blaze-Simms brushed aside Isabelle's ministrations, grabbing a walking stick as he headed for the door. Dirk followed after him.

"Wait!" Isabelle hurried after them. "Where are you going?"

"Chap we met on an old case," Blaze-Simms called back over his shoulder.

They hurried down the stairs and through the lobby, Blaze-Simms tipping his hat to an elderly neighbour who stared in concern at his battered face.

"If you tried hard you could be less specific." Isabelle's voice was sharp with annoyance. "What chap?"

"Chinese guy," Dirk said. "Called himself the Manchurian. Knows most of the oriental folks in London, and has his sticky fingers in half their business."

"You'll like him," Blaze-Simms said. "He's a people person."

#

Chinatown was a piece of a foreign land flung down in the middle of London. Its inhabitants had adopted the narrow, crowded streets so beloved of urban landlords, and the frantic, noisy lifestyle that made Londoners who they were. But theirs was still an alien presence, from the wide hats and loose tunics to the strange languages and sharp cooking smells. It was like entering another world.

Dirk knew just enough to know that these folks weren't all Chinese. This was a medley of a dozen different lands, the mixed races of the Orient flung together, indistinguishable to your average Englishman or American. Haughty Japanese, stooped Szechuanese, Hong Kong con-men, even the odd Korean sailor looking lost in the crowd. This was the Orient seen through a European lens – dirty, crowded, muddled, everything and everyone united in their primitive lifestyles.

The shop that fronted the Manchurian's operation was down a narrow back alley, hidden from the street noise. Dirk pushed aside a bead curtain and stepped inside, followed by Isabelle and Blaze-Simms.

The room was crowded with old things. Jars of shrivelled leaves and pickled roots for exotic medicines. Dusty statues of fat, laughing men. Brass bowls and faded parchments. In the middle of it all sat a wrinkled shopkeeper with a long moustache and elaborate but frayed robes.

The old man looked up at the rattle of the curtain. He bowed his head and shuffled around from behind the counter. The movement stirred the incense smoke that rose from burners around the room, wafting over a sweet, smoky scent.

"Welcome to humble shop." He steepled his fingers and lowered his head in a bow. "You looking for gift, yes?"

"No," Dirk said. "I'm looking for the Manchurian."

"Finger bowl is Manchurian." The old man pointed to a shelf of earthenware. "Some statues."

"Not Manchurian decorations, the Manchurian." Dirk folded his arms. It had been a long day already, and he wasn't up for games. "Well connected guy, works out back of your shop."

"Sorry, not know what you mean."

"Don't give me that." Dirk bristled with indignation. "I've been here before. Met you before. Been into your back room before and done a deal with your boss."

He pointed at another bead curtained doorway leading out of the back of the shop.

"Sorry, not know what you mean." The old man held his long nailed hands wide, pulling a face of exaggerated bemusement. "I am own boss. Only tea set in back room."

"Oh, for goodness sake," Blaze-Simms said. "It was only a year ago. You must remember us."

"Year long time. Many shoppers buy fine products, very reasonable price. I still own boss."

"Now listen here." Dirk loomed over the shopkeeper, bringing the full physical mass of his presence to bear. "Tell your boss we're from the Epiphany Club. We'll pay well for his time, but we ain't gonna be messed around by his cover man. Understand?"

The old man just shrugged his shoulders and treated Dirk to another bemused grin. Dirk replied with a scowl. This had been straightforward last time. They'd thrown around some cash and careful words, found the Manchurian's lair and been invited in. What was the problem this time? Had they stumbled over some stupid piece of gangster etiquette? Had he moved on? Was he just the kind of guy to mess folks around?

What the hell was the problem?

"Is this original Longquan Celadon ware?" Isabelle held up a small blue-green vase with handles shaped like animals. "It looks like a very early example."

"Yes." The old man shuffled around Dirk, eyes glittering as he zeroed in on Isabelle. "Very fine piece. Good glaze. Hard to find. You want?"

"A fine early piece like this could fetch all sorts of interest." Isabelle smiled. "I'm sure if I tell people you'll have a virtual sea of customers flooding into your shop. Everybody from artists to judges."

"Ha! I joke." The old man's grin became fixed, his body stiff. "Is imitation. Very fine imitation. Good glaze."

"So you just tried to sell me a fake?"

"Not fake. Imitation. Best quality. Chinese craftsmanship."

Blaze-Simms peered at the pot. "I don't think it is. The quality of the clay's wrong. More likely from Stoke, or possibly Manchester."

"Stoke pottery very like Chinese. Learn Chinese ways. Hard to tell difference."

"How fascinating." Isabelle's smile widened. "Perhaps I should find a policeman and see if they can confirm that?"

"No need! I sell you very cheap, yes? Specially price for friendly customer. No need for bother..."

The shop keeper's words faded to a nervous grin.

Behind him, the bead curtain twitched and a young woman's head emerged.

"The Manchurian will see you now," she said.

Dirk gave the bowing shopkeeper one last glare as they were led down a narrow corridor and into a small room panelled with smooth, unvarnished wood. The man who sat in it was much as Dirk remembered him. Anonymous, westernised clothes, shirt crisply starched, tie ruler straight. A calm face with the slightest smile. Dark, hooded eyes.

"Welcome." He waved them to seats with a hand whose bottom two fingers had been cut off at the knuckles. "Sir Timothy. Mr Dynamo. It is a pleasure to see you again."

Dirk lowered himself onto a wooden stool too small to comfortably take his bulk.

"And who is your charming companion?" the Manchurian asked as he poured tea.

"My name is Isabelle McNair." Isabelle didn't wait for the formality of introductions, settling with perfect poise on another of the stools and looking directly at their host. "And you are...?"

"I am simply the Manchurian." He passed them each a small bowl of green tea. "In my work, names are too important to spend lightly."

Dirk looked down at his tea. The bowl was barely more than an inch across, a drink for ceremonies, not quenching thirst. His fingers felt large and clumsy around the tiny object.

"Might I ask what your work is?" Isabelle held her cup lightly in her lap.

"I help people to find what they want, away from the glare of the open market." The Manchurian met Isabelle's gaze. If this was a staring match then it was the most sedate Dirk had ever seen. Neither showed any intensity of emotion, just the calm, quiet smiles of people chatting comfortably. People whose looks were fixed unwaveringly on each other.

"What some might call a fence?" Isabelle made the accusation sound polite.

"Of course not. That would be a crime." The Manchurian sipped his tea. "I am simply an enabler, a trader in information and services."

"And paintings," Blaze-Simms said.

"Did I sell you Lord Skelmersdale's painting?" The Manchurian set his cup down. "No. I merely directed you towards a man who could help. And now, I expect that you want my help again. So, what can I do for you today?"

"We're looking for some folks." Dirk set aside the futile little teacup. The damn thing didn't hold enough to quench a mouse's thirst. "They're in the enabling business too, only they enable with swords and knives. Black-clad, skulking types. Not Chinese, but from your side of the world."

"You wish to hire ninjas?" Their host raised an eyebrow.

"Find, not hire." Dirk leaned forward. If he could have done, he'd have cut straight through this conversation and on to the chase. "It's a particular group of ninjas. Big crew, been up in Manchester earlier in the year, stole something from us earlier today. We want our property back."

The Manchurian refilled his teacup, offered more to his guests. Silence grew around him. It scratched at Dirk's nerves but he kept himself still and quiet. He might be happiest with action, but if you wanted folks to do as you asked, sometimes you had to let them have things their way.

"I know of a group of ninja." The Manchurian sipped his tea. "They were in London in the spring and have recently returned. They are known as the Striking Snowflake, for they melt away in a moment."

"I say, that sounds like them!" Blaze-Simms beamed at the discovery, but his words were followed by an awkward silence. "Sorry, didn't mean to interrupt."

"Really?" The Manchurian played with the tea set again, letting attentive quiet build before he continued. "I do not know these people, but I am aware of their movements. The lands you call the Orient are a wide world of empires and oceans. London is one small city, and here it is much harder to hide."

He rose, smooth and formal.

"Wait here." He bowed his head slightly and turned toward the door. "Enjoy your tea. I will return shortly."

Once he was gone, Isabelle turned to face Dirk and Blaze-Simms.

"What an interesting gentleman." She sipped from her cup. "How did you meet him?"

"There was this painting," Blaze-Simms began. "Or at least, we thought there was, and it had been – ouch!"

"What he meant to say," Dirk said, retracting his foot, "is that there's some things we ain't at liberty to talk about, on account of promises and laws, and this is one of them."

"Of course." Isabelle's smile wasn't quite as warm as usual, but she made no further comment.

They sat in silence, Isabelle drinking her tea, Timothy scribbling in a notebook, Dirk using a spare stool as an improvised dumbbell. It felt odd, falling into regular habits so far from a regular moment, but there was no sense in letting time go to waste.

"I say." Blaze-Simms looked up from his notes. "If we can track down these Striking Snowflake fellows, maybe we can find out why they're after the tablet. I mean, I know it's meant to lead us to all sorts of knowledge, but – ouch!"

"Timothy." Isabelle retracted her foot. "Some things are best discussed in private, and not in the waiting rooms of gentlemen who sell information for money."

"Wise as well as beautiful." The Manchurian stood in the doorway, a teenage girl behind him. "If you ever need work, please come to me."

"So kind," Isabelle said. "Do you pay well?"

The Manchurian smiled and stepped back into the room, leaving the girl on the threshold.

"You are in luck." He settled back into his seat. "The Striking Snowflake passed near here a few hours ago. Arrogant Japanese, they assumed no-one would notice them among so many easterners."

He poured himself tea, the liquid still steaming as it emerged from the spout. Dirk figured that the block on which it rested must be heated from within, and he noticed Blaze-Simms craning his neck, trying to get a view of how it worked.

The girl stood silent, her head bowed, face half hidden by her hair.

"Li Fen here can lead you to where they left my... area of influence," the Manchurian said. "After that you will have to find your own way. I would not encroach on another man's manor, as these Londoners have it."

"Thank you." Isabelle reached inside her bag. "And what do we owe you for you kind assistance?"

"I would not be so crude as to ask payment for this small matter," the Manchurian said. "Merely a favour later, when it is needed. Your club has many contacts and resources, and will assist me in some equally trifling matter, when the time is right."

"You are too kind," Isabelle said. "Are you sure you won't accept payment now?"

"Very sure. Now if you will excuse me, I have other guests waiting. Li Fen will show you out."

#

Li Fen silently gestured them down the corridor and through a back door, then walked ahead of them down a maze of alleyways, glancing back at each turn to make sure she was still followed. Dirk wondered if she spoke any English at all. She didn't respond to Isabelle's enquiries about her health and background, or Blaze-Simms's queries about the meanings of oriental signs and graffiti.

The last alley they walked down was a dead end, its slimy cobbles leading to a brick wall. Buildings crowded around them, blocking out the light, and though the smell made clear that something was rotting, Dirk couldn't see whether it was food scraps, human waste, or some poor cat that had come here to die.

Li Fen stopped a foot from the wall and pointed at the ground. Dirk peered down, trying to make out anything in the gloom. He crouched on one knee, something cold seeping through his trousers, and saw a wide circle sunken into the street.

"You got a light, Tim?" he asked.

"Oh yes," Blaze-Simms said. "Would you like matches, or this new device I've been working on? It has a clockwork powered mechanism which-"

"The device." Dirk peered at the manhole cover. "'Cause guess where we're going?"

"Same as Venice?" Blaze-Simms fumbled through his pockets.

"Same as Venice."

"What is the same as Venice?" There was an irritable edge to Isabelle's voice.

"Funny story," Blaze-Simms said. "We'd been on the trail of a hoard of pre-Columbian treasure brought to Europe by Italian sailors. We knew it was... Oh, do you want this?"

He held out a small box with a crank on the side.

"Just give me a second." Dirk ran his hands across the steel disk, ignoring the unpleasantly slick film that coated it. If something hadn't died here then something fairly primitive was trying to live.

"The gold part of the treasure was purely incidental," Blaze-Simms continued. "What was really of interest was a set of Mayan carvings, believed to be..."

As Timothy kept talking Dirk continued his search. Finding two holes in the manhole cover, he crammed a couple of fingers through each, braced himself and heaved. For a long moment he strained for nothing, years of rust and dirt having fixed the cover in place. But he kept pulling, muscles hot with tension, ragged edges biting into his fingers, breath harsh in his smoke-ravaged throat. Finally, with a screech of metal against metal, the manhole came loose, one side rising up towards him.

Isabelle lunged forwards, slamming the cover back down so hard Dirk felt the clang through his boots.

"What the hell are you doing?" He shook his scraped and aching fingers. His fondness for Isabelle was fading fast.

"What am I doing?" She glared at him. "What are you doing, more like!"

"I'm goin' down into the sewers."

"Just like that? No protection, no permission, no papers, just down into the sewer?"

"Well, yeah." Now Dirk glared at her, frustrated at the feeling that he was being treated like an idiot, and that it wasn't his fault. He didn't like to be ignorant, liked to have his ignorance pointed out even less. "Why not?"

"You do that and you'll be dead within the hour. Not to mention leaving us to deal with the consequences."

"What's gonna kill me? An extra large rat? Angry cockroaches? The sewage monsoon?"

"Honestly, don't you know anything?"

They stood glaring at each other, both with arms folded and chins jutting in indignation. Dirk looked to Blaze-Simms for explanation, but the Englishman only shrugged.

"I don't see how it can be worse than Venice," he said.

"Come with me." Isabelle turned and strode back toward the sound of busy London streets. "I'll sort this out, before you get us all killed."

Chapter 4: Going Underground

Dirk watched Isabelle glide effortlessly through the crowded pub. She should have been a fish out of water, the society lady with her sharp, calculating mind in a dank, smoke-darkened hole full of labourers, sailors and drunks. But as she squeezed past, and they glanced down at her unblemished skin and costly dress, she'd make a small gesture or say a few words, and they'd smile and nod and go back to their drinks, comfortable with her presence. To Dirk, she was so obviously not one of them it was almost painful to see her here, like spotting a thoroughbred stallion dragging carts with pack mules. But to the people she passed she was one of the crowd.

It was weird. These English folks lived their lives defined by class, yet seemed oblivious to its implications, like fish who didn't know they were wet. Every fragment of their lives, from the moment they burst squealing into the world to the last thud of earth on their grave, was coloured by class, but they were so used to it they didn't even notice. Marx and Engels could scream from their rooftops while agitators stirred people to riot and the authorities to repression, yet those same rioters would never see the little ways in which their every manner, every move, announced and reinforced their status to the folks they met.

But Isabelle knew. She saw and understood, and with that understanding came power. The power to overcome class barriers and join any crowd, to play up to those colours and find complete acceptance.

She emerged from the belly of the pub with a little old man following in her wake, and led her companions outside.

It was an ordinary London street, with cramped buildings, dirty cobbles and a thin draping of smog. There was a beggar at one end and a cluster of kids playing jacks at the other. The folks passing by looked poor but respectable, heads held high, coats worn and patched.

Blaze-Simms leaned against a lamppost across the street, trying to look casual while one hand gripped his cane and the other dangled by the gun-shaped bulge in his jacket. Dusk was falling, and the flickering gaslight threw his face into shadow beneath the brim of his top hat. Together with the bruises, it gave him a ghoulish look.

Isabelle made the introductions. "This is Boris the Boat. He's kindly agreed to take us beneath the city."

Boris tipped his cap, revealing a wild spray of hair that matched the startling white of his beard.

"Couldn't we just have gone down the nearest drain?" Dirk's admiration gave way to exasperation at the reminder of why they were here. He'd bow to Isabelle's superiority when it came to grace, beauty and dealing with people, but she still hadn't explained anything and that was getting on his last spare nerve. Apparently chasing ninjas left time for side trips to dingy pubs in shady parts of London, but not for explanations.

Boris snorted.

"Maybe you want get shot or drowned in sewage by Underlord." His accent was Russian, tinged with the odd strained syllable from years of living around Cockneys. "I am poor immigrant and I know this. How you not know how your country works, huh?"

"It ain't my country." Dirk caught himself speaking in an exaggerated western drawl. He might not be a man of any fixed state, but he was still a proud American.

"I'm starting to wonder if it's even mine." Blaze-Simms twirled his cane. "I've barely spoken with an Englishman all day."

"Is this really what we've come to?" Isabelle sounded like an exasperated schoolteacher. "Casual jingoism and alarmist claptrap?"

"No ma'am." Dirk shuffled uncomfortably from one foot to the other.

"Terribly sorry." Blaze-Simms, like Dirk, was now looking at the floor.

"I should think so too." Isabelle turned to Boris with a smile. "Perhaps you could lead the way?"

"Da."

They followed the Russian around the back of the pub and past a couple of sheds to a canal. A pair of ducks sent ripples through the oily water as they paddled in slow, leisurely circles. A dirt path ran along each bank, shored up with concrete emplacements and wooden posts decorated with a few tiny clumps of weed.

A narrowboat was moored at the near bank, most of its length enclosed with walls and roof, with only a small patch of open deck at each end. Smoke drifted from a bent chimney pipe, past the hooked poles and coils of rope that covered the roof. Boris stepped on board, helping Isabelle on after him.

"You cast off," he said as Dirk and Timothy prepared to join them. "You know how to do this?"

He opened a hatch and disappeared into the bowels of the boat while Dirk and Blaze-Simms untied the ropes holding her in place. The coarse hemp had swollen with damp, and even with Dirk's frontier living experience it took a couple of minutes to get the knots untied. He coughed at the smoke billowing from the stack as the engine purred into life.

"One of you help with coal." Boris popped up at the far end of the boat, waggling a shovel.

"I'll go." Blaze-Simms strode excitedly toward the boatman. "I want to peek at the engine."

He scurried off to the rear of the barge while Dirk settled down on a bench at the front, his back to the low rail. They were drifting away from the path, gathering speed down the canal. The backs of factories and houses loomed above them, brick cliffs broken by the light of an occasional window.

Isabelle sat beside Dirk and let out a long sigh. Her whole body slumped, hands hanging by her sides. They'd all been going strong for hours, and now she looked exhausted, but Dirk still had questions. He needed to know where they were going, and why, and what she had planned along the way. On top of that was the issue of sharing information - he was sick of not knowing what was going on, and if they were working together he needed that to stop. But it was hard to start such a conversation when she could barely sit upright.

"It's been a long day," he said.

"The longest." She tilted her face to look at him, a curl of dark hair plastered to her forehead. "You may be surprised to hear this, but chasing ninjas and fleeing burning buildings aren't normally part of my day."

"Well, you know, every day's a ninja day back home." Dirk smiled. He couldn't help it around her. "So I can say with confidence that you're doing great so far."

"Thank you." She leaned against him, her head resting on his shoulder. "That means a lot to me."

Any questions and challenges went rushing from Dirk's mind. All he could think of was the gentle pressure of her body against his, the smell of her sweat and perfume close enough to overwhelm even a London canal. She made a small sound, almost a purr, and wriggled a little, making herself comfortable.

Slowly, tentatively, he stretched out his arm and placed it protectively around her.

They drifted down the canal like that, Isabelle dozing by his side, Blaze-Simms's voice a happy background chatter from the stern of the boat. Dirk knew from the stars and the last fading light that it took them about half an hour, though the perfect moment of it seemed gone in an instant.

"Almost there!" The calm was broken by Blaze-Simms as he strolled along the top of the boat. Isabelle jerked upright at the noise, blinking and rubbing her eyes. Dirk pulled back his arm and glared up at the Englishman.

"Still not sure where there is, though." Blaze-Simms thudded down onto the deck and settled on the bench opposite them. His front was smeared with coal dust, his hands black with it.

"We're going into the sewers," Isabelle said. "But we're going the polite way."

"So what, we go knock on the outhouse door?" Dirk raised a quizzical eyebrow.

"Very funny." Isabelle shook her head. "We're going in through the front door of the man who rules down there, and we're going to ask for help as well as his permission to travel."

"Someone rules under London?" Dirk asked.

"People live under London?" Timothy sounded even more bemused.

"Oh dear," Isabelle said. "What world have you two been living in, with your tea parties and libraries and adventures with paintings? People live everywhere. From the frozen rim of Siberia to the sun-blasted Sahara, from the wide American plains to a tiny island made of bird droppings. Everywhere. People. They adapt, they learn, they build civilisations.

"There are miles of tunnels under London, and all manner of materials to build a life from. Of course people live there. Their ruler swears fealty to the Queen once a year, in a darkened back room of the palace. But they have their own rules, and it would be both dangerous and terribly impolite to forget that."

The barge had turned down a side channel and was heading towards a lock, its entrance illuminated by the full moon. In the white light, silhouettes scurried around the top of the lock, turning handles, pushing beams, opening the wide gates. The narrowboat slowed as it passed through the gates and ropes dropped out of the darkness, lassoing the boat's mooring pins and pulling tight. It was an impressive display of rope work, small loops hitting first time in moonlight. Dirk was so out of practice that he wasn't sure he would have made those shots.

"We gettin' to this front door soon?" He stood to stretch his legs and catch a glimpse at the fellows on the path. They remained elusive, shadows in the night.

"We're there," Isabelle replied.

With a thud the front of the barge hit the inner lock gate. Ropes strained and men groaned as they inched the boat back, then the other gate slammed shut behind them. Cries of "Clear!" came from both ends of the lock, immediately followed by a rattling of gears. The sluice gates opened with a roar, murky water foaming white into the lock below, and they sank into darkness, walls of filthy grey stone rising around them, dripping with slime and weeds.

Dirk reached out and ran a finger over a passing block, acquiring a layer of green slime that stank of pure, unfiltered rot. It wasn't lovely, but he'd dealt with far worse. He flicked the slime away into the canal.

As the moon disappeared over a man-made horizon the churning water fell silent, the boat settling into its new level, and the gates swung open towards them. Ahead, illuminated by the boat's lantern, a tunnel mouth gaped, jagged with fallen masonry like the shattered line of a boxer's teeth. A wooden board hung above the entrance, one word scrawled in wide strokes of red paint across the crumbling planks.

"STYX."

The whole place gave Dirk the creeps.

On the towpath a figure sat hunched under a hooded robe, one withered hand clutching a dented tin bowl. As they drew level he shook it, rattling whatever was inside.

"Penny for the Underlord, lords and ladies?" he called out in a hoarse croak. "Them pays what comes to hell."

Dirk glanced at Isabelle, who nodded and pulled a purse from somewhere in her dress. She reached over the bow and tipped the contents into the battered bowl with a clatter that echoed into the darkness. Timothy followed suit, leaning out as they drifted past the huddled figure, dropping more coins into the pot. Finally, Dirk stretched out behind him, leaving a few glittering disks in the dish.

"Hope you take small change," he said, surprised to find himself feeling a little embarrassed. "I don't carry much."

"I takes whatever I can get." The man winked at him. Even that gesture added to Dirk's nervous edge.

In the tunnel, the workings of the narrowboat made their presence felt. The sound of its engine echoed around them and the smell of coal smoke, rather than drifting off into London's already murky air, hung around them, the tunnel's air flow carrying it forward faster than the boat moved.

The tunnel was brick lined, its smoothly curved surface dotted with weeds and moss. The sound of the boat was accompanied by the drip of water into the canal, a far louder sound than Dirk expected, each pointed sound echoing round and back, becoming magnified in the confined space.

"Hello?" Blaze-Simms called into the darkness, grinning as he listened to his voice return to him a dozen times over. "I say!"

"Timothy," Isabelle whispered, "do remember that people are watching us."

"Oh yes. Sorry." Blaze-Simms grinned sheepishly as these last words too echoed back to him.

It was cold in the tunnels. Up above, the air had been warmed by the summer sun. Not so down here. Dirk found it soothing after the heat and labours of the day, but Isabelle was shivering. He took off his jacket and draped it across her shoulders. She smiled at him and as he stepped away their fingers brushed. This time Dirk shivered.

The tunnel opened up into a circular chamber, still brick lined, with moorings at the far side. Gas lamps flickered on the wall beyond the moorings, their flames tinged with green.

Boris brought the boat round in a graceful curve, bumping sideways against the moorings. Dirk grabbed a rope and leapt onto the bank, tying them in place while Blaze-Simms and Isabelle climbed onto dry land.

"Thank you, Boris," Isabelle called down to the boat.

"No problem," the old Russian said. "You want I take you back also?"

"No, thank you. We'll find our own way home."

"Is good. Tomorrow is Sabbath. I don't work on Sabbath."

Dirk cast off the rope and the boat chugged away, back along the tunnel to the world above.

Isabelle led them through a doorway and down a long line of stairs. The theme of gas lamps and slippery brick-work continued until they emerged into another man-made cavern. This one was at least fifty feet across and half that high, its walls lined with piles of crates and barrels, heaps of warped timber and mismatched bricks. The ceiling disappeared not into walls but into the shadows behind these stacks, hiding the true size of the space.

They strode out into the middle of the room, then stopped.

"What now?" Dirk asked.

"Patience," Isabelle replied.

Something was stirring around the edge of the room. Shadowy bodies emerging among and above the crates. Faces peering out between the heaps. The shuffling and tap of footfalls. Whispers, coughs, deep breaths.

"Hello!" Blaze-Simms waved, then paused, squinting. He'd clearly spotted the same thing Dirk had.

The denizens of London below were emerging from the shadows, the first trickle of arrivals growing to a crowd. Among them were midgets and a pasty giant, folks with half a face or a missing limb. Hunchbacks, lepers and slack-faced loons. One man whose every inch of skin was covered in hair, and another who dragged himself along on a wheelbarrow, double-elbowed arms dipping to the ground.

Not a single one of them was normal and whole.

"What the hell's with this place?" Dirk whispered as he stared at the mob of warped bodies. "Everyone looks like they've escaped from Barnum's freak circus."

The crowd closed in, surrounding Dirk and his companions in a small circle of bare floor. Their uncanny nature sent a shiver down Dirk's spine. He could rationalise it all he wanted, think they were normal folks inside, that this was all just accidents of birth or life or both. He could tell himself that these things happened all the time, that you just didn't normally see so many of them at once. He could urge himself to be grateful, that there but for a whim of the world went he. But for all that, the revulsion still welled up within him, a baser instinct at which he felt ashamed.

The giant leaned over, long blonde hair hanging past her face, and stared Dirk in the eye.

"You're the freak down here, straight-boy," she said. "You'd better not forget it."

Surrounded in darkness by a hostile mob, Dirk had to fight the itch to reach for his gun. He cursed his own stupidity for saying anything at all, never mind saying it loud enough to be heard. They were on someone else's turf, looking for their help. Getting into a fight would be the worst possible start.

Well, the worst start short of getting lynched without fighting back. But the crowd had stopped closing in, and now they too were waiting expectantly, not leaping forward to make good on the giant's implied threat.

"I'm sorry to intrude, and for my friend's frightful comment." Isabelle looked serene as ever, smiling at the people around them. "But is one of you the Underlord?"

A chuckle echoed around the ceiling, bounding and rebounding until its soft stutter became a chorus of mirth. It seemed to come from all around, trickling with the condensation from the walls, rising worm-like from the ground. Dirk spun around, searching for the source. Tension gripped him.

The chuckling gave way to a voice that rasped like rusty steel.

"Over here, boys and gals."

At the far end of the chamber a man towered above them, raised up on a stack of wooden crates. A semicircle of miner's lamps lit him from below, casting his shadow up the wall in gigantic proportions. One hand spun a fob-watch on a tarnished chain, while the other held up a hand-rolled cigarette like it was the most exquisite cigar in all of London. He smiled a shrivelled smile from beneath a moustache like a tiny, greasy rat.

"Looks like we've got guests. Should I be getting out the good china?" He took a deep drag on his cigarette, blew a smoke-ring. "And before that, is there any reason I should let you live?"

Chapter 5: The Underlord

Dirk had faced enough self-styled masterminds in his time to hear the words coming. Before the Underlord had even finished his threat, his hand was on his gun and halfway through drawing. He'd be happy to shoot this smug villain full of lead.

But before he could get the Gravemaker from its holster Isabelle's hand was on his, restraining him.

"You think you have a choice, old chap?" Blaze-Simms's swordstick snicked clear of its sheath. "You're not the first villain to try to kill us, but as you can see, we're still standing."

"Timothy, put it away." Isabelle's tone clearly struck a chord, the blade disappearing almost on reflex.

"You've got them well trained, haven't you?" The Underlord's smile had something of the sneer to it.

"Their training is entirely their own," Isabelle said. "Unfortunately, so are their manners. I am Mrs Isabelle McNair. This is Sir Timothy Blaze-Simms and Mr Dirk Dynamo, of the Epiphany Club. We would like to permission to enter your domain, and the honour of a conversation with you, if we may."

"Epiphany Club, eh?" The Underlord tilted his head, catching the lantern light. Swept-back hair glistened like fish scales. "I knew several adventurous types at Cambridge who went on to join the club. I don't suppose you know Roger Harcourt-Phipps?"

"Of course." Isabelle smiled. "Splendid boxer."

"Small world, even above the ground." The Underlord took a last puff on his cigarette and ground the butt beneath his heel. "You can relax. I've no intention of killing you. Not yet, anyway. You found the ferryman, you paid the gatekeeper, and you had the good manners not to wander round my manor without permission. The least I can do is offer you tea."

#

The receiving room was another brick vaulted chamber, better lit and with less dripping from the walls, but still without the air of something designed for human habitation.

The Underlord sat in a wooden throne, clearly ancient and clearly battered by wear and damp. It creaked as he leaned forward, placing his elbows on the end of a long table. His three-piece suit was old and patched, and flecks of mud marked his sleeves.

Seated in high backed chairs along the sides of the table, Dirk and Blaze-Simms glanced at each other, waiting for Isabelle to take the lead. Aside from the Underlord, she was the only one looking relaxed, apparently unruffled by the filth and menace of their surroundings.

They'd been herded here by the malformed crowd, which had then retreated, forming an audience from doorways and alcoves around the edges of the room. Now that he'd got used to them, Dirk mostly felt pity for these poor souls, worn down by fate and left to linger here in darkness.

The décor of the room was mildewed mock gothic. Banners hung from the walls, decorated not with ancient heraldry but with slogans from regatta days or the logos of merchant fleets ploughing the Thames. Red velvet covered the table, but it was a patchwork affair, half a dozen pieces of faded cloth stitched together with their worse stains out of view. The candlesticks were mostly beer bottles, given a decorative aspect by the mixed dribblings of wax that coated their sides.

"I built some of these tunnels." The Underlord pointed at the brickwork above their heads. "Not the ones you've been through today, but others. I was a civil engineer, doing public works. North London sewers mostly, and a couple of covert links between government buildings. That's what made me aware of this hidden realm. You can't see so much of the darkness and not start to think how it might all add up."

He clicked his fingers and a dog padded into view, a tea-tray strapped to its back. Settling back into his battered throne, the Underlord proceeded to pour out four cups of tea, passing them to his guests.

"I've got to thinking that the Chinese have it right when it comes to tea." He dropped a lump of sugar into his cup, added a careful splash of milk. "It's not just a drink, it's a sacred rite. It's the uniting strand that binds us together. High and low, rich and poor, we all take time for tea."

"Some get finer tea than others, though." Dirk stirred his own cup. He might not like the Underlord's taste in dramatic menace, but he was always happy to discuss politics and society. Might as well make the most of a bad situation.

"You believe in class distinctions, Mr Dynamo?" The Underlord's eyes narrowed.

"I believe that they exist, not that they should." Dirk sipped his tea. It was better than he'd expected.

"I believe in neither. True, some are wealthier than others, some have finer homes or better health. But the bonds that matter stretch across that. Those of shared spirit, of character, of nationhood, of living a unique moment in history.

"What sort of class would you call us down here? Proletariat, perhaps? Or do we even qualify for that? A downtrodden mass, forced to live in the darkness below the privileged and powerful?"

He leaned forward, eyes glinting with intensity in the candlelight.

"You think that I am forced to live down here? An engineer, a man of learning such as myself? I choose to live here, for the wonders and joys that it brings. As much as a prince or parliamentarian, I live surrounded by the glories of our age. Look around you. What do you see?"

Dirk turned his head, gazing around the chamber. Not that he needed to look. He'd taken in every detail by the time he'd been there ten seconds. But this was a moment for social games, and this was one he could play. So play he did, acting out an exaggerated turning of his head, a roaming of the eyes, a thoughtful nodding. He stared again at the dripping walls, bricks running together as the foulest of the waste slowly dissolved their surfaces. The muck-trodden floor, brown with things it was best not to consider. The rickety table and the improvised candlesticks, chipped china and mismatched napkins, not hiding the grimness of this world but enhancing it, forcing the eye and the mind to address their surroundings however squalid and absurd.

He turned back to the Underlord and paused for a long second, wondering what answer the man was after. He settled on the obvious.

"Sewers," he said at last.

"Exactly right!" The Underlord grinned like he'd been handed a barrel of gold. "That one word captures the wonders which we have achieved. A marvel of engineering and infrastructure, miles of public construction beyond anything our ancestors could have envisaged, humbly hidden beneath the feet of the nation. We keep our real glories hidden.

"Like these men and women. To the ignorant masses who walk our streets they are just wretched, dirty and broken beneath industry's wheel. But they are so much more. Their toil, their spirit, these are wonders of the age. See Toby here..."

He waved over a tall, muscular man with weather-beaten skin and a massive grin. One shirt sleeve dangled empty by his side.

"Toby," the Underlord said, "tell our guests what you did for a living."

"I was a navvie, m'lord." Toby's tone was deep and rattling, a rock-slide of a voice. "I dug canals and laid railway tracks."

"You enjoyed it?"

Toby's smile widened, almost splitting his face in two. "I see coal in London, come all the way from Yorkshire, and I think to myself 'I done that'. I'll love my job forever."

"Sam!" The Underlord waved at someone in the shadows. "Tingling Sam, get yourself over here!"

A small man, crouched over his clasped hands, scurried out of the crowd. He bowed his head, nodding as he walked, like a pigeon hunting crumbs. When he reached the Underlord he looked up, revealing a face torn by a patchwork of scars, whole swathes of skin smooth and red or deathly pale.

"Sam." The Underlord lowered his voice, as if talking to a small child. "Sam, what do you like to do?"

Sam glanced around nervously, eyes flitting over the visitors and then back to his master. His lips twitched uncertainly.

"It's alright, Sam," The Underlord said. "You can talk in front of these people. What is it you like?"

"Splosions." Sam shot a furtive look at Isabelle as he said it, breaking briefly into a smile. "I make splosions."

"What do you make your explosions for, Sam?" The Underlord leaned forward eagerly.

"Stuff." He paused thoughtfully, then counted off on thin fingers. "Bombs. Guns. Digging. Fireworks. Fun."

"Could you do that if you weren't a Victorian, Sam? If you didn't live in this great and glorious age?"

Sam scrunched up his face, as if trying to remember some long-forgotten lesson. Then he shook his head.

"Sam is a chemist," the Underlord explained. "An artisan of explosives. Through science, he can control the details of his work. Size, intensity, colour, effect. He is a master of a craft that could not exist in any other age. Isn't that right Sam?"

"I like when they're tall and red." Sam was looking at Isabelle again, imparting a shared secret. His voice shook with quiet intensity. "It makes me tingle."

"Some people don't see the world I live in." The Underlord waved a hand at the broken masses huddled around him. "They believe that there is only shiny, clean wonder in our age. Wilfully or obliviously, they do not notice. Others see the blemishes, frailties, injuries, and see corruption in everything. The wiser see both, but see them in conflict, a battle between corruption and perfection, whether embodied by culture, class or race.

"But down here we see the truth. The two are not separate. They are not opposing forces grinding away at each other, or principles caught in some delicate balance. They are aspects of one and the same thing, a single uniting power seen from a million different angles. It exists in every space and every moment, and all are made equal by its touch. It is the march of history, the touch of divinity, the living soul. It is the modern."

The Underlord fell silent. Dirk felt numbed by the barrage of words, and Blaze-Simms's face reflected his own feelings of stunned bewilderment. It was hard to tell how much of what they'd just heard made any kind of sense, there'd been so much of it. But Isabelle, like the Underlord's followers, was nodding thoughtfully, as if taking in an insightful lesson. Somewhere in the chamber, condensation dripped from the ceiling, its irregular beat puncturing the quiet.

"Enough of my ramblings." The Underlord picked up his teacup. "What can I do for you?"

"We believe that someone else has come into your domain." Isabelle raised her own chipped cup, holding it as delicately as one would the finest china. "A group of orientals. They stole something from Sir Timothy's house, and we would like it back."

The Underlord poured himself more tea. He did it carefully, filling the cup to a precise level, watching the colour as he poured in the milk.

"I don't know anything about orientals." His spoon clicked against china. "If they are down here then we haven't seen them."

"All the more reason to get involved," Isabelle said. "Surely you can't let people wander around your territory without your permission?"

"A good point. What's a lord without authority over his lands?" The Underlord sipped his tea. "So you want my help tracking down these orientals, and you want your property back when they're found. But what's in it for me and mine? These could be dangerous sorts. I might be better off just letting them leave. Or ambushing them and taking whatever you're after for myself. You've gone to quite some effort to get here, so it must be valuable."

"As you admitted, there's the authority issue." Isabelle set her cup aside and crossed her gloved hands, taking on a deeply serious look. "All your good subjects watching us now know that you've been invaded, and you'll need to show them that you can deal with that.

"As for why you should let us take our property, the answer is because you will get our help. These are dangerous men. Very dangerous men. We have fought them several times, and beaten them, but they keep coming. Look at Mr Dynamo. Do you think any but the most deadly and determined opponent keeps running up against him? We'll help you exert your authority, and you'll help us get our property back. What do you say?"

The Underlord opened a wooden box of cigars and proffered them around the table. They all took one, even Isabelle, to Dirk's surprise and the Underlord's clear amusement.

"I like you, Mrs McNair." The Underlord lit his cigarette, paused thoughtfully as he took his first mouthful of smoke. "You're not afraid to stoop to my level."

"We're all on one level, your lordship." She lit a match on the arm of her chair. "Didn't you just tell us that?"

Dirk took a drag on his cigar. It was cheap and nasty, but it had been a long day and he didn't reckon it was over yet. Any little pleasure to see him through.

He stole a glance at Isabelle. Any little pleasure.

"I don't suppose you're widowed?" The Underlord was still looking at Isabelle.

Smoke caught in Dirk's throat. Any liking he had for this greasy little guy was fading fast.

"No, your lordship." Isabelle blew a smoke ring. "Mr McNair is merely busy elsewhere."

"Curious," the Underlord said. "And here you are, wandering the sewers with two other men. You'd have thought a husband would get concerned."

As they looked at each other, Dirk got that old, familiar feeling that he was missing something. There were many things that got him frustrated, but that feeling was top of the list.

"Can we get goin'?" He pushed back his seat. "The longer we wait, the further ahead of us those ninjas will get."

"Of course." The Underlord waved his cigar, smoke trailing through the air. "Plaguepit!"

Someone emerged from the shadows, hunched over in what looked like a monastic habit, the edges frayed and trailing. A sickly miasma hung around the figure, a smell of rot and vomit. Dirk took a deep drag on his cigar, trying to drown it out.

"If you're from the Epiphany Club I'm guessing that you're scholars,' the Underlord said. 'Are any of you men of science?"

"I'll say." Timothy looked up excitedly.

"Then you should have a look at old Plaguepit here."

The Underlord flicked back the figure's hood, revealing the most horrible face Dirk had ever seen. It might have been a handsome face once, a face that inspired lust and envy. Maybe it had once been plain, or merely ugly. But now it was a devastated mess, blistered, pocked and scarred, the muscles of one side hanging loose, pus seeping from spots and boils.

"Plaguepit here's a whole gallery of biological curios, all by himself. Isn't that right, Plaguepit?"

Plaguepit nodded, his ear wobbling like it wasn't quite fixed in place. Despite his wretched condition he managed a sloppy smile. He seemed familiar with this role as an object of curiosity for strangers.

"A lord needs to take care of his subjects," the Underlord said. "So I've developed my knowledge beyond engineering and into the medical sciences. I've read the works of Mr Jenner, and those who've come after him. That's why I keep Plaguepit around. He comes from a long line of very resilient people. Any time someone in my realm gets a new disease they pass it to Plaguepit. He beats it down, then passes it back harmless to my subjects. Nothing beats Plaguepit."

"But that shouldn't..." Timothy began, and was silenced by a kick from Isabelle.

"Ingenious," she said. "You're clearly a man who knows how to make the most of what he has."

"You're right." The Underlord grinned. "But there's so much more to that than Plaguepit."

He leaped from his seat, cigar tip carving red arcs through the air as he waved it about.

"Come on, I'll show you the real work."

Striding across the room, he set off down a tunnel, his subjects parting to let him through. Dirk and his companions followed. As they passed the lines of twisted bodies and scarred faces, Dirk felt like he was in an inversion of a freak show where normal, well-formed men were the objects of fascination. Roll up, roll up! Come and see the amazing upright man and his companion the thinker!

They twisted and turned through the dank spaces beneath London, up stairs and down slopes, along tunnels so narrow they had to walk sideways and through caverns so vast the ceiling disappeared into darkness.

Much of the journey took them along paths beside the capital's busiest sewers. There were some smells, like battlefields and infection wards, that you never got used to. This was one of them. Dirk felt the bile rising in his throat. He'd have held his nose, but he wanted to keep his hands free in case he slipped on the slimy path.

"Nothing gets wasted down here." The Underlord's voice echoed proudly from the brick vaults.

They emerged half way up the wall of a wide chamber, like the hall of a great palace, but one made of brick, pillared with sewage-weathered stone and painted with putrid slime. People bustled about in the space below them, sorting through piles of rubbish, making heaps of old and rotting food, of broken down furniture, of torn clothes, bricks and rubble. Everything was sifted through, the repairable retrieved from the irredeemably damaged and the unusably vile. What was left was piled into mine carts and pushed through the doors at the far end of the hall.

"This is where we find our treasures." The Underlord beamed with pride. "The things wastefully abandoned or pointlessly thrown away. You'd hardly believe the stuff people will discard. A man could get rich just picking out the gems. But through here, here's the really inspired bit."

He led them along a raised walkway and through an opening in the sewer wall. On the far side was another large chamber, this one filled with the crunk and clank of busy machinery and the smell of well-oiled mechanisms. A dozen sweaty labourers were shovelling heaps of refuse into receptacles like reinforced bath-tubs, then standing back as glowing piston-driven presses crashed down on the rubbish. There was a hiss of steam and a smell as acrid as burning hair. Then the pistons rose and the tubs tipped, dropping solid sheets of who-knew-what onto a conveyor belt.

The Underlord paused.

"The Compactor." He had to shout to be heard above the noise of machinery. "We use it for the real waste, the stuff even we can't reuse. Everything gets sprayed with an acidic formula that loosens its shape, melts it a little. Then the mix is heated under high pressure causing a reaction in the formula, binding everything together. We use the results for construction, and occasionally for fuel."

"What are you constructing down here?" Timothy asked, peering eagerly down at the Compactor.

The Underlord smiled his tight little smile. "Wouldn't you like to know."

Unease crept through Dirk. He understood that the world was full of secrets, but folks who gloated about them were usually up to no good. Yet there was much to admire in the Underlord's work, and so he pressed the feeling down. The man was helping, there was no need to let prejudice get in the way.

The walkway was scrap-built, like everything else in the Underlord's domain. But it was solid enough underfoot, barely creaking as Dirk made his way across the room. Below him, the Compactor chambers glowed, clanging shut then swinging open with a hiss of acrid steam. This was how the superstitious imagined hell, rows of fierce jaws opening on the glow of the flames below. To Dirk it was something glorious, the ultimate expression of the human will. Here anything could be remade, anything could become useful. There were no limits. No need to leave anything or anyone behind. God was dead, heaven and hell with him. Man ruled all, and man could make himself great.

He leaned over the rail, trying to get a better look at what went into the process. Mostly broken, indistinguishable fragments and twisted shapes he would once have thought beyond all use.

Anything. Anything could be remade.

Something slammed into his back. He went over the rail, into the air. The compactor opened wide.

Dirk tumbled in toward fire and steel.

Chapter 6: On the Trail

Dirk shot out a hand. Skin brushed rusted metal, terror taking hold as the railing slipped through his fingers. He was falling, the compactor gnashing its teeth below him.

His hand hit a strut and he grabbed on tight, quivering with tension as he dangled above the rending jaws. Steam spurted past him in super-heated bursts, the hiss and roar of machinery surrounding him. Above, a hunched figure shifted furtively back from the rail and disappeared.

Dirk could feel his grip slipping, his fingers losing their hold on the strut as its rusted surface rubbed away beneath them.

"Help!" he called out, his voice lost in the noise of the vast, echoing chamber. "Help me, dammit!"

He shifted his body, swung from left to right and managed to get enough momentum to swing his other hand up onto the strut. He grabbed it firmly, even as his initial purchase became nothing more than a painful finger hold.

Frustration bubbling up within him, he fought to stay calm. How had he been so careless as to let someone creep up on him? Why had he relaxed so much in a place full of strangers, freaks and lunatics?

"Help!" he called out again. Both hands were sliding away now, slippery with sweat and steam, their grip closed on little more than layers of rust and flaking paint. He looked around below him. Maybe if he could swing himself forward as his grip went he could fall past the machines. Sure, it was twenty, thirty feet that way, and he wouldn't have much momentum. Even under the best of circumstances it was a long shot, and this definitely wasn't the best of circumstances. But if that was the only chance he had...

Hands closed around his wrists and he found himself hauled upwards. He almost swore with relief as they dragged him over the edge of walkway. He lay there for a moment, enjoying the firm ironwork beneath him and the lightness in his arms, now released from the burden of bearing his whole weight.

"I say, old chap, you gave us quite a scare." Blaze-Simms looked at him with concern. "Were you hanging there long?"

"Too long," Dirk said.

"Sorry about that." Blaze-Simms fished a notebook and pencil out of his pocket. "Didn't notice at first. This place is just so fascinating."

The Underlord stepped forward, a little grin twitching up the corner of his greasy moustache.

"You should be more careful, Mr Dynamo," he said. "Leaning over like that, slipping into my crushing pans, you'll end up as bricks."

"I didn't slip." Dirk took a deep breath to keep his temper in line. This would be the test of their host's intentions. He didn't want to pre-judge the man, but it was hard not to as he sniggered at Dirk's discomfort. "I was pushed."

"Not again." The Underlord's eyes narrowed. "Stupid sods."

He whirled around and bellowed to the room. "Machines off! Everybody stop! We're having a meeting."

#

The alcove was dark, the walls slimy and cold. Dirk sat forward rather than smear his shirt with the clinging goo, and Isabelle did the same.

He clenched and loosened the hand with which he had grabbed the railing. The palm was badly grazed, the skin rubbed raw, flecks of rust buried in tender flesh. It was the sort of low key, slow burning pain that was hard to ignore, especially given it made his hand next to useless. It was going to hurt to pull a door handle, never mind carry any weight or squeeze the trigger of a gun.

"Let me look at that." Isabelle leaned forward, gently but firmly prying his fingers apart. Her touch was warm and reassuring in the darkness.

She pulled a handkerchief from her pocket, a white lace square with delicate, embroidered edges. With long finger nails she pulled the slithers of rusted metal from his hand. Each time, the pressure of those nails sent a shiver of pain up Dirk's arm, but he kept from flinching, holding steady with his hand in hers. With the visible rust gone, Isabelle wrapped the cloth carefully around Dirk's wound, turning his hand over to knot it around the back. Then she held his hand in both of hers, examining her handiwork.

"That should keep it clean for now," she said, and Dirk realised how close their faces were, leaning forward in the darkness. Her warmth radiated against his cheek.

"Thank you kindly, ma'am," he murmured.

"Please." She looked up at him. "Call me Isabelle."

Outside, the Underlord was still arguing with his followers, berating some, cajoling others, trying to rouse the crowd without setting more of them against the visitors. Blaze-Simms could occasionally be heard answering a point - calm, reasonable, and so very English.

"How come he's the one talking to them?" Dirk asked. "Ain't that more your area of expertise?"

Isabelle shrugged. "It seemed more appropriate. Even people who will listen to a woman in private may not when she's speaking in public."

"That ain't right." Dirk felt an unexpected burst of indignation. "You've a way with words more than any man I've ever met, and a kindness with folks that'd get any man doing what you please." He paused, realising how awkward his last point had been. "I don't mean that like it sounded. Not that you're manipulative, or-"

"Relax." She laughed and squeezed his hand. "I understand. And thank you. I try to be kind to people, to make people happy. It is one of the few ways a woman can make a difference in this sad, strange world of ours. But some people's happiness matters more than others."

Dirk gazed into her eyes, saw that gentleness looking back at him, so different from himself or from any woman he'd been with.

"I..." Words failed him. She leaned forward, her lips pressed against his. The taste of her was like electricity jolting through him. Their hands tightened together, his pain forgotten in the intensity of delight.

He pulled back, overcome by a moment of guilt.

"You're married," he said. "I can't..."

She looked away, but her hands were still around his, their fingers intertwined.

"What if..." She hesitated. "What if I weren't. What if-"

"I say!" Blaze-Simms thrust his head into the alcove, squinting into the darkness. Isabelle and Dirk jerked back away from each other. Cold soaked into Dirk's back as he pressed against the wall.

"I think they've finished talking," Blaze-Simms continued. "The Underlord wants us all out here."

Dirk and Isabelle both rose at once, bumped into each other in the confined space. She laughed softly and he stepped back.

"After you, ma'am." Feeling confused and awkward, he slipped back into the comfortably familiar.

"Thank you, sir." She led the way out into the chamber.

The Underlord's people stood in wide a ring, the Underlord and another man in the centre. The man's shoulders sloped down to the left, and the right side of his body was substantially more muscled than the left. His face was downcast beneath a matted grey beard.

The Underlord beckoned Dirk forward into the circle.

"Dirk Dynamo, this is Frederick Raddles," he said with the casual ease of a man introducing two friends at a party. "Mr Dynamo, say hello to Old Fred."

"Howdy," Dirk said, holding out his hand. "Pleasure to meet you."

There was a pause. Around the circle people shuffled their feet and whispered to one another.

"Fred." A hard edge rose in the Underlord's voice. "What do you have to say to Mr Dynamo?"

Old Fred mumbled indistinctly.

"What was that?" the Underlord said.

"Sorry," Fred muttered, finally meeting Dirk's eye. "For trying to kill you."

Dirk stared in disbelief at the lop-sided cripple. The idea that this man had pushed him over the bannister at the edge of the walkway was absurd. He wondered if the Underlord was covering for something. It was the only explanation that seemed to make any sense.

Then Fred shifted his weight, the muscles of his right side visibly rippling, popping the seams of his stained and much repaired shirt. Now it made a lot more sense.

"Not everyone down here likes or trusts outsiders," the Underlord said. "That's what comes from being mocked and beaten any time you show your face in daylight. Ain't it, Fred?"

Fred shuffled on the spot, eyes down cast once more. Just watching his discomfort made Dirk uneasy.

"It isn't right for my people to take matters into their own hands," the Underlord continued. "Is it, Fred?"

"No, sir," Fred mumbled.

"And he won't do it again, will you?"

"No, sir."

"Right!" the Underlord pulled a wrinkled cigarette from behind his ear and struck a match. "That's settled then. Isn't it, Mr Dynamo?"

Dirk glanced around the circle of warped faces, some eager, curious and welcoming, others filled with wariness and fear. He wasn't sure it was settled at all. But what else was there to say? They needed these folks' help. But now he'd take that help with a backward glance and a wariness of his own.

"Sure is, your lordship." Dirk stuck out a hand towards poor Fred. The lopsided elder ran his hand across his nose with a loud sniff, then took the handshake. His right hand was like a vice squeezing Dirk's fingers, but his left hung withered and twitching at his side. Dirk squeezed back, accepting the challenge of Fred's gaze.

"Grand," the Underlord said. "Now, I've got a realm to rule, and you've got some intruders to catch. Turpin here will be your guide. He's a simple soul, but he knows the tunnels like the back of his hand."

Dirk looked down at the dirt-slathered cherub staring up at him, and the pudgy paw now being held out. He sure hoped their guide knew more about the tunnels than would fit on the back of that hand.

"Well Turpin," he said, "I hope you're real smart."

#

With his high voice, round face and chubby fingers there was something endearingly childlike about Turpin. He was an adult, the hair spurting from his ears and his incongruously low voice said as much, but even his wide smile was that of a toddler at play as he waddled along the path beside the sewer. At times the tunnels would split and he paused to examine his surroundings, peering at the walls and the ground, kneeling down for a close view of the dirt.

Dirk stayed close to their guide, holding up one of the lanterns they'd been given by the Underlord. He had done tracking in tunnels and sewers before now, but it was a long way from his area of expertise. Give him the sun and the open plains and he could follow week-old prairie dog tracks. But spotting a trail in the darkness and ooze below London took knowledge you couldn't learn in the new world. He wanted to know more.

"This way." Turpin beamed and shone his lantern down a side tunnel.

"How d'you know?" Dirk asked.

Turpin pointed at a green smear among the grey and brown coating the brick wall.

"It's growing back." His voice was full of pride in his skills. "If it's growing back now then it's been hurt today. Someone leaned here."

He turned down the side tunnel, singing softly to himself as he walked. Dirk paused to observe the mark on the wall, the layers of mould and filth, memorising the pattern and what it meant.

"I say, isn't this exciting?" Blaze-Simms asked. His bruised face was still smudged with soot from their journey on the canal boat and he had muddy spatters half way up his carefully tailored trousers. He kept stopping to scribble in his notebook, but Dirk could hardly complain at the delays, given that he was taking tracking lessons as they went.

Besides, he was more concerned with Isabelle than with Timothy. She had been quiet since the alcove, letting Dirk and Blaze-Simms finish off their conversation with the Underlord, giving him the briefest of parting words. She was not meeting Dirk's eye either, though that was a hard thing to judge in the darkness as they trudged down paths often wide enough only for one man, sometimes less than that as they clung to the wall, toes perched on a precarious few inches of slippery brickwork with a rotting mess of sewage below.

Dirk tried to keep his mind on the task, but it was mighty tricky with the memory of her lips brushing his. She was a married woman, and a man had to stand by his principles no matter how hard that was. But it was pretty damn hard right now.

"Down here." Turpin led them down a tunnel so low only he could stay upright, Dirk and his companions stooping to follow through. "You'll get to see something really special."

He closed the shutter of his lantern, urging them to do the same. Without the lamps' orange light, a silvery glow could be seen coming down the tunnel ahead, glistening off the walls, making the gaps between bricks stand out like a web of dark veins.

"Sometimes," Turpin said in an awed whisper, "I think even the walls themselves might be alive."

They stepped out of the end of the tunnel into a chamber filled with the same eerie light. It was like stepping out into moonlight, but moonlight that flowed from every surface, leaving no hiding place for shadows. Every inch of Dirk and his companions was illuminated, from the stains on the underside of Timothy's sleeves to the warts beneath Turpin's straggly hair. But even in the harshly overwhelming light Isabelle remained as beautiful as ever.

The light seemed to come from the walls themselves, from the floor beneath their feet, and most of all from a pool in the centre of the room. Once part of the sewage system, it had been cut off by the deliberate damming of one end and a masonry cave-in at the other. It should have been stagnant and grotesque with trapped waste, or dried out over time, reduced to a layer of slime and crusted sewage. But instead it was full of water that seemed to glow from within, the silhouettes of fish shimmering back and forth beneath its surface.

Dirk placed a hand on the wall and it came away glowing. His skin tingled and shimmered as something writhed on its surface.

"I don't know what it is," Turpin said, "but I've never seen it nowhere else. There must be something special in this place, cause I tried taking some away once and it stopped glowing after a couple of hours, left me with nothing but a jar of grey slime." He shook his head sadly. "I come here when I can. It's the most amazing place."

Blaze-Simms had pulled a magnifying glass from the depths of his pocket and was peering at the stuff on the wall. The light distorted as it shone through the lens, becoming a bright circle in a wide, dark ring. He had a notebook pressed against the wall with his elbow and was scribbling in it with the other hand.

"Amazing," he said. "Something in the walls must be reacting with agents in the water to feed them. But how did they develop down here, with no natural light? Did they migrate in some more complex form, or do they exist elsewhere as well? This could be-"

"Could be a big distraction from what we're really about." Dirk hated to say it, the room was mighty pretty and he was as curious as Blaze-Simms to know how it worked, but they had other concerns. "Those ninjas ain't gettin' any closer."

"You're right." Blaze sighed and put his pencil away. "Lead on."

#

Turpin led them through a narrow doorway in the far side of the chamber and down a winding series of tunnels, along sewer-side paths and up access ladders. Dirk was learning to spot the signs their guide followed. The scuff marks on the walls that were made by people passing, and those that belonged to whatever else was living down here. The ripples in the filthy water that showed a disturbance down a distant tunnel. The footprints he might have missed, formed only of the faintest hint of mud amid a layer of slime.

The glowing room wasn't the only odd thing growing in the space beneath the city. Spiny fins sliced the surface of the sewer. Mosses and fungi clung to the walls. Dirk leaned against one while he adjusted his boot, and it felt like the cold grey thing was trying to grow over him. Of course there were insects - beetles, millipedes, cockroaches as long as his hand, buzzing clouds of flies.

"Don't you get rats this far down?" Timothy paused again to scribble something in his notebook.

"Oh yes." Turpin's eyes went even wider. "Gosh, we haven't seen any in while, have we?"

"Surely that's a good thing?" Isabelle looked as calm and comfortable as a person could seem, despite hitching up her skirts to avoid the sewage.

"Oh yes, I'm sure it is." Turpin said. "It's just odd."

Dirk walked on ahead and peered around the next corner. He could hear a whistling, like the warble of a bird, but not one he had ever heard before. There was a scurrying in the dark, something scuffling over stone. The sound grew louder, faster, closer.

Raising his lantern, he lit up the path ahead. Instead of flagstones he saw a seething mass of fur and claws. It scampered toward him out of the darkness, lantern light glinting from hundreds of pairs of rodentine eyes.

He called back to the others. "Reckon I've found your rats."

Chapter 7: Different Ways

The rats rushed along the path, a tumbling, malevolent mass of hunger, scything the air with filthy claws and jagged teeth. Tension gripped Dirk as he backed around the corner and toward the others.

The creatures scurried after him. A high pitched whining followed them, seeming to drive them on, to agitate them as it rose in pitch. They gnashed their jaws and scrabbled madly with their paws, still heading straight towards Dirk. A terrible image filled his mind, of being swamped by these creatures, drowning in a tide of claws, fur and filth.

He drew his gun, hand stinging from the scrapes he'd taken at the compactor, and snapped off a shot at the front of the pack. The roar of the Gravemaker echoed in the closed space of the tunnel. Dozens of rats were flung through the air in a blast of stone chippings and bloody rodent remains. But the swarm kept coming, leaping over and through their fallen kin, something like madness in their eyes.

Dirk fired again and again, desperately trying to hold back the tide, but they were on him - scrambling up his legs, dropping from the wall, crashing over him like a wave as they leapt and gouged to overtake one another. Claws dug through his shirt and into his skin. Teeth bit his hand as he tried to batter them off. He kicked some of them into the filthy water but they kept coming. The horrible mass of filth and fur threatened to overwhelm him.

Even his lantern was covered in rats, weighing heavy in his hand. Fighting back a sense of claustrophobic panic, he swung the lantern against the wall and it smashed open, oil igniting as it spilled across the path, blocking the rats' way. A few tried to dive through it, but their agonised screeches and the stink of burning flesh deterred the others behind them. The swarm split, some still scrabbling up the top of the wall and over onto Dirk's head, others diving off into the water and swimming on, pointed heads bobbing in the stream.

Dirk slammed his body against the wall. There was a sickening crunch as tiny ribcages were crushed between his chest and the stones, and he could feel the warmth of their blood soaking through his shirt. He pulled two more from his face, their last scrabbles a sickening sensation against his skin, the smell of filthy fur making him gag. He flung them out into the water then ran his hands back over his head, knocking a dozen more clear.

The torrent of rats had ended, and he was almost free of them. A multitude of tiny scratches and bits stung his flesh as he shook a last furry body from his boot and turned down the tunnel towards the others. Timothy was swinging his lantern wildly as he tried to shake the attackers off. Isabelle had curled up on the path, sheltering her head in one hand as they scrabbled all through her dress. Even Turpin was lashing out wildly, knocking them away with blows from his chubby fists and small feet.

Dirk reached Timothy first, sweeping a score of rats from his back and dragging two large specimens off his arm. Timothy yelped as the creatures' teeth were torn from his flesh, and large drops of blood spattered the path. With only a few rats left, Dirk squeezed past him along the edge of the path, slipping on a slime-slathered stone and almost toppling over into the sewage below. He managed to keep his balance, just, and to step around Blaze-Simms to Isabelle.

Her defensive posture had done little to deter the rats. They could still smell flesh and feel the warmth coming through her clothes. They were scrambling over each other in a heap on top of her, biting and scratching in their desire to be warm and fed. Her sword stick protruded from the heap, lashing back and forth with flicks of her wrist. But all that did was sweep a few from the path, while the rest kept scrabbling and scratching across her. She screamed as Dirk picked her up, swinging her out above the water and shaking her about. Rats plopped into the sewer, spattering Dirk and Isabelle with sewage.

When Isabelle was almost clear, Dirk set her back down on the path and turned toward Turpin. But the little man was in no need of help. The water near him was foaming with the frantic movements of scores of rodents, and dozens more lay scattered and broken on the path, heads crushed, necks snapped, backs broken. Turpin had a sack out and was dropping the bodies into it, humming a tune to himself as he worked.

"A use for everything!" He grinned.

Dirk dabbed at a trickle of blood running down his cheek. He didn't want to know what the Underlord and his followers would do with a sack full of rats. If he asked them for a meal he'd be keeping an eye out for claws and tails.

However efficient these people's way of life was, there were still parts that turned his stomach. It wasn't rational, but even as a man of reason he felt nauseous at the thought.

"I say, that was pretty ghastly." Blaze-Simms straightened his jacket, now torn as well as stained.

Isabelle glared in embarrassment at the path.

"I..." she began, but faltered before she could even begin the meat of the sentence.

"Don't worry." Dirk placed a hand on her shoulder. "That was pretty damned grim for all of us. Was all I could do to keep from screaming myself."

His small lie was rewarded as she leaned close to him, her body trembling. He wanted to wrap her in his arms, to give her comfort and a shoulder to cry on, but didn't know if he should, if he even could. Frozen by indecision, with Timothy and Turpin stood nearby, he waited too long. By the time he moved his arm she was stepping away, straightening her skirts and rearranging her hair.

"Are we likely to face that again?" She looked at Turpin, her usual calm fighting to restrain the panicked tone still in her voice.

"Never seen that before." Turpin shrugged. "Not the sort of thing rats usually do, but I'll know what to do with it next time."

He shook his bag of broken rats.

"Don't reckon that was just about the rats." Dirk thought back to the moment he'd seen the seething mass of fur. "There was a whistling sound. Someone driving them on, maybe."

"A sonic agitator to manipulate the native fauna." Blaze-Simms was making notes again. "How ingenious."

"The ninjas?" Isabelle asked.

Dirk nodded. "It sure ain't the cockroaches."

#

They almost lost the trail. The rats, drawn in from all over the surrounding tunnels, had left such a mess of tracks that it obliterated any trace of human passage. But Dirk had learned from Turpin's earlier lessons. Peering at the traces around a series of tunnel mouths, he found one where the resident bats had been scared away by something larger passing through. Carefully following the passage, he studied the walls, ceiling and floor, until human footprints emerged from the dwindling rat tracks.

They set off down the tunnel, but their pace slowed, Blaze-Simms and Isabelle struggling to keep up. They'd all had a long and exhausting day, and no rest for a good few hours. The thought of it made even Dirk's muscles feel cramped and weary.

"Hey, Turpin," he called out.

The little man turned from examining an intersection, a big smile across his face. "Yes?"

"Is there anywhere round here we can take a rest?"

"Of course!" Turpin said, then paused uncertainly. "Um... Oh yes, I know."

He led them down a winding series of tunnels, away from one sewer, along a plank across another, and through a brick archway into the echoing space beyond. Dirk tried not think about what dripped on them from the arch.

Turpin swung his lantern up and set it on a shelf to the left of the archway. A wide lens in front of the shelf caught the lamp's light and dispersed it, filling the chamber beyond with a soft yellow glow. The room was about thirty feet square and seemed to be newly built. Though made from old bricks and blocks of compressed rubbish, the cement was still fairly new, its surface not worn by time or smoothed by the damp that seeped down every wall in the sewers. Bunks were set into the back wall of the room, and a row of wooden cots ran beneath the shelves on the left hand wall. To the right were rows of cupboards, again set into the walls, their doors made of scrap panels or chunks of timber nailed together in irregular fashion.

The centre of the room was filled with tables and chairs. Its barracks hall feeling was reinforced when Dirk glanced to his right and saw a selection of weapons, from old fashioned rifles to sabres, axes and knives, all hanging from hooks. It was a ramshackle arsenal in keeping with the whole of the Underlord's realm, the weapons mismatched and mostly outdated. But they were in good repair. Even the oldest blades, which looked like they'd been forged in the sixteenth century, had been ground to a sharp edge and greased to protect them from the damp.

"What a charming place." Weariness crept into Isabelle's voice as she sat at one of the tables. "Is this the Underlord's doing?"

"Oh yes." Turpin rummaged through one of the cupboards, pulled out a couple of large cans and a package wrapped in oiled cloth, its edges sealed with wax. He placed them on the table by Isabelle, along with four chipped plates, some forks and cups and a dusty wine bottle.

Dirk and Blaze-Simms pulled up chairs, the furniture creaking beneath them. Dirk opened the cloth package, wax cracking and crumbling away as he tugged it open. An oaty smell rose from within as a pile of biscuits were revealed. Meanwhile, Blaze-Simms had pulled a finger sized gadget from his pocket, unfolded something between a knife and a spanner from one end, and was using it to open the tins.

"I say, it's stew," he exclaimed, sucking gravy from one thin finger. "Not bad, either."

They shared out the biscuits and gravy while Turpin poured the wine.

"It's not strong," he explained. "But it keeps better than water."

"Not terribly good either," Blaze-Simms said after a sip. "But anything would be refreshing right now."

"And it is very kind of you to do this for us." Isabelle shot a quick glare at Blaze-Simms.

Turpin grinned. "Happy to help."

Dirk tucked in, scooping up the stew with one of his biscuits. There was meat floating in the brown gravy, though it was hard to tell what sort, and the same went for the lumps of root vegetable. The biscuits were hard and brittle, even after a soaking in stew. But after all that walking it was like the most delicious banquet. His stomach rumbled into life and he glanced at Isabelle in embarrassment, but she was too busy eating to notice.

After the first few mouthfuls, with the edge taken off his hunger, Dirk slowed down and took the time to properly observe his surroundings. This place seemed to have been built to hold twenty men and keep them comfortable for some time. There were chess sets out on a couple of the tables, and chests labelled "Books" and "Blankets" in one corner. Beneath the weapons were the tools needed for their maintenance - oil, cleaning rags, whetstones, cases of ammunition. Beneath the home comforts, this place had the trappings of war.

"Underlord built this, huh?" He looked at Turpin, then back down at his stew, trying not to seem like he was offering any challenge. "What'd he build it for?"

"For more people to live with us, of course." Turpin spat fragments of biscuit and beef in his enthusiasm to reply. "He says this is the future, hundreds of us beneath the great cities, taking up less space, keeping out of sight, just getting on with our lives."

"Seems he's stocked for more than that." Dirk knocked his fork against one of the empty cans. "Those cupboards must hold enough food to feed an army."

Turpin laughed.

"We might even be one!" He lowered his voice. "The Underlord worries that one day there will be war. That the government can't last, and there will be revolution, like they've had in France and America and places like that. He says that we must be ready to protect ourselves, and anyone who comes to us for protection. We aren't to take sides, but we aren't to give in either. If we can protect people then they will want to stay. That's what he says."

"Is that why you stay?" Isabelle was looking up from her empty plate, dabbing at her lips with a handkerchief.

"Um, I suppose. But it's more than that." Turpin waved a hand around, taking in the room and all it contained. His voice rose in confidence, losing the uncertainty that had marked his speech. "He gives us a home, food, people to be with. But there's something else. Before he found me I was lost. I'd fallen out with my family, lost my home, no work, barely more than the clothes I stood up in. I was sleeping in Regent's Park, getting moved on most nights by men with sticks and badges. But worst of all, I had no aim, nothing to aspire to, nothing more to do than hunt for scraps and a place to sleep. But the Underlord gave me that purpose, gave us all that purpose. We're building something down here, and it will be beautiful." A tear welled at the corner of his eye. "We were rejects, unwanted, cast out by the modern world. But thanks to the Underlord, we are the future."

Dirk pondered the little man, his face so serious, his tone so determined. That brief outburst of eloquence had come as a surprise after the snatches of limited conversation they'd had working their way through the sewer. The Underlord's plans brought out something in Turpin that wasn't normally there, and it sounded like the same happened for many of the Underlord's followers. Now at least he knew how the guy had pulled this lot together. As for why, if Turpin wasn't telling the truth, or the Underlord wasn't telling it to his people, then the surface world had something to worry about. An army growing beneath its feet, alienated, excluded, and wondering about its own fate.

Turpin rose and went to another cupboard.

"One last treat." He pulled out a jar. The stopper popped out and he pulled something from inside, a dried, brown thing cover in white crystals. "Sugared rats." He passed one to each of them. "My favourite!"

Isabelle squirmed in her seat, while Blaze-Simms peered at his with curiosity and pulled a scalpel and tweezers from his pocket.

Turpin looked at them both with puzzled disappointment. "Don't you-"

Dirk slapped Turpin on the back, took a big bite from his rat.

"It's fantastic." He grinned as he chewed on the stringy, sweetened flesh. "Makes me glad you're on our side."

He looked once more at the weapons lining the wall. It was hard to avoid the suspicion that the Underlord was on a side all of his own.

#

Rested and fed, they set out through the sewers with renewed energy. Dirk could hear the change in tone, Isabelle and Timothy talking in hushed but excited voices, rather than trudging along in the weary silence that had come to dominate their journey. He wanted to fall back and join them, to listen to the sound of Isabelle's laughter, to be the one telling anecdotes of his adventures. He could feel a hot lump of jealousy at the fact that it was Blaze-Simms making her laugh. But he pressed down the childish thought, focusing on what he really needed to do, helping Turpin to follow the trail.

Despite the break, it soon became clear that they were making progress, getting as close to the ninjas as they had all day. The tracks were fresher, splashed puddles still empty, the dirty water not yet refilling the tracks. Turpin's previous excitement was receding into nervousness.

"What will we do when we find them?" he asked. He was still grinning, but the smile was starting to look forced.

"It'll be fine." Dirk patted his holstered Gravemaker. "Fightin' ain't for everyone. Just do what you can, and if all else fails keep your head down." He tried to sound more confident than he felt. "Ninjas ain't so tough."

In truth, he was feeling more confident than he had before. If they were catching up that meant that their prey were slowing down. Whether they were starting to tire or struggling to navigate their way through the unfamiliar tangle of tunnels, it put them off guard, and that was what he wanted to see. True, there were more of the ninjas than of Dirk and his friends, but in the narrow confines of a sewer that wouldn't count for much. Maybe it was just the release of energy that came from being well fed, but he reckoned the odds were swinging in their favour.

They reached a junction and Turpin frowned.

"It's all scuffed up," he said. "They're trying to lose us."

Dirk lowered his lantern and peered at the path. It was no more than a foot wide, a narrow lane of stones beside a turgid river that flowed, thick and slow and covered in flies, through two brick arches up ahead. The path split like the tunnel, one fork following a rusted iron bridge across the stinking flow, the other sticking to the wall. He looked at the way the dirt lay on the way onto the bridge, the way it had been kicked around in both directions.

Behind them, Isabelle and Timothy stopped and peered around, for all the world like a pair of walkers pausing on a stroll through the park.

"I say, is something the matter?" Blaze-Simms called out.

"It's just gettin' a little tricky," Dirk said.

"If anyone can follow them, I'm sure you can." Isabelle's confidence filled Dirk with a warm glow of pride, and a determination to prove her right. He looked even closer, scouring his memory for anything he'd seen before that might help with this.

There'd been that time in Chicago, hunting Confederate agents through the grimy streets as the smoke stacks billowed. They'd split, one heavy footed and slow going, the other trying to take paths that left no prints. But he'd still caught them both, and got the blueprints back.

Then there was that time on the plains, with the rogue Sioux brave who stepped back through his own prints to throw Dirk off. That had ended in a bloody fight, but not through any failure in his tracking.

And of course that night in the Alps, with Gabo the Monkey Man hanging over their heads the whole time they traced his followers through the snow. If not for his mad sniggering they'd never have known he was there, and his criminal empire would still be going strong.

Dirk stepped past the end of the bridge, careful not to disrupt what passed for tracks. There was something leading away down the path to the left. Footprints, scuffed but still visible, a trail someone had tried to hide.

Or had they? The prints were a little larger than before, a little less distinct than they had been, just like the footprints of that Indian brave. A trick to lead them down this path. They'd head that way, find that the tracks ran out somewhere hard where a person might not leave a trail, but there'd be no prints coming off the far side.

He turned, shone his light over the bridge.

"Check over there," he said.

Turpin clattered across.

"No footprints," he called out. "But there's nothing to leave them in."

Dirk let himself smile a little. 'That's the way I'd go,' he said.

He stepped forward, about to cross the bridge, when something caught his eye. A thin track in the mould growing up the wall, as though something had been dragged down it, or a string had dangled through the slime.

"Hold up." He peered at the line and at the walls around it. The slime was scuffed in other places too, just a little, as if by someone taking great care to apply the least pressure they could. He tilted the lantern up, following the marks up to the top of the wall, and onto the ceiling.

Metal hooks glittered in the lantern light, shiny and new, steel hoops just big enough to provide a hand or toe hold, jammed into the cracks between bricks. The ceiling itself was scuffed where hands and knees had brushed against it.

"Son of a bitch," Dirk whispered. These guys must be incredibly strong and agile, to hammer those climbing hooks into place while hanging upside down, never mind to crawl along like that, hanging from the roof, but it was a hell of an effort to do anything else. He whistled in admiration. 'Triple bluff.'

He waved Turpin back across the bridge and, one eye still on the ceiling, led them down the path. They walked on for another fifteen minutes, as the tunnel narrowed and the sewer flowed faster past their feet. Beetles scurried across the stones and millipedes wriggled their way up the walls, pale and fragile, their antennae twitching at the passing people. The odd rat scurried nervously past them, but not the hordes that had overwhelmed them earlier.

After a while the hooks in the ceiling ended and there were footprints on the ground once more, leading past a narrow opening to their left and continuing on down the path. Dirk followed them for a moment, the others with him. Then he stopped, looked down at the blurred edges of the tracks, the clearer prints leading away and the gap in the wall behind them.

"Well I'll be," he whispered. "They've done it again. They've doubled back."

"Very good, Dynamo san." A voice echoed around the tunnel, bouncing back to surround them from every direction. "But not good enough."

Silent as shadows, black-clad figures stepped out onto the path behind them and emerged from the darkness up ahead. Eyes sparkled from the narrow bands of skin visible on their faces, and the edges of swords glittered in the lantern light. All around the ninjas closed in, blades raised and ready for the kill.

Chapter 8: The Striking Snowflake

Shuriken hissed out of the darkness, glittering points of death skimming past Dirk's head and pinging off the walls. He ducked and rolled forward along the slime-coated path, slamming into the nearest ninja. The black-clad figure tumbled into the water, sending stinking waves up and down the sewer.

Dirk sprang up, shoulder first, into the next ninja. There was a crunch of breaking ribs and a hiss of breath as the man went over. Dirk flung him after his comrade, another splash echoing around him.

A pistol cracked somewhere behind him, followed by the clash of steel on steel as the ninjas closed with the others. They were coming from every direction, but the greatest number were up ahead. Dirk saw one of them giving out orders, pointing to him and then past towards Isabelle. A hot wave of anger rose through him.

"Push back," he called out. "You can break clear. I'm goin' for the boss."

He yanked his gun from its holster, firing before it was even fully raised. A ninja fell, his shin giving way beneath him in bloody ruin.

Another was scampering towards Dirk along the wall, for all the word like a giant spider. He leapt, clawed gloves stretched forward, but Dirk had better reach and his fist collided with the ninja's face just before those gouging metal fingers could reach his own. But the ninja still had momentum, his body colliding with Dirk, sending them sprawling on the path, rolling over and off into the sewer.

Dirk gagged as he was plunged into sewage, the filth forcing its way into his mouth and nose while bladed fingers dug into his lower arm. He lashed out frantically with his feet, collided with something just soft enough to be flesh, and the blades released their grip. He kicked once more for luck, then started to swim, bobbing to the surface in a wave of sewage. He spat out what he could and sucked in deep lungfuls of air, desperately trying to clear the sickening taste from his throat.

Something hissed out of the darkness and Dirk dived back down, mouth firmly closed. With quick, powerful strokes he swam to the edge of the path and reached up, hooking someone's legs out from beneath them as he heaved himself upward. He swung wildly, lashing out at anything nearby as he blinked water from his eyes. The tunnel was a blur of flailing lanterns and twisting shadows, the clash of swords fading down the tunnel through a cloud of grunts and groans. The Gravemaker still somehow in his hand, he rose and turned to aim.

A force like a ton of masonry slammed against the back of his head. As he slid forward into blackness, he wondered for one dazed moment if the ceiling had fallen down.

#

The first thing Dirk felt as he rose into consciousness was the stone, cold and wet, pressing against his face. He tried to turn away from it, but his head was pounding and something was pressing him down, stopping him from rising. He couldn't quite remember where he was, but it clearly wasn't anywhere good.

He suppressed the urge to struggle, to twist and writhe and mindlessly throw his weight into shaking off whatever was oppressing him. Instead he took a long, deep breath and tried to ignored the ache in his brain, instead focusing on what the rest of him could feel.

He was flat out on a stone path. He was soaked to the skin and something stank. He hoped it wasn't him. This place was dark but not pitch black, and as well as the throbbing in his skull he felt a sharp pain in his arm.

He'd been in a fight. He kind of remembered that. Something about books, or maybe a stone. He'd been with someone. Probably Blaze-Simms. It was usually Blaze-Simms. But Blaze-Simms was always on his side, so who'd done this to him?

"I know that you are awake," a voice whispered by his ear, breath creeping across his skin. A woman's voice, hard and determined.

Of course, Dirk thought as memory came flooding back. Ninjas.

She barked some words that meant nothing to Dirk and the pressure disappeared from his back.

"You may sit," the ninja leader said. "We have your gun, and the knife from your boot. Try to stand and Hasegawa-san will knock you out again."

Dirk blinked and levered himself up, sitting with his back against the wall. His brain must have been more rattled than he thought. The name Hasegawa rang a bell, but he was damned if he could work out why. And now that he paused for thought, that woman's voice seemed faintly familiar too, like a politician he'd heard at hustings or some guy he'd met twice at a party.

"Do you want to live, Dynamo-san?" She crouched down next to him, eyes glittering like diamonds amid the swathes of black silk that covered her face.

"Who doesn't?" Dirk rummaged through the back corners of his memory, looking for something to hook on that voice. He thought of the orientals he'd met, running through the names and faces carefully filed away, linked by mnemonics and mental constructs like any other thought he'd considered worth preserving. That martial arts master in San Francisco, with his eager young followers and his predilection for dope. The visiting professor who'd spoken about the mathematics of people at the Epiphany Club. The guys hauling fish and cloth around the East End. That Chinese couple on Hakon, the guano trader and his wife. Last time he'd seen them she'd been chasing after him into the jungle, while that mad bear roared and charged about.

The guano trader's name was Hasegawa Minoru.

"Stop following us, Dynamo-san." The woman's voice was harder, sharper than it had been on Hakon. No more the shrinking wife, timidly following her husband around. But there was enough the same. "We have what is ours. This can be over."

"Whatever you say, Miura Noriko." Dirk looked her in the eye, watching for a reaction.

These guys had discipline. No one around him even flinched as he said the name, never mind turning their heads to see their boss's response. But the silence grew sterner somehow, their stillness stiffer, warier than before. They stood silent, waiting expectantly.

At last she reached up and pulled the cloth from across her face. The lantern light picked out a stern, thin lipped face.

"I am surprised it took you this long," Noriko said. "Disappointed even. The great adventurers and investigators of the Epiphany Club, unable to make the connection between our presence on Hakon and that of the ninja."

"I was a little distracted, what with the locals and all." Dirk tilted his head, trying to find an angle at which it didn't ache. "And there were some things throwing us off the trail. After all, ain't ninjas normally Japanese?"

"Yes." Noriko raised an eyebrow.

'And you're Chinese.'

"No."

"Oh." Dirk almost laughed. "So you were pretending to be Chinese on Hakon?"

"No." Noriko's small brow furrowed. "I never claimed to be Chinese."

"But you let us keep believing it."

"You believed I was Chinese?" She sounded indignant, her voice rising, arms folded defensively.

"Well, yes." Dirk shifted, uncomfortable at more than the stones and the damp. "You had a Chinese name, Chinese clothes-"

"Japanese name. Japanese clothes. Totally different."

"How were we meant to know that?"

"You are smart enough to know where ninjas come from, but can't tell the difference between Japanese and Chinese?"

"Um... Well, can you tell the difference between an American and an Englishman?"

"The English are better dressed, and can tell that I am not Chinese."

Dirk thought of Blaze-Simms, with his stained jackets, frayed cuffs and similar ignorance over what made a name Chinese. But this didn't seem the time to tell tales.

As Noriko stood, Dirk glanced around. There were a dozen ninjas lining the path, all clad from head to foot in black, with short swords at their waists and belts of shuriken criss-crossing their chests. One of them sat on the path while another splinted his leg, and a third was missing the sleeve off his tunic, which was being wrapped around what looked like a bullet wound. That left ten healthy bodies for Dirk to contend with. Fighting his way clear didn't seem too viable right now. He could take down ten men, no problem, when armed, in good shape, and facing ordinary guys. But unarmed, in a dark, slippery tunnel, his body already bruised and battered, against ten warriors of the Orient's finest fighting tradition? He didn't like those odds.

"You folks must set an awful lot of value by that stone," Dirk said. "You've gone to a lot of trouble to steal it."

"Steal?" Noriko snorted. "Is it stealing to take back what is ours?"

"How do you work that one out then?" Dirk asked. "Those slabs came from Egypt. Last I heard, Egyptians didn't pay homage to the land of the rising sun."

Noriko shook her head. "You think that the rest of the world does not interact, Dynamo-san, that we waited for westerners to bring us together? One of your slabs travelled the silk road long ago, a strange artefact of a fallen civilisation. It was kept at the Emperor's court for hundreds of years, a curio, rumoured to be a map to exotic knowledge. No-one found its source, though several tried. But it remained safe for centuries, relegated by slow steps to a small room of an obscure imperial dwelling house, valued by scholars and those who enjoy the obscure.

"Until last year, when a gang of thieves broke in and stole it away. They were apprehended, of course, but not before they had passed the tablet on to the mysterious gaijin who hired them. It took many months to track it down, in the hands of your Mrs McNair. Even when we followed her to Hakon, we were unable to find out whether she had it with her or where it was hidden. But now, at last, it will be returned."

"All those months of effort, all this violence, for something you yourself called obscure?" Dirk struggled to keep the annoyance from his voice.

"No, Dynamo-san." Noriko shook her head. "For pride."

Dirk looked around the tunnel at the slimy walls, the flowing sewage, and the filth that clung to all their clothes. He took a deep breath, almost choking on his own stench.

"So this is pride, huh?" His laughter echoed hollowly round the tunnel. "Tell me this. How proud are you gonna be if you get that stone back home and your scholars tell you it's the wrong one?"

Noriko glared at him. She had a good glare, the sort that would whither a lesser man down to a trembling mess. "It is the right shape, the right size. It has the symbols."

"Same symbols, or similar symbols?" Dirk asked. "You don't strike me as a scholar of Egyptian hieroglyphics. There's at least three of those things out there. I don't know if you've got the right one, but I do know you ain't got Mrs McNair's, and it don't seem like you can tell the difference."

Noriko turned away, talked in hushed tones with one of the other ninjas. Dirk could hear just enough to know they weren't talking any language he recognised. He guessed it must be Japanese, though after the whole Chinese fiasco he wouldn't place any bets.

While he waited he scanned the walls and floor, looking for anything that might work to his advantage. A stone, a decent stick, a rat he could kick to make a distraction. Nothing. Just a whole lot of ninjas with a whole lot of very sharp blades. He didn't know what they had planned for him, but he didn't hold out much hope.

Noriko turned back to him.

"Clearly there is more to do if we are to retrieve the correct stone," she said. "We are grateful to you for showing us the error of our ways. You are an honourable foe, and deserve to be treated as such. But we cannot have you following us." She raised her sword high above her head. "I shall make this quick."

The sword flashed down and Dirk's world went black.

Chapter 9: Pistons

Dirk dreamed he was back on Hakon, at the party at the governor's mansion. He was dancing around the room, Isabelle McNair in his arms. He was as poised and graceful as she was. They danced in the centre of the hall, moving faster and faster, leaving the rest of the room a blur around them. The faces of Cullen, Braithwaite and Noriko, spiralled away into a haze.

Her face moved closer to his and he felt her breath against his cheek as she whispered in his ear.

"Dirk." Her voice was faint amid the tumult of the ball.

The room smelled awful. Dirk realised it was the guano. Of course - the mansion was built on guano, just like the whole island.

"Dirk," Isabelle said. This time her breath stung his cheek, and her voice had become lower. "Dirk, you have to wake up. Dirk!"

He felt a slap across his face, raised a hand to defend himself.

"Oh, thank goodness!" Timothy Blaze-Simms exclaimed, staring down at him. Blaze-Simms was clutching Dirk's lapel with one hand, the other raised as if to strike him again. "I was starting to worry that might not work."

Dirk shook his head, trying to cast off the fog of unconsciousness. He was on cold, wet stone again. The same cold, wet stone he'd last woken on. Once more and he'd have to start calling this place bed.

He pushed himself up on his elbows and looked around. Except for a lack of ninjas, the tunnel was just the same as before. Isabelle and Turpin stood behind Blaze-Simms, looks of concern and curiosity respectively filling their faces.

"You always were one hell of a nurse, Tim." He raised a hand to his forehead, where a lump like half an egg was throbbing painfully. It hurt more when he touched it, so he stopped. "How long have I been out?"

"Not too long." Blaze-Simms took a step back. "An hour, tops. We managed to fight clear and catch our breath, then crept back as soon as things had quietened down."

"I'm sure you were real stealthy." Dirk hauled himself upright. His knife and gun were lying a few feet down the path. Someone had even cleaned the sewer muck off of them. Guess that's what they call honourable, he thought as he slid the knife back into its sheath.

"It is true that our opponents have the edge on us when it comes to sneaking," Blaze-Simms said. "But we did our best. And so far, no more ambushes."

Dirk wondered about pointing out that "so far" amounted to sixty minutes of sitting still. But he couldn't deflate his friend's proud grin.

"We need to keep on them," Dirk said. "They'll go after Isabelle's stone next." He felt a stirring of gallantry as he strode protectively towards her, wobbling as his head adjusted to being upright. "Don't worry, that ain't gonna happen."

"Thank you, Mr Dynamo." Her lips curled in amusement. "Perhaps you can tell us more as we walk?"

Turpin took the lead, hunting for tracks through the twisting darkness. He seemed very familiar with this stretch of the tunnels, hurrying past alcoves and side passages, fobbing them off as inconsequential in his rush to catch their prey.

Still woozy from being knocked out twice, Dirk struggled to keep up with their guide. His dip in the sewer had left him soaked and the cold was seeping through his body, stiffening his muscles and sending shivers up his spine. He swung his arms and tipped his head from side to side, trying to loosen up muscles left tight and awkward from lying flat out on the path, to get some warmth back into them. As they walked he talked, filling the others in on Noriko and her mission. Struggling to collect his thoughts, he stumbled tongue-tied through an account of what he'd learned.

"How embarrassing," Blaze-Simms said when the Chinese-Japanese mix-up was explained. "I shall have to apologise if we meet again."

"They stole from you, beat me senseless, and now you want to apologise to them?" Just occasionally, Dirk struggled to keep his patience with the Englishman. This was one of those times.

"That's terribly sweet, Timothy," Isabelle said, "but perhaps not the best approach?"

"Hm." Blaze-Simms seemed to give the point serious consideration. "Maybe the swordstick instead."

He stopped in his tracks, pausing at the entrance to a side passage that Turpin had just rushed past.

"I say, what's down there?" He pointed to where something gleamed in the light from his lantern.

"Nothing!" Turpin called back sharply. "Come on, this way."

"There's definitely something." Blaze-Simms's voice became muffled as he disappeared down the narrow passage. "How intriguing."

"We should keep going." Turpin scurried back toward them, his voice rising with tension. "The ninjas might get away."

Dirk paused. He wanted to keep moving, to settle the score with Noriko and her sword-wielding pals. After all this, he didn't want to let the tablet get away on one of Blaze-Simms's whims. But they'd built a career out of following those whims, the wild instinct and flights of fancy that caught Blaze-Simms's mind and led him toward the truly extraordinary.

Isabelle was looking at him, one eyebrow raised, as if to ask whether he was going to get his friend to focus this time. Turpin peered down the passage in agitation, muttering about invaders as he shifted from foot to foot.

After a moment's reflection, Dirk followed Blaze-Simms down the passage.

"What is it?" he asked as he emerged into a surprisingly large chamber. It looked to have been built recently, the bricks still clean and red, not pitted together through years of erosion. In the middle of the room was a silver-brown cylinder nearly ten meters across, with pipes running in from the direction of the sewer and an opening like the hatch on a steam train's firebox. It disappeared up into the roof of the cavernous chamber.

"Some sort of piston, I think." Blaze-Simms ran a hand down the side. "I don't know what the alloy is. Something messy and impure, by the look of it. Between that and the scale of the thing, I wouldn't want to try firing it more than once."

He walked around the outside of the device, pencil scratching across the page of his notebook.

"Good welding," he muttered, talking more to himself than to any of his companions. "But what's it for?"

"This one of yours?" Dirk turned to Turpin who, along with Isabelle, had followed them into the chamber.

The little man's child-like excitement was gone, replaced by a nervous chewing on his cracked lip.

"Um, well..." he murmured uncertainly.

"It's alright, Turpin." Isabelle placed a reassuring hand on his shoulder. "Whatever it is, I'm sure the Underlord put it here with the best of intentions, didn't he?"

"Yes." Turpin nodded slowly, eyes darted back and forth. "Best intentions. Good things. But we really should go." Something lit up behind his eyes and he turned to Dirk. "The next bit of the trail, it's tricky, but I found this smudge..."

As they headed back to the tunnel, Blaze-Simms lost in scribbling equations, Turpin pointing out trail signs no-one else could have seen, Dirk caught Isabelle's eye. She glanced at Turpin, then back down the side tunnel, then back at him, and arched an elegant eyebrow. Dirk gave a small nod. Something here stank. Something other than him.

#

After a while, they found themselves at the mouth of a wide side tunnel that sloped upwards, its paved surface broken by wagon rails. There was a slight indent in the path where the two met, layered with a rich crust of ancient mud. Dirk crouched near the floor with Turpin, peering at a mess of criss-crossing footprints. It was hard not to get caught up in the little guy's excitement as they worked to disentangle what had gone on, pointing out odd discrepancies in the layers of prints to each other, trying to figure out the order of events.

"Look." Dirk point at several sets of prints to their left. "I've seen that before, with plains Indians laying an ambush. Walking backwards from a spot to make it look like more folks going forwards. But the way the feet fall ain't quite right. Angles are a little out, and it scuffs the dirt backwards."

"Oh yes!" Turpin gave his eager to please grin. "I see. So in that case... One." He pointed to a set of prints leading up the tunnel. "Two." A second set, leading out. "Three." A third set, some the backwards ones, apparently going in when some were really heading out.

Dirk nodded. "That figures. But why?"

"They didn't know what I do." Turpin's grin grew bigger with pride. "That used to be a way out for works carts. But some of the other works nearby shook the roof loose and it caved in."

"Other works?" Now it was Blaze-Simms's turn to sound excited.

"Underground trains," Turpin said. "The Underlord let them dig lines round here. They're meant to stay clear of the sewers, but they don't know them like we do. They broke a tunnel up there in the spring." He pointed ahead down the main sewer. "It's still broken."

He peered once more at the footprints, then gave Dirk a satisfied smile. "The ninjas went up, found they had to come back, then tried to trick us into going up there too."

Dirk nodded, checked his pistol was in place. "Time it took them to make that mistake, we must nearly be caught up."

The trail led them on down the sewer, up a ladder whose crust of rust had been dislodged by recent footfalls, and into a very different space. It was still man made but cavernous, rough walls held by wooden braces and iron brackets, with the beginnings of more permanent brick walls around the lower parts. The earth was packed flat, rutted by the wheels of the large, hand-pushed wagons that sat idle along one side like an abandoned mine, and by larger tracks like an inverted railway gouged through the rock-strewn soil. Lamps hung from a pipe along the ceiling, lighting the tunnel with their sickly green flames, disappearing down the tunnel openings in two opposite walls.

"I say," Blaze-Simms called out, "there's another of those piston things."

"This really ain't the time." Dirk looked around for footprints.

Blaze-Simms had wandered over to the far side of the works, where a section of the tunnel wall had crumbled away, revealing another chamber beyond. He poked both head and torch through the gap, light gleaming off a huge brass cylinder, then emerged, scribbling something in his notebook.

"Turpin." Blaze-Simms's voice had gone distant, a sign Dirk had long learned to associate with moments of triumph and disaster. "How much of London is the Underlord planning to bring down?"

The little man's mouth hung open.

"Timothy." Isabelle's eyes drifted between the aristocrat and their diminutive guide. "What do you mean?"

"It's obvious, when you think about it." Blaze-Simms was still scribbling in his book. "The size of the pistons, the way they're placed. I couldn't work it out based on one, but they're positioned to exploit key points in the sewer network. And other tunnels, of course. Fire up enough of these machines, and you could bring down a sizable portion of the city. Just drop it into the ground."

The chill Dirk felt came from more than just the temperature in the sewers. He thought of the devastation that would come as London fell to a massive cave-in. Thousands, perhaps millions of people caught up in a madman's scheme to make the city above him part of his domain.

"My word, that is impressive, isn't it?" Isabelle said, smiling at Turpin.

He nodded uncertainly.

"And then you'll all move in and take the scrap, I imagine?" She was still smiling like a hostess setting a difficult party guest at ease. "Show the people above who's really in charge. That's what the weapons are for, and the little barracks rooms, isn't it?"

Turpin nodded.

"We'll be in charge. It'll be..." He looked around, seemed to remember who they were and where their priorities lay. "Oh."

He turned and leaped down the ladder. Blaze-Simms went as if to follow him, but Dirk caught his arm.

"We can deal with the crazies later," he said. "Right now, we've got us some ninjas to catch, and they ain't been as careful as they think."

He pointed to a lone footprint, barely visible in the packed earth at the base of a track.

Dirk turned to Isabelle.

"You stay here," he said.

"After everything we've done, you think I can't handle myself in a fight?" She flourished her pistol.

"No ma'am." In truth, he wasn't comfortable leading a lady into a dead end full of oriental warriors. But there were other considerations too. "Just need someone to deal with any that get through."

Not that he had any intention of letting them through, not with Isabelle here.

She stood for a moment, staring at him like she might bore through the half truths and see the protective instinct buried behind his words. But if she did she kept quiet about it.

"Alright." She opened the chamber pistol and checked the rounds. "But please don't dawdle. We've been down in this ghastly place quite long enough."

Dirk led Blaze-Simms down the tunnel. After a few minutes an end came into view, the flickering lamps stopping where the half-finished tunnel had ground to a halt.

At the head of the tunnel was a machine the size of a railway engine. Its front consisted of two huge wheels with shovel blades around their edges and a foot-wide drill bit between them. Rubble lay around and beneath them, with more on the conveyor belts that ran from behind the wheels down the machine's sides. There was no sign of movement.

"Looks like old Croddlesby's handiwork." Blaze-Simms gave the machine an appraising glance. "Looks a dashed sight more useful than that steam powered octopus he built back in sixty-five. I admire an articulated tentacle as much as the next man, but it was an absolute nightmare to dock."

"LNWR?" Dirk read off the brass plate on the machine's side.

"London and North Western Railway." Blaze-Simms said. "I heard they were building a new line for the outer suburbs, but they've been keeping it quiet in case the District try to steal their patch."

"Very quiet now." Dirk looked around. "Can't see the Underlord letting them stick around with that piston exposed."

"Still, someone's been tending the machines." Blaze-Simms pointed beneath the wheels.

A man in overalls lay unconscious in the mud, his hands dark with engine oil. A round bruise stood out from the middle of his forehead.

Dirk peered around by their feet. A spanner lay next to a crushed oil can, its dark contents seeping into the dirt. On the conveyor above it was a glistening footprint, and a black smear gleamed on the side of the machine.

"Hey Tim." Dirk took care not to look up as he inched his hand around towards his gun. "You remember that time in the Lonely Mountain pass, when we were being chased by the Sultan's troops?"

"Was that the time in sixty-seven or sixty-eight?" Balze-Simms asked with detached curiosity.

"Sixty-eight."

"Oh yes! They got onto the slope above us, and we had to get ready while pretending not to have..."

A shadowy figure leapt from the top of the machine. The Gravemaker was already in Dirk's hand, its roar deafening in the confines of the tunnel. The ninja's sword tumbled from his hand as he was thrown back, lifeless, onto the conveyor belt. Not another body stirred.

Dirk snatched up the sword and raced back up the tunnel.

"Was I meant to get ready?" Blaze-Simms panted as he ran behind.

"Yes!"

"Sorry!"

They burst out into the main excavation. Ahead of them, Isabelle was backing towards a wall, pistol drawn, half a dozen ninjas closing in on her. They looked around at Dirk, their eyes twinkling points in the black cloth swathing their faces.

"You'd all better back off from the lady," Dirk bellowed, his gun out in front of him, "or you'll end up as dead as your friend back there."

Glittering slithers of light hissed out of the darkness overhead. Dirk dived to one side and three metal discs tinged off the wall behind him, their sharpened edges raising sparks from the rock. Dirk raised his Gravemaker to return fire, but a shadowy shape was falling on him from above, knocking the pistol from his hand and slamming him against the floor. His vision flashed black and white as pain throbbed through him, but he swung a fist around, knocking his opponent flying.

Instincts kicked in as he scrambled after his opponent, grabbing him by the throat and lifting him from his feet. As his grip tightened the mask slipped away, revealing Noriko's bruised face, caught in a grimace of pain and anger.

"There's no need for this," Dirk said, as she squirmed in his grasp. "We can work together."

Her knee slammed into his gut, a burst of pain that buckled him over and broke his grip.

"No need?" She lashed out with the edge of her hand, bruising Dirk's arm as he hurried to defend his head. "You stole what is ours."

"We didn't steal anything." Dirk backed away, frantically blocking a flurry of lightning fast blows. "We just followed what we found."

"And now we found it." She aimed a high kick at his face.

Dirk caught her foot, twisted, flung her to the floor.

"You can have the damn thing." He tried to pin her arm with his foot. "Hell, have the whole set. We just want to know what they say."

She rolled clear, somersaulting up onto the side of a waggon.

"Why should I trust you?" She glared down at him, fists raised, poised to strike. "Someone here is a thief. Someone here is dishonest."

"You left me my weapons," Dirk said. "You must trust me on some level."

She leapt straight at Dirk, landed so close he could feel the air move. Staring up at him, her expression was filled with icy ferocity.

"If I say no?" she hissed.

A silence had fallen across the room, ninjas frozen in action, watching to see what their leader would do.

"It really doesn't matter what you say," a voice called out from the end of the chamber.

Dirk turned to see the Underlord rolling a cigarette in the tunnel entrance. His followers were streaming out of the tunnel behind him, more emerging from the ladder by which Dirk and the others had arrived. Men and women with twisted limbs, scarred faces, hunched bodies, all armed and agitated.

"You've seen too much." The Underlord gestured with thin fingers toward the vast piston showing through the broken wall. "Like the chumps who worked this line, I'm afraid you're going to have to die."

Chapter 10: Going Down

"I'm sure this isn't necessary." Isabelle stepped towards the Underlord. "We've cooperated so far, why stop now?"

"You're not really so stupid as to have to ask," the Underlord said. Turpin had appeared beside him, wringing his hands and smiling sheepishly. "I can't have you warning people about my plan to bring down chunks of London, can I? If they find out there's a giant piston waiting to sink St Paul's and another for Parliament, they'll take action. The city's high and mighty might not lift a finger for the likes of us, but they'll raise arms and cry God for Harry if they hear we're plotting to ruin their skyline."

"Then why help us in the first place?" she asked.

"Seemed the easiest way to get rid of you all." He shrugged. "Next time I'll stick with simpletons and steam engines."

The under-Londoners were closing in, raising a range of weapons from chunks of broken lead pipe to grimy pistols and broken-tipped swords. Individually they didn't look like much, but there were dozens of them.

Dirk glanced around, looking for a way out. The Underlord's men had both exits covered, and by the way they kept streaming through it looked like there were plenty more coming. He'd been in tight spots before and found a way out. But for that to work there had to actually be a way out. You couldn't stick around and fight with odds like this, but he couldn't see any other options.

Resignedly, he pulled out his knife. These were decent people, just looking to make a life in the cast-offs that civilisation had left them. Sure, their leader had turned into a moustache-twirling lunatic, but still, these were the ultimate proletariat, preparing to throw off their shackles. In a different world, he have fought on their side. But in a different world, he and his friends wouldn't be about to die.

"At least we get to go down fighting." Head throbbing from injuries and exhaustion, he couldn't think of anything smarter to say.

"Oh, I don't know." Blaze-Simms stood beside him, sword-stick in hand, an excited gleam in his eye. "It's a long shot, but I have a plan."

They were close together now - him, Blaze-Simms and Noriko, back to back amid a growing sea of hostile faces.

"It had better be damn good," Dirk said.

"Oh, it is." Blaze-Simms nodded down the dead end tunnel where the works continued. "Ms Miura, could you please get Mrs McNair and the others into the tunnelling train. It should be sturdy enough. Dirk, we need to go that way."

He pointed through the hole in the wall to the vast piston, which gleamed in the light of a growing throng of lanterns.

"You know that's two dead ends, right?" Dirk asked. His friend could build a steam engine from newspapers and solve quadratic equations in his sleep, but he sometimes forgot the little details.

"Oh yes," Blaze-Simms said. "That's why they'll let us get through."

There were fewer under-dwellers between them and the piston than there were blocking the ways out. Still "let us get through" wasn't how Dirk would have described what happened next.

With a roar and a swing of his lantern, Dirk plunged into the mob. The lantern collided with someone's head, shattering glass and spilling both oil and blood. Then he was down to his knife, lunging and slashing and screaming like a madman, creating an arc of fear into which few of his opponents dared to tread.

He fought for show not damage, making a big display of his size and ferocity, opening up a path by force of personality as much as force of arms. Blaze-Simms followed, keeping the enemy from closing on Dirk's back.

Out of the corner of his eye he saw Noriko leap off in the opposite direction, her ninjas closing in around her from the edges of the chamber. He wondered for a minute if this was the last he would see of her, if she would take this chance to get away and leave him and his allies to their death. But it seemed that Noriko had drawn the same conclusion he had, that their best chance was to stand together. She grabbed Isabelle McNair with one hand, a sword with the other, and led her people in a running fight toward the tunnel.

For all Dirk's ferocity, not all of the Underlord's men were filled with terror. Two of the bigger ones stood their ground, great pillars of rag-clad flesh with shaved heads and tattoos over every square inch of skin. They blocked his way, clubs raised, teeth bared in ferocious grins. Dirk ducked as one swung at him, just avoiding having his head caved in. He stepped inside his assailant's arc, slamming a knee up between the guy's legs. As the man mountain crumpled before him, the other one grabbed Dirk from behind, squeezing the air out of him in a brutal bear hug. Dirk jerked back, smashing the man's nose with the back of his head, elbows jabbing backwards as he squirmed from the loosening grip. The world span around him but he couldn't stop to steady himself. One last punch for good measure and he was moving on, stumbling over the groaning bodies and through the broken wall into the piston chamber.

"Could you keep them out for a minute, old chap." Blaze-Simms darted past Dirk. He started fumbling around at the base of the piston, one hand fiddling with a box of matches while the other pulled a couple of small bottles from his coat.

Dirk turned to face the mob. At least now he only had to fight in one direction, keeping them from entering the chamber. He was sure it would be easier said than done.

The next few minutes were a whirl of flying fists and angry snarls, battered flesh and bloody knuckles. The under-Londoners just kept coming, an endless flow of dirty, desperate men and women, swinging at him with whatever came to hand. For Dirk the fight was as much mental as physical, struggling for focus through a haze of adrenaline and exhaustion, mind reeling from the blows to his head. How long had they been down in this dank, stifling place, walking and fighting and walking some more? At least in the war they'd stuck to one battle a day. But this kept going, and the bruises were piling up faster than the unconscious bodies around him.

There was a hiss behind him and a chugging sound. Slow at first, like the beat of a shaman's drum, it grew in volume and urgency until the walls rattled and the ground shook beneath his feet. The whole cavern lurched and Dirk almost fell across the man he was fighting.

"This your plan?" he yelled.

"Nearly!" Blaze-Simms grabbed his shoulder and yanked him back. They tumbled together onto the floor of the piston chamber.

The mob wavered at the gap in the wall, then parted. The familiar figure of the Underlord stepped forward, a ragged cigarette dangling between his lips.

"Looks like you've started my work for me," he sneered, stepping back into the crowd.

"Sort of," Blaze-Simms said over the growing racket of the piston.

A lump of masonry bounced off the Underlord's shoulder. He looked up in annoyance, then in growing alarm, as bricks and mortar started raining down on his people.

There was a roar, a loud collective scream, and the cavern roof caved in on the Under-Londoners.

In the shelter of the piston room, Blaze-Simms reached for the off lever.

Dirk breathed a sigh of relief.

#

"How did you know that was gonna work like that?" Dirk asked. "That it would bring down that roof and nothing more?"

"Simple maths." Blaze-Simms brushed dust from his hair. "Together with some observation on tunnel engineering - this really has been a most enlightening day."

They stood in the rubble of the railway workings, amid the smells of brick dust and blood. From time to time one of the injured under-Londoners would crawl out of the rubble and away into the sewers, under the silent glares of the ninjas. The black-clad warriors, along with Isabelle, had been protected from the cave-in by the sturdy railway car, and had been surveying the damage by the time Dirk and Blaze-Simms dug themselves out of the piston room.

"I'm sorry about your friends." Dirk turned to Noriko, ready to face the difficult consequences of the blood he'd spilt. "Especially the ones I killed."

"We had our task," Noriko said. "To die for it is acceptable. Would you not die for yours?"

"Not if I can avoid it." Dirk touched the lump on his head. It was starting to go down. "And if one of my friends died, I'd make damn sure someone regretted it."

"And when their friends came to bring you the same regret?" She shook her head. "You gaijin think too highly of your own emotions."

She slung a black sack from the dark folds of material in which she was enveloped, peeling back the cloth to reveal a familiar block of stone.

"So," she said, eyes fixed firmly on his, "we have a deal?"

Dirk nodded. "No more fighting. We collect the stones together. The Epiphany Club gets copies, and whatever they lead to. You get to go home with three instead of your one. More pride for you, more knowledge for us."

He reached out and, after a moment, she shook his hand, bowing her head as she did so. Dirk didn't know when he'd last felt so relieved.

"What now?" Noriko asked.

"Paris!" Blaze-Simms said. "The third stone was lost in the Seine. Hopefully it's still around there somewhere."

"Don't tell me we're going underground again." Dirk was sick of tunnels. He wanted to spend some time in bright, wide open spaces, enjoying fresh air and sunshine.

"Maybe." Blaze-Simms pulled out a notebook. "But the last report was hundreds of years old. Who knows who has the stone by now."

"Lets not get into a fight with the locals this time," Isabelle said.

"But they're French." Blaze-Simms let the weight of national prejudice hang in the air. "I mean..."

"Don't you read the papers?" Dirk asked. "The French are plenty busy enough without fighting us. They've got a war on."

Book 3: Aristocrats and Artillery

Chapter 1: The King in Shadow

"I preferred this place in the spring." Dirk Dynamo tilted his hat and water poured from the brim. A small trickle escaped down the back of his neck, running inside his long waxed coat.

"It was certainly warmer." Sir Timothy Blaze-Simms hunched in his overcoat, his upturned collar and top hat making him look like a bespectacled chimney. "And livelier."

They peered out of the cramped alley and down the rain-sodden Paris street. Everything around them - the sky, the street, the tall terraces - was a dark, lurking grey that swallowed optimism and spat out gloom. Autumn had come early to the city, or else the sky itself was weeping at France's military defeat by the Prussians and their allies, and the second fall of the House of Bonaparte.

"The hotel manager was telling me that they can hear guns on the north side of the city." Blaze-Simms glanced upwards, as if expecting to see shells fall on them at any minute. "Probably Krupp's breech-loaders."

"That's bull." Dirk shook his head. "It might only take a day for a message to come from Sedan, but it'll take an army a hell of a lot longer. It ain't that bad yet."

"A sentiment shared by the Government of National Defence," a familiar female voice said from the darkness behind them.

Dirk grinned as Blaze-Simms started at the sound. In his Pinkerton days, Dirk had tracked fugitives across the plains using skills learnt from the Indians, sensing the sound through the earth. When it was quiet he could hear a penny drop three streets away. He could certainly hear a high society lady sneaking over cobbles.

"They're talking about settling down for a siege." Isabelle McNair stepped around puddles and took up a place between the two men. In her fashionable blue dress and grey jacket, she looked every inch the elegant lady about town. An umbrella blocked the view of her face, but Dirk could hear a smile in her voice. "It appears that the Republic is as determined to defy the Prussians as the Emperor was."

"Good for them." Dirk smiled at more than just Isabelle's company. "Time for the proletariat to cast aside the oppressors who got them into this mess. Government by the people for the people, that's what Europe needs."

"Steady on, old chap." Blaze-Simms looked at him in alarm. "It's that sort of sentiment brought the Bonapartes to power. Hardly a peace-loving lot."

There was a rumble of thunder, the sort of sound a civilian might mistake for artillery. But Dirk had seen his share of warfare, and he knew the difference between angry clouds and exploding shells. Knew it all too well.

"Timothy's right." Water trickled past Isabelle's face as she turned toward them. "Sweet as your sentiment is, Mr

Dynamo, I'm afraid it hasn't been that sort of revolution. We can expect a nice, safe republic of bureaucrats and shopkeepers, not labourers in the halls of power."

"We'll see." Dirk said. "If the Prussians and their Black Forest buddies get here it could all be up for grabs."

He reached for a cigar, but rain had filled his pocket, leaving a brown mess of uncurled leaves.

"Don't worry." Isabelle took his arm. "We'll soon be warm and dry."

Dirk smiled. The gentle warmth of Isabelle pressing against him was more comfort than any cigar. He'd set out on this journey in search of treasure, seeking the stone tablets that would lead them to the lost Great Library of Alexandria. But with two tablets in their grasp and the third supposedly in this city, he was starting to think that he'd found something more precious in Isabelle McNair.

Except that she was married, a bitter corner of his brain reminded him.

Isabelle led them across the street and through a small, inconspicuous door. This district was far enough out from central Paris to have avoided the vast upheavals of urban reform. There were no broad boulevards or gaslights brightening the streets here, just the tall, cramped buildings that had piled up over centuries of growth.

Through the door, guttering candles lit their way down a long spiral staircase, along a tunnel and across a wrought iron bridge.

"Not another damn sewer." Dirk screwed his face up in revulsion as he caught the stink of the place.

"Not for long." Isabelle seemed unphased by their surroundings. "And remember both of you, when it comes to Paris's secrets this man could make or break our investigation. Please be on your best behaviour." She squeezed Dirk's arm. "No singing the Marseillaise or talking about guillotines."

"Right you are, ma'am."

Isabelle rapped on a pair of heavy oak doors, steel reinforcements staining the wood with rust. A grille shot open revealing two feverish eyes above a waxed moustache, and a faint smell of perfume.

"Oui?" The voice was sharp with impatience.

"Our letters of introduction." Isabelle spoke in flawless French. Dirk's time in Quebec had taught him enough of the language to make conversation, and to recognise when someone was speaking it better than him.

Handing an envelope through the hole, Isabelle smiled brightly at those shifting eyes. There was a shuffling of papers, a few moments of murmuring, and the sound of bolts drawing back.

As the door swung open a wave of warm air swept over them, heavy with the smell of bodies sweating in a confined space. An attempt to drown out the stench of humanity with expensive perfume had failed, only adding a cloying note that made Dirk gag, accustomed though he was to barracks air. They stepped from damp darkness into a world of bright lights and busy chatter.

"Sir Timothy Blaze-Simms, Mrs Isabelle McNair and Mr Dirk Dynamo." A man in a bright tabard announced them in clear, aristocratic French. "Representatives of the Court of St James."

Dirk raised an enquiring eyebrow in Isabelle's direction.

"A little borrowed prestige," she murmured, "to help us through the door."

The door in question led onto a marble staircase at the head of a wide, vaulted room. The place looked like a stage set of a palace. A brick-walled cellar had been whitewashed so thickly that, where the paint was cracking in the corners, it peeled away in strips as thick as roof-slates. It was lit by a chandelier made irregular by missing pieces of its glittering glass crystals. Paintings lined the walls, some proprietorial country scenes, others elaborately rendered melees of horse, gunsmoke and glory. Their regular spread around the room made the absences stand out, spaces of blank wall where some masterpiece had once hung, as sad as empty chairs at a family dinner table.

They were led down the stairs, into a chattering chorus of frock-coats and bloated ball gowns. The clothes mingled the fashions of the decade with those of a hundred years before, sometimes on one person. Four-in-hand ties and cravats, powdered wigs and sideburns, bodices high-cut and low. Up close, Dirk caught glimpses of rework and patching, all meticulously done but none as invisible as their wearers seemed to hope.

No-one turned to greet them as they approached, to nod hello or catch an eye. These people were entirely wrapped up in each other and their world of hand-me-down aristocracy. Pale faces and wide eyes spoke of a life lived in darkness, like fearful lizards hiding from the sun.

Their guide, a footman in knee-length breeches, top-hat and tails, led them to a cluster of chairs by a fireplace.

"Would madam or sirs care for a drink?" His French was nasal - Parisian gentry carried to parodic extreme.

"Sherry." Isabelle settled decorously into a seat.

"I'll have a brandy." Blaze-Simms stepped past her to warm himself by the blazing fire.

"Coffee please," Dirk said. "Couple sugars if you've got them."

The footman winced at Dirk's heavily accented French, nodded, and departed into the crowd.

Dirk threw himself down in one of the armchairs. It was made of elaborately carved oak, but luxuriously padded, threadbare cushions hugging him close. The arms were worn with age, edges smoothed away by years of men at rest. And the fire, after the cold and wet outside, came like manna from a kindly god. Faint wisps of steam began to rise from his sodden coat.

"What the hell is this place?" Dirk reverted to English. As no-one around cared for their company, they were unlikely to care what he was saying.

"This is the court of Louis XXI," Isabelle said. "Otherwise known as the King in Shadow. But don't use that to his face. Louis is a little sensitive about his situation."

The footman reappeared with a silver tray and passed them their drinks.

"I say," Blaze-Simms exclaimed, staring at the smeared side of his glass, "this isn't really – ouch."

He stopped short as the toe of Isabelle's boot knocked against his shin.

"Thank you very much," she said, and the footman, still grimacing slightly, backed away through the room.

"Timothy." Her voice was soft but firm. "These people have convinced themselves that the old order never fell and the monarchy with it, that the revolution and Napoleon I were nothing but passing disturbances, King Louis Philippe and the Emperor Napoleon III pretenders to the throne. They have spent decades as the ghost of a court whose corpse was long ago left for the crows. This bubble of illusion may not be all they have, but it is the dessicated stalk upon which this dead flower hangs, and if you break it then you throw away our best lead. So please, no matter what you see, remember that you are among monarchy, and everything is as perfect as it could be."

"Right ho." Timothy sat down with over-egged grace, sipping at his drink with a beatific smile.

"And Mr Dynamo," Isabelle turned her gaze on the American, "I sympathise with your aversion to airs and graces, but in this place everyone is equally pathetic, and so equally entitled to play the grandiose part. This is nothing but a figment of grandeur, so there is really no harm in joining in."

Dirk sighed, nodded his acquiescence, and turned to his coffee. One sip and a smile rose across his face. It had the unmistakable flavour of chicory and charred acorns, cheap substitute coffee for when the supplies ran low. He thought of standing guard during the war, watching the lights of the Confederate pickets on the night before Bull

Run - just him, his rifle and the stars. The certainties of a righteous cause.

Something wet touched his fingers and he looked down to see a bloodhound looking up at him with sad eyes. It was strapped into a harness which held a tray of canapés steady on its back. Ignoring the food, Dirk instead patted the dog and was pleased to hear its contented growl. It was nice to have company that appreciated the simple things.

"I say, how do they let the smoke out?" Timothy was gazing at the fireplace, dirty glassware forgotten. "I mean, without anybody noticing."

"The houses above are occupied by friends of the King," Isabelle explained. "These fires link to their chimneys, so the smoke comes out where it's expected. Most of this district is loyal to Louis these days. He may not be the ruler he would like them to believe, but he is a decent employer, and his followers look after their own."

A new servant appeared, this time draped in a tabard of royal livery that might once have been a flag.

"His majesty will see you now."

They followed him across the hall, past dancers and diners, swaggerers and servants. Despite the decadence and inequality, Dirk struggled not to laugh. These folks were so pompous, with their upturned noses and their powdered faces, but it was nothing but a costume party, a band of rich fools in second-hand ball-gowns wishing the real world away.

"It has a certain tragic nobility, don't you think?" Blaze-Simms whispered. "Preserving the life they love by sheer force of will."

"That life was built on oppressing peasants." Dirk shook his head. "I don't see much nobility in it."

Louis XXI sat on a raised throne at the rear of the hall, draped in a pale fur cloak despite the heat, a thin circlet of gold atop his head. The men and women around him were serious in their bearing, sterner of demeanour than the crowd that filled the hall.

Louis was cadaverously pale, his eyes sunken and dark-rimmed. He drummed thin, manicured fingers against the arm of the throne, staring at the approaching guests with a feverish intensity.

"Your Majesty, may I present Sir Timothy Blaze-Simms, Mrs Isabelle McNair and Mr Dirk Dynamo." The herald bowed and backed away.

Dirk hesitated a moment, then joined the other two in bowing to the king. Now wasn't the time to stand by his principles. Besides, he was no more bowing to royalty here than he would have been to a small child playing at King Arthur.

"Mrs McNair." Louis crooked a finger, gesturing Isabelle closer. "It has been too long. Are you really working as an ambassador now?"

"Some friends in the Foreign Office were good enough to extend us diplomatic papers," Isabelle said, holding them out to the king. "And we will be happy to relay any messages you have for the British government. But though the glory of your company would be reason enough to come, my colleagues and I are here on business."

"Of course." Louis arched an eyebrow. "The Proceedings of the Epiphany Club is always a most interesting read, and an edition seldom goes by without reference to Sir Timothy and Mr Dynamo's exploits. Such busy men"

"Your majesty is a step ahead of us."

"Any step that takes me closer to you is a pleasure, madame. But how is Mr McNair?"

"Very well. He sends his best wishes."

"His manners remain impeccable. I look forward to meeting him one day in the flesh. Remind me, where in Africa is he working?"

"The Cape Colonies, your majesty."

"And yet when Viscount Renard was there earlier this year, he could not find word of him, never mind passing on my regards."

"As your majesty knows, Africa is a large place."

"Yet I would expect any man who married you to be a figure of some repute. But no matter. Now that we have the diplomatic niceties out of the way, what can I do for you, madame?"

"We are looking for an ancient tablet, an archaeological curio that the club's scholars believe may help to identify a further site of interest. We know that it was brought to Paris, and suspect that it may have been hidden in the Shrine of Charlemagne. We seek your permission to visit the shrine and, if we can find the tablet, to borrow it."

Dirk glanced over in confusion. Hadn't the stone headed into the Seine? What was this about a shrine, he wondered.

There was a gasp from one of the assembled advisors.

"Outrageous!" said a woman sat next to the king. "We should have them taken out and whipped!"

Louis waved her into silence. "That you know to ask for this reveals the poor state of my own security. But your boldness, in asking to intrude upon the most secret and revered temple of my family, reveals more. What do you have to offer me?"

Isabelle pulled a slim envelope from her handbag and handed it to Louis with a soft smile.

Louis cracked the black wax seal and sat silent, reading the contents of the letter. At last he looked up, casting a curious glance over Dirk and Timothy.

"I will need confirmation that this is real. Especially given..." He gestured towards their diplomatic papers.

Isabelle nodded. "Arrangements have been made."

"Once I have my proof..."

Isabelle shook her head. "Events above us are moving too fast. We need to complete our mission and leave Paris."

The King stared at her, then back at the letter. His fingers drummed again on the arm of the throne.

"I am the absolute monarch of France," he said. "Yet my country is a mystery to me. I walk her streets only at night, in secrecy and silence. The faces I see are ghosts, grey and lifeless, mere memories of the glory that this nation once was.

"Long have I planned my return. Gathering weapons, sifting intelligence, raising and training those who will fight at my side. But it was never enough. And now, you bring me this. Is this real, or just another ghost, an imitation of hope that will crumple at the touch of action?"

He and Isabelle stared into one another's eyes, locked in the moment of decision.

"Can you afford not to take this opportunity?" she asked.

Louis nodded. "You have me, madame."

He snapped his fingers and the herald reappeared.

"Your majesty?"

"Make our guests comfortable once more. And fetch me Father Gaston. They are going to need a guide."

This time, they were led to a secluded alcove near the rear of the hall. It was large enough to boast half a dozen chairs and a set of fine inlaid cabinets, but small enough to feel strangely cosy. A tall man in a tightly tailored suit sat in one of the chairs, a leather case across his knees. Opening pleasantries revealed him to be a man named Noiriel from the Banque Cantonale de Genève, one of Switzerland's newest and most reputable banks.

"I take it that you are a diplomatic party?" he said, peering over the top of his wire-framed spectacles.

"What makes you say that?" Isabelle asked.

"This area is normally reserved for ambassadorial representatives."

"Thought you were a banker," Dirk said.

"Well, yes, but on this occasion my duties are more political. His majesty had a falling out with the Portuguese ambassador some months ago and banished him from court. Now the Portuguese wish to discuss certain matters with his majesty, and my employers have been asked to make representations in their place. Informally, of course – it would not do for King Louis to accept a Portuguese representative under such circumstances."

Shouting broke out above the general din of the hall, followed by the distinctive rattle of rapiers. Dirk sprang to his feet, looking around for the source of danger.

Noiriel sighed. "Calm yourself, Monsieur Dynamo. They are just duelling again."

"I didn't realise that duelling was still common at court," Isabelle said.

"For a community with so many enemies, his majesty's followers have a quite unnecessary tendency towards self-destruction. The nation's current upheavals are over-exciting the younger generation, as they believe that with Napoleon III gone their time in power may soon come. This is the fifth incident I have witnessed in three recent visits."

"Perhaps they are looking to impress you, monsieur?" Isabelle smiled, an expression Noiriel seemed incapable of returning.

"Only two things impress me," he replied. "A well-starched shirt and a well-balanced book."

His gaze flickered with disdain across Dirk and Blaze-Simms, settling once more on Isabelle.

"There is no shortage of charm and beauty at court," he said. "But I believe that you outshine them all."

Isabelle laughed. "You are too kind."

"I am a man of careful measures - seldom kind, and never too much of anything."

Isabelle moved her seat closer to Noiriel. "Tell me more about your work," she said. "I hear good things about the Banque de Genève."

Dirk found himself liking this banker character less and less. The fellow was rude and arrogant, and not half as charming as Isabelle seemed to think. His blood was boiling just being around him.

"Going for a walk," he muttered and stomped off across the hall.

It wasn't just Isabelle's liking for Noiriel that turned him against the man. She was friendly with folks all the time, and he had no hold over her, no call to go getting jealous. Sure, she was a fine lady, but that wasn't such a rarity either. The world was full of fine ladies, there wasn't any reason to worry about one. But the way that sleazy banker had sidled in towards her made Dirk's skin crawl.

He was so lost in his thoughts that he never saw the dancers before he crashed into them. He jolted to a stop, looking uncertainly down at the woman sprawled in a heap of lacy skirts, at the man in the blue tailcoat and feathered hat helping her to her feet, at the other couples staring at him, and at the band sitting silent in mid-movement.

"Awful sorry," he mumbled, turning away from them.

"Don't you dare turn your back on me," the man in the blue jacket said.

Dirk paused, took a deep breath. They were meant to be diplomatic. The guy might be dressed like a cockerel and dripping disdain, but if he punched him out there'd be hell to pay. He could imagine Isabelle giving him grief, while that Noiriel stood by and smirked.

He took another long step away.

"Where are your manners, sir?" the man snapped.

Dirk spun around. "My manners are all that's keeping me from punching you," he snarled.

"Oh really?" The man sneered, his hand settling on the pommel of a rapier. "But what can one expect from an American? As if assaulting a lady weren't enough, now you threaten me too."

"I ain't assaulted anyone. It was an accident, and I already apologised."

"Not to my satisfaction, you didn't."

Dirk took a deep breath again. Diplomacy, he thought. Isabelle and diplomacy.

"I am excruciatingly sorry," he said.

"Apology accepted." The man gave a narrow little smile as he turned away. "Maybe there is hope for you backwoods colonial barbarians yet."

"Sorry I ever set foot in your glorified cellar," Dirk snapped, his pulse pounding at the insult. "Sorry to have set eyes on such an over-dressed, over-stuffed, over-indulged kid and his fancy dress friends."

Dirk caught the man's hand as it sailed toward him. He held it an inch from his face, squeezing the wrist until something clicked and a white glove fell from trembling fingers onto the chipped tiles.

"You challenging me?" he asked.

"Oh yes," the man breathed through gritted teeth.

Dirk released his opponent. "What'll it be then? Swords?"

"Of course." The man twirled his injured hand around and, apparently satisfied with the results, drew his rapier.

The hiss of steel over silk seemed to drown out the whole room.

"Somebody lend me a damn blade?" Dirk asked.

A sword clattered at his feet. He picked it up, felt its passable weight and balance, eyed up the notched but well oiled blade.

The man cast off his jacket with a flourish. It clattered to the floor, a string of medals knocking against the tiles. He twirled his blade, moving faster and faster, slashing the empty air to left and right. Dirk watched in awe as the blade became a blur filling every corner of his vision.

Awe turned to apprehension as he remembered why he was seeing this display. He'd never been afraid to go down fighting, but it ought to have been for a better cause than this.

"Oh, Dirk," Isabelle sighed from somewhere behind him. "What have you done?"

Chapter 2: Surprises

A growing space opened up around Dirk as he and the swordsman circled each other, blades raised. He tried to remember the books he'd read on fencing and swordplay, the few lessons he'd taken, the fights where he'd faced swords. Sword fighting wasn't like brawling, where you could count on endurance to see you through against a skilled opponent. Take one good thrust to the chest and you were gone. Worse, take one to the guts and you faced a long, slow bleed out. He'd borne witness to that more times than he cared to count - the stink of blood and bowels, the haunted eyes and trembling breaths of a man dying in fear and pain.

He tried to think of anything that might give him an edge. Some trick of the wrist, a clever manoeuvre to see him through. But all the ones he knew relied on an opponent he could match, or fighting three at once, or using the furniture against them, and as the ballroom opened up around them, and his opponent's blade danced in the light of the dusty chandelier, he knew there wasn't much hope of any of that.

Worse, now that he faced the very real chance of death he was feeling frustrated at himself for getting into this stupid position. He pressed that feeling down, but still the buzz of frustration niggled at his brain, distracting him from the task in hand, leaving him even more doomed. He cursed his intrusive emotions as he tried to focus.

Something touched his elbow and he jumped, caught unawares by a woman in a black dress. She held his arm in a surprisingly steely grip. Dirk's opponent gave a small, gracious bow to the lady, but his foot tapped impatiently on the floor.

The woman's face was hidden behind a black lace veil, but there was something familiar, something clipped and exotic in the way she spoke.

"Dynamo-san." She bowed her head.

"That you, Noriko?" He didn't know many orientals, and only one he was expecting to see in Paris.

"I believe that, when a westerner cannot fight a duel, they are allowed a second." Miura Noriko spoke loud enough for the crowd to hear.

"Reckon you're right," Dirk said, "but I'm fully fit and capable for this here fight."

"Really?"

There was a flash of movement. Noriko's index finger jabbed Dirk's neck just above the collarbone, and his whole body went rigid. He tried to protest but even his mouth betrayed him, jaw locked, lips frozen in place. All he managed was an animal grunt.

"Ninth Scorpion Punch," she whispered. "It is all about the nerves."

She tapped his chest and he fell back on the floor, rigid as a plank. Whatever she'd done didn't stop the pain as his head smacked against the tiles. Black spots danced across his vision.

Picking up his rapier, she stepped out into the glare of the watching crowd. By the time she cast aside her hat and veil, the leader of the Striking Snowflake ninja clan had the room's full attention.

"Honourable sir." Noriko tested the weight of the sword as she tested her opponent's gaze. "Dynamo-san is incapacitated. I will take his place."

"The Counts of Veradieux do not duel women." The man lowered his blade. "Never mind orientals."

The crowd, a single judgemental mind, murmured their approval.

There was a blur of movement and a pearl-white button rolled away across the tiles. The Count stared down at the frayed cotton thread dangling from his shirt.

"A trick fighter," he said. "How... refreshing."

Another black blur, another button fell to the floor.

The Count's lips thinned. "Madame, only propriety keeps me from running you through. Propriety and pride at never having wet my blade on inferior blood."

Another blur of movement. This time the Count moved to defend himself. There was a brief clash of blades before both fighters stepped back into their defensive stances, waiting.

The Count made a show of counting his buttons.

"Your aim is off," he said, the tension in his voice belying his forced calm. "My shirt remains intact."

Noriko flicked her blade and a drop of blood spattered the floor, crimson across white tiles. The Count's face fell as he saw the clean cut through his sleeve, white cotton turning red.

Titters of laughter rippled through the crowd.

The Count of Veradieux snarled and leapt to the attack.

Dirk might not be much of a swordsman, but he knew enough fighting to tell the good from the bad. Hours spent watching other folks' form, reading manuals on different styles, analysing and imitating manoeuvres, had left him a finely honed spectator at any bout. Sure, his view was limited from down here on the ground, but what he saw was a master class in humiliation.

Veradieux darted towards Noriko with the proud energy of a champion in his prime. He made two swift feints, shifted to the left and stabbed upwards inside Noriko's guard. But even as the blade darted towards her face Noriko turned, spinning like a ballerina, out of reach and around behind Veradieux. A kick sent him stumbling forwards, a bootprint on the seat of his pants.

The Count turned back, all vestiges of control shredded with his dignity. He lashed out left and right but Noriko barely moved, effortlessly avoiding his blows. Rushing at her, he became a bull raging at this black rag, but she knocked his lone horn aside and slid past, the hilt of her sword reddening his cheek with a loud thwack. As Veradieux raged back round she twisted the blade, slid it smoothly through his right arm and caught the sword that came tumbling from his grasp. As he stared in shock at his skewered limb she sliced off one last button, leaving his shirt hanging open.

A trickle of blood ran down the jewel-hilted blade as she pressed its tip against his chest.

"Enough?" Her whisper filled the room.

"Enough," he gasped.

#

By the time they left the hall Dirk was walking straight. It took a little more concentration than he was happy with, looking down to check that he wasn't tripping at thresholds or broken patches of paving.

The network of passages beyond the grandly dilapidated ballroom had deteriorated still further, their walls dirty and dejected with paint flaking away beneath the creeping march of mould. Velvet curtains hung around murals to create the illusion of windows. Moths flew from them as footsteps echoed by, wings fluttering like the haggard servants who still rushed down these halls, a few dozen greying figures maintaining the illusion of a full staff. The further they walked the more certain Dirk became that Louis was deluded in his talk of armed revolt, that there was nothing but him and a hall full of discarded aristocrats. If the time ever came, they would charge forth into the face of a full modern army and never be seen again.

But then they came to the barracks.

Father Gaston, their guide through the halls, paused at that door. His black robes brushed the floor as he shifted nervously from foot to foot.

"Guests don't normally come this way," he explained, stubby fingers fretting at his straggling white hairs. "But the west passage is flooded, sewer flooded in fact, and, well..." He turned the handle and ushered them forward. "We'll be quick."

At the start of the Civil War, Dirk had found himself in a company of irregulars guarding an ill-prepared patch of the Union's midwest. There had been a grim determination to the men in that company, many of them veterans of the pre-war fighting in Bleeding Kansas, abolitionists with no formal military training but with the tenacity, the scars and the hard-earned experience of a fighting dog. Their canvas roofed barracks had been a place of lowered voices, serious conversations and distant, lost stares. Dirk was surprised to recognise that same atmosphere on the other side of the door.

This was one of a series of underground chambers, with others visible through the red brick doorways to either side. The weapons on the walls were mostly museum pieces - old muskets, rows of pikes, swords from half of human history. They gleamed in the gaslight, a sure sign of care and maintenance, and the banners draped along the ceiling gave the same impression of history on display, of pride and pomp to match the rest of Louis's court.

But not so the men here. Sat alone or in clusters at battered wooden benches, they looked up from their meals as Dirk and his companions passed, watching them with unswerving suspicion. These were men who were ready for terrible things, their weapons ancient but fit for purpose. Dirk couldn't help but feel some sympathy for their resolve.

Isabelle and Noriko walked side by side, leaning in close to whisper to each other.

"What do you reckon's gotten into those two?" Dirk murmured to Blaze-Simms.

"Perhaps they're talking about fashion." Blaze-Simms peered at their surroundings in fascination. "I hear that's what ladies do when together."

"Probably not these ladies." The thought of the ninja master discussing bustles and skirts made Dirk laugh out loud.

They tramped through two barracks chambers, connected by a tunnel where Dirk had to duck or risk scraping his head. As Gaston opened the door at the far end, a cacophony of animal noises erupted into the silence of the barracks. Blaze-Simms and Isabelle jumped at the noise, and for the first time the grim-faced soldiers laughed.

Seeing the nervous looks on his companions' faces - even Father Gaston looked less than eager to continue - Dirk marched through the door, Noriko unflappable beside him. He'd faced wild cougars, a mutated bear, once even a pack of giant rats each taller than a man. He wasn't worried about whatever Louis was keeping in some crazy underground menagerie.

This room was darker than the barracks halls, lit by just enough guttering candles to show the way through. There were cages in the darkness to either side, and animals pressing up against their bars. Dirk peered at them, trying to make out their shapes in the darkness. These first few seemed to be hunting dogs, taller than most he'd seen and with teeth so long they cut their own lips barking. He couldn't make out much of what was in the next cage, but saw what looked like two raggedly furred heads hidden in the shadows, and only a single body. Then came a lion, growling low in its throat and pacing the tiny space of its cage, strong and lean despite the clumps missing from its mane.

"This ain't right." Dirk looked with sorrow at the proud beast trapped in such tiny confines.

But Gaston was already ushering them along, hurrying from the room into the tunnel beyond. There he paused, lit a pair of oil lamps hanging from hooks on the wall, and passed one to Dirk.

"What's all that about?" Dirk jerked a thumb back over his shoulder.

"Army," Father Gaston replied. "Army, army, army." He closed the door they had just come through and then scurried on down the tunnel. "Come along, come along."

"Not the barracks," Dirk said. "The beasts."

But the priest was already disappearing around a corner, intent only on getting them where they had to go.

This time they were led down a series of narrow, winding tunnels, with no animals to howl at them or ragtag soldiers to watch with scorn. There weren't even rats for most of the journey, except on two occasions when the tunnels emerged into sewer lines, narrow bridges carrying them above the filthy flow. Dirk was glad not to get as acquainted with Paris's rivers of waste as he had with London's - the rats were welcome to their stinking home.

After half an hour of walking, their only company their own footsteps and Blaze-Simms's observations on tunnel architecture, they arrived at another door. Its oak was old, warped by centuries in the cold and damp below Paris, yet still sturdy in its frame. The metal fittings were worn smooth with care and use, not rusting away as might have been expected.

"This place..." Father Gaston took a hefty key from within his robes and turned it in the lock. The mechanism turned smoothly, effortlessly, the faintest of clicks announcing that a sturdy bolt had moved back to let them in. "This place is the most holy in France, and therefore the world. You are privileged in a way few commoners have ever been, and even fewer foreigners. Please treat it with the reverence it is due."

This didn't seem the moment for Dirk to mention how little that meant to an atheist. He just nodded his head and followed Gaston through the door.

It was like walking into the cave of a beast from legend, a dragon hoarding his wealth against thieves and adventurers. The light of their lamps sparkled off a hundred gold surfaces and a thousand gleaming points. It shone through gems, fracturing and scattering bright colours across a pale marble floor. It wasn't a large room, but it had more precious metalwork per square inch than Dirk had ever seen in his life. At the far end, incense smouldered in the braziers in front of a shrine, its sweet, smoky scent overwhelming the lingering sewage smell.

Behind the altar rose the figure of Christ on the cross. This statue, three feet tall and hanging from the wall, was made from silver, the figure's features crude and simply made, the head exaggerated, eyes wide and staring. The cross was a thing of stunning intricacy by comparison, a curling mass of Celtic knots and Viking-style curves whose ends split into roots and branches. The faces of past kings, some familiar, some not, surrounded the crucifix, each a pale silver visage against a warm golden background.

Gaston knelt before the shrine. Isabelle followed his lead, tugging at Blaze-Simms's sleeve as she did so, leading him into a stance of prayer, even as he flicked his notebook open to a blank page.

Dirk folded his arms and watched. He didn't know the prayer the father was reciting, the Latin meaning little to him and the spiritual essence of it even less. Noriko stood blank-faced through the small ceremony, even more of an outsider than Dirk. But Isabelle and Blaze-Simms joined in the "Amen" at the end, and that seemed enough to appease Gaston.

"Why's all this still here?" Dirk asked as they rose to their feet. "Given the state of the court, I'd have thought all this wealth-"

"Monsieur Dynamo!" Father Gaston looked appalled. "This shrine is a link between the monarchs of France and God most high. A connection reforged in gold by each generation since Charlemagne. Its value is beyond that of mere money or soldiers for hire. To even suggest such an outrage-"

"Forgive my friend, father." Isabelle laid a hand on the priest's arm. "His expectations have been set by being raised in a republic."

"Hmph." Gaston frowned. "Well, whatever you want to see, let us get it done. It shows little enough respect to bring such a person in here, I would not want him lingering longer than is needed."

With a final glare he turned away from Dirk and returned to kneeling before the altar, leaving them to look around.

At first glance there was little to see beyond the display of blinding wealth. But Blaze-Simms had already proved how little first impressions were worth, opening a hatch in the gold frieze nearest to him and peering into a small stone-lined alcove.

"Not the stone that we want, I'm afraid." He stepped back to reveal a large ruby sitting on a velvet pillow. "But there are plenty more like this."

They made their way around the room, opening the little cupboards in which generations of French royalty had left offerings to the divine. Some of them were simple - small stone statues, finger bones and fragments of wood, things that Dirk concluded must be religious relics. Others like the ruby held a more secular value, gold and jewels sparkling in the light of their lamps.

At last they had opened all the cupboards, without seeing any sign of the tablet.

"Now what?" Dirk asked. He'd been on the back foot since they entered Louis's court, and he still didn't feel like he knew enough to get things moving.

"Back to the books, I suppose." Isabelle frowned. "This is terribly vexing. I was sure it would be here."

Noriko still stood by one of the cupboards, her hand resting on its door. It was one of the larger ones, a panel a foot and a half high and half that across, carved with images of a bridge and of fish leaping from the river below.

"Who looked in here?" she asked.

"I did." Blaze-Simms was making sketches of their surroundings, to the obvious unhappiness of Father Gaston. "There's nothing in there."

"True." Noriko opened the door, revealing a simple wood lining. "But look at the size of what is not in here."

"I suppose it would fit a small briefcase," Blaze-Simms said. "Or... Oh."

"Yes." Noriko nodded.

"Or a tablet like the ones we have." Blaze-Simms let out a huge sigh, but then brightened. "I say, it's a good thing we have you with us, isn't it?"

Father Gaston stood by the cupboard, his face a picture of shock.

"All the cupboards contain artefacts." He stared into the empty space, hands knotted in agitation. "All of them. Artefacts. Precious artefacts."

"Here, Father." Isabelle took the trembling priest by the arm and led him to a seat in the corner of the room. "Mr Dynamo has worked as a detective for the famous Pinkerton Agency. He can find a clue to what happened."

The look of faith she gave Dirk boosted his confidence, but as he approached the box he was all too aware that the conditions were against him. There was no dirt in this room for footprints to have been left in, no guards to see who came and went. Unless they checked all the cupboards regularly, the tablet could have been gone for weeks, along with any hope of finding a clue.

But if Isabelle wanted him to find that tablet then he'd damn well do it.

He peered inside the cupboard. Its walls might once have been fine carpentry, but time and damp had warped them. There was a crack in the timber of the ceiling and a gap half an inch across between the doorframe and the base. A few scratches where the stone had scraped against the timbers. Other than that, the whole thing was featureless.

"I could do with more light." Dirk felt around the interior, not sure what he was looking for. Sometimes that was how you had to start, just looking for anything that might be out of place.

"I've got the perfect thing!" There was a rattle as Blaze-Simms rummaged through his pockets, and then he placed a small ball in Dirk's hand. "One-use light. I've been looking for a chance to give it a go. Agitate it until you hear something break, the chemicals will do the rest."

Obediently, Dirk shook the ball until something crunched, then watched as it began to glow with a clear, white light.

"Great work, Tim." He turned back to the cupboard, holding out the increasingly bright ball, and peered around once more.

Now he could see details he had previously missed. More scratches on the ceiling; some old, faded writing on one of the walls; something glinting in the gap at the front of the cupboard. But the light was still growing, becoming so bright that it hurt his eyes. The ball was heating up too, and he dropped it as a burning sensation spread across his hand.

"Dammit, Tim!" He stepped back.

Smoke trickled out of the cupboard. The chemical light, still glowing brightly, was burning the bottom of the case. As Dirk looked around for something to move it with, Noriko stepped forward, picked it up calmly between the tips of her thumb and one finger, and dropped it on the floor.

There was a tinkle of shattering glass, and for a moment a pool of bright light spread across the floor, before it finally started to dim.

"Not bad for a first field trial." Blaze-Simms had his notebook out. "How would you describe the light? Bright? Piercing? Iridescent?"

"Burning." Dirk shook his stinging hand.

"Let me have a look at that." Isabelle took hold of his arm, but for once Dirk had higher concerns.

Hitching up one leg of his pants, he drew the Bowie knife from his ankle sheath. Careful not to stand in the glowing chemicals, he slid the tip of the knife down the crack at the front of the cupboard, hooked it beneath the thing he'd seen gleaming, and drew it carefully out. A brass button fell from the back of the knife and into his upturned hand.

"Found a clue." Dirk beamed. "Now we've just got to work out what it means."

Chapter 3: A Moment of Rest

Dirk prodded gently at the burn on his hand. It wasn't as bad as he'd feared. It would sting for the next day or two, but he'd worked on through far worse injuries.

He lit a cigar and peered once more around the hotel bar. The place was gas lit, making it easy to see just how empty it was. Last time he was in Paris this place had been full of businessmen and pleasure seekers enjoying the City of Light. Now there were only two sorts of people in Paris - locals and politicians, the latter hoping to gain power in a country that had thrown out its ruler mid-war.

The Prussian army might still be miles away, but everybody knew it was coming, and most of them had gotten out of the way.

"It's from a National Guard uniform." Isabelle passed the button to Noriko. "There were sixty battalions in Paris before the war started. Now there are nearly two hundred, all ready to defend France against the Prussian invaders."

"The tablet was stolen by a soldier." Noriko peered at the button for a moment, as if setting its details to memory, and then placed it on the table next to the two stone tablets they already had.

Isabelle had found a safe place to hide the stones while they were out of the hotel, but there didn't seem any point pretending not to have them. The other interested parties, including the Dane and his criminal gang, already knew what they had and what they were after. Given a choice between a futile attempt at secrecy and giving Blaze-Simms a chance to translate, they had opted to speed up their search. Dirk hadn't been convinced of the logic at first, but Isabelle was adamant that it would all work out, and she was the one who had set them on this path in the first place.

"National Guard ain't real soldiers." Dirk took an ornament from above the fireplace, a stone bust of Napoleon I. As he talked he lifted it up and down like a dumbbell, getting some exercise in while he could. "More like a militia. Bunch of bourgeoisie dressing up fancy and strutting around, and now a load of common folks conscripted by the government."

"Bourgeoisie?" Noriko turned to look at Isabelle, who said something in Japanese, and Noriko nodded. "I see. So we find these not-soldiers, and we take the stone from them."

"It ain't as simple as that." Dirk spoke around his cigar as he shifted his improvised weight from one hand to the other. "Button like that means it was someone from the old battalions, the rich guys in their fancy uniforms. But that's still thousands of men split across sixty units."

"I think we can focus on two." Isabelle picked the button up again and pointed to a ring of leaves embossed around its edge. "I visited some tailors after our expedition today. As Dirk has implied, these men dress as much for fashion as for war. Different units use different buttons, and only the seventh and twenty-third battalions use these."

"So all we need to do is investigate two battalions of armed men during a time of war?" Dirk sank into a padded armchair and grinned at his companions. "It's a challenge, but I reckon we're up to it."

He waved a waiter over and ordered more drinks - might as well make an evening of it. As their order was delivered, Dirk noticed a burly figure in an ill-fitting grey suit lurking at the bar. A guy he'd last seen in a fight on a boat.

"Aha!" Blaze-Simms looked up from the tablets, his eyes wide with excitement. "Do you remember I said there was something odd about this tablet?"

He pointed at the one they had brought back from Hakon.

"No." Dirk scoured his memory, following all the mental connections he'd used to keep the pieces of this puzzle together in his head, but nothing came to mind. "When did you say that?"

"Back in London, just before Noriko and her chaps attacked us." Blaze-Simms smiled at the ninja. She shifted uncomfortably in her seat, though Dirk figured that was as likely due to wearing a fancy dress as it was to being reminded of the fight in Blaze-Simms's tailors.

"Sure." Dirk sipped at his brandy. No point telling Blaze-Simms he had been too distracted to remember the conversation. "What about it?"

"This one has it too." Blaze-Simms pointed at one of the many indecipherable squiggles covering the stone. "They used a mixture of codes and languages, and it's taking me a while to disentangle it all. But one of the first things that stood out was this." He pointed at a word, then another one, and four more, scattered across the two stones. "Do you see?"

Staring at the letters and symbols, Dirk felt his head spin. He tried to focus on the few pieces Blaze-Simms had pointed out, but he couldn't see the connection. It sounded like this was something that should be obvious, and it drove him nuts that he couldn't see it, hard as he tried. He clenched his hand on the armrest, and the burned skin stung.

"I'm afraid you may have to help us, Timothy," Isabelle offered Blaze-Simms a gentle smile. "Not all of us are as strong on classical languages as you."

"Oh. Yes. Of course." Blaze-Simms sat back, pushing his glasses up his nose. "Frightfully sorry, I sometimes lose perspective on these things." He picked up a glass of wine from the small table beside him and took a sip, face crumpling in thought. "All those words are written differently. Different languages, scripts, dialects, even codes. But once you pay attention to the sound of them they're all the same. They're all variations on the name of the river Nile. If the library had been moved far then we might expect the Nile to feature early in the directions to its new location, but it's all over the text. Which means that the library is almost certainly still in Egypt, and probably not far from its great river."

He leaned forward, picking up his notebook and scribbling something again.

"Of course we'll never have a complete picture until we find the third tablet, but..."

His voice trailed off. There was a far-away look in his eyes.

"You got an idea?" Dirk asked eagerly.

"Yes." Blaze-Simms stood. "If I restrict the flow into the pressure chamber, I think that I can double the range on my gun."

"Your gun?" Dirk sank back into his seat. He should have known his friend couldn't stay focused on one task for this long.

"I have it in my room." Blaze-Simms picked up his glass. "I'm going to go and make some modifications."

Noriko stood. Her eyes always sparkled, but now that brightness spread to the rest of her face, and she almost seemed to smile. It was like catching a glimpse of the young child from before she had grown into a stone cold killer.

"This is the gun you had on Hakon?" She stared eagerly at Blaze-Simms. "Long range. Great power. Killed the bear."

"That's right!" Nothing excited Blaze-Simms like talking about his inventions. "Would you like to see it?"

"Yes." Noriko bowed her head. "Show me."

"Noriko." Isabelle touched the woman's arm. "It would be rather unseemly for you to go to Sir Timothy's room with him."

"Thank you for explaining your customs." Noriko bowed her head again. "But there is no-one here to misread my intent, and I wish to see this gun."

She followed Blaze-Simms toward the stairs, turning at the bottom to look back at Isabelle.

"If Sir Timothy tries anything unseemly, I have many knives." The ninja's face looked deadly serious again, but Dirk had to laugh at Blaze-Simms's nervous expression as Noriko ushered the inventor up the stairs.

By the bar, the man in the ill-fitting suit carefully didn't watch the pair of them disappear.

"'Scuse me a minute." Dirk rose from his seat.

"Going to talk to our old friend?" Isabelle's eyes flicked briefly in the direction of the man.

Adventuring with Blaze-Simms, Dirk wasn't used to working with someone who thought like he did. It made him all the happier to spend time with Isabelle.

"Don't go anywhere." There was a spring in Dirk's step as he walked across the room.

By the time he reached the bar, Dirk's suspicion had turned into a certainty. The man was one of the two "secretaries" of the French businessman they'd met on Hakon, men clearly more suited to busting skulls than taking minutes. Men sent to steal the tablets by the man known only as the Dane, western Europe's king of crime.

To the thug's credit, he didn't look up as Dirk approached. That might have come from a cool head or from not being smart enough to know what was going on. Either way, it made it less likely that things would turn violent.

"Tell your boss we ain't got the third tablet yet." Dirk met the man's gaze in the mirror behind the bar. He had angry, beady eyes and a face only a rhinoceros could love. "He might as well wait and rob us once we've got the whole set."

"I don't know what you mean." The man said it without feeling. He downed his beer, dropped a couple of coins on the bar, and walked away.

Dirk bought a couple more drinks and returned to Isabelle, taking the seat beside her.

"I..." Dirk was very aware of being alone with Isabelle. Everything became jumbled in his brain, and he could barely string together a thought, never mind a sentence. "I..."

"Would you like to know a secret, Mr Dynamo?" She turned toward him, smiling as she leaned across the arm of her chair. A strand of dark, curling hair fell across one cheek.

"Guess I would, Mrs McNair." Dirk leaned forward too, found his face inches from hers. All he could think about was their moment together in the sewers beneath London, that one kiss. It muddled him up even more.

"It's not a secret I've shared with anyone else," she murmured conspiratorially, then took a sip of her wine. "I can trust you, can't I, Mr Dynamo?"

"Yes, ma'am," he managed, palms sweating.

Isabelle leaned forward until her lips were almost brushing his ear.

"I'm not really married," she whispered.

Slack-jawed, Dirk waited for the words to sink in. They just seemed to float on the surface of his brain, not connecting with the other thoughts that lay within.

Isabelle stood, put down her wine glass and picked up one of the tablets.

"Could you look after the other one tonight?" Her voice was back to normal - sweet yet efficient. "I'll hide them properly in the morning."

"Uhuh." Dirk stared as she walked away, skirts rustling around her, never looking back as she disappeared up the stairs.

The waiter came over and started loading their empties onto a tray. Dirk placed his half-finished whisky among them.

"You do not want the rest?" The waiter pointed at the glass.

Dirk shook his head.

"I've had all I can take for one night," he said.

Chapter 4: Friends and Enemies

"I say, things don't look too bad, do they?" Blaze-Simms held up a newspaper with one hand, while with the other he shovelled scrambled eggs into his mouth. Or at least mostly into his mouth - yellow flecks of breakfast were joining the soot stains on his jacket. It looked like he'd had a night of inventing, not sleep.

The hotel dining room was as empty as the bar had been the night before. They were the only people eating, and a single waitress sat at the back of the room, looking bored beside a sideboard loaded with breakfast food.

"Never trust war reports." Dirk set aside his coffee and took the paper, scanning past the patriotic passages meant to stir the French soul, instead looking for what few real details were hidden there. "This ain't good. None of these troops would be near Paris if the war wasn't damn near lost already."

"Really?" Blaze-Simms reached for the toast. "But there's all this talk of forts and bringing in armies and-"

"An army rushing to stand still is an army that has lost." Noriko sawed a bread roll open with a single efficient stroke and reached for the butter.

A movement in the doorway drew Dirk's attention away from the food. He felt a childish grin spread across his face as Isabelle McNair glided into the room, blue skirts swirling around her.

"Good morning." She smiled as she approached the table.

"I saved you some of those pastries you like." Dirk gestured at the plate beside his own, piled with crisp, golden croissants and other baked treats. Then he glanced in embarrassment at the untouched heaps still sitting at the side of the room. "I'll admit, it don't seem so necessary now, but I didn't want you to miss out."

"Thank you, Mr Dynamo." She laid a hand on his shoulder as she sat down beside him. "It was very sweet of you, though I fear you may have over-estimated my appetite."

"I just figured..." Dirk blushed.

"The advantages of not sustaining such a spectacular frame as yours." She smiled as she poured herself a coffee and refilled his cup. "I can get by on far less."

He knew he was still blushing, but it didn't feel so bad any more. Having no idea what to say, he nodded and reached for his cup.

"What do we do today?" Noriko pushed her plate away. In her black dress she almost looked like a regular Parisian woman, apart from the table knife balanced menacingly on the tip of one finger.

"I'd like to take the gun out for some testing." Blaze-Simms looked up from carving gears out of toast. "See how the modifications do."

"There's already two armies getting ready to fight for this place," Dirk said. "Last thing we need is to look like we're getting involved."

"I'll find somewhere out of the way. Some rooftops, or a-"

"Mr Dynamo is right, Sir Timothy." Isabelle shook her head. "We can't have you out taking potshots at pigeons with Paris in this state. And besides, Noriko is going to need your help."

"She is?"

"I am not." The ninja launched her knife across the table, expertly skewering the croissant Isabelle held.

"Yes you are." Isabelle looked at Noriko, and there seemed to be another message in that glance, something Dirk couldn't quite read. "You two will be going to investigate the twenty-third battalion of the National Guard, to see if you can find a connection to King Louis and our tablet. Dirk and I will be talking with the seventh battalion. I know that Mr Dynamo and Sir Timothy are used to working together, but I think it best that there is a man in each group, as soldiers may treat them more seriously. And one of us, of course, to look out for other details."

"I see." Noriko bowed her head slightly. "This is wise."

"Sure works for me." Dirk stood, not wanting to leave time for the plan to change.

Before he got anywhere Isabelle laid a hand on his.

"Please, Mr Dynamo." She pulled the knife from her croissant. "At least let me finish breakfast."

#

Dirk wasn't sure what he'd expected of the Seventh Battalion's barracks, but it wasn't this. The guards outside indicated that this old warehouse building housed soldiers, whether permanently or for the duration of the current crisis. The sounds of marching boots, clattering equipment and shouting men emerged from beyond its walls into the otherwise deserted street.

Two guards stood by the doors in their blue jackets. Neither was missing a button.

"Is this Major of yours going to be long?" Dirk asked in French, trying to keep the impatience from his voice. They had been waiting for nearly half an hour, and there was still no sign of anyone worth talking to.

"It may not be the Major." One of the guards shrugged. "He is a busy man. More likely the Captain."

"Though the Captain is busy too." The second guard spoke solemnly, as if dispensing some deep nugget of wisdom. "There is, after all, a war on."

"Like I said, that's why I'm here," Dirk said. "I fought in my country's war, and I heard things were getting tough. Figured I'd see if I could offer any tactical advice."

It wasn't the worst excuse he'd ever used. One time he'd talked his way into a Canadian brothel by pretending to be a government health inspector. The initial response here had been friendly, one enthusiastic guard running off to find an officer to talk with him. But maybe that had just been a sign that the guy wanted off of guard duty.

"Relax." Isabelle smiled up at him. "Diplomacy is all about the careful deployment of patience."

"Sorry." He realised how far his face had slid into a scowl. "I'm more used to the deployment of fists is all."

There was a creak of rusted hinges and one of the doors swung open. The guards jerked to attention as a man emerged - short, rotund and balding, with a neatly waxed moustache and gold braiding running like waterfalls from his shoulders.

"You are the American?" He raised an eyebrow as he looked up at Dirk. "You do not look like much of a soldier."

It was one of the dumbest comments Dirk had ever heard. Sure, he might not have gleaming buttons and bright red trousers like these folks, but did this man really think that he was the one who looked soldierly?

The officer stared at him impatiently. Suddenly remembering how these things were meant to work, Dirk took a card from his pocket and handed it over. It was crumpled from neglect, but at least he had it on him.

"Dirk Dynamo," he said. "Formerly of the United States Infantry."

"Captain Renard." The man peered at the card. His scowl deepened as he read it. "Thank you for your time, Mr Dynamo, but we are in no need of your advice."

He pocketed the card.

"Let's not be hasty," Dirk said. "I know your boys ain't got much fighting under their belts, and I've-"

"You will go now, Mr Dynamo." Renard turned on his heel and disappeared back inside.

"What the...?" Dirk glared after him.

A hand gently but firmly grasped his elbow.

"Thank you, gentlemen." Isabelle smiled to the guards as she led Dirk slowly away down the street. Once they were out of earshot she turned, looking back toward the warehouse, and spoke again. "What does it say on your card, Dirk?"

"My name." He reached inside his pocket, but didn't have any more. He'd only ever carried them to humour Blaze-Simms, and had never replaced the few he handed out. "Epiphany Club. The Club's Manchester address. That's about it."

"He didn't react to your name," she said. "It must have been the Club."

"Someone's put the word out against us?" Dirk nodded. "Makes sense, but who?"

Deep, loud laughter echoed down the street as the warehouse door opened. A tall man in a suit emerged, slapped one of the guards on the shoulder, and started walking in their direction. With his enormous, rambling beard he was instantly recognisable, and somehow completely out of place.

"Braithwaite?" Dirk said in surprise. He hadn't seen the merchant since their visit to Hakon, had barely even thought about what he was doing. Yet here he was.

Braithwaite grinned at them.

"Dirk bloody Dynamo." He stomped up the street, grabbed Dirk's hand and pumped it up and down. "And the lovely Mrs McNair. Didn't expect to see you here."

"Didn't expect to see us?" Dirk stared in bewilderment at the Yorkshireman. "Don't tell me you're sellin' guano in a war zone."

"There's more to my business than just bird shit, I'll have you know." Braithwaite grinned even wider. "I'm here on behalf of Johnston's Beef Fluid."

"What?"

"Johnston's Beef Fluid. I were over making a delivery when the war started. Didn't look like it'd come to nowt, so I thought I'd stay, see if I could get some more orders. How 'bout you?"

"What the hell's Jackson's Fluid Beef?" Dirk knew that Braithwaite, an ex-quartermaster and army butcher, knew meat better than him, but this sounded like gibberish.

"This butcher from Edinburgh came up with it. He gets the bits of cow you can't sell, boils 'em down, sticks it in a tin and sells it to the French army. Calls it Beef Fluid. Soldiers get something like meat, so they're happy. Generals feed their troops cheap, so they're happy. And Johnston's selling scraps for cash, so he's laughing all the way to the bank."

"How utterly repulsive," Isabelle said.

"Waste not want not." Braithwaite glanced back toward the barracks warehouse, where more soldiers had emerged, watching them warily from the doorway. "What about you, why are you lurking around the rough end of France?"

"We're after..." Dirk glanced at Isabelle. They hadn't expected to meet anyone from the trip to Hakon, and he didn't want to give away too much. He liked Braithwaite, but was it possible the man was involved with their current difficulties? It was one hell of a coincidence for him to turn up again here.

"We came on a research trip." Isabelle took Braithwaite's arm and led him away from the barracks. Dirk, frowning a little, walked along to one side. "I'm afraid it turned out to be terribly badly timed."

"Research, is it?" Braithwaite winked. "Some sort of Epiphany Club adventure, I'll be bound. I read one of your journals after meeting you on Hakon. You're probably after buried treasure or summat like that, ey?"

"Something like that, yes."

They turned a corner into a residential street. Scruffy children chased a ball across the cobbles.

"Whatever it is, I bet that little turd Louis's up to his arse in it." Braithwaite laughed. "King in Shadow my foot."

"You know about King Louis?" Isabelle's voice had lost some of its gentleness.

Slow and careful so as not to be too obvious, Dirk eased open his jacket, ready to go for his gun if he needed to. Braithwaite seemed to know a surprising amount.

"You think I could sell exotic bird shit without His Pretend Majesty wanting some?" The merchant shook his head. "Bloody idiot's been buying anything with half a chance of a military use. I heard he blew up half a block trying to turn it into explosives, then blamed the mess on a gas leak."

He looked back over his shoulder, eyes narrowing conspiratorially.

"Mark my words," he said. "There'll be more than two armies fighting for this city when the Prussians arrive. Some bugger's been stirring the sort of shit even I can't sell."

Dirk caught Isabelle's eye. This sounded like something they needed to know more about. But she gave a tiny shake of her head, discouraging him from further questions.

They turned another corner. This time there were no children in the street, and all the doors were closed. It was strangely quiet.

Tension twisted inside Dirk, and he inched his hand ever closer to his Gravemaker revolver.

Half a dozen men appeared at the far end of the street, all dressed in the familiar blue jackets of the National Guard seventh battalion. Footsteps behind Dirk announced the arrival of half a dozen more. All of them carried long wooden batons, headless handles for spades and axes.

"Nay, lad." Braithwaite shook his head as Dirk laid a hand on his gun. "Tis never a good idea to turn a fist fight into a gun fight."

"Can we help at all?" Isabella called out as the men approached, surrounding them in a ring of uniformed menace.

"You are taking an interest in things you should not." It was Captain Renard, his ridiculous braiding wobbling as he swung his baton from side to side. "Think of this as a lesson, all the information you are going to get."

"Best you get behind me, ma'am," Dirk said to Isabelle. "This ain't gonna be pretty."

"Really?" she snapped. "After all we've been through together, that's still your attitude?"

Her hand disappeared into her bag, emerging a moment later dressed in knuckle dusters.

"Is a little chivalry so very wrong?" He raised his fists as the French soldiers came closer.

Then Renard snapped an order and there was no further talking.

The first attacker came at Dirk with a wild swing, an amateur unaware that he was facing a real soldier. Dirk leaned back, grabbed the improvised club as it sailed past, and jabbed it into the man's face. There was a crunch of breaking bone, a grunt of pain, and Dirk found himself armed with a length of solid pine.

With a crack of wood against wood he parried the next attack. Then he barged into the attacker shoulder first, knocking him to the ground, and stamped on his knee to keep him down.

Something hit his shoulder and his arm went numb, the baton dropping from his fingers. Without thinking he swung with his other fist, connected with a flabby belly and saw Renard stumble away. But others were coming in from left and right, and there was no time to follow through against the Captain.

After that the fight got into its ugly, confused phase. Dirk was aware of blue bodies all around, of blows against his legs, arms and ribs, of the clatter of wood and thud of bodies. It wasn't instinct that carried him through, but years of careful training, lessons learnt so deeply he could act on them with just the slightest thought. A guardsman went down to an elbow strike, another to a kick in the groin. A glancing blow left Dirk's nose bleeding but not broken, while a more solid one winded him. He ducked, twisted, sent another man flying and headed back into the fray.

Except that there was no more fray. Half a dozen of the guardsmen lay on the floor, groaning and in one case bleeding. The rest, Renard included, stood back nervously. Braithwaite's cheek was red and swollen, and he was avoiding putting weight on his left leg. Isabelle's hand was spattered with blood.

"And I was told the National Guard were gentlemen." She stood up straight, brushed a muddy bootprint from the front of her dress, and tucked back a loose strand of hair.

"You should leave Paris while you have the chance." Renard's strong tone was undermined by his wheezing.

"And you should stay out of my way, unless you want me to rip off that ridiculous moustache." Isabelle raised her fist, brass gleaming across her knuckles.

Renard glanced up the street, where Dirk caught a brief glimpse of a figure in an ill fitting grey suit, a briefcase in his hand. Then the Captain nodded to his men. Picking up their wounded they skulked away, back toward the barracks.

The man in the suit disappeared around the corner. For a moment, Dirk considered running after him in search of information. But he was tired and battered, and at that distance he didn't like his odds of catching up. Instead he turned back to Isabelle.

"You OK?" he asked, looking at her with concern.

"Don't you dare," she said. "I've been patronised quite enough for one day."

She put her weapon back in her bag and strode off up the street.

"I just meant that-" Dirk began in bewilderment.

"Your meaning was quite clear," she snapped back at him.

"Well done lad." Braithwaite slapped Dirk on the shoulder. "Whatever it were you did."

"You coming with us?" Dirk pointed up the street after the rapidly disappearing Isabelle.

Braithwaite shook his head.

"Nay, lad. I've work to do. But you'd best get after her right quick. And remember, someone's stirring, so you take care."

That thought echoed around the inside of Dirk's head as he ran after Isabelle. Somebody was stirring up trouble, adding to the conflict already descending on Paris. But who, and why? And why had Isabelle stopped him from asking more?

A memory froze him in his tracks. Isabelle handing a mysterious letter to Louis XXI. Elusive snippets of conversation that had made little sense. Was she a part of this? It seemed he couldn't trust her temper, or that she'd listen to him when he explained himself. How far could he trust her at all?

Chapter 5: The Smell of Failure

There were more guards on watch around the Seventh Battalion barracks. Even in the darkness Dirk could make them out, illuminated by the light spilling through the windows. From the rooftop opposite he'd watched three patrols pass in the past hour. Was this effort for the sake of the Prussians, or was it for them?

"What if this Renard chap doesn't know what's going on?" Blaze-Simms was wearing a specially adapted top hat, a collection of lenses hanging from the brim, turning his eyes into giant white orbs amid a metal framework. Wires hung from there to a box on his belt, and every few minutes he would crank a handle on its side, generating a fresh intensity in the machine's low whine.

"Then maybe he'll know who does." Dirk slapped his hand against a chimney. "Dammit, you're as bad as her. Don't you want to know what's going on?"

"Um..." Blaze-Simms shuffled uncomfortably. "Dirk old chap, I don't mean to pry, but is something going on between you and Mrs McNair?"

"You've sure got a funny way of not prying." Dirk kept his glare firmly fixed on the building opposite.

"Well, yes, but..." Blaze-Simms took a deep breath. "It's just rather hard to plan for a group when two of them aren't talking. Remember when Harcourt-Phipps and Prof Barrow had that bust-up over the Club race day. The expeditionary committee was in chaos for weeks."

"OK, I get it." Dirk looked at Blaze-Simms, and there was sympathy behind those ridiculous mechanical eyes.

It hadn't taken Dirk long, on the awkward, silent walk back to the hotel, to work out what he had done wrong. After all, Isabelle McNair was a scholar and an adventurer, not some damsel in distress. Sure, his attempt to protect her had been well meaning, but he should have known better.

Still, she'd completely over-reacted. She had to deal with this all the time, couldn't she cut him some slack for getting it wrong this once? It had only happened because she mattered to him. That left him feeling mad and struggling to find the right words, which had led to another row over dinner, this time about where their investigations led next. The treacherous part of his brain that had taken over in the street now kept asking the same question - what if she was the one stirring trouble in Paris? A question which made no sense when she was on their side.

He couldn't say any of that to Blaze-Simms. How did you discuss thoughts that made no sense?

"It's complicated," he said at last. "I'll deal with it. I promise."

"Good enough for me." Blaze-Simms smiled awkwardly. "And if you ever want to, you know, talk about it..."

His voice trailed off and they looked away from each other.

"So... Barracks?" Dirk looked back around the chimney, wanting something practical to focus on.

"I can get there." The soft voice made Dirk jump. He looked to his right, but there were just shadows.

"That you Noriko?" he asked.

One of the shadows slid over to sit beside him.

"I can get to the roof from here," she said. "I will throw a rope back for you."

"I'm afraid it won't be that easy." Blaze-Simms cranked the handle on his device again. "I got a better view of the rooftop with my light accumulating lenses. There are sentries up there as well, and they've scattered caltrops on the flat parts. Even if you don't get shot you'll get feet full of nails."

"If we cannot go over the walls then we go under." The shadow that was the ninja waved them toward the back of the rooftop. "Come with me."

#

"At least this time they're relatively clean sewers." Blaze-Simms sounded almost cheerful as his voice bounced around the tunnel. "It's done in a rather ingenious way, actually. They have these giant wooden balls that..."

No-one interrupted as he kept talking, explaining the intricate mechanisms used to keep the sewers of Paris flowing. Noriko was far ahead, scouting a route to take them up into the Seventh Battalion barracks, while behind the Englishman, Dirk and Isabelle trudged along in uncomfortable silence.

Clever as Paris's cleaning machines might be, they didn't stop the sewers stinking, or make it pleasant to wade through filthy water. Dirk tried not to look at the things bobbing past or the shadowy shapes his lantern illuminated.

"I'm sorry," Dirk whispered, just loud enough for Isabelle to hear him over Blaze-Simms's enthusiastic babble. "About how I acted at the fight."

There was no answer from Isabelle, just the squeak of a rat behind them in the darkness.

"What else is it you want me to say?" His heart was pounding. He felt like his brain was being squeezed in a clamp. Pressure seemed to bear down on him from out of thin air, forcing him to try to make her talk. But he had no idea how to get through. "Just... What?"

"That's your solution, is it?" she hissed at last. "Tell me what you think I want to hear? Because isn't that what any woman wants?"

A slap would have hurt him less.

Light appeared ahead, Noriko coming back toward them with a lantern in her hand. When she came close Dirk could see that she too was glaring.

"Filthy soldiers," she said. "I do not think the barracks is connected to the sewers."

"Is there another way up nearby?" Dirk asked. "A street opening next to the warehouse maybe?"

"Not that I have seen."

"I have an idea." Isabelle stepped forward. "Noriko, come with me. You two stay here."

"Why?" Dirk hadn't meant the word to come out so sharp, but he couldn't help himself. What was the point in leaving him back here? He told himself that things were looking suspicious again, that he had a decent reason to feel mad.

"Why not?" Isabelle demanded.

"Because we're all in this together." Dirk gestured around the group. "And that means we all work together, right Tim?"

"I really don't think..." Blaze-Simms backed away. "That is to say..."

"Enough." Noriko's always stern expression had an extra layer of steel. "We have work. Dynamo, Blaze-Simms, wait here."

She strode off up the tunnel with Isabelle. As they reached a turning, the two women paused, talking quietly out of Dirk's earshot. They peered around the corner, and then back toward where Dirk stood, struggling to bring his attention to the mission they were on.

"What do you reckon that's all about?" He nodded up the tunnel toward the pool of light around their companions.

"Didn't they say it was about a plan to get into the building?" Blaze-Simms had his notebook out and was drawing a patch of mould he'd found on the wall.

"A plan they can't discuss with us?" Dirk frowned. "What the hell would that be?"

"Maybe they just wanted to get on with it?" A look of confusion crossed Blaze-Simms's face as he looked at Dirk. "I mean, that makes sense, doesn't it?"

"I..." Dirk clenched his fist. It did make sense, sometimes action was more important than explanations. But an angry corner of his brain still kept telling him that it wasn't right.

As he fought the urge to pace impatiently back and forth, a chill made the hairs stand up on the back of his neck. He crouched, lowering his lantern to illuminate the ripples lapping across the foul water.

"Feel that?" he asked.

"Hm?" Blaze-Simms looked up from his notebook again, a distant look on his face. Then enlightenment hit and he smiled. "Gosh, there's a breeze."

"Not so common underground," Dirk said.

"Well no, but not so very rare either. Perhaps someone has opened a vent up-tunnel from here."

"And the waves?"

"Formed by the breeze?" Blaze-Simms peered at the water lapping impatiently against his leg. "Some sort of mechanism upstream, working up into gear? Or getting closer? Yes, getting closer. Perhaps a boat, or a pump for clearing backlogged pipes, or a -"

"Giant wooden ball?" Dirk peered back up the tunnel. Something was rumbling toward them, seemingly filling the whole space.

"Maybe, yes, or a mule-drawn cart or a-"

"Giant wooden ball."

"Well, yes, it's good you have an idea too, but-"

"Giant wooden ball!" Dirk grabbed Timothy's arm as he pointed back down the tunnel.

"Oh."

Blaze-Simms stared for a moment at the thing approaching them, filling the tunnel like a bullet in a gun.

Sewage crested in waves before the ball as it rolled ever-faster toward them.

"Run?" Blaze-Simms asked.

"Run," Dirk agreed.

They turned and sprinted up the tunnel. Filth flew from their footfalls. A noxious miasma, filled with the stink of churning waste, followed them. Each deep, rushing breath made Dirk gag.

"Run!" he yelled as they approached Isabelle and Noriko. Isabelle turned to frown, then her eyes went wide as she looked past him.

Now they were all running, chased by waves of sewage that lapped first around their knees, then their thighs, then up to their waists. They rounded a corner and a tunnel stretched into blackness ahead of them, past the reach of their lamps. Still they kept moving, the noise of the ball growing closer, the water slowing them as it rose higher and higher.

Blaze-Simms slipped and fell, sliding through sewage. Dirk hauled him to his feet and thrust him forwards.

"Too slow." The Englishman smeared ooze from his eyes as the grinding sound of the ball grew ever closer.

He was right. If they kept on like this, they would soon be over-taken and crushed in the filthy ooze. With an extra burst of speed, Dirk ran ahead of the others, forcing his way through the sewage, looking for anything that could help.

There it was - a black space in the ceiling, an opening leading into an upward tunnel. There was no ladder up to it, but he could see rungs attached to its side.

He ran back. The ball was less than fifty yards behind his companions, the rising tide of sewage starting to slow them down. Yet again, there was no time for explanations. He just pointed to the opening, visible at the edge of the lantern light. Then he slung the flagging Blaze-Simms over his shoulder and ran.

Noriko reached the opening first. In a single fluid motion she leapt, hooked her feet through the ladder rungs and reached down to haul Isabelle up.

The rumble of the ball was overwhelming as it echoed around the tunnel, waves of sewage crashing against Dirk as he reached the opening. Noriko swung back down, grabbed Blaze-Simms and vanished into the darkness. Then Dirk leapt after her, pulling his legs clear just as the ball roared past on a wave of fetid air.

#

"I don't suppose anyone was paying attention to the air pressure?" Blaze-Simms asked as they climbed, sewage-soaked and bedraggled, up an access tunnel.

"What air pressure?" Dirk asked resignedly.

"In front of the ball." Blaze-Simms sounded chirpy, despite the filth dripping from his tailcoat onto Dirk's head. "I've never seen one in action before, and I'm intrigued as to how they manage the air flow while still using it to unblock the lines. Presumably that's how it's driven, but-"

"Tim." Dirk bit back the harsh words that first came to mind. In their place he took a deep breath. "Even if we'd paid attention to air pressure, now ain't the time."

"But the longer we wait the more likely someone will forget what they-"

"Really not the time." Dirk couldn't keep the anger entirely from his voice, and his friend fell quiet. He felt guilty about it, picturing the look of hurt and confusion that would be filling Blaze-Simms's face, but he didn't have the patience. Ninety percent of the time his friend's inquisitiveness was a joy to hear. But right now there were too many other things on his mind.

Most important, in theory at least, was how they were going to make any progress in their investigation. Even after the close encounter with the sewer cleaning ball, they still hadn't found a way up into the barracks warehouse. That meant they either had to find another way in, which no-one was in a state to do right now, or find another lead in their search for the tablet. How they'd manage that should have been the first and only thing on his mind. Not the sewer cleaning system, not Blaze-Simms's hurt feelings, and certainly not the issue that kept pushing its way to the top of his mind.

Looking up the ladder, he caught a glimpse of Isabelle's skirts flapping wetly around her legs. With all due haste he returned his gaze to the rungs in front of him. Not that decency was a high priority right now, but looking at those legs now felt like grubby opportunism.

Yet he couldn't keep from glancing up again, or from thinking back to their argument in the tunnel. He knew he'd gotten things wrong, but he didn't know how to get them right. Hell, he wasn't even sure there was anything he could do - her anger had seemed so damned unfair.

A rat stared at him from a hole in the wall, its eyes glittering with accusation in the light of their lanterns.

"You're right," Dirk muttered. "A real man doesn't give up. There ain't nothin' can't be done with the right sort of hard work."

"What was that?" Blaze-Simms called down.

"Nothing," Dirk called back, embarrassed to realise that he'd spoken out loud, letting his feelings show.

Maybe that was the answer. If he couldn't make himself into whatever she wanted, maybe he could show her who he really was, and hope he lived up to her standards.

With things the way they were, what did he have to lose?

Lost in thought, Dirk didn't realise they'd reached the top until he stretched for the next rung and instead found Noriko's hand gripping his, pulling him up with amazing strength for her small size. Emerging onto a narrow cobbled street, he glanced around.

"Any idea where we are?" he asked.

"Two streets from where we started." Noriko's face was blank. If she felt half as frustrated as he did then she was hiding it well. "Dawn soon. We should return to the hotel."

Dirk hurried to catch up with Isabelle as she stomped away, leaving Noriko to deal with Blaze-Simms, who was once again furiously scribbling in his notebook.

"Can we talk?" Dirk asked as he caught up.

"What about?" Isabelle's tone was polite but frosty.

"I..." Dirk's mouth hung open as he tried to work out where to start. "That is to say, I-"

He was cut mercifully short by a click and two heavy footsteps. Ahead of them a large man stepped out of the shadows. The flicker of a streetlamp revealed the burly, suited man who had been spying on them in the hotel bar.

"Hands up," the man said. "Or I shoot you both."

"Listen pal, this ain't the time." Dirk raised his hands but kept walking forward. "I'm cold, I'm wet, I'm tired and I'm covered in shit. I've had a night of frustration and disappointment, and it ain't put me in the best of moods."

"Why should I care?" The man frowned as Dirk kept walking slowly forward. He wriggled his fat fingers, unable to get a comfortable grip on his gun. "Stop walking!"

"Fine."

Dirk leapt. He had half a second before the goon got his finger back on the trigger, but it was enough. Grabbing the man's wrist he twisted it aside. The gun fired, a bullet grazing Dirk's shoulder.

Ignoring the pain he kept moving, swinging the man against the wall, knocking the breath out of him. He slammed his forehead into the man's face with all the force of his pent-up frustration. There was a crunch, a crack of a head against the wall, and the gun clattered to the ground.

"What the hell do you want?" Dirk growled.

"Stones." Blood bubbled from the man's broken nose. "Dane wants some stones."

"Then he'd better come and get them himself." Dirk pulled his fist back. "Because the folks he's sending ain't up to the job."

#

The thud of artillery could be heard as they entered the hotel lobby.

"Bombardment's getting closer." Blaze-Simms reached inside the pocket where he kept his notebook, then caught Noriko's gaze and stopped. "I'll make a note after I've cleaned up."

"Sleep." Noriko followed the inventor up the stairs. "Tomorrow we find a new plan to deal with the National Guard and the third stone."

"Technically it's today, not tomorrow." Blaze-Simms's voice faded away along the landing.

"Technically, I do not care."

Dirk looked through a door at the chairs of the hotel bar. They seemed too nice to sit down on in his current state, but damn he needed a drink.

Not that there was anyone here to serve it.

"Here." Isabelle placed two glasses on the reception counter and poured a good measure of whiskey into each. "I could do with something for my nerves. They've been a little on edge tonight."

Dirk took one of the glasses. The drink trembled in his hand, a sign of weakness he didn't expect to see in himself.

"Listen," he said. "I've got something to say, and I ain't great at this stuff, so-"

"Please." Isabelle put a hand around his. "Let me."

She took a sip of her drink, eyes closing for a moment, and then followed it up with a deep breath. A sense of dread seized Dirk's heart. What was she about to say?

"I have had bad experiences, Mr Dynamo." She looked up into his eyes. "I have trouble trusting people. Men in particular. Men I like most of all. I spend my life hiding behind the mirage of an imaginary husband. Those times when I most want to lower my guard are the times when I least trust myself, or the person I am with. I am sorry I took that out on you."

If there was a word for what Dirk was feeling, then he didn't know it. There was surprise, confusion, relief, guilt, a whole messy mix that he couldn't untangle. So he just did what he'd meant to do anyway.

"I'm sorry too," he said. "For how I treat you. The way I was brought up to see women, I'm starting to see it ain't really respect. But that's no excuse."

"Thank you." She took the whiskey bottle from the counter. With her other hand she took Dirk's, and led him toward the stairs.

"Where are we going?" he asked, following along behind, his belly warm with more than just spirits.

"To take a bath." Isabelle tucked back a strand of sewage-soaked hair, then turned a smile on him that made his heart skip a beat. "Then once we both feel clean and human again, to do something much more fun."

Chapter 6: Beneath a Sheet

Dirk couldn't remember the last time he'd felt this good. Not that this was the first time he'd woken up in a tangle of bedsheets, a beautiful woman lying next to him. Not even the first time it had happened in a fancy hotel room, with fine carved furniture and soft sheets. But there had never been a woman who'd left him feeling so amazed, so overjoyed to wake up to the sight of her.

"Guess we ain't going out investigating today." He nodded toward the window, where a thin sliver of dusk was visible between the curtains.

"I think we earned that rest." Isabelle sat up smiling and ran a finger across his chest. Everything about her was stunning, but that smile was what really made Dirk's heart skip.

Then he remembered the last time she'd left him feeling stunned, and a question blurted out, unwitting, from his befuddled brain.

"Was there ever a Mr McNair?" he asked.

"Oh, Dirk." Isabelle shook with laughter. "You really know how to judge the mood, don't you?"

Dirk didn't like being mocked, but it was hard to be cross at her. He found himself laughing too.

"I'm not the one pretending to be married," he said. The damage was done, he might as well go with it.

"Alright, you have me." She stood, a figure out of some renaissance painting, and set to rummaging in the clothes scattered across the floor - the clean ones they'd both changed into after bathing, not the filthy heap piled up beside the bathtub back in Dirk's room. "There was a Mr McNair, a missionary in west Africa. I was a servant in his household, the only one left by the time the cholera passed through our community. Poor Mr McNair was the last to go, and the only European apart from me for a hundred miles around. He left me what money he had. The name I simply took. He didn't need it any more, and I knew I would have more freedom as a married middle class lady than as Miss Isabelle Jones, maid and tutor."

She pulled her underskirts on, then turned to look at him, an all too familiar defensiveness returning to her face.

"No-one was harmed," she said firmly. "He had no family left, no-one else who was losing out. I have met many men who have done far worse."

Dirk slid to the end of the bed, reached out and took her hand in his.

"You don't need to justify yourself," he said. "Not to me, not to anyone. We've all done some bad things to get by, or because they seemed like good things at the time."

He stood, letting the sheet fall away, but that wasn't what left him feeling naked. It was the thought of what he was about to say. He'd decided before this, long before this and yet less than a day ago, that he was going to be open with her. However tough that was, now was the time to do it.

"My name ain't my name either," he said.

"Really, Mr Dynamo?" She smiled a lopsided smile. "You surprise me."

He hesitated, the words frozen in his chest by the mockery. She must have seen something of that on his face, because her own expression softened.

"I'm sorry." She placed a hand on his belly, then gently pushed him back until they both sat on the edge of the bed, hands wrapped around each other. "Please talk. I'll try not to interrupt."

Dirk took another deep breath. He could do this.

"I was born in Kentucky," he said at last. "My Ma didn't survive the birth, and my Pa... Well, I ain't sure if he was bitter at me for that, or if he wasn't really my Pa at all. Either way, he wasn't what you'd call kind.

"Around where we lived, there wasn't much but mining. By the time I was eight I was down the mines - pushing carts, carrying tools, doing whatever work I could to help keep us fed. I was good at judging fuses, so soon they got me setting explosives. A ten year old kid, risking blowing himself up every day so that the men around him could get paid better. Little Dirk Dynamite.

"My Pa was bitter. Way he saw it, no-one had ever done him any favours in life, so why should he do them any? Me, I saw it differently. No-one had done me any favours, Pa included, and that meant I had to work harder for myself. I exercised to get strong, so that he'd stop beating on me. I paid attention to my letters and learned whatever I could, hoping one day I could be something other than a miner. That one day I'd have control over my own life.

"There weren't no slaves where we lived, but I heard about them. Whenever Pa or his cronies wanted to justify the way they worked me, they'd tell me it could be worse, that I could be a slave. Except they used uglier words for it. All that did was make me hate slavery, hate the idea that there were folks even more miserable than me, folks who had no control over their lives.

"One day this pastor came through town. An old-fashioned southern man, ranting and raging against the abolitionists causing trouble in Kansas, how they were going to destroy our way of life by setting the slaves free. Half of town was cheering him on, Pa included. That hateful talk got me so angry I up and knocked that old man out, did the same to the sheriff when he tried to arrest me, and finally to my Pa when he tried to stop me leaving town. Fifteen years old, and I'd never had the courage to make myself free until I heard about those others in chains. Kind of stupid, huh?"

He looked at Isabelle, and tears were running down her cheeks.

"Not stupid." She leaned forward and kissed him. "Not even a little."

A while later they lay among the sheets again, her underskirt once more abandoned on the floor. It was fully dark, the two of them alone in the room, only the sound of distant artillery interrupting their solitude. Dirk was hungry, so hungry that most days it would have forced him out of bed and straight to the nearest source of food. But he didn't want to let go of the woman in his arms.

"What happened after you left home?" Isabelle asked, and he could feel her breath against his chest.

"I went to Kansas." Dirk was surprised at how easily the words came. He'd spent years skirting around these memories, hiding them from the world. But now he'd started sharing them, there seemed no reason to stop. "Bleeding Kansas they called it, abolitionists and slavers fighting each other long before the war began. I had to give folks a name, but I was damned if I was going to see my Pa's name live on through me. First time someone asked I got so muddled I almost said Dirk Dynamite. Dynamo was my way of softening it a little, taking a name folks had given me and making it my own."

"And did you find something better there?"

"Hell no." A bitter, snarling laugh escaped from Dirk, and he felt Isabelle flinch against him. "I saw bad things there, things more ugly and hateful than most folks can imagine. Did bad things too, even though my cause was good."

"And you were only fifteen?" she whispered.

"Yup." Dirk swallowed, pressing down the horrified feelings that had almost overwhelmed him at the time.

Maybe he wasn't quite ready to talk about this yet. About what it felt like to fight for your life at that age. About his first kill being another young man no older than himself. About being led away from that body by the same kindly folks whose eyes he'd just seen filled with hate. About watching a town burn and being told it was God's work.

About Dirk Dynamite once again being asked to light the fuse, and not knowing how to say no.

"I should go." He stood, peering around in hopes that the darkness might recede and reveal his pants. "I'm hungry."

There was a hiss of gas, the flare of a match, and the lamp was lit beside Isabelle. He didn't look back at her, couldn't bear to have that beautiful image tarnished by these awful feelings.

"I heard a cleaner in the corridor." Sheets rustled as Isabelle got out of bed. "Wait a few minutes, then you can get to your room without being seen. When we come down for dinner we can both say that we needed sleep."

Dirk tensed. Here it was, the shadow hanging over what had seemed like something beautiful. The dark descent of their true situation, and the deceptions that would wrap this up.

"That's how this is gonna be, huh?" he said.

"Of course it is." Isabelle sighed as she stood behind him, wrapping her arms around his body, her warmth soaking into him. "If a man is caught behaving like we have, he gets a raised eyebrow and drinks bought for him. If a woman gets caught, especially a married woman, she is disgraced."

"I'm sorry." Dirk turned guiltily around and looked down at her, wrapping her once again in his arms. "But..." He almost didn't dare ask, but he had to know. "Was this just about today, or is there more to come?"

"More, I hope." She squeezed him tight. "But first I need to go and flirt with another man. Because unless I'm very much mistaken, Louis can still help us get that stone."

#

There was a tension in Louis's court that had not been there before. The jollity of the couples dancing, the drunken laughter of the courtiers, the hushed chatter of gossip, all felt more forced. Around the King was a flurry of activity, servants dashing back and forth in their tabards and tailcoats, nobles debating with an urgency and seriousness that had been entirely absent the last time around.

Even the least professional war room had a particular atmosphere, and this was the least professional war room Dirk had ever seen. Noriko shook her head at the sight, but Blaze-Simms showed his usual curiosity, peering at the swords, guns and armour being carried past.

As Dirk and his companions approached, the banker Noiriel was stomping away from the royal presence and toward the door. He paused for a moment as Isabelle greeted him, a battle between manners and temper written across his face.

"Mrs McNair." He nodded sharply. "I hope you have more luck with these lunatics than I did."

"My dear Mr Noiriel, what do you mean?" Isabelle asked.

Blank professionalism returned to Noiriel's face, his anger only visible in the way his eyes flickered across the servants accompanying them.

"I know little of politics," he said in a less than sincere tone. "But I know money, and if yours is invested in France than get it out now."

With that he flounced out the door.

They waited a short distance from the throne, joining the queue in front of a harassed looking royal secretary. But before they could reach the front of the line Louis looked up, grinned, and waved them over. His smile was sly as a pickpocket on the docks.

"Your Majesty." Isabelle curtsied before the King. "So good of you to see us at this difficult time."

"How could I refuse such charming company?" Louis waved over a servant, who pressed a glass of champagne into each of their hands. "And more importantly, how can I help you?"

Dirk's impression of Louis as a pompous fool was only reinforced by the way he was dressed. Medieval plate armour covered his legs, while an eighteenth century rapier hung by his side. A string of medals was pinned to his shirt. Despite all of it, Isabelle treated him as seriously as ever.

"As you know, we are here on an academic mission." She sipped at her champagne, then gave a surprised smile. "We believe that someone in the 7th Battalion of the National Guard may have information that can help us, but we are having trouble getting access to their barracks. I imagine that you are well informed on the movements of such men."

"The National Guard?" Louis paused to drink from his own glass. Another sat empty on the arm of his throne - it seemed that he was celebrating his success in advance. "Republicans, most of them. I have few friends there."

"All the more reason to assist us," Isabelle said. "It is possible that the 7th Battalion will become quite busy with us, if we can get into their barracks."

"You are looking to distract the National Guard just as my city comes under attack?" Louis pulled a face of mock shock.

"You aren't?" Isabelle's gaze shifted pointedly toward his sword.

"Indeed." There was a secretive little smile at the corner of the King's mouth. "The Prussians draw ever closer, and we both know that a republican government cannot stop them. Someone else must take control of the situation."

"Who could possibly have predicted such a crisis?" Her voice was heavy with irony. "And the opportunity it brings."

"An opportunity for which I am most grateful." Louis raised his glass to her. "But still, the city is in danger."

"A point which only makes my plea more urgent." Isabelle looked him in the eye. "Paris is full of priceless artefacts, sources of knowledge that might be endangered by the war."

"Or by the ignorance of the Prussians." Louis nodded. "Take this for example."

He drew back the cloth on the table next to him, revealing a stone tablet. A tablet like the two they had hidden back at the hotel. This time he favoured them all with his knowing smile.

Dirk stared at the stone, then up at the King as he stood, cloth in hand from his big reveal, looking like nothing so much as a cheap stage magician. This whole time, he'd been playing them. Leading them on a wild goose chase to distract a National Guard unit, while he got ready for his royalist revolution.

Clenching his fist, Dirk held back his anger. They had waded through sewage for that damn tablet, and this petty would-be king had it all along. Given free rein, he'd have punched Louis out cold, and to hell with the consequences. But they still needed the tablet, and the King was still surrounded by his followers.

"To some it just looks like a rock." Louis ran a finger across the engraved surface. "But to persons of learning it could be a source of great knowledge."

"Indeed." Isabelle remained calm. "We should ensure that it is safe."

"We should ensure that the whole city is safe from the invaders. And for that I need all the support I can muster."

"You will need supporters abroad." Isabelle made a gesture with her hand, taking in their small group of international academics and adventurers. "People with influence in foreign governments. Respected organisations that can quickly win diplomatic support for your regime."

"And I would reward such friends greatly." The King smiled and pulled the cloth back across the stone. "Once my city and my country are secure. But for now what I need are experienced people who can fight at my side." He looked at Noriko, and then at Dirk. "Do you know any?"

#

Dirk knocked back his drink in a single gulp, put the glass straight back on the waiter's tray and ordered another. Brandy wasn't normally his drink, but there was no whiskey here. Other than that, this was by far the best place

Isabelle had ever taken them, a proper bar with notches in the tables, wood shavings on the floor, and darkened corners a man could lose himself in. In a better mood, he would have enjoyed the change of pace from courtly, artistic Paris.

But he really wasn't in the mood.

"I ain't doing it," he said. "I'll go a long way for learning, but I ain't helping overthrow a government, least of all for that man."

"He's not all bad." Blaze-Simms sipped at a glass of red wine. "He's been really quite hospitable, and he has what we're after."

"Quite hospitable?" Dirk snarled. "He lied to us from the start. Someone told him we were coming, and why. Then he hid the tablet and left that button, to trick us into picking a fight with the National Guard. Only reason he's given up on that is 'cause he wants us in his army instead."

Blaze-Simms frowned, then shrugged.

"When you put it like that, he does seem a bit of a rotter." He turned the wine glass in his hand. "But we still need what he has."

"What do you think?" Isabelle looked at Noriko. "Would you be willing to fight for him?"

The two women looked at each other for a moment. Not for the first time, Dirk feeling like he'd missed some silent meaning.

"No." Noriko shook her head. "There is no honour in fighting for such a man."

Isabelle frowned at Noriko, then sat back with a sigh.

"In that case we need a new plan." She drummed her fingers against the handbag in her lap. "Delusional he might be, but King Louis has a lot of people around him. We need to steal that tablet from what will soon be a war zone. So, ideas?"

"I have a concept for a digging machine." Blaze-Simms flicked through the pages of his notebook. "If we could find the parts then we could tunnel up beneath the court and steal the tablet."

"I can sneak in past the guards." Noriko drew a long knife from the folds of her black court dress. "But getting out with the stone would mean a fight, and they are numerous."

"Any thoughts, Dirk?" Isabelle asked.

Noriko shot the other woman a slight frown.

"I think we've got more urgent problems." Dirk reached inside his coat, placing a hand on his Gravemaker pistol. "All the waiters have left, and I see a familiar face at the door."

The others followed his gaze, taking in the muscled man in a suit who stood by the entrance to the bar. His face was bruised, a plaster strapped across his nose, and a vicious snarl curled the corners of his mouth.

"I didn't get your name last time," Dirk called out to the Dane's thug. "I'm Dirk, but I'm guessing you know that."

"Maurice." The man walked slowly toward them, more men in grey suits fanning out behind him. Some held guns, others clubs. "Dane wants a word."

"I don't see that happening." Dirk scanned the room. There were more men coming in through the door behind the bar, hemming them in with a ring of muscle and bull-faced menace. Through the wide windows filling the café front, he could see a single passer by hurrying away from the threatening mob.

"Then this will hurt." Maurice grinned.

Pushing back his seat, Dirk rose to his feet.

"You got the bill, Tim?" he asked.

"We're paying the people who let us get ambushed?" Blaze-Simms looked aghast.

"Doubt they had much choice." Dirk caught Noriko's eye, then flicked his gaze down to the table and on to the window. She gave the slightest of nods.

"Very well." Blaze-Simms placed a handful of coins on the tabletop. "But I'm not leaving a big tip."

By now they were all on their feet and ready for action. Outnumbered at least four to one, and in an awkward corner, it wasn't a fight Dirk was looking forward to.

Not that he often looked forward to a fight.

He gripped the edge of the table, fingers white with tension, as Maurice started to raise his gun.

"Now," Dirk yelled.

He lifted the table one-handed, flinging it straight at Maurice. The thug stumbled out of the way and the table smashed through the window. Guns fired wildly as men leapt out of the path of flying furniture and shattered glass.

Gun in hand, Dirk snapped off a couple of shots that sent their attackers crawling for cover. Then he grabbed the bewildered Blaze-Simms and flung him through the broken window.

"I say!" the Englishman yelled as he hurtled through the air.

Noriko was behind him, dragging Isabelle with her. Then Dirk fired his last rounds and leapt after them, out onto the cobbles.

Following Noriko's lead they rushed down the street. The sound of distant artillery was accompanied by the crack of gunfire behind them, and of footsteps hurrying in pursuit.

Blaze-Simms stumbled, clutching at his leg. Not waiting to see what was wrong, Dirk flung his friend over his shoulder and kept running.

"If you hadn't thrown him..." Isabelle looked crossly at Dirk as she turned, pistol in hand, and fired. Her gun's adapted ammunition exploded the cobbles in front of the pursuers, scattering them as they leapt back from the blast.

"You had a better plan?" Dirk skidded on a patch of smooth cobbles, righted himself just before he fell, and kept on running.

"Noriko might have."

"Save your breath," Noriko snapped. "Run."

Bullets rattled off the street, windows shattering and chips of stone flying. One clipped the ninja's leg and she slowed, glaring over her shoulder.

"Too many guns," she hissed.

The breath was growing hot and fierce in Dirk's lungs, his shoulder aching from the weight of Blaze-Simms. Looking for a way clear, all he saw was closed door after closed door, and the open boulevards with which Napoleon III had remade his capital.

Then a large, bearded figure stepped out of one of those doors.

"In here," Braithwaite roared.

Dirk didn't need asking twice. With an extra burst of speed he reached the doorway and was through, Isabelle and Noriko behind him. Bullets thudded against woodwork, followed by the heavier sound of a bolt sliding into place.

"By 'eck, you lot look like you've been through the wars." Braithwaite led them down a short corridor and into a wide, bare hall, while angry shouts and the rattling of the door let them know how close Maurice and his men had come.

"Damn glad you were here to help us." Dirk looked around. Rows of muscled men stood around the room. Some were lifting clubs and balls, others exercising on the floor, and one was using a skipping rope. All except Braithwaite seemed to be dressed in long johns or shorts and shirts.

"Friend of mine runs this gymnasium." Braithwaite nodded to a tall, lean man. "Some bugger's messing with your door, Gaston."

"Not for long." The man waved them on, then picked up a pair of the heavy clubs and headed toward the sounds of trouble, several other muscular men following him.

The gymnasium consisted of an open hall full of mats and weights, with corridors off both ends and a servant standing ready in the entrance. Braithwaite led them straight through and out into the open air, where a carriage was waiting.

"Thought you might need a quick getaway," he said as he opened the carriage door and helped lift Blaze-Simms inside.

"Why did you think that?" Suspicion flowered in Dirk's mind. Why would an English businessman know what sort of trouble they were in?

"I heard word that the Dane were causing someone trouble tonight." Braithwaite winked. "Seemed likely that someone were you."

"How the hell do you know about the Dane?" Dirk grabbed Braithwaite and slammed him up against the side of the carriage, only for Braithwaite to shove him away. The two stood glaring at each other.

"Do you really think this is the time?" The Yorkshireman's vast beard wobbled as he nodded toward the gymnasium, from which sounds of violence were emerging. "I can get you to safety. Question is, do you trust me enough for that?"

Looking at Isabelle, Dirk could see that she was as hesitant as him, as uncertain of what was going on. Half the appeal of the Braithwaite they'd met on Hakon had been his simple, straight talking ways. This was another man entirely.

"It will be fine." Blaze-Simms wobbled a little as he leaned out of the carriage. "I trust him."

Dirk didn't reckon Blaze-Simms a great judge of character, but it was his safety at stake here, and that made it his call.

"Alright." Dirk took a step back. "Noriko, go with Tim. Even wounded, I reckon you can deal with any trouble."

"And me?" Isabelle tipped the spent casings from her pistol and pulled fresh ones from her bag. "Are we going to have a chat with the Dane's friends?"

"Oh no." Dirk offered her his arm. They hurried away from the noise of the gymnasium and the rattle of the carriage's wheels. "We're going to see a king."

#

Dirk didn't have much of a plan. He just knew that they couldn't keep reacting, that they had to take control of the situation. That meant finding a point they could press at to move things forward, and that meant Louis.

They strode through the chill night together, like a couple out for a late night romantic stroll. A couple with guns in hand and a determined pace.

A sound caught Dirk's attention. A group of people was coming toward them from the opposite direction, and after the way the night had gone that made him wary. Tugging Isabelle back into the darkness of an alley mouth, he peered out into the night.

As they stood in the crisp darkness, a soft pattering sound emerged, rising into the drumming of fast footfalls. A loose column of silhouettes appeared around the corner, like shadows going to war. Each held some weapon - a sword, musket or club - and ran wordlessly down the street, never slowing nor breaking formation until all had gone by.

"Someone is on the march," Isabelle whispered, one foot stepping forward out of the alley. Dirk took her arm, pulling her back into concealment as he nodded up the street at the next mass of moving shadows.

These were cavalry, proud men on once-noble steeds. They carried flaming brands, their orange light illuminating a long parade of tradition. Theirs were the uniforms of their forefathers - navy blue jackets that had taken the field at Waterloo, silver buttons gleaming; cuirasses that had led a hundred charges across war torn German principalities in the name of god and king; tabards of musketeers and palace guards that had hung on study walls next to old oil portraits. Some even wore plate mail, their faces made monstrous by iron helms, lances raised in salute to the same sky that had gazed down upon French warriors since their nation's birth. The clatter of hooves and jingle of spurs were all that showed these men as more than ghostly reflections of dead glories.

Then another formation came, slower this time. Snarling, furred beasts lumbering out of the darkness, a mass of claws, teeth and hunger. Some were inbred hunting dogs, flat-faced and furious, squinting from beady eyes. Others looked like giant rats, tall as a man, shoulders hunched and tails swishing. Heat rose off them in damp waves, a scent of salt and a sensation of fury. Dirk could see it rising in a mist through the chill morning air. They sniffed and snarled as they approached, and a few turned from snapping at each other to peer in his direction. But they kept moving, herded by a band of nervous men with whips and prods.

Dirk tugged Isabelle's sleeve and led her back down the alley, to a narrow backstreet running parallel with the army's march. They hurried down it, glancing from time to time at the torchlight flickering between the buildings, the two of them dogging the footsteps of that marching, striding, shambling force.

At last they stopped in a cobbled square. At the far end a figure stood on a balcony, gleaming in polished plate armour and a long white cloak, a crown on his head. The King in Shadow had emerged.

"This is not just a war." Louis's eyes burned with an intensity so terrible that Dirk could see it across the square. "This is a holy crusade. A new White Terror like that which scourged the revolutionaries of old, blasting away all that is unclean, all that is impure. The rebels, the dissenters, the Republicans and collaborators, they will feel the fire of our wrath. I will see them gutted in the streets and hung from the eves of their own homes, a testament to our power and majesty. Paris shall rise like her King from the ashes of history. But first, let her burn!"

Chapter 7: Decisions and Revelations

"This is pure nonsense." The hotel manager, a portly man with thinning hair, peered at them disapprovingly over his half-moon spectacles. "If there were an army in the streets all of Paris would know it."

"They will soon enough." Dirk glanced out the main door toward the gaslit street. "Best guess, Louis and the government are keeping the fight between themselves as long as they can, rather than risk other folks interfering."

The manager shook his head.

"I will not have you barricading up my hotel for some invisible war. How would my customers get in?"

"What customers?" Dirk waved a hand around the empty bar. "You reckon anyone's coming out drinking tonight?"

As if to reinforce his point, the sound of distant artillery once again drifted in through the open door.

"I can't say that I like your tone." The manager folded his arms across his belly.

Dirk could feel himself reddening, his temper rising at the man's idiocy. Then a soft hand touched his arm, and he felt his frustration recede.

"Perhaps Sir Timothy could help?" Isabelle smiled at the manager.

"I'm sure I can." Blaze-Simms looked over from where he was holding up a chair, comparing the size of its back with a small window. "But how?"

"If you were to hire this bar for a private function, there would be no need to let other guests in," Isabelle said. "And of course you would pay for any damage to the fixtures and fittings."

The manager's eyes lit up as Blaze-Simms pulled out his pocket book and extracted a series of notes.

"Will this be enough?" The expression on his face was far less innocent than his tone of voice. "I'm afraid I don't know the going rate for private parties in France."

The manager snatched the notes, his eyes wide as he counted them. The snap of Noriko removing legs from a table made him frown again, but then he looked down at the money, smiled, and headed back around the counter.

"I will fetch you hammer and nails," he said as he disappeared.

Taking a chance, Dirk took Isabelle's hand, squeezed it, and then let go before the others could see.

"Thanks," he said.

"My pleasure." She smiled, then took a moment to brush imaginary dirt from his lapel. "And now to business. If we're going to wait out the violence while Louis exhausts himself, then we should at least do it in comfort."

She closed and bolted the door, then set to organising their preparations - deciding which furniture to use for barricading and which to keep intact; investigating the back ways into the hotel; ordering tea to keep them going and a meal for later. She only paused long enough for a brief, quiet and intense conversation with Noriko. It made Dirk smile to see the way she dealt with everyone's concerns, keeping them all working together. He was still mulling over what Braithwaite was up to, the Yorkshireman apparently having left after bringing Blaze-Simms and Noriko home. But that, like many other concerns, would have to wait.

It was no surprise to hear, in between the hammering of nails and heaving of tables, the occasional sounds of violence out in the night. It had the intense, furtive quality of a New York gang war or a night-time raid out on the Plains. Brief clashes of arms, muffled grunts, and then swiftly receding footsteps. If Dirk hadn't known what he was listening for, he might never have realised what it was, especially when it came from several streets over. But he knew, and the occasional howls of animals confirmed that King Louis's strange forces were at the heart of this semi-secret war.

More surprising was the moment when, just after dawn, a newspaper was thrust through letterbox. It fell between the planks with which they had sealed the door and tumbled with a domesticated thud onto the doormat.

Dirk hopped down from the bar stool where he had been perched with his gun, having volunteered to keep this watch while the others slept in arm chairs and a sofa. Figuring that he might as well keep his mind active, he strolled over and picked up the paper, perusing its headlines on the way back to the bar.

The staunchly outspoken press had always been one of Dirk's favourite things about France. With the war going badly, it was hard for the government to keep the papers in check, and he didn't have to read between the lines any more to see that things had gone to hell. Across the north,

French forces were in retreat or completely out of contact. And as of last night, the Prussians had Paris surrounded.

"I say, is that Le Figaro?" Blaze-Simms rolled over on the couch, suit crumpled but eyes bright. He picked up a half-empty glass of wine from the coffee table beside him, emptied it and let out a satisfied sigh. Then he sprang to his feet and walked over to join Dirk at the bar.

"Do you think we might get coffee?" he whispered, glancing back at their sleeping friends.

Dirk reached over the bar, picked up a cup and up-ended the jug they had kept handy on the burner all night. What emerged was little more than a black, tar-like dribble.

"Let's investigate the kitchen." Blaze-Simms nodded toward the back of the bar. Seeing Dirk's reluctant expression he laughed. "The sun's coming up, old chap. The fighting's over for the night."

"You really think Louis will stop for daylight?" Dirk wasn't convinced that the would-be King, with his intended reign of terror, was really that subtle.

"Oh yes." Blaze-Simms walked back toward the kitchen. "At night, Paris can't see how dirty he fights. Glorious things could be happening in the dark. This way, the story is far better later."

It was a surprisingly practical observation for Blaze-Simms, and Dirk smiled in pride at his friend. The logic he'd spelt out wasn't the sort Dirk could get behind, but then Louis wasn't the kind of leader he would back either. Feeling a huge yawn escape, he decided that he could take the risk, and followed Blaze-Simms into the hotel kitchen.

The place was impeccably clean, stone worktops and wooden tables gleaming as they lit lamps. Every utensil had its place, from pots hanging from the ceiling to knives racked against the walls. The coffee pot sat on its own burner right by the door, and while Blaze-Simms fetched water Dirk rummaged through cupboards in search of coffee.

"There's something I wanted to talk about, old chap." Blaze-Simms nudged the door closed and turned to look at Dirk. He seemed even more awkward than usual, shoulders hunched, fingers frantically twiddling.

"What's that?" Dirk opened a bag and was assailed by the rich smell of coffee beans. Smiling, he poured some into a grinder on the counter top. Enough for all of them - fresh coffee would be a nice surprise for Isabelle when she woke up.

Except that she was English, so she'd probably want tea. He went back into the cupboard, trying to work out which bag the tea leaves would be in.

"I noticed..." Blaze-Simms hesitated. "That is to say, I was starting to think that maybe..."

"No need to worry so much." With a sense of satisfaction, Dirk placed a teapot next to the coffee grinder. "You know you can talk straight with me."

"Well, yes, this just isn't my normal area of expertise." Blaze-Simms took a deep breath. "The fact is, I wouldn't even mention it if you weren't such a good friend."

"What's the matter?" Dirk looked straight at Blaze-Simms, brow crumpling with concern. "Are you sick? If it's a debt, I've helped folks out of that before."

"No, nothing like that. It's just... You seem to be getting rather attached to Mrs McNair."

Laughing with relief, Dirk ducked back into the cupboard, now looking for a strainer.

"Guess I am," he said.

"Yes, well..." There was another pause. "She and I had a bit of a thing."

Dirk bolted upright so fast he slammed his head against the top of the cupboard. He clutched the injured spot, but the pain seemed nothing compared with his shock.

"What the...?" Now he was lost for words.

"It was just the once," Blaze-Simms blurted out. "A bit of fun, as you do. A gentleman doesn't like to talk about these things, especially where a married woman's concerned. That's the most distasteful sort of bragging. But with everything else, I wanted you to know. I wanted you to hear it from me."

#

It wasn't quiet up on the roof of the hotel. Paris was still a busy city, and Prussian artillery could be heard, whether shelling the outskirts or bombarding some distant French force. But there was a sort of peace that came with solitude, and that was what Dirk needed. He spent half the day up on that rooftop, walking back and forth as he tried to find some focus, smoking his remaining cigars, sleeping for a brief while underneath his jacket. None of it did what he needed it to do. He couldn't even think about Isabelle without feeling his pulse race, his thoughts scatter in confusion and distress.

He'd thought there was something special between them. She'd broken the cover of lies that kept her protected, so that they could be together. She'd slept with him despite the front she kept up of being a married woman. Naive as it now seemed, he had assumed that only happened for him, and that he meant something important to her.

It seemed he'd thought wrong.

One thing was certain - he couldn't face staying cooped up here with her any longer than he had to.

Around noon, he finally got calm enough to face going back inside. He slid back down the drainpipe onto the nearest balcony, levered the window open without concern for the damage he did to its frame, and walked with heavy footfalls back through the hotel. Empty corridors and echoing stairwells led him to his room to grab his single bag, and from there back to the barricaded bar.

Isabelle looked at him with concern, Noriko with a single raised eyebrow. Blaze-Simms just looked away, and Dirk felt a pang of sympathy in among the tumult of tumbling emotions. He could never stay mad at his friend. He'd known Blaze-Simms too long to ever see him as someone worthy of real blame.

"I ain't cowering here through a three-way war." Dirk slammed his bag down on the counter. "Between Louis, the government and the Prussians, this place is going to go to hell. Folks get killed in a time like that. Treasures get lost. We need to go grab the tablet and get out of here."

"We had a plan." Noriko's voice was as steely as her gaze.

"Waiting does seem safer," Blaze-Simms mumbled.

Dirk glared at Isabelle, waiting for her too to shoot his idea down.

"Dirk's right," she said after a reflective pause. "I would love to be able to sit this out, but with the Prussians here the fighting isn't going to burn out, it's just going to intensify. We should get the tablet before it falls into the wrong hands." She turned to Noriko as she spoke those last words. "Isn't that why we're here?"

Noriko's eyes narrowed, but after a moment she nodded her agreement.

"Tim?" Dirk said, as warmly as he could. "You in?"

Blaze-Simms looked up at him, his smile wobbling.

"Of course," he said. "Whatever you want, old chap."

"Alright then." Dirk hefted his bag as he looked from Blaze-Simms to Noriko. "Get your things together. Anything vital comes with us. The rest goes behind the bar, and we hope we get a chance to pick it up later."

"What constitutes vital?" Blaze-Simms asked. "For example, should I bring both spanner sets, or..."

Noriko grabbed his arm and dragged him, still chattering but at least not resisting, up the stairs toward their rooms.

In the silence of the hotel bar, Dirk was very aware of being alone with Isabelle.

"Is something the matter?" The touch of her hand on his sent a shudder through him. A day before it would have been a shudder of excitement. Now he didn't know what to make of it.

"You'd best get the tablets," he managed, not looking her in the eye.

"Dirk, what on earth has got into you?" She sounded concerned, though a dark part of his mind wondered which of them she was concerned for - him, or herself and her ability to get him to do what she wanted.

He tensed, trying to come up with an answer.

"I-"

There was a roar from the street, and the barricaded windows burst inward. Dirk grabbed Isabelle and ducked behind the bar. Half a table flew through the space where they had stood, carried on a spray of splinters, shattered glass and cobblestones.

Fragments of rubble were still pattering down as Dirk sprang to his feet, gun drawn, and turned to face out through the ruined windows. Through the remnants of their barricade he saw the edge of a crater thirty feet across. The building across the street creaked like death's own door and then crashed down into the hole, sending out another spray of flying rubble.

Footsteps raced down the stairs and Blaze-Simms appeared, a suitcase in one hand and his experimental rifle in the other. Noriko was beside him, so quiet even in haste that her footfalls made no sound.

"We should go." Isabelle had drawn the sword from within the shaft of her parasol.

"Where did you stash the tablets?" Dirk asked.

"I have them." Noriko held up a black sack, weighed down by the distinctive shape of the two stones, while with her other hand she flung a small bag to Isabelle.

"You told her where you hid them, but not me?" Dirk glared at Isabelle.

"What is wrong with you?" she snapped.

There was a shout from the street and the bark of a rifle. Men in blue Prussian uniforms were pouring out of the crater.

"I say, Krupp did it." Blaze-Simms peered excitedly at the crater. "I owe him ten guineas."

"What the hell are you on about?" Dirk asked.

"You know, Krupp, the Prussian armaments chap." Blaze-Simms turned to them with a smile. "I bet him ten guineas he couldn't make a tunnelling torpedo before I did. Only then I got distracted with the gun and that serving machine, and we-"

"That's your fault?" Dirk pointed his revolver at the Prussians emerging into the street, pointed helmets gleaming in the late afternoon sunlight.

"Fault is a very strong word." Blaze-Simms looked away. "I mean, he was working on it anyway, I just-"

"Let's not worry about that now." Isabelle's tone was soft and conciliatory, at odds the sword in her hand and the pistol she had drawn from her bag. "We should be getting out of here."

"Halt!" a voice shouted from the shattered doorway.

Without thinking, Dirk turned his pistol toward the voice. A rifle roared and Dirk's pistol echoed the sound as it bucked in his hand. The mirror above the bar shattered, while a Prussian soldier groaned and slid to the tiled floor in the doorway, blood streaming from his shoulder.

More uniformed bodies appeared, pointing guns in through the window. Once again, Dirk dived for cover, crouching with Isabelle behind the bar as bullets pelted the walls.

"Well done." Her tone was icy. "Now we have to fight the Prussians too."

"Not my fault," Dirk peered around the corner of the bar, snapped off a shot and then drew back into cover.

"Oh really?" Isabelle reached up above her head, firing blindly at their attackers. "You seemed happy enough to lay blame on poor Timothy."

"Poor Timothy now, is it?" Dirk rose, bullets whizzing past him as he took out five men with as many shots.

"And what is that supposed to mean?" Isabelle finished reloading and rose to stand beside him. But the Prussians were gone - all except those lying dead or injured - and a moment later they saw why.

A band of mismatched cavalry galloped past the window, some in tabards, others in jackets, one dressed in full plate armour. They carried bloodied swords and smoking pistols, and their leader flew a fleur-de-lis flag. Three massive dogs and a mangy lion ran with them. It seemed the royalists were willing to fight in the open now the Prussians were here.

"Typical man." Isabelle murmured. "I knew Louis couldn't resist turning it into a real fight."

"Huzzah for King Louis!" Blaze-Simms raised his top hat, and in return received a salute from a passing rider. Seeing the others' expressions he shrugged. "Would you rather have them attacking us too?"

Dirk picked up his bag and strode to the doorway. Peering out, he saw that the street around the crater was clear, the royalists and Prussians fighting each other a hundred yards down the road.

"Well, if this ain't a golden opportunity." A little of the weight lifted from his heavy spirit. "Louis's got two armies to fight. Seems like the perfect time to go steal his stone."

Chapter 8: The Subterranean Strike Force

"What about the Dane?" Noriko asked as they hurried through the rundown district where Louis kept court.

"He'll have to wait." Dirk opened the nondescript door that led to the King Under Paris's secret lair. "We've got to deal with Louis and the Prussians first."

"Noriko has a point," Isabelle said as she followed him through. "His people have come after us several times now."

"Sometimes you've got to deal with one guy at a time," Dirk growled. "Don't you know that?"

"Oh, for goodness sake." Isabelle's low grumble was almost lost amid the clatter of their feet on the iron staircase and across the sewer-spanning bridge and its base. "What is your problem now?"

Not pausing to answer, Dirk knocked sharply on the sturdy little door that led into the court. When no-one answered, he gave it a shove and it creaked open.

"So much for security," he said.

The ballroom was emptier than when they had last been there, but no less bustling with activity. Messengers ran in and out, hurrying distractedly past priceless works of art and gossiping knots of courtiers. Trained dogs still wandered back and forth, trays of drinks and canapes strapped to their backs. Louis stood by a table on his dais - taking messages, snapping orders, and toying impatiently with the hilt of his sword.

He looked up as they entered, then back down at a map spread in front of him. A wave of his hand sent the black-robed figure of Father Gaston scurrying toward them.

"I'm sorry." The priest said, tugging at strands of his thin white hair. "His Majesty is too busy for visitors. Too busy. Too busy."

"That's quite alright," Isabelle said. "We can wait."

Father Gaston nodded, smiled unconvincingly and hurried away.

"We can wait?" Dirk asked. "Last I checked, we were in a hurry."

"The stone is not with the king." Noriko turned from scanning the dais to look around at the art and artefacts scattered around the room, more visible now that half the court had gone away to war. "He is arrogant. It will be on display."

"Then let's go look for it." Blaze-Simms took a glass of champagne from one of the dogs that still roamed the hall, trays strapped to their backs.

"Good idea," Isabelle said. "You two split up and start looking. Dirk and I will catch up."

Blaze-Simms sauntered off with the casual stride of a man completely at home, while Noriko slid discreetly away.

"We should split up too," Dirk said, eager to leave Isabelle and his uncomfortable feelings behind.

"Oh, no." She turned to glare at him. "You don't get off the hook that easily. You've been acting like a petulant child all the way here. What has got into you?"

"What's got into me?" Dirk snorted. "It's what's gotten into you."

He regretted the words as soon as he'd said them. Flippancy was no way to deal with this, and it certainly wasn't the place for the conversation. But some words once spoken couldn't be taken back.

"What do you mean by that?" she asked, her sharp tone making him grit his teeth.

"I mean I know about you and Timothy." Now he was glaring at her too. "You made out like there was something special between us, turns out you're just sleeping with whoever comes to hand."

"Really?" She waved her hands at their surroundings, a look of incredulity on her face. "You choose now to get petty about this?"

"Now's when I found out. And you're the one wanted to talk, so let's goddamn talk."

"Fine. You know what you are? You're a complete hypocrite."

"How's that? You think I've been banging Noriko?"

"You're certainly no blushing virgin. Those were some experienced moves you made the other night."

"Reckon you'd know."

"And why shouldn't I? Are only men allowed to-"

The chamber groaned and lurched like an ailing stomach. Dust shivered from the cracks in the walls, tumbling like waterfalls in the wavering candlelight.

"What the-?" Dirk staggered as the floor heaved beneath him.

There was a crash as a statue fell from its pedestal and shattered on the floor, fragments of perfectly sculpted muscle disappearing beneath the threadbare velvet sofas. Half a face slid to a halt at Dirk's feet, one eye staring up at him in shock.

Louis stood on his dais in the centre of the room, ordering his courtiers to save the art, to tell him what was happening, to make it all stop. His voice rose as they failed to fulfil each contradictory demand in turn, rushing about and past him in bewilderment, an unfocused swirl of lace fringing and official sashes. He grew louder and louder, taller and taller as he stretched up onto his toes, trying to rise above the anarchy and grab their attention. One arm raised high, his body stretched into an angrily quavering arrow, until the ground followed him upwards. The floor rose, tiles flying as the centre of the room exploded, flinging him to the ground.

In a spray of dirt, a vast machine burst from the hole. A metal cylinder eight feet in diameter and thirty feet long, its front end was a cone covered in mechanical tools. Rows of drills and shovels spun through the air, hurling dirt and rocks around the room. Given space to vent, steam poured from the tunnel it had dug, surrounding the machine in a dense white cloud as it reared up and then crashed down onto the ballroom floor.

One courtier screamed. Another fired a pistol, the shot ricocheting off the machine's steel hull.

Dirk drew his Gravemaker and looked around the room.

"Where's Tim?" he asked.

"Where's the tablet?" Isabelle asked.

"You go left." Dirk headed right.

A hatch swung open in the side of the machine, clanging back against the hull. There was a smell of sweat and gun oil as Prussian soldiers poured out, rifles firing as they tried to get clear of the machine.

Louis was lying in the dirt, staring in shock at the chaos that had been his court. All around, the supposed cream of French society were rushing around like headless chickens. Half were arguing about who was in charge, half running for the door, only those closest to the Prussians getting to the dirty business of defending their home.

"The stone." Dirk grabbed Louis by the collar, hauling him to his feet. "Where is it?"

"Get your hands off me, you filthy ruffian!" The King's cool demeanour was entirely shattered, his eyes wild and mouth twisted in outrage.

"The stone." Dirk pointed his pistol at Louis. "I'm not messing around."

"Got it!" Blaze-Simms bounded over. He held his sword stick in one hand and a revolver in the other. Tied to his belt was a rare steak.

Behind him ran one of the serving dogs, a bloodhound with drool running across its long tongue, eyes fixed on the steak. In place of a drinks tray, it had the stone tablet strapped to its back.

"I thought I might need my hands free," Blaze-Simms explained, waving his gun for emphasis.

"Indeed you do." The voice was crisp, authoritative, and German. "Now please raise them."

Dirk turned to see a dozen Prussian soldiers, all with their rifles pointed at him and Blaze-Simms. Behind them stood an officer, gold braid glinting on his shoulders, hands clasped behind his back.

"I would not like to hurt you, Herr Dynamo," he continued. "But I need His Majesty."

It was hard to tell with the accent, but Dirk thought there was a hint of irony in the way he referred to Louis. More pressingly, he wondered how this stranger knew his name.

"Dirk," Blaze-Simms said quietly, "should we do like we did under London?"

Dirk thought back to that fight, in which they had overcome a far greater number of opponents than this. But the Underlord's men hadn't been professional soldiers armed with the latest firearms.

"No." He placed his revolver on the ground and raised his hands. "We should do like he says."

Blaze-Simms dropped his weapons. The dog leapt up, snatched the steak from his belt, and ran off through the rubble and steam.

"Ha!" Louis brushed the wrinkles from the front of his jacket. "I told you to unhand me."

"All of you into the carriage please." The Prussian officer pointed to the door on the side of the tunnelling machine.

"What?" The outrage was back in Louis's voice. "We had a deal-"

"A deal your troops have broken at every turn." The Prussian smiled smugly. "As we expected. Now get into the machine, Herr Bourbon, or get ready to meet your Maker."

#

The inside of the tunnelling machine was cramped and uncomfortable. Squeezed into a tiny compartment next to the rear engines, the metal floor was hard and hot beneath them. Rivets in the wall pressed into Dirk's back as he sat against it, running over escape plans. Next to him, Blaze-Simms was eagerly sketching the machine in his notebook, while Louis sat silent, looking like he'd smelled something bad and was sure it wasn't him.

The gas light held possibilities for escape. If Dirk smashed the front he could use a piece of glass as a knife. It would be too dangerous for the Prussians to fire their guns in here, though that only got him safely as far as the exit.

Maybe they could get through to the engine room and sabotage it. The door didn't look to have a lock, and you could stop most machines just by smashing things up. How that would help them get free he wasn't sure, but it was a starting point.

He glanced up at the soldier standing guard over them. Over six feet tall, his uniform bulged in all the places muscles went, and he held his rifle with casual confidence. All the Prussians they'd seen here so far had that look about them. Maybe this breakout wouldn't be so easy.

"Herr Dynamo." The officer appeared through the doorway into the main troop chamber. "Excuse the delay in dealing with you. We are mopping up courtiers before we resubmerge."

"That's the second time you've called me by name," Dirk said. "Have we met before?"

"I wish, Herr Dynamo." The officer undid two shining buttons on his jacket, reached inside and pulled out a slim book. Its well worn pages were fraying at the edges, but Dirk recognised the cover. "Proceedings of the Epiphany Club, Volume Seventy-Two. Your paper on self-improvement. The power and focus of your thoughts has been an inspiration to all of us in the Subterranean Strike Force."

The man next to him nodded.

"Is good, yes?" he said.

Dirk was used to being lost for words, but not like this. It was the one and only paper he'd ever contributed to the Club journal, and that after months of badgering by Blaze-Simms and Professor Barrow. Learning was his thing, not instructing.

"I didn't really write it," he said at last. Despite the circumstances he felt a swell of pride. He had dedicated so much of his life to knowledge, dreaming rather than expecting that his own thoughts might one day earn him praise. "Tim did that part. I just gave him ideas."

"But what ideas!" The officer opened the book and held out a page on exercise routines, complete with engravings of Dirk lifting weights. Mrs York, the club's artist in residence, had done a damn fine job of capturing his likeness. "Your focus, your commitment, your discipline, it perfectly matches the ethos of our unit. We have followed your exploits ever since. When I heard that you were in Paris, I dreamed that I might find you after the conquest, two like minds sharing the brotherhood of great men. I never dreamed I would meet you in the field. Yet I should have known that Dirk Dynamo would not miss out on a chance to shape the fate of nations."

"I'm not really a fate of nations guy." Dirk rose slowly to his feet. He didn't want to alarm the guard and get them shot, but this was starting to look like an opportunity. Nobody told him to sit back down. "To be honest, there ain't no reason we can't cooperate here. This war's between you and the French. I'm just looking for a stone."

"A stone?" The officer gave a disbelieving smile. "Really, Herr Dynamo, there is no need to lie. Whoever you are working with, there is no shame in taking a side when the world is at stake."

"No, really." Dirk pointed at Blaze-Simms. "You think I'd bring him to a war?"

"I say!" Blaze-Simms looked indignant for a moment, then seemed to think better of it. He shrugged. "No, fair point, I'm terrible in battles."

He went back to making notes.

"We're looking to get an archaeological artefact from this guy." Dirk pointed at the stiffly silent Louis. "Let us do that and we'll get out of your way."

The officer sighed and slid the journal back into his pocket.

"You disappoint me," he said. "Why do you waste your time scrabbling after trinkets? A man like yourself should not be limited in this way."

"I know my limits." Dirk spread his hands, as if to reveal himself. It gave him a bit more space to manoeuvre, and a shorter stretch to the guard and his gun. He shifted his weight, readying himself as he spoke. "I keep pushing those limits further every day. But what's the point of all that work on body and brain if I don't use it to make the world a better place?"

"The purpose is to become greater still." The officer laid a hand on Dirk's shoulder. "Greatness is its own reward. Most people are just small scraps of the world. You can be so much more. You have dominated yourself. Now make yourself greater, and dominate the world that surrounds you."

"I've seen what happens when men dominate one another." Dirk remembered the screams of battle, and those of slaves in the fields. "Ain't nothing great about that."

Something in his voice raised the Prussian's guard. His eyes narrowed and his hand tensed on Dirk's shoulder.

"I was told to bring this so-called king back alive," the Prussian said. "Everyone else is disposable."

Dirk didn't give him time to step back. Fast as a rattlesnake, he grabbed the officer's arm and twisted. The man turned in response to the pain, and Dirk slammed him into the guard.

"The gun!" he exclaimed as he grappled with the Prussians. "Grab the gun!"

The officer slammed him back against the wall, and the tiny compartment descended into a mass of flailing limbs and thudding bodies. There was no space for agile manoeuvring or well swung punches, just the awkward wrestling of close quarters combat. Choking, gouging, twisting, fighting for enough space to land a decent blow. Dirk found himself pressed against a metal grille, then on top of a heap of writhing bodies, then slamming his knee up into the guard's groin. At last he managed to knock the two Prussians' heads together, and they slumped to the floor.

Taking a deep breath, he looked around to see Louis and Blaze-Simms fighting over the rifle. Impatiently he pushed them apart, grabbed the gun and smashed the lock from the engine room door.

"I say!" Blaze-Simms followed him through the door. The air in here was hot and damp, filled with the clunk of busy pipework and the squeal of escaping steam. Most of the room was filled with fiercely pumping pistons, gnashing gears and loops of pipes, with dials and levers protruding into any available space. The parts were all shiny new, but they had been forced together in a chaotic, even desperate fashion, and some joins had already been rebuilt with rough solder and steel splints. This was a work of passion, not rational design – engineering as art.

"No time for notes." Dirk stopped his friend as he reached for his notebook. "I just want to reduce the number of complications we're dealing with."

"But..."

"No buts. What's the quickest way to break this thing?"

Blaze-Simms stepped past him and started examining the pipework.

"Maybe we could..." He stopped, staring at a mass of funnels and chambers attached to one wall.

"Time for action," Dirk said, "not inspiration."

"But look." Blaze-Simms pulled the device free, sighting along it like a rifle. Steam hissed from the place where it had fitted. "Someone has used my turbine design."

"Good for them." Dirk looked around. "Will that stop it?"

"No, you don't understand." Blaze-Simms held up the pipes. "I've never published this design. The only time I ever showed it to anyone was the party on Hakon. How has it ended up in a Prussian war machine?"

"I don't know." Dirk bit back a more forceful response. "But more guards could come this way any minute, so unless that turbine can wreck the machine-"

"Oh, of course it can!" Blaze-Simms grinned. Turning back to the steaming machinery, he twisted the turbine around and slotted it back into place, adjusting some pipes as he did so. He pulled a wrench from his pocket, unfastened and refastened several valves, while Dirk stood watch in the doorway. No-one stirred outside - Louis was gone, and no soldiers had come to find their unconscious commander.

Screeching, groaning sounds emerged from the engines.

"Time to go," Blaze-Simms said, as something popped loudly and a valve flew across the room.

They rushed through the door and down the tunnelling machine, which was now shaking beneath their feet. As they reached the exit hatch an alarmed looking Prussian soldier peered inside, and Dirk slammed the rifle butt into the side of his head. He fell and they leapt out over him, still running as the tunnelling carriage shook, rattled, and finally exploded with a roar of escaping steam.

The blast flung them to the ground, gears and chunks of metal plate whirling past their heads, and the world went black.

#

Dirk found himself drifting in a calm, yellow haze. A warm glow lifted him up. He was floating in a sea of positive energy.

Then real consciousness kicked in, and sharp reality with it. Rubble sticking at sharp angles into his back. A pounding head. Choking dust and smoke.

He opened his eyes.

Many of the room's inhabitants, French and Prussian alike, had been knocked from their feet by the blast. The rest stood dazed, staring in confusion as they clutched their weapons.

Dirk's ears were ringing as he rose to his feet and looked around. Across the room, he saw the bloodhound with the tablet strapped to its back. It stepped over a broken statue near the door, coat dusty and legs wobbling.

With the weary resilience of a veteran, Dirk forced himself to his feet and staggered after the dog. With each step he felt his strength and resolution returning. Spotting his pistol on the ground he stooped to grab it, only to see Isabelle and Louis arguing a half dozen paces to his left. The ringing in his ears blotted out half the words, but Louis was talking angrily about a letter and a bargain, while Isabelle frowned as haughtily as she could with her skirts and hair all blown to one side.

Still scrambling to get his thoughts together, Dirk grabbed Isabelle's arm and dragged her with him after the dog.

"Tablet." He pointed ahead of him, shouting to be heard.

"What?" Isabelle bellowed in his ear.

"Tablet!" He turned to face her. "The dog with the tablet, he's over there."

He turned to point again. Another figure stood in the doorway. A bruised, burly man in an ill-fitting grey suit. The bloodhound wasn't small, but he'd lifted it as casually as he might a glass of wine. Maurice sneered at Dirk, then turned and ran, out of the ballroom and away through the sewers, carrying the stone tablet with him.

Chapter 9: Vive la France!

There was a place for tracking in war zones. That had been Dirk's role often enough, as the blue and grey tried to outmanoeuvre each other across the length and breadth of a divided United States. Once you knew where to look, tracking an army was easy. Even tracking a patrol, if the area was undisturbed and you knew they were nearby. But tracking one man through a city that had turned into a battlefield? That was as close to impossible as these things got.

Try as he might to look for clues in the street outside Louis's court, he couldn't bring his usual focus to the task. His frustration at this failure was one of two internal distractions, an irrational, whining voice getting in the way of the work at hand.

"Have you found anything?" Isabelle leaned in close. The aftermath of the explosion was fading, their hearing returning to normal, but the city was still a noisy place.

"Still no," Dirk snapped. "And you're in the way."

He could have looked somewhere other than where she was standing, but why shouldn't he look there?

"Oh, for the love of God." Isabelle flung her hands in the air. "Will you please stop making life harder for the rest of us."

"I'm making life harder?" Dirk turned on her. "You're the one running round making secret deals between the Prussians and that mad bastard Louis. Or did you think I'd be too stupid to work it out?"

That was the other internal distraction, the piecing together of things he'd heard and seen. The letter Isabelle delivered when they first arrived at court. The Prussian's mention of a deal with Louis. The things that the so-called King had been shouting at Isabelle. Put it all together, and Dirk felt more hurt and betrayed than he had at the hotel.

Isabelle hesitated, her normally smooth demeanour faltering for the briefest moment.

"Yes," she said. "I made deals. That's how you get help. That's how you get information. That's how you create distractions and opportunities, if your favourite solution isn't just to punch everything in the face."

A band of Louis's irregulars retreated down the street, men in mismatched outfits carrying swords and clubs, a large dog with twisted muscles limping ahead of them. They were followed by the snap of gunfire as National Guardsmen followed, but the whole thing seemed half-hearted, the swagger gone from the royalists, the guardsmen advancing slowly and firing only occasionally.

"I say," Blaze-Simms called from the doorway behind them. "What now?"

A bullet clipped Dirk's sleeve and ricocheted off the nearby brickwork. He leapt for cover behind an abandoned wagon, Isabelle hurrying after him.

"Now we need to find the Dane." Dirk glanced back up the street. "Though I ain't entirely sure how we're going to do that."

More of Louis's troops were retreating toward them from another street, these ones pursued by Prussians. Everywhere Dirk looked, the streets were turning into a chaotic three-way melee, through which the organised Prussian assault troops were slowly but surely fighting their way toward domination.

"We should find Braithwaite," Isabelle said.

"What good's a merchant going to do us?" Dirk asked.

"Don't play the simpleton," she retorted.

"I'd rather be a simpleton than a schemer." Part of Dirk's brain screamed at him to pay attention to the fighting. But he couldn't drag his mind away from her or from the anger he was feeling. "You gonna make another deal with Braithwaite, get him caught up in this too?"

"He's already part of this." Isabelle glared at him. "Haven't you been paying any attention?"

"I've been a little busy saving our lives at every-"

A hand clamped across Dirk's mouth. Noriko was at his side, staring at him with a look as hard as steel.

"Dirk and I will scout," she said. "You two stay here."

"Of course." Isabelle's triumphant tone made Dirk want to disagree, but Noriko's hand was like a vice around his arm, dragging him from doorway to doorway up the street until he began following her of his own accord.

She was right, and he knew it. They needed to get the lay of the land.

The end of the street opened into a wide square full of ruined market stalls. Cavalry had been in action here, and the ground was scattered with the broken bodies of horses and riders. A nearby horse raised her head, looking at Dirk with sad eyes, blood dribbling from the corner of her mouth. The injustice of it was heart-rending - this wasn't the horses' fight. It never was.

There was still fighting nearby, but not in the square itself. Dirk was about to head down a side street when Noriko once more grabbed hold of him, slamming him up against a wall. He knew that she was strong, but he still found himself amazed to be lifted from his feet by a woman a foot shorter than him. It was that amazement that gave her time to speak before he could fight free.

"You bring shame upon yourself," she snapped. "You are like a small boy who has broken his toy, and now punishes his mother for not buying another."

"I don't know what-"

"Isabelle." Noriko tightened her grip. "She does not deserve your hate."

Dirk could feel his cheeks reddening with embarrassment.

"I know it ain't the time," he admitted. "But it burns me up. You don't know-"

"I know." Noriko set him back on his feet, but did not release her grip. "I know that you two shared a bed. I know you have learnt that there were others, including your friend, and that this upsets you. But unlike you, I understand. This is not a fair world. A woman's life is bound around by the limits set by men. Rules, laws, expectations. You think she takes a false name for pleasure? You think I chose a path of violence because it excited me?

"You have the life you want by being forceful and open. She must do it through secrets, facing the strain and the sorrow that comes with that. Do not mistake what is soft for what is easy. And do not think, just because you have a penis, that you are entitled to take pleasure in what a woman cannot."

Right then, Dirk wished the whole war would come pouring down on them. He would rather face three armies than the shame Noriko's words had stirred. Without the self-righteous fury that had defended him from Isabelle's arguments, he found himself defenceless, knowing full well that he was in the wrong.

"You're right," he mumbled, staring at his feet.

"Good." Noriko let him go. "I do not want to die because you are distracted." She looked away, casting an evaluating gaze over the square. "Nor for my friend to have chosen poorly in love."

Those last few words stirred a fonder feeling in Dirk, a reminder of the joys that had got him to this point. There was something here he wanted to save, something far more precious than a stone tablet or a victory in war.

The sounds of violence grew louder back the way they had come.

"We should go get the others," Dirk said.

"No." Noriko pointed to the street mouth. Isabelle and Blaze-Simms were dashing their way, the inventor limping from his injury of the night before. Behind them came a dozen French guardsmen, their faces wide with panic.

"I know you said to wait," Blaze-Simms gasped between breaths. "But things got a little hairy."

There was a roar, and the roof of a nearby building exploded. A hot air balloon floated into view, Prussian colours painted across its canvas. The crew leaned over the sides, round objects in their hands.

"Aerial grenadiers." Blaze-Simms was grinning despite the danger. "The future of warfare!"

"I'm more worried about the future of us." Dirk led them in a dash from cover to cover across the square. French troops of both sides were emerging from the surrounding streets, as many of them firing upon each other as upon the Prussians, even as another grenade shattered the waggon behind which the first soldiers had hidden.

Together with Noriko, Dirk leapt through the broken window of an otherwise undamaged café and turned to help the others through. The walls looked sturdy enough to protect them from stray bullets, and the ceiling would shelter them from the balloon bombers.

As he turned to grab a table and reinforce their defences, he saw that they were not alone. In a corner of the room stood Captain Renard, the same National Guard officer who had led his men in attacking them. He held a sabre out unconvincingly in front of him. The redness of his face looked to be more embarrassment than exertion.

"I am regrouping," Captain Renard declared.

"Course you are." To Dirk's eye, Renard didn't look ready for any kind of fight. Experience had taught him that a lack of readiness didn't always stop people. "You going to cause us trouble?"

"That depends." Renard glanced out the window. "Are you really Prussian agents, as my men believed?"

"We're hiding in here from Prussian soldiers," Dirk said. "What do you think?"

Renard nodded. "I see no reason for trouble."

Dirk shook his head and turned to his companions. "Mrs McNair, you were saying something about Braithwaite?"

"Um,yes." Isabelle blinked. "But all this..."

She waved toward the battle growing in intensity outside the window.

"This war has become a hindrance, not a useful distraction." Noriko watched the ebb and flow of combat, sword in hand. "But we cannot leave it without the shame of defeat."

"This war is an absurdity," Renard called out from his corner. "You think true Frenchmen want to fight each other when invaders are here? It makes a mockery of us all!"

"Reckon you're making yourself mockery enough, Captain." Dirk pointed at the man's dropping sword and the dusty gold frocking of his epaulettes.

Renard frowned but said nothing more.

"Any smart ideas?" Dirk looked from Blaze-Simms, who was sketching pictures of strangely shaped hot air balloons, toward Isabelle. He fought the urge to look away, instead holding her gaze and keeping his voice as steady as he could. "Seems you're better at being smart than I am."

It wasn't much of an apology, but maybe it would do for now.

Isabelle laughed and shook her head.

"I was all ready for another fight," she said. "But it seems that making peace is the way forwards." When she looked up there was a spark in her eye. "And maybe not just for us."

She turned toward Captain Renard.

"You strike me as a good officer," she said, despite the evidence. "If the men in the square, royalist and republican, were to focus on fighting the Prussians, could you get out there and lead them against the invaders?"

"Of course!" Renard puffed up with pride. "But these royalist scum, they keep attacking us."

"Then let's see what we can do about that." Isabelle strode over to the window and peered out at the grey sky above Paris. "Noriko, gentlemen, I want the Prussian balloon."

"Which one?" Timothy pointed across the rooftops. More of the craft were drifting in, some with men leaning over the sides, others with rifles pointed from the baskets.

There was a clunk as something hit the ground outside.

"Down!" Dirk yelled.

They all dropped to the floor as the grenade exploded, smashing the remaining glass from the window and leaving a blackened scar on the pavement. Despite the bombing the struggle continued in the square. The French had mostly stopped fighting each other, but they were divided and disorganised, being pushed back by the steadily advancing Prussians. The Royalists' attack dogs had scattered into hiding behind shop fronts and fallen bodies.

"How on earth are you going to make peace out of that?" Blaze-Simms asked.

"Get me a balloon and I'll show you," Isabelle said.

Dirk poked his head out of the window, looking to see where the lowest balloon was. If he could get up onto the rooftops, and then got lucky about which way the balloons drifted, maybe he could lasso one. Though he didn't have rope, and he wasn't sure what the lasso would catch on. He could try jumping from a rooftop, but he was tired, stiff and aching. He'd need the balloon to be really close to one of the buildings, at which point the occupants would be shooting at him or dropping bombs as he balanced on sloping tiles. Any way he looked at it, he didn't like his chances.

He took a deep breath, getting ready to give it a go.

"Keep them from shooting at me." Noriko stood with one foot on the edge of the shattered window, swords sheathed at her sides. "I will do the rest."

Before they could reply she leapt, grabbed the top of the window frame and pulled herself out of sight.

"You heard the lady." Dirk pulled out his pistol. "Let's give her some cover."

A dozen yards away, a Prussian was pointing his rifle at Noriko. Dirk jumped through the window and charged. The Prussian turned too late. Dirk knocked him out with a single punch, catching the rifle as it fell and throwing it back to Blaze-Simms. He grabbed another from beside a fallen royalist and flung that one to Isabelle, along with a cartridge belt. Settling in behind the cover of a bench, he set to firing on anyone who looked like aiming at Noriko.

Her ascent up the building, when he had a moment to watch, was a wonder to behold. Using the slightest of protrusions she climbed as easily as a spider, and yet her movements had a dancer's easy grace. She hung single-handed from the gaps between bricks, balanced on one foot on the back of a flagpole, jumped five feet sideways and grabbed a window ledge without the slightest hesitation.

Meanwhile, Dirk and the others laid down a hail of fire, as much for a distraction as to hurt anyone aiming at their ally. Royalists, guardsmen and Prussians all ducked for cover or ran off in search of easier targets. That didn't stop some of the Prussian soldiers pausing to return fire, bullets ricocheting off the café and surrounding buildings.

Given a moment's pause, Dirk became briefly aware that there were already two bullet wounds on his arm, the injuries forgotten in the rush of events. They weren't bleeding enough to be a problem, and he turned back to the fight.

An explosion shook the air to Dirk's left as one of the balloons came close, the crew dropping explosives on whoever was unfortunate enough to be below them. He looked up, expecting to see a cluster of men in Prussian blue, and was surprised to see that one of the four wore a grey suit.

"People of Paris." The man in the grey suit was speaking through the funnel of a loudhailer. His French was clearly and unmistakably that of a native. "Do not resist. If we surrender to the Prussians all will be well. Lay down your arms."

A black shape flew across the gap between the building and the balloon. As she hit the basket, Noriko knocked one of the Prussians out of it. His arms flailed briefly as he plummeted to the ground. Another followed him, and Noriko disappeared into the basket. It rocked back and forth, then the man in grey came tumbling over the side, screaming as he fell. He landed near Dirk with a wet thud and a clang as his loudhailer hit the pavement.

Even spattered with blood, the cut and colour of the suit were very familiar. Dirk wondered if all the Dane's goons went to the same tailor, or if this was just standard Parisian gangster chic.

The last member of the crew appeared at the side of the balloon and flung the end of a rope down to the ground below. Noriko was just visible, holding a blade to his throat.

Grabbing the rope, Dirk held it steady as he waved to Isabelle and Blaze-Simms.

"Let's get out of here," he shouted.

As Isabelle ran over she grabbed the loudhailer, sliding her hand through a strap on the handle. She looked back to Renard.

"Get ready," she shouted at him. "You need to take charge of your men."

As she began climbing the rope Blaze-Simms followed, slowed by his injured leg. Dirk turned to fire a final shot at a royalist looking their way, and then scrambled up, climbing hand over hand as fast as he could. A single bullet whistled past, but most of the combatants were too busy to care about three civilians and a balloon that had stopped bombing them.

He reached the top just as Isabelle raised the loudhailer to her mouth.

"Soldiers of King Louis, you have been betrayed!" Enhanced by the loudhailer, her passionate, commanding tone filled the embattled streets beneath them. "His so-called majesty arranged this invasion by the Prussians, so that he could seize the throne. Is this the action of a true

King of France? To bring her enemies to your doorstep for his own greed?"

There was a mixture of boos and cheers from below. Another shot zipped past the balloon.

"I know you do not believe me," Isabelle continued. "I would not. But I hold in my hand incontrovertible proof - a copy of the letter by which Louis and Chancellor Bismarck sealed this wretched deal!"

She held up a handful of paper - blank pages torn from one of Blaze-Simms's notebooks. Dirk grinned. Any paper would look the same to the folks down on the ground. The success of this wouldn't be about truth, it would be about how much the French wanted to stop fighting each other. And judging by how bad things had been on the ground, he figured they might want that a lot now.

"See how the National Guard turn their guns away from you and onto the invaders." As Isabelle continued, Dirk saw Captain Renard moving through the nearest Guardsmen, ordering them to focus on the Prussians. Royalists followed their lead, or perhaps Isabelle's, happy to focus on the foreigners. Their battered looking lion roared, and then was sent charging into the Prussian ranks, to great cheers from all the French. "Do not spill the blood of your brothers, but act like true Frenchman, bound together by blood and by the love of mother country.

"Vive la France!"

She took a deep breath, and shouted the words again.

"Vive la France!"

The cry was echoed by the fighters below.

"Vive la France!

"Vive la France!"

Joining together, the French forces drove the Prussians out of the square and back down the street, while some fired at the balloons up above.

Isabelle turned to look at Dirk.

"Will that work?" she asked.

"Are you kidding?" He grinned at her. "You were amazing."

He turned his attention to the remaining member of the Prussian balloon crew, who stood nervously in the corner of the basket, Noriko's blade half an inch from his throat.

"Give it a few hours, and your whole army's gonna be chased from this city." In the cramped confines of the balloon, Dirk loomed over their captive. "You want to be handed over to a million angry Frenchmen, that's your choice. But if you want the chance to run away with your buddies, we need something from you.

"Tell us where you picked up the man in the grey suit. We want to have words with his boss."

Chapter 10: Café Danemark

Their first stop was an alleyway near Louis's court, only two blocks from where they had seized the balloon. They moored to the narrow balcony of a loft apartment, to the entertainment of the artist and his model who sat within, sipping absinthe beside a half-finished oil painting. Dirk looked away in embarrassment as the model raised her glass in salute, the movement dislodging the sheet that had concealed her breasts.

He scrambled down the rope to the ground below, followed by the Prussian balloon pilot. The man had told them what they needed to know, and keeping him meant having to keep an eye on him.

As the soldier disappeared out the far end of the street, Dirk turned to a pile of abandoned crates. Wincing from his injuries, he moved aside the upper crates, revealing the luggage they had hidden before confronting Louis.

He tied the first of the bags, including Blaze-Simms's ridiculous experimental rifle, onto the end of the rope and gave it a tug. As Noriko hauled it up, Dirk heard the sound of hooves. A horse was galloping toward him out of the dingier end of the alley, its eyes wild, tattered heraldry flapping from an embossed saddle. On top of the frantic steed sat Louis XXI, the King in Shadow.

"Out of my way, peasant!" he screamed. His once gleaming armour was dented and stained, his hair full of brick dust.

Dirk pressed himself against the grimy brickwork, and as the King galloped past there was a flash of recognition across his face.

"This is not over!" Louis yelled defiantly as he approached the alley mouth. "The rightful King of France will-"

A plank of wood swung into view, knocking him from the saddle. He hit the ground with a clang. The horse kept running, while its rider lay sprawled in the gutter.

A large, familiar figure leapt down from a cart beside the alley mouth.

"Braithwaite?" Dirk exclaimed.

"That were one hell of a swing, if I do say so myself." The Yorkshireman looked at him with a grin, the plank held easily in one muscled hand. "Maybe I'll play cricket for Yorkshire yet."

"What are doing here?" Dirk asked.

"This and that," Braithwaite said. "I heard you lot were round here too." He nodded and two pairs of hands appeared, dragging Louis out of sight. "You deal with His Nibs," he said to whoever had taken the King. "I'll meet you back at the embassy."

He strolled toward Dirk, stroking thoughtfully at his beard.

"Where's the rest of your lot?" he asked.

As if in response there was a rustling from behind Dirk. Isabelle dropped the last few feet from the rope to the ground.

"Mr Braithwaite." She held out her hand, as calm and refined as if they had met at a party instead of an alley smelling of rot and gunsmoke. "So good to see you."

"You too, Mrs McNair." Braithwaite winked. "And yon slab of muscle."

"What the hell are you doing here?" Dirk asked again. "These streets ain't safe for a merchant."

"Aye, lad." Braithwaite nodded. "But that's not all I do."

Dirk tensed. Here it came, whatever was really going on. Was Braithwaite about to become one more barrier to their mission?

"I've had about enough of tricks and lies." He reached for his pistol. "You'd better gimme a clue what's going on, or there's gonna be trouble."

"Mr Braithwaite is with British intelligence." Isabelle laid a restraining hand on Dirk's arm. "Isn't that right?"

"Aye, lass." Braithwaite grinned. "Well deduced."

"If you're a spy, shouldn't you be keeping that secret?" Dirk asked.

"Aye, maybe," Braithwaite said. "But then how could we work together on catching the Dane?"

#

Weighed down with their baggage and the bulk of George Braithwaite, the balloon drifted more slowly across the rooftops of Paris. Blaze-Simms, given access to his tools and materials, cobbled together a small engine that spun a rotor blade, propelling them in the direction they needed to go. Everyone was delighted to see him at work again until he started fixing attachments to the loudhailer. The first noise it made shook the teeth in Dirk's head and nearly blew out the flame on the balloon's burner. The next made him clap his hands over his ears in pain.

"Enough!" He snatched the loudhailer, and was immediately punished with a look of hurt on his friend's face. "Just save it for later, OK? Maybe get working on that gun of yours again, in case we get into trouble."

"Oh yes!" Blaze-Simms took the steam rifle from its case and began fiddling with the glowing green power source on the back.

Isabelle was still quizzing Braithwaite on his pursuit of the Dane.

"So you were after him on Hakon?" she asked.

"Aye." Braithwaite nodded. "He's been a pain in the arse of Her Majesty's Government for over a decade. I'd used the guano trade as cover before, so when we heard he were going to Hakon I got sent. Never managed to ferret the bugger out - he's good at hiding his identity - but after that there were rumours he was back in Paris. And as he and thee seemed to run into each other all the time, I kept an eye on thee too."

Much as he hated to be played, Dirk had to admire what Braithwaite had done. Following his enemy's enemy had got him to where he wanted to be - with them, on their way to the Dane's lair.

"There." Noriko pulled the string to let more air out of the balloon, beginning the slow descent to a square lined with pavement cafés. With the precision that seemed to come so naturally to her, she landed at the centre of the square. Leaping out, she secured them by ropes to a bench and a small fountain, leaving the balloon inflated and ready for a quick getaway.

The square was quiet and well kept, the violence of the city not having touched it. Piles of fallen leaves lay around the trees at the edge of the square. Beyond them were the narrow fronts of cafés, bakeries and delicatessens.

"I expected something grander," Blaze-Simms said as he clambered out of the basket, gun in hand.

"Then you haven't dealt with many criminals," Dirk said. "At least not the successful sort."

He thought of all the conmen, spies and felons he'd tracked in his time with the Pinkertons. The difficult ones weren't the ones living in luxury; they were the ones who hid their wealth and influence behind anonymous façades. Of course most couldn't resist at least a small, subtle tell.

A Danish flag hung from the window of a nearby café.

"Reckon we're in the right place," he said.

The Café Danemark wasn't the sort of business that would draw in many customers. Paint flaked from the woodwork in thin coloured scabs, revealing a long history of fading fashions. The awning was water-stained and spotted with black dots of mould. The windows were in desperate need of cleaning.

It was exactly the sort of place Dirk would have chosen.

As they approached the door, a large man in a grey suit emerged to block their path.

"Closed." He folded his arms and stared at them.

"I don't think so." Dirk punched him so fast the man didn't have time to react, beyond curling over around the pain in his stomach. They walked past him and into the café.

The place was far smarter inside than out. A shiny new coffee machine hissed away behind a counter decorated with plates of golden pastries. Another man in a grey suit stood at the counter, behind which a waiter stood, shirt sleeves rolled up, an apron hanging from his waist. But they didn't hold Dirk's attention. As he peered into the shadows at the back of the café he saw a small, pale man in a yellow jacket.

In that moment a lot became clearer. Now he knew who had given the Dane's thugs their orders on Hakon. Who had sold Blaze-Simms's technology to the Prussians. And at last, the identity of the Dane.

Dirk felt the satisfaction that came at the end of the hunt.

"Noriko, Braithwaite, Tim, you keep these gents company." As Dirk spoke, there was a cracking of knuckles and a hiss as the ninja drew her sword. Blaze-Simms pulled out the loudhailer and started playing with its mechanism once more. "Isabelle and I are going to have a chat with this gent."

He pulled out a chair for Isabelle across the table from the man in the yellow jacket, then sat in the one next to it. There was a calculating look in her eyes as she shifted her gaze from the man in yellow to Dirk and then back again.

The man, unperturbed, continued to drink his coffee.

"We meet again, Mr Dynamo," he said. "And of course Mrs McNair. Always Mrs McNair."

Isabelle's grip tightened around the clasp of her handbag, but she remained silent.

"You gave us a French name when we met on Hakon," Dirk said. "Regy something."

"Regis Marat." The man put down his cup and dabbed at his lips with a napkin. "That is correct."

"So that's part of how you get away with your crimes, huh?" Dirk stared at the Dane. "By pretending to be from other countries."

The Dane sighed and put the napkin down.

"English is such a literal language," he said. "Its lack of nuance clouds your thinking. As always, you Anglophones cannot achieve the shades of subtlety needed for the real world."

"You really think this is the time to insult me?" Dirk pulled out his Gravemaker, pointed the heavy pistol at the Dane's chest.

"Absolutely." The Dane gave no more than a flicker of the eyes, but it was enough to make Dirk look behind him.

A dozen men in loose grey suits had appeared outside the café windows, pointing guns in at Dirk and his friends. As he stared, a door at the back of the room opened and three more emerged. Among them was the bruised yet triumphant looking Maurice, with whom was a bloodhound, the stone tablet still strapped to its back.

"Please lower your weapons," the Dane said softly. "I am very fond of this place. Having kept the Prussians away, I would not like to see it ruined by you."

Dirk lowered his gun.

"What did you think, that this would be like something from Shakespeare?" The Dane held up his cup, and one of the men in grey refilled it with coffee. "The rogue confesses himself and gently accepts defeat, content with 'at least I am an honest villain'? I control half the crime in Europe. I was hardly going to be defeated by a war-weary colonial and a childish inventor. Not even once they allied with Britain's crafty Mr Braithwaite."

"You two know each other, huh?" Dirk sank back into his seat. Robbed of the momentum they had been building, he felt his injuries and exhaustion weighing him down.

"Of course." The Dane's smile was a small, miserly thing. "We worked in the same field, once upon a time. But though I love my country, I love it as a republic. I could not continue to serve under another Napoleon."

"Wait." Dirk blinked. "You're with intelligence. French intelligence?"

"I am no more a Dane than you are a Dynamo. Amazing the power of words, is it not, to throw men off our trails?"

Taking a croissant from the plate beside him, the Dane held it out to the dog. It took a few eager steps forward, sniffed at the pastry and then gobbled it down. With one hand the Dane patted the dog, while with the other he unfastened the tablet from its back.

"You're part of all this chaos, aren't you?" Dirk gestured toward the door and the war-torn city beyond. "Working with the Prussians to sink Napoleon's regime, hoping to bring back the republic."

"That is one part of it." The Dane looked up from the stone to Isabelle. "Like others, I have played many sides against each other, to create the conditions I desire. And of course there is the bigger picture." He held up the tablet. "So much of what I stole was meant to fund my activities. But these stones, this path to the Library of Alexandria, they represent so much more. A fresh intellectual renaissance for whichever nation finds the Library. A resurgence in learning that I can use to restore national pride." He shrugged. "Of course their value also helps. As a criminal mastermind, one becomes accustomed to a certain lifestyle."

Reaching across the table, he took Dirk's gun.

"Another fine piece." He pointed it at Dirk. "And a most fitting way for you to die."

Dirk looked at the table in front of him, the armed thugs all around, and his own gun pointing at his chest. There had to be a way out of this, but he wasn't seeing it. He turned to look at the others. Noriko's sword had been taken by the Dane's men, as had Blaze-Simms's gun. The inventor still held his loudhailer and a handful of wires, but no weapons.

"Sorry, buddy," Dirk said.

"Me too." Blaze-Simms looked down meaningfully at the loudhailer and then back up at Dirk. He winked. "This is going to hurt."

Dirk got his hands over his ears just in time. As Blaze-Simms touched two wires together, the loudhailer let out an ear-splitting shriek. The windows exploded, and the Dane's goons fell, clutching their heads, one of them vomiting from the pain. The noise lasted a second before smoke poured from the loudhailer and Blaze-Simms dropped it, but that was enough.

Slamming the table back, Dirk trapped the Dane against the wall. He grabbed his gun with one hand and the tablet with the other, then bolted for the door. Maurice was trying to pull himself upright, and Dirk kicked him in the teeth as he passed, knocking him out cold.

He rushed into the square, his friends staggering after him. They had all taken the same hint he had, and though Braithwaite looked nauseous, no-one was in as much pain as the Dane and his men.

Overhead, a Prussian balloon drifted past, its crew dropping grenades into the nearby streets.

Reaching their balloon, Dirk turned to cover the criminals with his gun. Isabelle passed him and vaulted into the basket, followed by Noriko, while Braithwaite stood, hands on knees, dry heaving. Blaze-Simms ran to unfasten the ropes.

"Let's get out of here," Dirk said.

Cold steel pressed behind his ear.

"I'm sorry about this," Isabelle said. "But I'm afraid the time has come to part ways."

Chapter 11: There Is More At Stake

"I need you to drop the tablet into the basket." Isabelle sounded regretful as she pressed the barrel of a gun against Dirk's skin. "Make any other move and I'll add your brains to the Prussian firework display."

"What the hell?" Dirk froze. If this was a joke then it was one hell of a poor one.

"The stone." Her voice was like ice now, hard and cold. "I'm very fond of you, Dirk, but I won't ask again."

Dirk reached back over the edge of the basket and dropped the tablet inside. As he did so he inched his gun around.

"Stop that at once," she said. "After everything we've been through, do you think that I can't spot you trying to be furtive? And Timothy, hands out of pockets. You've such a splendid mind, I'd hate it to end up decorating the cobbles."

Dirk flung his pistol away across the square. He had never been one to surrender easily, but he couldn't even think of fighting back against Isabelle. He could barely even believe that she was doing this, and the thought of it opened a chasm in his mind, an overwhelming darkness over which he hung helpless.

The Dane emerged from the café.

"Bravo, Mrs McNair," he called out. "I knew that you would see reason in the end."

The chasm opened wider. If Dirk had believed in souls then he would have believed that his own was utterly and irretrievably crushed.

He loved Isabelle McNair, and she was betraying him with the man they were fighting against.

"Why?" he asked. "How?"

"I'm sorry, Dirk." Was it his imagination, or could he feel the gun trembling where it pressed against his skull. "But it was always going to end something like this. If I find the Great Library with a man, any man, then the discovery will be his. The fame, the glory, the status, it will all go to him. Worse, all the secrets hidden there with fall into the hands of the same men who bring us futile wars like this one, who keep us pinned in marriages and kitchens, who do not even realise how much worse life is for the other half of humanity."

A Prussian grenade exploded near the Café Danemark, sending the Dane's recovering men running back inside. The Dane himself walked slowly toward them, his pale face triumphant.

"Stop there, Regis," Isabelle called out.

There was a click as Noriko raised a gun and pointed it out of the balloon. The Dane frowned.

"I thought we had a deal," he said.

"You all did." Isabelle sounded weary. "I had an agreement with the Epiphany Club too, so that I could use their skills and resources to find the stones. But here is the only deal that matters. Whatever Noriko and I find at the Great Library, its fate will be decided by women, not men. For once, the future will be in our hands.

"Mr Braithwaite, which do you care about more, the tablets or the Dane?"

A smile split Braithwaite's face.

"This fella." He gestured toward the Dane.

"Then you can have him, as long as you cover these chaps too while we leave."

"It's a deal." Braithwaite picked up Dirk's gun, then moved to cover him, Blaze-Simms and the Dane. "I weren't expecting this, but tis better than a poke in the eye with a dog turd."

Isabelle pushed Dirk gently away from her and the balloon basket. He turned, stunned, to look at her.

"But I love you," he whispered, only then realising how heart-rendingly true it was.

"And I..." She couldn't look him in the eye, though she kept her pistol trained on him. "I'm frightfully fond of you. But I cannot let another man stand in my way. There is more at stake than just us."

There was a twang as Noriko sliced through the last mooring rope, and a roar as she turned a valve on the balloon's burner. It lifted off the ground and sailed upward, past a descending Prussian balloon, rising faster with each passing moment.

The sounds of war had grown quieter. Dirk was distantly aware of panicked movements from the crew of the sinking Prussian balloon, and of a flapping from their vessel's damaged canvas. The invasion of Paris, a technological assault that came up from the ground and down out of the air, was coming to a messy end, and an inglorious one for the invaders. One more thing Isabelle had achieved.

She was amazing.

"Is this really it?" The Dane sneered at Dirk. "A woman deceives you and you give up?"

Dirk turned, sadness turning to anger.

"I ain't given up on dealing with you," he said, and pointed at the gun-wielding Braithwaite. "If it weren't for him I'd come over there and knock that smirk off your face."

"And if it weren't for him I would be gone." The Dane pointed at Braithwaite too. "But we cannot all have our way."

"Maybe you can't," Dirk growled, "but I'm done taking other people's shit." He turned and advanced toward Braithwaite. "You really gonna shoot me, George?"

"I might." Braithwaite fired a warning shot at Dirk's feet.

The threat would have stopped any reasonable man. But Dirk wasn't feeling reasonable. Slowly, step by step, he advanced toward Braithwaite.

"No need for this." Braithwaite spoke firmly as he pointed the gun at Dirk's chest, all his attention now that way. "I don't want to-"

The Dane slammed into Braithwaite. The Frenchman was so slender that he bounced off the massive British agent. Braithwaite turned in surprise and Dirk leapt, grabbing the gun with one hand and punching him with the other. He wrenched the Gravemaker from Braithwaite's hand, sent him reeling with another punch, and turned to see a dozen grey-suited gangsters advancing from the café and across the square.

At the far side, the Prussian balloon had almost hit the ground. One of the crewmen leapt out and it bobbed briefly upward again.

"Back off!" Dirk pointed his gun at the Dane. The criminal goons stopped uncertainly. "Tim, you think you can get that balloon to fly?"

"Of course!" Blaze-Simms limped excitedly across the square, as the Prussian craft dipped once more toward the ground. "There's plenty of ballast to lose, and in my pocket I have a-"

"Yes was enough." Still covering the Dane and Braithwaite, Dirk backed across the Parisian cobbles.

"Frightfully sorry." There was a thud as Blaze-Simms dragged the remaining Prussian from the balloon and then clambered aboard. "I say Dirk, there's lots of unnecessary ballast."

There was a thud and then another. Dirk turned to see the balloon starting to ascend, Blaze-Simms looking around excitedly and then in some concern.

"Ah," the inventor said. "Need to get you on board."

Dirk didn't wait for a solution. Holstering his gun, he sprinted across the square and leapt, catching the edge of the basket. As he clambered on board, Blaze-Simms was flinging bombs and other military equipment out over the side.

Looking back, Dirk saw the Dane's men chasing George Braithwaite out of the square. The master criminal himself stood, a distinctive figure in his yellow jacket, waving at the balloon with a sardonic grin.

"Bon chance!" the Dane shouted.

They rose out of the square and up above the rooftops. Below, the last of the Prussians who had tunnelled into the city were being rounded up by uniformed guardsmen and the ragtag irregulars who had followed Louis. The sky was grey overhead, the wind cold.

Dirk turned to look east, the way Isabelle had flown. Sadness weighed at him again.

"I'm sorry, old chap." Blaze-Simms laid a sympathetic hand on his shoulder. "All really isn't fair in love and war."

"No it ain't." Dirk gripped the edge of the basket, sorrow turning to resolve. He wasn't going to let a betrayal stand, no matter who had done it.

"I think I have enough parts for another navigational propeller." Blaze-Simms pulled a handful of gears from his pocket. "Shall we head home?"

"Hell no." Dirk pointed into the growing gloom of dusk. "Don't you remember, we've got a library to find."

Book 4: Sieges and Silverware

Chapter 1: The Red Castle

Night was falling as the hot air balloon reached the walls of the Red Castle.

"You sure this is the place?" Dirk Dynamo peered through the grey shroud of dusk toward their destination. It was quite unlike the fortifications he had seen in the Civil War. Those had been lines of trenches with wooden palisades and heaps of earth. This was a fortress out of the distant past, towers stretching up from the tree-lined German hillside, reaching like crimson fingers into a grey sky.

"This is it." Sir Timothy Blaze-Simms stood beside him, a screwdriver in one hand and a clutch of gears in the other. "Given the supplies Isabelle took on at that last town there were only two options, and recent weather means-"

"Yes was enough." Dirk drew his Gravemaker, the revolver's heavy cylinder gleaming in the last light of day. Glancing at Blaze-Simms, he saw a hesitant look on the face of the English inventor. "Don't worry, I'm not going in all guns blazing. I just want to be ready."

With a sputtering sound, the motor Blaze-Simms had rigged on the back of the basket propelled them toward the castle. Dirk released some of the hot air, lowering them smoothly across the battlements.

An elderly servant in a tailcoat stood staring at them, hands clasped behind his back. At his nod, two teenagers in livery sprung forward and took the ropes Dirk had lowered, securing the balloon to the crenellations. Even before they had finished, Dirk leapt down onto the stonework and looked around in the light of burning torches. Behind him, Blaze-Simms scrambled from the basket, accompanied by the rattle of gears and gadgets in his pockets.

The elderly servant held out a gloved hand and said something in German.

"You catch that?" Dirk asked.

"Sorry, what?" Blaze-Simms looked up from a gargoyle cut from the same reddish stone as the walls around it.

"Ah, you are British?" The butler's expression didn't change as he shifted into English, but Dirk thought there was less of a formal edge to his voice.

"He is." He pointed at Blaze-Simms. "I'm American."

"Oh." Was it possible for a man's face to fall without moving a muscle? If it was, then the butler managed it. "May I have your card please?"

"Do I look like I'm carryin' a card?" Dirk said, gesturing toward the battered balloon, his shirt and pants, and the bruises still fading from his face.

"I'm afraid I don't know what passes for normal in America." The butler managed to make the last word sound like a curse, and it made Dirk's blood boil. With the least possible movement, the servant turned to face Blaze-Simms. "Sir, do you-"

"There's no need for that." Isabelle McNair stepped out of the shadows of the nearest tower. Cool and refined in a blue silk dress, she treated them to a welcoming smile. "I know these gentlemen."

Dirk felt like someone had grabbed hold of his insides and twisted them until everything was knotted with tension. Rage and longing battled inside him at the sight of the woman he had thought he loved and who had betrayed him. He fought to take long, deep breaths, calming his hammering heart.

"Mrs McNair." He couldn't keep the edge from his voice. Everything about her reminded him of Paris, both the good and the bad. It was the bad that threatened to overwhelm him as he pressed his anger down. "We've come a long way to talk with you."

"And I look forward to that conversation," she said. "Though I must confess, I barely know where to start."

"Sorry would be nice." Blaze-Simms looked absurd in indignation, his scowl so serious atop his incorrectly buttoned tailcoat. At least he could put into words what Dirk couldn't. "I think it's the least we deserve. We worked just as hard as you to find those stones, and you just snatched them away."

"If I were sorry, I would not have done it." Isabelle took a step forward, her attention on Dirk. "But I hope that, with time, you might forgive me."

"That don't seem likely," he said through gritted teeth.

"Of course not." Isabelle smiled, though there was sadness in her eyes. The wind caught a lock of her black, curling hair as she offered him her arm. "Shall we go inside?"

Dirk thrust his hands into his pockets and nodded toward the stairs.

"After you," he said.

"You could at least be civil." Isabelle's voice was cold and sharp as broken ice.

"I'll save that for those who deserve it. I ain't a hypocrite like you."

"Oh no, Dirk." She strode away through an elaborately carved doorway. "You're an entirely different sort of hypocrite."

Fists clenched, Dirk watched her disappear from view. It was all he could do not to run after her demanding an apology and answers.

"My card." Blaze-Simms passed an oil-stained white rectangle to the servant. "Perhaps you could take us to the gentleman of the house?"

The servant narrowed his eyes, gaze shifting from Blaze-Simms to the curiously elaborate rifle he had taken out of the basket.

"This way," he said at last.

#

There were no gas lamps in the corridors of the Red Castle or in the receiving room where the servant left them. Instead the place was lit by silver candelabras between the bookshelves and by the warm glow of an open fire.

"How did you find me?" Isabelle sat in a high-backed padded armchair. Across the fire from her, Blaze-Simms sat in an identical chair, thin legs sprawled in front of him, cup and saucer in hand. The place was too warm and stuffy for Dirk, who strode to the arched window and opened a shutter, letting in the late autumn night.

"Weather patterns were the most important part." Blaze-Simms waved his cup, spilling tea down his front. "I knew you had no propulsion, and so-"

"She doesn't really care, Tim." Dirk clenched the windowsill. "She's just being polite."

"Oh." Blaze-Simms went quiet, his enthusiasm dead. "Of course."

"Would you rather I were needlessly callous, Mr Dynamo?" Isabelle took a sip of her own tea.

"You'd know all about that." He turned to glare at her. "You made me think-"

"Think?" she snapped. "If you even started to think you'd realise that-"

"Oh, so now I'm an idiot?"

"I'm sure you've been an idiot for a long time."

"I don't have to stand here and-"

"Enough." A shadow shifted in the corner of the room and Miura Noriko stepped into view. With silent footsteps, the ninja went to stand beside Isabelle, placing a hand on her shoulder. The other hand rested, calmly but deliberately, on the handle of the katana at her waist. "Timothy, tell us what you want."

Blaze-Simms set aside his tea and stood, right hand outstretched.

"I say, Noriko," he said. "It's splendid to see you."

With the slightest of smiles, Noriko shook his hand, bowing her head as she did so.

"Damn it, Tim." Dirk almost exploded with fury. "She betrayed us too!"

"Oh yes!" Blaze-Simms stepped back and shook his fist at the two women. "Ghastly behaviour. Scoundrels, the pair of you."

He turned an apologetic look toward Dirk.

"I'm sorry, old chap," he said. "I'm not terribly good at this sort of thing."

"That's probably for the best." Dirk leaned back against the wall. "Noriko's right, someone calmer than me should do the talking."

"Why don't I start?" Isabelle's calm demeanour only aggravated Dirk more. How could she just brush off the anger between them, acting as if he weren't here? "You've come to demand that we hand over the stones that will guide you to the lost Library of Alexandria. You feel outraged that we took them, and you feel entitled to them after our efforts together."

"Well, yes," Blaze-Simms said. "We went through a lot to get those tablets. What you did just wasn't cricket."

"Anything else?" Isabelle raised an eyebrow. "Conditions, time frames, insistence on compensation?"

"We should probably be quick about it." A thoughtful look crossed Blaze-Simms's face. "This German unification business is very new, and none of us know how people will react. I'd like to get somewhere more stable as soon as I can."

"I really don't think you need to worry about that." Isabelle's smile stopped just short of condescending. "We're a long way from the heart of Bismarck's new Empire. No-one is going to make a fuss about a tiny out of the way duchy."

"Still..." Blaze-Simms shrugged. "About the stones..."

"I'm sorry to have wasted your time, but you can't have them." Isabelle picked up a poker. "I have travelled too far and worked too hard to give them up."

"We did that work too!"

"Yes, but you receive the fruits of your labour all the time." Sparks flew as she prodded at the fire. "Praise, wealth, credit for your finds."

"We could have shared that."

"Oh, Timothy." She shook her head as she turned to face them. "So naive. If women received the credit they were due, or one fraction of the power they deserve, the world would be a very different place."

"Enough of this." Dirk stepped away from the wall. "We were working together. You chose to abandon that. You don't get to take the stones with you."

"And how are you going to stop me?" The poker rose like a rapier in Isabelle's hand. "By force, perhaps?"

"If that's what it takes."

Dirk didn't wait to see if things would get ugly. No-one was going to bend here. They had spent so much energy getting to this point, no-one had any left to craft a compromise. Not waiting for Isabelle to turn the poker against him, he darted forward.

It was a move he'd made a hundred times before. Against street thugs with knives and outlaws with six shooters, plains braves with axes and barroom drunks with broken bottles. A quick grab, put pressure on the wrist, and see your opponent disarmed. Given the first move, it always worked.

A black blur filled his vision and his hand was knocked aside. Ducking, he felt the rush of air as Noriko's fist passed an inch from his face. Relief was replaced by pain as her other hand jabbed at his gut. He grunted, staggered back, and took a swing at her. She barely even made the effort to dodge, simply stepping out of his way.

They were all on their feet now, Dirk and Blaze-Simms on one side of the room, Isabelle and Noriko on the other, both sides tensely silent.

Between them, the door creaked open. A woman stepped in with a swirl of full black skirts, red ribbons dangling from the waist. Clasping dainty hands to her daringly low cut bodice, she stared at them in shock.

"Ruffians!" she exclaimed, her shrill voice lightly accented with German. "There are ruffians in my home!"

She leaned against the door frame and fanned herself, strands of bright blonde hair dancing in front of her face.

"We didn't mean to-" Dirk began.

"I'm frightfully sorry if-" Blaze-Simms exclaimed.

"Really, Beatie?" Isabelle cut across them both. "You're going to give poor Heinrich a heart attack."

Outside the doorway, the elderly butler raised his eyebrow half an inch.

The woman made as if to swoon, then burst out laughing.

"Oh, Isabelle." Her voice was lower now - rich, smooth, and delicately accented. Her English was near perfect. "You are such a spoilsport."

She straightened her skirts and walked into the room, taking a seat by the fireplace. As she passed, Dirk caught a hint of expensive perfume. Having finally settled, the woman looked up expectantly at Isabelle, who sighed and smiled.

"You seem to have restored the room's manners, so let me not forget mine." Isabelle sounded calm and relaxed, as if the fight of moments earlier had never happened. "Gräfin Beatrix Klingemann, may I introduce Sir Timothy Blaze-Simms, a scholar and inventor of the Epiphany Club, and Mister Dirk Dynamo, his travelling companion."

"Gräfin's an odd sort of name for a lady, ain't it?" Dirk whispered to Blaze-Simms. Most of the others pretended not to hear him, though Noriko kept her eyes fixed on them and her hand on the hilt of her sword.

"It's her title." Blaze-Simms was even worse at whispering than Dirk. "Roughly equivalent to a countess."

"You are his travelling companion?" Gräfin Klingemann glanced excitedly from Dirk to Blaze-Simms and back again. "This is - how do you say it? - a euphemism?"

"No, ma'am." Dirk flushed.

"No need to be ashamed," Gräfin Klingemann said. "We all want someone to keep us warm at night."

"I ain't... It's not..."

"Two handsome men, spending so much time together, it would be a shame not to."

"Dammit!" Dirk snapped. "Travelling companion ain't a euphemism. We travel. We explore. That's it. Nobody keepin' anyone warm at night."

For a moment, he thought he saw Isabelle suppress a smile. He glared at her.

"He's very serious, isn't he?" The Gräfin touched Isabelle's hand. "I can see why you like him."

"Liked." Now Isabelle scowled.

Taking a deep breath, Dirk stepped forward and smiled at the Gräfin. Charm wasn't his strong suit, but he could pull a little together when he needed it. If the lady of the castle had taken a liking to him then maybe he could take a leaf from Isabelle's book, use folks to his advantage and get what he wanted.

"It's a pleasure to meet you, ma'am." Reaching down, he took her hand, bent low and pressed it to his lips. He didn't try to force a smile as he looked up into her eyes - if the lady liked drama she could have that instead.

"And you, Mister Dynamo," the Gräfin said, smiling back. "Tell me, are you an athlete? You certainly have the build for it."

"No, ma'am." He straightened. "Just an ordinary miner's son, trying to make his way in the world. Most athletic I've ever been is on a battlefield, and I doubt you want to hear about that."

"Oh, but I do." She leaned forward, looking up at him as eagerly as a hungry hound. "Have you suffered, Mister Dynamo? Have you seen the worst of man and glimpsed the darkness within your own soul? Have you felt the blood pump in your veins, and that of other men plaster you as they breathe their last?"

"That I have, ma'am." Now Dirk knew where he stood. He had met women like this before, in big cities well away from any real war, women excited by the poetry of horrors they would never have to see. "It cuts me deep, but I'd be willing to talk about it with a kind soul like you. There's just a little business we've got to deal with first."

He risked a glance at Isabelle. Her arms were folded and her lips pursed, but she looked nowhere near as annoyed as he had hoped.

"This business is the Great Library of Alexandria?" The Gräfin beamed. "By all accounts, you have had a thrilling adventure this far. And such a noble cause, to retrieve learning so long tragically lost."

"That's right, ma'am." Uneasiness crept over Dirk. How much had Isabelle told this woman? And how close were they, that she would share the information? Whatever the case, he had to press the chance he had. "We collected the clues together, but Mrs McNair stole them from me and Sir Timothy. Ain't that right, Tim?"

"I should say so." Blaze-Simms turned from examining the innards of a cuckoo clock. "Dashed dastardly move."

"How can I help with this terrible injustice?" The Gräfin fanned herself once more.

"By ordering her to hand back what's ours." Dirk channelled his indignation into a hurt expression. "This is your castle full of your people and you can make it happen. Help this poor wounded veteran get what's rightly his."

"Such a sad story." Gräfin Beatrix stood, her face close to Dirk's, her hand on his arm. Her perfume enveloped him again. "My heart bleeds for you. But of course I will not help."

Dirk clenched his fist.

"Guess this is just between us, then." Taking a step back, he looked directly at Isabelle.

"Again, no." Beatrix went to stand beside Isabelle and took the Englishwoman's arm. "There will be no threatening or stealing from Mrs McNair. She is my guest, just as you are, and she is my friend."

"Is she friends with your husband?" Dirk glared at the two of them. "Castle like this, it's gotta be run by a lord, right? Most lords I've ever met weren't keen on letting theft go unpunished."

"What did I tell you, Beatie?" Isabelle leaned her head against the Gräfin's.

The two of them laughed as if at the antics of an over-indulged child.

Dirk clenched his fists.

"Heinrich." He turned to the butler. "I'd like to see your master. Seems only polite, seeing as I'm in his castle."

"I'm afraid that won't be possible." Heinrich's expression was perfectly blank.

"It is rather late," Blaze-Simms said. "If he's busy, it might be better to wait until the morning."

"I'm afraid he won't be available then, either," Heinrich said.

"After lunch?"

"Graf Victor will not be available for some time. The Gräfin runs the household while he is indisposed."

Clenching his stomach around the growing knot of frustration, Dirk walked over to the window. He took a deep breath and stared out into the darkness, trying to calm his mind. It got hard to think straight sometimes, when he found himself running up against a world that didn't make sense to him, that didn't behave the way he expected it to. Sure, folks were never going to act exactly like he wanted, but they could at least behave in a way that was halfway predictable. One thing he'd learnt to recognise from Isabelle was how unfair it was that women never got their say in the running of the world. Now he needed that bias to act in his favour, and it wasn't there.

Lights twinkled in the valley below the castle. Neat lines of them, like glowing ants crawling back toward their nest. The rumble of waggons and tramp of marching feet drifted out of the night.

"Is there some sort of military camp around here?" Dirk asked. That might be another way to bring authority in on his side.

"Not that I know of." Gräfin Beatrix stood beside him at the window, staring out into the night. Her eyes sparkled with excitement.

A servant stepped silently into the room, her lips trembling nervously. Holding out a silver tray, she offered a single folded sheet of paper to the Gräfin. Next to it lay a business card.

"My, my." Beatrix glanced at the card, then picked up and read the note. "Someone named Colonel Wulff sends his regards. It appears that we are under siege."

Chapter 2: Turning Left

Dirk prided himself on being able to sleep anywhere and still wake up ready to go. Months in rain-soaked army camps; weeks exposed to the freezing desert air; the last three nights curled up in the corner of a wicker balloon basket - whatever the circumstances, he'd slept in worse.

Still, there was something refreshing about a soft bed and softer sheets. Like a steak dinner or watching a boxing match, he didn't need it, but he felt better for having enjoyed it. The world seemed a kinder place.

Waking up beneath a pile of blankets and silk sheets, he yawned and stretched cat-like as far as he could. The stiffness that had plagued him since the first night in the balloon was gone. Even the aches of recent fights - and there had been a few - had finally faded away.

He flung aside the bedding and brisk air hit his skin, bringing him fully awake. The stone floor was cold beneath his feet as he crossed a bedchamber larger than his whole rented apartment in Manchester and yanked the curtain open. The sun had just risen over a cold winter's day and clumps of mist clung to the wooded German hillsides. Through the haze, the orange glow of campfires was just visible in the valley below.

Making the most of the daylight, he took a proper look around the room Gräfin Beatrix had provided for him. Aside from the four poster bed and a looming closet of dark wood, there was a nightstand, a writing desk, several chairs, and a wall hanging he reckoned must be medieval, its faded blue threads showing a hunting scene. Cold ashes filled the fireplace.

Dirk examined himself in the mirror above the mantel. Most of his bruises had faded away, and nothing from Paris had added a scar to his collection. He could do with some exercise to tone up his muscles - that was hard to do in the basket of a hot air balloon - but as far as appearances went he'd gotten off lightly from his recent adventures.

Inside though, where it really mattered, that was another story. He thought of Isabelle and felt an icy fist close around his heart. This was the problem with feelings - they made you weak, made you vulnerable. He took a deep breath and pushed the emotion aside. There was a bigger picture here, a wealth of knowledge to be found. He could come to terms with Isabelle, if that was what it took.

A click behind him made Dirk spin around, snatching up a poker to defend himself. A servant stood in the doorway, her face red behind an armful of firewood. She jabbered something he couldn't understand.

"Sorry." Dirk set aside the poker and held up his hands. "Don't speak German."

The girl nodded, blonde hair bobbing. Her eyes kept flicking from Dirk to the firewood in her hands.

"Er... clothes?" she said in a heavy accent.

"Oh!" Dirk grabbed a bed sheet and wrapped it around himself. "That better?"

She said something he couldn't understand, then crossed the room and put the wood beside the fire.

"Down." She pointed at him and then the floor. "Um... food, yes?"

"Breakfast?" Dirk smiled. "Damn good idea. But I'd maybe better change first."

He waved at the sheet and his bare chest. The girl laughed, nodded and headed for the door.

"Wait a second." Dirk pointed at himself. "Dirk." He pointed at her. "And you are?"

"Ingrid." The girl curtsied, turned, and closed the door behind her as she left.

#

The dining hall of the Red Castle was a vast chamber in imitation medieval style, complete with a minstrel's gallery of wood too neat to be centuries old and a table that stretched the length of the room. They sat at one end, beneath a set of steeply arched windows and a grim-faced gargoyle, while servants hurried in and out with dishes of fruit, eggs, toast and plump sausages. Brightly polished silverware gleamed against dark wood, a constellation of candlesticks and cutlery. Ingrid was among the servants and she smiled briefly at Dirk as she passed. But his attention was fixed firmly on the people seated around the table.

Isabelle acted as if nothing had ever happened, chatting amiably with everyone except Dirk. Blaze-Simms's combination of good manners and forgetfulness soon led him to join in. Noriko sat vigilant, twirling a butter knife between her fingers with deadly precision, as wary as ever. The Gräfin, like Isabelle, acted as if she had ninjas and adventurers to breakfast every morning - for all Dirk knew she did. Maybe in time she might even have lulled Dirk into relaxing.

The problem was the other guest.

"This is Colonel Gerhardt Wulff." Beatrix made the introductions as they sat down to eat. "He arrived this morning to oversee the siege."

"You invited the guy attacking your home in for breakfast?" Dirk had always found the English obsession with good manners a little insane. Apparently the Germans were the same.

"Of course," Beatrix said, smiling across a steaming cup of coffee. "It is my dearly held hope that we can all be friends."

"That doesn't seem real likely," Dirk said, staring across the table at the Prussian officer. His blue uniform was impeccable and a fresh medal gleamed on his chest. That was probably related to the bandages swathed around half his head and the fresh red burns covering the exposed skin. There was something familiar about the little of his face that showed. "Have we met before?"

"In Paris." Holding his fork in one bandaged hand, Wulff stabbed a sausage, drops of fat spattering across his plate. His angry glare never left Dirk.

"I don't remember meeting any..." Dirk fell silent as realisation dawned. "You're that Subterranean Strike Force guy. The one whose tunnelling machine we blew up."

"Indeed." Colonel Wulff grimaced as the fork snagged his bandage. "A week ago I commanded the most prestigious unit in the Prussian army, leading a daring raid behind French lines. Now the doctors tell me my face will never recover from the explosion, and here I am, stuck quelling some backwater mess."

The Gräfin nibbled at her toast, smiling even as he glared at her.

"So why are you here?" Dirk didn't touch his own food. The smell of bacon was making his mouth water and he was ready to kill for coffee, but Wulff's tension had him on edge, ready in case of trouble.

"Because I failed." Flecks of sausage flew as Wulff spoke through a mouthful of half-chewed meat. "I failed gloriously, injured when the tunneller was lost, and so they pinned a medal on me. But then they sent me here, out of sight and out of glory."

"Why is the Prussian army here at all? Ain't you busy fighting the French?"

"I am afraid that is my doing." Beatrix heaved a sigh that made her elaborate corset creak. "The Prussians have such grand dreams of unifying Germany, but I was not willing to get involved. Imagine the embarrassment if a tiny mountain duchy refuses to join their new empire. So what they can't have by talking they will try to take by force."

"No trying." Wulff set down his fork. "We will simply take this place. What will you fight us with, a handful of servants?"

He stood and looked around at them all with a sneer.

"Such a fine castle you have here," he said. "But given the company you keep, I will take delight in tearing it down."

Without a word of thanks, he strode from the room.

"What a ghastly chap," Blaze-Simms said, shaking his head.

"Wasn't he a fan of yours?" Isabelle looked at Dirk with mocking curiosity.

"Guess I ain't picky enough in the company I keep," he replied.

"Well I am." Isabelle rose. "Thank you, Beatie, that was delightful."

Dropping her napkin beside her plate, she followed the Prussian officer out the door.

Sagging with relief, Dirk reached for his coffee. Then he remembered why he was here and what he'd been planning not an hour before. It would be hard to talk to Isabelle if he didn't know where she was.

"Excuse me." Cutlery bounced off the table as he bashed his knee in his hurry to stand. How was it that Isabelle McNair could so easily reduce him to a cumbersome, uncoordinated mess? "That was a fine spread, ma'am, but I need to get goin'."

"Is nobody hungry this morning?" the Gräfin asked with exaggerated exasperation. "I would hate for all this to go to waste."

"I'll help." Blaze-Simms shovelled sausages onto his plate and reached for the teapot. "And perhaps you could tell me more about this splendid castle?"

#

The gargoyle above the doorway looked a lot like the one Dirk had noted on his way out of the dining hall. But then, so had the last one he'd stopped at, and that door had only led to another confusing tangle of stairs. After two hours of wandering the Red Castle, he had to admit that he was completely lost.

It was crazy. He was good at this stuff. He could sail into any city on the globe and get an idea of his way around within an hour. But this whole place was a mess, a tangle of oddly aligned corridors, twisting stairwells, and unexplained doors. Every time he thought he knew what would be around the corner, he ran into something unexpected. There was no way you could make something so baffling by accident.

The lack of windows didn't help. The further down he went into the bowels of the place, the less light there was. Half the windows he saw were tiny slots high in the walls of echoing corridors, not illuminating the world but casting it into starker shadow.

There were no gas lamps - that would have been far too modern for this place - but old fashioned flaming brands and oil lamps sat in niches and brackets on the walls, their erratic light casting an amber glow across stone run through with the deep pink of the castle's exterior.

Standing in front of the gargoyle, he forced himself to reconsider what he was doing. He'd set off hours ago in search of Isabelle but immediately lost track of her. Since then he'd wandered pointlessly, trying to kid himself that he was still on her trail. He needed a different aim and only one sprang to mind.

He was going to work out the layout of this place. He'd learn its passages and hallways inside and out, because however events fell out here, that had to be useful.

Certainly a damn sight more useful than staying lost.

There were plenty of times he wished he was as smart as Sir Timothy Blaze-Simms, but this was the first time he'd wished that he had his friend's habit of constant note taking. A pencil would have been handy for what he had planned. But the only thing he habitually carried was his Gravemaker pistol, and that hadn't seemed like a polite thing to bring to breakfast.

In the absence of a writing implement, Dirk yanked a flaming brand out of its sconce. Holding it up against a door frame, he left a soot stain to show which way he'd come. The wisdom of an old maze maker he'd met in Peru sprang to mind.

"When lost, just keep going left."

If in doubt, Dirk tended to follow the advice of smarter folks than himself. So left he went.

It took a few turns before he heard someone moving at the far end of a corridor. He hurried after the sound and rounded the corner just in time to catch a distant glimpse of blue skirts. His spirits lifted. Maybe he'd found Isabelle after all.

Hurrying forward again, he strode through a doorway and into a spiral staircase running both up and down. A flicker of light was disappearing below, and he was about to follow when hurrying footsteps appeared from above.

Ingrid appeared around the stairs, a box in her hands. She looked at Dirk with confusion and then with shock as he turned from her to continue down the stairs.

"No!" she exclaimed.

"I'm just looking for my friend," Dirk said, pointing down the stairs.

"No down." Ingrid shook her head again. "Not allowed."

Dirk grinned. "Ma'am, if there's one thing makes me curious about a place, it's knowing I ain't allowed to go there."

Her face crumpling in frustration, Ingrid set the box down on the step beside her.

"Not down," she said again. "There are..."

She raised her hands claw-like in front of her, bared her teeth and growled. The whole business was so incongruous on the pretty young blonde, Dirk burst out laughing.

"Monsters?" he asked. "You reckon there are monsters down there?"

"Yes." She nodded, her expression absolutely serious, then did the impression again. "Monsters."

Dirk wanted to say that he didn't believe in monsters. But there had been those poor, malformed creatures in the royalist army in Paris; the giant rats he'd once encountered in a British sewer; and that twisted, vicious bear on the island of Hakon. After all that, who was he to say what didn't exist?

He'd delayed too long already. The light had disappeared from the stairwell and he didn't fancy his chances of finding whoever it was again.

"Alright, you win," he said. "But can you show me the way back to my room? I'm kind of lost."

By the look on Ingrid's face, she hadn't understood what he'd said.

"Up?" He pointed, then picked up the box from the step next to the servant. "Let me help you with that."

"Up," she agreed, nodding, and off they went.

#

Back in the familiar corridors of the castle's upper reaches, Dirk left Ingrid to get on with her work. With renewed determination, he set about learning his way around.

Knowing where he had started made it a lot easier. He found different routes between that study, dining hall, music room, his own guest room and the one Blaze-Simms had been put up in. Judging by the noises emerging from under his door, the inventor was creating something again, his ability to find parts and inspiration unhindered by unfamiliar circumstances.

Dusk was turning into night by the time Dirk found himself on a balcony overlooking the valley. Fires around the perimeter showed the outline of the Prussian military camp, which had crept closer to the castle. The light of flames glanced off the distinct cylinders of artillery guns.

"Feeling nostalgic, Mister Dynamo?" Isabelle's voice drifted softly from the shadows. Dirk tightened his grip on the battlements, not wanting to turn and let her see his face until he was in control. "It must be reassuring to you, the simplicity of war."

Dirk took a deep breath.

"There ain't nothing reassuring about war," he said. "Nothing noble or glorious. It's mostly just a lot of decent men doing terrible things to each other."

"I have trouble believing that so many men can ever be decent." With a rustle of skirts, Isabelle came to the edge of the balcony and stood looking out with him, two feet of cold air between them. "Especially given the way women get treated in war."

"Decent folks can do terrible things when they lose their way," Dirk said. "And sometimes the folks who seem decent turn out to be conniving beneath it all."

"I believe I detect a hidden meaning in your words."

"And you'd never have another meaning, would you?"

Now it was her turn to take a deep breath.

"I'm not going to apologise for what I did," she said. "The rules of the game are rigged against women, and unless we break them once in a while we will never win."

"I was on your damn side," he said, feeling anger flush his face.

"I wish that was true," she said. "And I know you believe it. But every time you try to re-explain a perspective I fully understand, you show just how badly you misunderstand the situation. I was always going to be second fiddle to you and Sir Timothy. This was the only way I could make this discovery my own."

"Bullshit." He slammed his hands against a crenellation, venting his anger against the impervious stone. There was a grinding sound and the stone fell away, tumbling down the side of the castle.

Isabelle stepped back, trembling. She had drawn a small pistol from the folds of her dress and eyed Dirk with a mixture of fear and determination.

"I ain't gonna hurt you," he said. The expression on her face was like a knife in the guts. "I'd never do that."

"I wish I could believe you," she said. "But I have heard that many times before."

There was a thud from beyond the castle walls, and then another. A flash in the darkness caught Dirk's eye.

Artillery.

"Down!" he yelled.

When Isabelle didn't move he leapt. She raised the gun, but not as fast as he reached her, flinging them both to the ground. Behind him there was an explosion and chunks of rock hurtled through the air. Another shell exploded somewhere below and one whizzed past over the castle.

"Get off me," Isabelle said, scrambling out from underneath him. She stopped in the doorway, then turned to stare out into the night. "This is it, isn't it? They're going to attack."

Dirk peered down into the valley. There was another flash and a thud, nothing too impressive.

"I don't reckon so," he said. "They ain't even firing the big guns yet."

Chapter 3: Graf Victor Klingemann

"Thank you, Heinrich." Gräfin Beatrix smiled at the butler as he led the servants in clearing the table. "Please tell cook that she excelled herself this time."

Dirk had to agree. He hadn't eaten a steak that fine since he'd left America, and the sausages had tasted like real meat, not the leftovers and sawdust most butchers filled them with. He leaned back in his seat, one hand holding a cup of coffee, the other resting on his replete belly. The only thing that could make this more perfect was a cigar, but he was feeling far too full to get up and leave the ladies behind for a smoke.

As if reading his mind, the Gräfin rose in a swirl of scarlet skirts and fetched a box from the mantlepiece. As she opened the lid, a rich tobacco smell joined the heady scents of wine and coffee.

"Please help yourselves," she said as she clipped a cigar and reached for a candlestick. Placing the cigar between her lips and puffing it into life, she smiled at Dirk from beneath lowered eyelids.

Noriko refused the offer, but Dirk was surprised to see Isabelle take her up on it, along with him and Blaze-Simms.

Just like the steak, the wine and the coffee, the cigar was better than Dirk could normally afford. He paused to enjoy a truly relaxed moment, but a glance at Isabelle set his nerves on edge again. The sooner this business was over with, the better for all of them.

"What's it gonna take to make you see reason and hand over those stones?" he asked.

Isabelle glared at him from behind her wine glass. Across the table, Blaze-Simms coughed awkwardly.

"I say, Noriko, splendid weather we're having, isn't it?" he said.

"It is raining shells," the ninja replied as a distant explosion shook dust from the rafters. "This is not splendid."

"I say, that's rather poetic," Blaze-Simms said. "Isn't it, Dirk?"

Dirk stared at Isabelle, waiting for an answer.

"My, but you are wonderfully direct, Herr Dynamo," the Gräfin said. "So forceful."

Rolling her eyes, Isabelle leaned forward, planting her elbows on the table.

"Nothing could persuade me to give up the stones," she said. "Your arrogant demands only make me more determined."

"I could just take them," Dirk said.

The Gräfin laughed.

"Please, Herr Dynamo, there is charming directness and then there is just being rude." Beatrix laid a hand on Isabelle's shoulder. "I forbid you from taking anything from this woman in my home. If you try, it will not just mean a terrible breach of good manners. It will mean you have to fight your way out of here past all my servants and fight me again in the courts when I sue you for theft and trespass. Believe me, I have very good lawyers."

"Guess I'll wait, then," Dirk said. "Sooner or later, Mrs McNair will have to leave."

"So you'll be here for a while?" The Gräfin winked. "Lucky me."

#

"I don't think this was what Beatrix had in mind when she asked you to make her feel safe tonight," Blaze-Simms said.

"I ain't in the mood to try guessing what a woman wants," Dirk said as he hammered a final nail through a plank, sealing shut one of the castle's small outer doors. "How's the trap coming along?"

"I'm rather pleased with it." Blaze-Simms stepped back from the picture frame he'd been adjusting. "There's a spring-loaded lever behind there now, with half a dozen metal darts attached. Any Prussian bounder who breaks through and hits that tripwire is in for a nasty surprise."

"Good work." Picking up the lantern whose light they'd been working by, Dirk carefully stepped over the near-invisible tripwire and followed Blaze-Simms back up the corridor. Their footsteps echoed from the cold pink stones, making it sound as though a whole squad was marching through the castle.

"Don't suppose you can improvise some more guns?" Dirk asked. "I don't know how well the servants here can handle themselves, but I'd rather not leave them unarmed."

"Sorry, old chap." Blaze-Simms shook his head. "I'd need better equipment than they've got in that old tool store. It's just down to your Gravemaker and my Elloise."

"You named your gun Elloise?"

"First girl I ever courted."

Dirk blinked in surprise. He'd never thought of Blaze-Simms as the courting type - he always seemed too distracted with learning and inventions. The Englishman was no monk, but there was a difference between casual seduction and building a relationship.

"What came between you?" he asked, strangely fascinated by the thought of Blaze-Simms carrying flowers and love poems.

"I added a special sort of rifling to her father's favourite gun," Blaze-Simms said. "Unfortunately I forgot to take the type of ammunition into account. The thing back-fired. Took two fingers and part of his cheek. I managed to work out the problem with the rifling, but the atmosphere was rather awkward between us after that."

"That gives me an idea." Reaching a junction, Dirk paused to regain his bearings. "The lord of a place like this has to be a hunter, right?"

"Oh, yes. With all these lovely forests around, it would be rude not to."

"So he must have guns."

"Oh yes!"

"And if it's to defend the castle, then folks will be willing to tell us where to find him."

"What a splendid notion! Let's ask."

They turned left and headed back towards the heart of the castle, the light from their lantern illuminating ancient tapestries and oil portraits of noblemen and their wives, regal figures with haughty expressions and a lot of gold jewellery over their silk doublets. They looked pretty pleased with themselves, and Dirk felt the same way about the plan he was formulating.

"I say." Blaze-Simms's eyes widened as inspiration struck. "If we find the Graf to talk about the guns, maybe we can ask him to help out with this business with Isabelle. After all, the Gräfin has to listen to him."

Dirk took a deep breath, but decided to let it go. Sometimes it was easier to let smart folks take credit for the obvious.

"Good thinking, Tim," he said.

#

"You think I am an idiot?" Heinrich said, his wrinkled face going red. He turned back to dusting a suit of plate armour, one of the dozen that lined the castle's entrance hall. "My mistress has told you already that you cannot see Graf Victor."

"But this is different," Dirk said.

The butler snorted. "No, it is an excuse, and you insult me by trying it."

Dirk turned to Blaze-Simms. The Englishman was more used to managing servants.

"It strikes me that we haven't expressed our gratitude for your splendid work here," Blaze-Simms said, drawing a pocket book from his inside jacket. "I mostly have francs and sterling at the moment, but I'm sure I have some Vereinsthaler in here somewhere."

"Really, Sir Timothy." Heinrich lowered his duster and turned to look at the Englishman, shaking his head. "Is this an appropriate way for a gentleman to behave? You have been spending too much time around Americans."

"Terribly sorry," Blaze-Simms said. "I didn't mean to-"

"Enough," Heinrich said, holding up a hand. "Just be glad that the Gräfin is tolerant in her attitude towards guests."

He stalked away down the hall, tailcoat flapping behind him, dust flying as he shook out his cloth.

"So much for that," Blaze-Simms put away the pocket book. "Back to reinforcing the doors?"

"There's still one option," Dirk said.

The servants' quarters were always among Dirk's first stops when in a new place. It was where all the honest graft went on and where most of the folks he considered worth talking with would be found. People with servants never knew where the soap was kept or which sorts of oats the horses liked - practical information came from practical minds.

The kitchen of the Red Castle was broad and spacious, with rows of old stone fireplaces along one wall. Most of them were empty, but the fires that did burn were well fuelled and warming. Knives, pans, and ladles hung from racks on the wall. Bundles of herbs added a sweet scent to the air.

As Dirk had expected, there were a few servants sat around the table, drinking tea, darning socks, and polishing the silverware their supposed superiors ate with. Ingrid was among them, and though she looked as confused as the rest to see Dirk standing in the doorway, she smiled and walked over when he waved.

"I was hoping you could help me with something," Dirk said as he led her out of earshot, into a corridor where aprons hung from hooks on the whitewashed walls. Blaze-Simms stood there with a notebook in one hand and a pencil in the other, scribbling down whatever inspiration had struck him this time.

"Uh..." She smiled uncomprehendingly at his English words.

"We'd like to talk with the Graf," Dirk said, but she still looked confused. He pointed at himself and Blaze-Simms. "Me. Him. Graf Victor."

He mimed shaking hands.

"Ah!" Ingrid said. "You want talk Graf."

Dirk nodded.

"Can you take us to the Graf?" he asked, pointing at her.

A look of fear crossed Ingrid's face.

"No," she said. "Not good."

"It's OK," Dirk said. "We won't tell anyone it was you."

She kept shaking her head and pointed down.

"The Graf's down in the tunnels?" Dirk asked.

Ingrid nodded.

"Yes," she said. "Tunnels."

"Then we'll go there." Dirk turned to Blaze-Simms. "You hear that?"

"No!" Ingrid grabbed his arm, turning him to look at her again. Then she bared her teeth and raised her hands like claws.

"Oh yeah," Dirk said. "The monsters are down there, right?" He patted the holster strapped to his thigh. "Don't worry, we can handle ourselves."

Her gaze shifting between Dirk's face and his pistol, Ingrid hesitated as if weighing something up. Finally she took hold of his arm and led him towards a stairwell at the darkened end of the corridor.

"Come on, Tim," Dirk called out over his shoulder. "We're going to meet the Graf."

"Not Graf." Ingrid shook her head as she led him into the stairwell. The stone steps spiralled downward in the light of oil lamps. She took one from its hook and led the way, hurrying in dizzying turns into the darkness below. Several floors down she suddenly stopped and stood pointing at a door.

"Through there?" Dirk reached for the handle.

"No." She shook her head and pointed again at the lower door frame.

At first glance, it looked as though someone had taken a heavy axe to the ancient wood. Three deep gouges had been cut close together, each strike strong enough to splinter the wood around it, leaving clumps of jagged points between the gaps. But as Dirk peered more closely at the damage, he realised that this was not the work of an axe. The wood had been torn at from one side, the apparent cuts turning into scratches at the far side. The damage was not neat enough for a man made weapon. It looked more like...

"Claws," he said. "What kind of creature has claws strong enough to do this?" Rising slowly, he slid his hand to his holster and looked around. "More importantly, what's a creature like that doing in a place like this?"

"Monsters, yes?" Ingrid pointed at the damage and then raised her hands in another impression of claws.

"It certainly looks that way." Blaze-Simms pulled a measuring tape and notebook from the pockets of his tailcoat. "I wonder what it could be? Perhaps a pet brought back from safari in the wilds of Africa, now running rampant in a habitat quite unlike its own? Or some ancient creature uncovered during the digging of the castle's cellars?"

"However it got down here, why haven't our hosts got rid of it?" Dirk asked. "That's what I want to know."

"Not go Graf, yes?" Ingrid said. "Monsters in tunnels."

Dirk hesitated. He didn't like to put a lady in danger, but he needed to find Graf Victor. He and Blaze-Simms could handle themselves against a dumb beast.

"You armed, Tim?" he asked.

"I've still got a hammer," Blaze-Simms said, hefting it. "You remember what I achieved with one of these in Zurich."

"That Habsburg agent ain't gonna forget," Dirk said, smiling at the memory of a close encounter they'd gotten out of with skill, ingenuity and more than a little brute force. He held up his gun. "Ingrid, we're armed and we know how to use it. We ain't gonna let a monster hurt you. Now please take us to Graf Victor."

The serving girl hesitated, eyes shifting from Dirk to the doorway to the stairs running back up to the safety of the servants' quarters. At last she gave a slow, reluctant nod.

"I take you Graf," she said.

"I say, maybe we'll get lucky and see one of these brutes," Blaze-Simms said, pointing at the gouged wood.

Dirk took a deep breath. It was going to be a long night.

#

The good thing about Ingrid's limited English was that she didn't understand what Blaze-Simms was saying. Even before he got into scientific jargon and Latin names of animals, she was staring at him blankly, unaware that he was dreaming of meeting the beasts she dreaded. Blaze-Simms, equally oblivious to her potential distress, talked excitedly as they descended by lamplight down cold stairwells and dank corridors. The prospect of seeing a lion adapting to European caves was almost as exciting to him as the thought of meeting something entirely new.

Dirk just kept his pistol ready and his mind alert, watching and listening for signs of danger.

At last they stopped at the end of a corridor, in front of a door made out of solid iron. Dirk tried the handle, but the door was sealed with two sturdy locks. Shaking her head, Ingrid pointed to a panel at eye height on the door. It was the sort of small, purposeful panel Dirk had only seen on one kind of door - that to a cell.

"Graf," Ingrid whispered.

Dirk slid back the well oiled shutter and peered through the viewing slot.

The room beyond the door was large, well lit and comfortably furnished. Lamps burned in a small chandelier hanging from the centre of the ceiling, illuminating a table scattered with tools and bottles. Beyond that were a writing desk, a plushly upholstered couch, and in one corner a curtained bed. The walls were hung with maps and diagrams, the floor covered with rugs apart from a bare area around the central table. As Dirk peered in, a man turned in his seat at the writing desk and looked at him with surprise.

The man spoke as he rose and walked slowly across the room. He wore a black tail coat over a white shirt with frilly lace at cuffs and collar. His movements had the easy grace of a man who never had to rush or to wait upon the whims of others.

"I'm sorry," Dirk said. "I don't speak German."

"Ah, you are English, yes?" the man said.

"American," Dirk replied.

The man nodded. "Thomas Jefferson. Abraham Lincoln. Cotton plantation."

"Uh, yep, that's the one," Dirk said, a little puzzled. "You wouldn't be Graf Victor Klingemann, would you?"

"Indeed I am!" The Graf grinned. "And who are you? I thought it unlikely that it was breakfast time already. Even less likely that Heinrich helps Beatrix recruit an American."

"The name's Dirk Dynamo," Dirk said. He considered trying to reach through the gap and shake hands, but the angle was awkward and he didn't know how a Graf would feel about handshakes. "I was hoping you might help me talk some sense into your wife."

The Graf's laughter began as a warm, genial sound that rolled out like warm syrup. As it went on it rose in volume, becoming an angry, jagged noise that echoed around the chamber. With a shriek of fury, he swept a row of jars from the table. Glass shattered against the wall.

Suddenly calm and quiet, the Graf ran a hand across his slicked back hair and turned to face Dirk.

"Really, Herr Dynamo, look at where you find me," he said. "Do you think I have any influence over my wife?"

At last Dirk was ready to admit the obvious.

"You're a prisoner, huh?" he said. "Why's she got you locked up down here?"

"Beatrix says that I am mad," the Graf said, his stare boring into Dirk. "She says that I am a lunatic who will ruin us both. So she locks me up down here, leaves me with my books and experiments in the hope that they will keep me occupied, that I will not commit my every last waking moment to escaping her clutches."

He slammed his fist into the palm of his hand. Then the intensity slipped from his face and he shrugged.

"In that, at least, she is right," he said.

"You just accept this?" Dirk said, incredulous. He couldn't imagine taking confinement with anything like the calm the Graf showed.

"Of course not," the Graf replied. "I never see daylight. My plumbing is a crack in the rocks with a stream below. But what can I do? She has the servants in the palm of her hand. I cannot reach the outside world, and even if I did, who is to say that they would take my side? My family has a history of troubled personalities.

"Now excuse me. It is long past midnight, and I must sleep."

Ignoring Dirk's protests, the Graf strode over to the bed, clambered in through the curtains, and within moments had begun to snore.

"Damn." Dirk's fist hit the door with an almighty clang. "We're gonna need another plan."

Chapter 4: Under Attack

"Have you not listened to a damn word I've been saying?" Dirk said, clenching his fist in frustration. "We're not just facing an army on the outside - there's a monster in here with us too."

"I heard you." Isabelle stirred her tea, eyes idly following the steam as it rose towards the rafters of the study, beams of pale mid-morning sunlight turning it into a silver fog. "What I mostly heard was you finding more excuses to tell me what I should do."

"Excuses!" Dirk bellowed. "There are threats all around us here. We have to get out."

"If you feel a need to leave, then go," Isabelle said, carefully setting down her spoon. "You won't be missed."

"You won't listen to me? Fine." Dirk turned to Blaze-Simms. "Tim, you were there too. Tell her."

Blaze-Simms looked up, blinking in surprise at the mention of his name. He was sprawled in a vast armchair, one thin leg stuck out in front of him, the other folded across it, a notebook resting on his knee. He'd covered a dozen pages with scribblings in just five minutes. To his right, Noriko stood silent by the fireplace, running a cloth along the blade of her katana.

"What?" Blaze-Simms said, wriggling uncomfortably. "I mean, I think we're all free to-"

"About the monster," Dirk said. "Tell her about the monster."

"Oh!" Blaze-Simms sat up, tapping a finger against his open page. "It's fascinating, really. I've been trying to calculate the strength it would have taken to do that damage, and we're looking at something at least as strong as the mutated bear we met on Hakon. Probably shorter and slimmer, or it would have difficulty navigating the castle's passageways. So strong, manoeuvrable, and stealthy enough that no-one's seen more than the briefest movements in the shadows. I asked the servants, and they were very clear on that. Honestly, this may be the deadliest predator I've ever encountered."

"You see?" Dirk said to Isabelle.

"I can't wait to go back down and get a closer look," Blaze-Simms said.

"What?" Now it was Dirk's turn to blink in surprise.

"Nets won't help in catching it, but it looks like the Graf has a jolly good chemistry set. If I can use it to produce a sedative, make some darts for Elloise..."

Blaze-Simms's voice drifted off as he resumed scribbling in his notebook.

Not to be stopped by the parrying of his first attack, Dirk turned to the next topic.

"That's another thing," he said. "Your friend Beatrix has her husband secretly locked up in the dungeon, like some kind of criminal."

"Oh no!" Isabelle pressed her hand against her forehead in exaggerated shock. "Pass me the smelling salts, for in my womanish frailty I may faint clean away."

"You knew, huh?" Dirk said, sagging.

"Of course I knew. She's one of my best friends, and he's a terrible lunatic. Honestly, Dirk, debating really isn't your strong suit, is it?"

Raw, angry heat blazed in Dirk's cheeks, the sensation adding to his embarrassment. It only became worse as Gräfin Beatrix swept into the room in a rustle of skirts and a cloud of perfume, her fingers brushing his shoulder as she walked by.

"Have I missed anything exciting?" she asked.

"The boys are trying to be smart," Isabelle said, her gaze a challenge to Dirk. It froze the words in his mouth, making him feel like all the cogs in his brain had become stuck, thoughts straining for release but unable to move.

"I... I..." He forced back an angry yell. "Come on, Tim."

Grabbing Blaze-Simms by the arm, he dragged the Englishman out of the room, delicate laughter following in their wake.

"I say, old chap, are you alright?" Blaze-Simms asked.

"No, I'm not alright," growled Dirk. "Damn upper-class women with their ridiculous damn manners and their stupid damn laughter."

"Ah." Finally released from Dirk's grip, Blaze-Simms scurried to keep up as they strode deeper into the castle. "Would you like to talk about it?"

"No, I'd like to hit something."

"Thank goodness." Blaze-Simms sighed with relief, then looked up brightly. "In that case, I have a splendid idea."

#

With a hammer in one hand and a lantern in the other, Dirk crept down a darkened corridor. Beside him, Blaze-Simms also held a shuttered lantern and a net he had improvised out of wires and chains. Even moving with the stealth of a trained tracker, Dirk's footsteps echoed softly back to him from the stone walls. Blaze-Simms's efforts at stealth were barely worthy of the word.

Still, Dirk had to admit that this had been a good idea. Sure, he'd wanted to use the monster as an excuse to get them all out of there, but running away had never really suited him. The familiar activity of a hunt, even a hunt as strange as this one, was far more satisfying.

They'd started out at the damaged door frame Ingrid had shown them and worked their way down from there into the bowels of the castle, looking for the monster. This was a strange place, full of dusty storerooms and abandoned niches, man-made corridors morphing into natural tunnels and then back again. Supposedly it was the work of past lords, though no-one knew why they'd done it. If the tunnel network was meant as a maze then it wasn't a fun one to navigate, and if it had some other purpose then it couldn't possibly be suited to it.

Taking the left fork at a junction, Dirk walked up a short flight of stairs and into a familiar corridor. As far as he could tell, they were near the Graf's cell. Something dripped from the ceiling into a shallow puddle, long seconds passing between each drop, and the beginnings of a stalactite pointed down at them from the cut stone.

Crouching beside the puddle, Dirk widened the aperture of his lantern, illuminating patterns on the floor.

Something had stepped in the water. It had large, clawed feet, and judging by the dampness of the prints it had come through in the past half hour.

"Found something," Dirk whispered.

"I say, how exciting." Blaze-Simms crouched beside him and started sketching the prints. "This matches what I-"

"Ssh." Dirk grabbed his friend's arm and pointed up the corridor. Footsteps were approaching the t-junction at the far end of the passage.

Drawing his gun, Dirk carefully drew back the hammer. Blaze-Simms might want this thing alive, but Dirk was more worried about their survival.

The glow of a lantern appeared at the junction, and by its light Dirk recognised Ingrid hurrying past with an empty tray, away from the Graf's cell. She was visible for just a moment before disappearing from view.

"Don't reckon you'd need a net to catch her," Dirk whispered.

"You certainly wouldn't," Blaze-Simms replied. "I'm not sure I'm her type."

"That's not what I-"

A scream pierced the darkness, followed by a hideous howl.

Dirk didn't stop to think. His feet were moving before the sound had even fully registered, propelling him up the corridor as fast as he could move. Revolver in hand, he rounded the corner just as a clang was followed by another scream.

The thing he saw was seven feet tall and stooped to fit in the narrow corridor. It stood on two legs, with two more held out in front of it, all ending in claws as long and deadly as bayonets. From the tip of its reptilian snout to the end of its curled tail it was covered with scales. Ingrid lay on the flagstones beneath it, shielding her face with the buckled tray.

Dirk fired a single shot, the gun bucking in his hand. The bullet glanced off the side of the creature's head in a spray of thick, dark blood. It reared and looked at Dirk, narrow eyes glittering. Behind it, in the darkness, other creatures bared their teeth.

He held his gun steady, ready to fire again but reticent to do so in the corridor, where a ricochet might hit Ingrid.

With a growl, the beast turned and ran. The others ran with it, footsteps fading away into the tunnels.

Dirk sighed in relief.

#

They were halfway back to the servants' quarters, a trembling Ingrid leaning on Dirk's arm, when he heard a sound he'd been waiting for since Colonel Wulff's visit.

Rifle fire.

To some people, it might have sounded like rocks falling in the distance. But Dirk could tell that noise apart from any other in the world. There were times when his life had depended upon it.

"Do you think they're taking pot shots from their camp?" Blaze-Simms asked when Dirk pointed out the noise.

Dirk shook his head. "It's too close. And what good would that do against a castle?"

Unease spread through him as he tried to work out where the firing came from. He worked his way through the map of the castle he'd been piecing together in his head, trying to connect the different rooms, to gain a sense of direction in the bewildering mass of tunnels and half-forgotten rooms. As he came closer to a conclusion, unease turned to fierce determination.

"They're at one of the side doors," he said. "Must have snuck someone in and unbarred it, or blown it open while we were too far away to hear."

"I hope the traps we laid worked," Blaze-Simms said. "They should give the ladies an edge if it comes to a fight."

An image of Prussian troops storming the castle filled Dirk's brain. He imagined grey-haired Heinrich and Gräfin Beatrix trying to fend them off. Worse yet was what followed across his mind's eye - Isabelle McNair, bloody and battered, disappearing beneath a sea of guns and blades.

He passed Ingrid, wild-eyed with fear, over to Blaze-Simms, and sprinted off towards the sounds of violence.

#

As Dirk raced along the corridors, the sound of gunfire was joined by the clash of steel and angry Germanic shouting. He rounded a corridor and came into a square room with sculptures and vases on pedestals around the walls. Several had been smashed. Gunfire emerged from a doorway to his left, bullets bouncing off a nearby wall.

Noriko stood across the gallery from him, the steady stream of gunfire separating them. Around her lay a dozen bodies in blue uniforms, their guns and clubs scattered, their blood staining the black and white tiles. Her katana was in her hand, blood dripping from the blade, as she calmly watched the bouncing bullets.

"What happened?" Dirk asked, counting the seconds between bullets.

"They came in through upper windows," Noriko said. "Tried to seize me and Isabelle. They were looking for you and Timothy too."

"Guess Wulff's making this personal." Dirk opened the chamber of his Gravemaker, picked out the shell from the bullet he had fired earlier, and slid a new round in. Bullets continued to strike the wall, as steady and disciplined as a clock counting away their lives.

"Or he wished to remove the best warriors," Noriko said. "I have watched the servants. Isabelle and Timothy remain the third and fourth best fighters in this castle."

"Which of us is number two?"

"You."

"Seems fair." He closed the gun.

Beyond the gunfire, grunts of pain were accompanied by the clash of weapons.

"Where's Isabelle?" Dirk asked, frowning.

Noriko pointed down the corridor.

"Penned into a storeroom," she said. "I was nearly through to her, but then..."

She pointed at the bullet-scarred wall.

"Now there's two of us," Dirk said, tensing ready to charge. "Doubles our chances of getting through."

"Too many guns." Noriko shook her head. "You are not normally so stupid."

Taken aback, Dirk stared at her. He couldn't remember Noriko ever speaking like that. Worse yet, she was right.

"What do we do, then?" he asked. "We can't just let them capture her."

"How strong are you?" Noriko pointed at the oriental vase next to Dirk. Underneath it was a stone plinth four feet high and nearly as wide as a door.

Dirk holstered his pistol and bent his knees, placed a hand on each side of the plinth, and lifted. Stitches popped at the shoulder of his shirt as his muscles bulged, straining to bear the improvised stone shield. The vase wobbled and then fell to the ground, shattering at his feet.

"Let's go," he said between gritted teeth.

Three sideways steps took him in front of the doorway. A bullet cracked off the pedestal, ricochet from the ceiling and shattered a floor tile. The briefest moment of black-clad movement told Dirk that Noriko had moved up behind him.

He began to advance, his steps slow thanks to the extra weight. Momentum took over as he picked up speed. The stone dragged him forward, threatening to topple him if he didn't move faster. The sounds of gunfire grew more rapid and chips of stone sliced the back of his fingers, while a commanding voice yelled in frantic Prussian.

Then there was a thud. A soldier fell in front of him, hit by the unstoppable mass of stone. Dirk just managed to avoid tripping over him, then became tangled in the legs of the next soldier to fall. The rock slipped from between his fingers as he struggled to stay upright, and the pedestal crashed to the ground. A man screamed as his leg was crushed beneath the stone, but Dirk just kept running, leaping over the obstacle and straight into the enemy, not giving them a chance to regroup.

Grabbing the barrel of the nearest Prussian's rifle, he yanked the man around, slamming his head against the wall. Hands slid from the weapon, letting Dirk swing it as a club, taking down another soldier. Then he spun it around, sank to one knee and snapped off a hasty shot. Twenty yards down the corridor, by a door onto the battlements, a Prussian fell.

Three more men moved into the doorway. As they raised their weapons, Dirk dived forward and to the left, rolling into a side room as bullets hit the flagstones behind him.

Soldiers turned in surprise as Dirk appeared in the room. Using the momentum of his forward roll, he propelled himself to his feet, each fist coming up beneath a Prussian jaw. A third man fell as Isabelle stepped out of the corner and ran him through with a narrow sword.

Three Prussians remained in the room. With the element of surprise gone, they had the advantage over Dirk, armed as they were with bayoneted rifles instead of just their fists. He dodged two flashing blades while the third held Isabelle at bay.

One Prussian stabbed at Dirk from the left and one from the right. Unable to dodge both, he leaned into the attack from his left, catching it on his forearm. The bayonet scored a hot line of pain across his skin and blood flowed freely as he came inside the man's reach. He head-butted him.

As the Prussian slid to the ground, Dirk took hold of his rifle and spun around. He parried an attack from the other soldier, then drove him out into the corridor with a series of swift jabs.

More shouts were coming towards them down the corridor. Shoving aside the remaining Prussian, Dirk grabbed Isabelle's hand and dragged her out of the room, his heart hammering. She parried a rifle butt, sliced its bearer across the guts, and then they went racing back towards the heart of the castle, bullets and shouts following them up the corridor.

As they reached the gallery of shattered sculptures, Blaze-Simms appeared.

"Look what I found in my pocket!" he exclaimed, waving a stick of dynamite.

Before Dirk could respond, Blaze-Simms lit the fuse and flung the explosive down the corridor.

"What about Noriko?" Dirk asked.

"Here." She emerged from behind one of the pedestals. A thin stream of blood was running down her thigh and her frown was deeper than Dirk had ever seen it.

There was a roar as the dynamite went off. The floor shook. A blast of hot air and dust swept into the room. As Dirk fought to catch his breath, Isabelle snatched her hand out of his. By the time the air cleared she was gone and Noriko with her.

As the last echoes of the explosion cleared all other thoughts from his mind, Dirk looked down at his hand and realised a terrible truth. That one brief moment, the urgency with which Isabelle had pulled away from him, had hurt more than the bayonet cut.

"That got them," Blaze-Simms said, peering down the corridor. "Completely blocked it, and they won't be able to bring heavy lifting equipment up here. A fine job, if I do say so myself" He dusted off his hands, face slowly falling as he did so. "Unless it weakens the structural integrity of the the castle, of course. Or the Gräfin makes me pay for the damages. Or-"

"Tim," Dirk said, still staring at his hand. "Can I tell you a secret?"

"Of course you can, old chap." Blaze-Simms looked at him with concern. "What is it?"

"I think I'm still in love with Isabelle."

"Sorry, old chap," Blaze-Simms said, patting him on the shoulder, "but the only person you kept that secret from was yourself."

Chapter 5: To Prove That You're Better

"Don't you have a servant who could do this?" Dirk asked.

Beatrix finished tying the bandage around his forearm, tucking the ends neatly away. Her fingers lingered a little longer than was needed, just long enough for Dirk to feel a small squirm of discomfort. This time he was sure that the woman attending to him was married - he'd even met her husband.

"After you saved us all from those ghastly Prussians?" Beatrix asked, smiling at him. "This is the least I could do."

She smiled at him, eyes half closed. Dirk cleared his throat and looked away, out through the open shutters of the parlour window, down into the valley below.

By the last light of dusk he could see the Prussians milling around their forward camp. They had been all bustle since Dirk and his comrades drove back their attack. Maybe they were planning something new, maybe they were busy arguing over blame, or maybe they just needed to keep busy to distract themselves from their losses - he'd seen all those responses to failure in his time. What mattered to him now was that they couldn't get into the castle.

A knock on the door announced the arrival of Heinrich holding a silver tray. On it was a letter in a white envelope, the letter "B" written on the outside in a curling script.

"From the Graf," Heinrich said, bowing his head to Beatrix.

"Again?" She took the envelope and sliced it open with a single elegant nail. Her scowl deepened as she read the contents. "More nonsense, as I expected. I know the Prussians have him agitated, but if I agreed with him on his science then he wouldn't be where he is."

She strode over to the fireplace and flung the letter into the flames. Then she turned to face Heinrich.

"Tell him to stop this nonsense," she said.

"I will do my best," Heinrich said. "But he is my lord, there is only so much I can do."

As the elderly servant turned away, Dirk saw a flicker of sadness cross his face. Then Heinrich was back to his indignantly efficient self, striding out the door and away.

"Now, where were we?" Beatrix returned to the window with slow, swaying steps. Lipstick gleamed, matching the scarlet of her dress. "Do you read gothic novels at all, Mr Dynamo? Tales of adventure, horror and romance. Something to make the pulse pound."

She stepped close to him, looking up with sparkling blue eyes.

"Really, Beatie." Isabelle stood in the doorway, arms folded, one eyebrow raised. "Are you still using that line?"

Beatrix laughed and stepped away from the blushing Dirk.

"Can't a countess have some fun?" she asked.

"Can't a lady have some dignity?" Isabelle replied.

Both women smiled and laughed, but Dirk thought there was an edge to Isabelle's tone. A flicker of hope stirred in his heart. Was Isabelle jealous?

He took a deep breath. The longer he waited, building up the courage to say what he wanted to say, the harder it would get. He should just bite the bullet.

"Gräfin Beatrix," he said in his most respectful tone. "Would you mind giving us a moment to talk alone? I reckon Mrs McNair and I need to have a conversation."

"How intriguing!" Beatrix said. "Are you sure I can't listen in?"

Despite her words, she was already on her way towards the door. As she passed Isabelle she laid a hand on her friend's shoulder.

"You must tell me all the juicy details later," she said, and then was gone.

Alone in the parlour with Isabelle, Dirk became intensely aware of every detail of the moment. The fall of her blue silk dress. The candles in the sconces around the room, taking over from the sinking sun as the main source of light. The fire in the hearth, its warmth battling the cold of the stones and the autumn air. Motes of dust drifting in front of the bookshelf. With terrible care, he pulled back one of the armchairs by the fireplace and offered it to Isabelle. As she sat cautiously on the edge of the seat, he settled into the one opposite.

Isabelle's face was a perfect heart shape framed by two ringlets of dark hair. Not for the first time, Dirk found himself at a loss of words in front of her. He knew what he wanted to say, but he struggled to find the words he needed. Poetic sentiments and romantic gestures had never been high on his list of studies, and he was struggling to remember the bits he knew. They were crowded out of his mind by the vision before him.

"You said we need to talk," Isabelle said, tapping a finger against the arm of her chair. "So talk."

"Gimme a moment," Dirk said. "This ain't easy."

"It never is with you, is it?" Isabelle said.

"OK, here's the thing." Dirk leaned forward, meeting her unwavering gaze. "Earlier today, when you were in danger, that made me realise something. Something I ain't comfortable with, but that I ain't gonna deny.

"Right now, I should hate you. After everything that happened between us, the way you turned around and betrayed me in Paris, that hurt like hell. It was like taking a knife in the guts, and trust me, I'd know. But when you were in danger, when I thought you might be killed or carried off by Prussians, that hurt just as bad. It was like having everything light and good snatched away. Like that knife had been pulled out then plunged straight back in again. And that's when I knew.

"Despite what you did, despite what we're both after, despite all the craziness around us right now - I love you like I've never loved anyone in my life. I can't imagine ever not loving you. I'm not one of those men who lies easy to get a woman to go with him, or one who can say how he's feeling without a struggle. So believe me, I wouldn't be saying this if it weren't the most important damn thing in my whole world right now.

"I love you."

He sank bank into his chair, exhausted at the effort of getting the words out, anxious over what might follow, waiting for a response.

Isabelle just sat staring at him, her expression unchanging. Darkness had descended outside and the flickering light of the fire gave her face its only movement. The silence pressed in upon Dirk until he couldn't bear it any more.

"That's why I had to rescue you, you see," he continued. "I ran all the way across the castle to make sure you were safe. Went in against all those Prussians to rescue you. I couldn't take the thought of-"

"Someone to rescue," Isabelle said, the word as cold and hard as steel. "That's how you see me, isn't it?"

"Sometimes, yes. Hell, a lot of the time, given our work."

"Then let me put your concerns to rest. I am not some damsel in distress, waiting for you to sweep in, rush me off my feet and romance me with your heroic charms."

"That ain't what I meant."

"Really? Because that's what it sounded like."

"I meant..." Dirk grimaced as he battled to find the words. He felt like his brain was a mass of stuck gears, clogged up with feelings he could barely control. "I just... Oh, forget it."

"Gladly." Isabelle strode across the room. "If I wanted some arrogant, muscle-headed maniac chasing around after me, I could be back in England, screwing sons of noble families for diamonds and favours."

Dirk stared at her. He knew that was something that happened, but to hear anyone say it out loud, especially to hear the words coming from Isabelle's lips, that was something he'd never expected. And to think that she might choose that life, that she could treat someone as just another opportunity for advancement...

"But I love you," he said, unable to find another thought.

"And I have no idea why I ever felt anything for you."

Isabelle slammed the door behind her as she left.

Sorrow and bewilderment gave way to anger as he stared after her.

If that was how things were, then why should he treat her with any damn consideration? Why should he be the reasonable one?

He'd show her. He'd steal the stones and get out of here, as far away from Isabelle McNair as he could. There was no hurt he couldn't get over by throwing himself into action. No pain he couldn't escape with a good enough distraction. All his memories of the mines and the battlefields proved that.

Soon Isabelle McNair would be just one more bad memory.

He could do anything he set his mind to. He could get over this gut-wrenching pain.

#

Any effective military operation began with reconnaissance and planning. So that was where Dirk started - scouting out the turret of the castle that held the best guest room, the one given over to Isabelle McNair.

This was a part of the castle Dirk had spent less time in. A space inhabited by men with titles and women who preferred to be known as ladies. Rooms that included the Gräfin's grand bedchamber and two more for her favourite guests. There was a safety in life below stairs. Up here there were fine paintings and ancient tapestries on the walls - things Dirk would have liked to study, things that belonged in a museum where ordinary folks could get to see them. Houses with that sort of thing put him on edge.

Isabelle's room wasn't as high up the tower as he'd expected. It seemed that the Red Castle's builders preferred to keep guests at arm's length, with only the family rooms on the upper floors. Instead, Isabelle was housed in a large south-facing room where a tower rose out of the main castle, right by the stairs leading down to the dining hall and servants quarters.

It should have been easy enough to find. Isabelle was the sort of person who left her shoes out for the staff to clean. In Dirk's opinion, a person should take care of their own boots - it wasn't hard, and boots were important. But as an investigator, it was a habit that came in handy when he was tracking down someone wealthy, old-fashioned, or aspirational.

To Dirk's surprise there weren't many lamps or torches lit along this stretch of corridor. He almost tripped over the tell-tale shoes before spotting them.

He tried the door handle, for form's sake, and as expected it was firmly locked. So he knelt by the keyhole and examined the lock. He was no expert in the not-so-fine art of lock picking, but there were some mechanisms that could be opened with the right application of brute force.

The low light made it hard to see inside the lock and he was considering fetching a lamp when he heard a disapproving cough.

Turning, Dirk saw Heinrich stood in the entrance to a stairwell the servants used to discretely roam the castle. He held a tray loaded with plates and silverware for that night's dinner.

"Americans." The butler shook his head. "When the Gräfin hears about this you will be gone, and good riddance."

"I don't know." Dirk stood, trying to look unconcerned. "I reckon Gräfin Beatrix is mighty fond of me. Might give me a pass this one time."

"Gräfin Beatrix is no fool," Heinrich said. "And your insulting tone will not help."

A shadow moved in the stairwell behind Heinrich. Something tall and angular that set Dirk's nerves on edge.

"Behind you," he said, pointing.

"I am no fool either," Heinrich said. "You think you can trick me like this? And then what? Hit me over the head and lock me in a cupboard? Push me down the stairs and call it an accident? I think naaarrrgghhh!"

His clipped words turned into a scream as a claw sliced through his left arm, shredding the sleeve of his tailcoat and spraying the corridor with blood. The tray fell from his hand with an almighty crash.

It was dark in the corridor and the thing had gotten tangled with Heinrich. Dirk had his revolver, but a shot was as likely to strike the servant as to hit its mark. Instead he pulled a Bowie knife from his boot and leapt forward.

The creature had the flexing tale and long jaw of a lizard, sharp teeth gnashing up and down. Its arms were thick and muscled like those of a bear, but with claws like kitchen knives. Its legs bent in three different places and it stood on one foot while the other grasped the door frame, claws splintering the wood. Eyes flashed bright and cold as lightning on a midwinter night.

It was the craziest creature Dirk had ever seen, but that wasn't going to stop him. Grabbing the creature's right wrist, he shoved the arm upwards, lunged forwards, and drove his knife towards the vulnerable spot under the armpit. The arm seemed to writhe in his hand and the creature leapt over the attack. It caught the top of the doorway and hung there.

The creature's claws were mostly taken up with clinging on. Dirk slashed at it with his knife but the blade slid off a layer of thick scales.

Fire appeared to Dirk's right. The monster screamed as Heinrich thrust a blazing torch at its face. It clawed at Heinrich. The torch fell to the ground. Long strips of flesh hung loose amid the rags on the servant's arm.

"Are you crazy?" Dirk shouted at the pale faced and blood-soaked man. "You're half dead already. Get behind me!"

"You'd like that, wouldn't you?" Heinrich said as he staggered back, leaning against the wall. "The chance to save me. To prove that you're better. To put me in your debt."

"What?" Dirk darted forward as the creature leapt back into the stairwell. The air smelled of scorched flesh and Heinrich's blood. This time Dirk stabbed at the creature's face. It raised its arm as he had expected, and he turned the point of his knife into the blow, ramming it through the scales. Thick blood spattered Dirk's hand, hanging in dark globules, and the creature jerked back, taking the knife with it.

"I see through you, Herr Spies Through Keyholes." Heinrich's voice grew faint as he slid down the wall, leaving behind a scarlet smear. "This is how men... how men of... how... get... way..."

Teeth bared, the creature leapt at Dirk. It was as heavy as he was, and he'd already seen the incredible strength in its legs. It knocked him back, pinning him to the ground, and wrapped its tail around him. Dirk grabbed its throat, but still the teeth snapped an inch from his face, the weight of the creature pushing them slowly closer.

"Heinrich!" he yelled. "Heinrich, dammit, do something!"

The German didn't stir.

In desperation, Dirk took one hand off the creature's throat. The beast pushed down, Dirk rolled his head to one side, and the creature landed flat on top of him, pressing him against the stones.

His fingers closed around the handle of his knife. The creature screamed as he pulled it free, then screamed again as he rammed the blade into its guts. This time he kept his grip on the knife as the creature staggered back, howled once more in pain, and vanished into the darkness of the stairwell.

Scrambling across the blood-slicked floor, Dirk reached Heinrich and grabbed him by the shoulders.

"Come on," he said. "We've got to get you some help."

Empty eyes stared back at him, glassy and unmoving. Dirk tore off his shirt and started wrapping it around Heinrich's ravaged arm, but already the flow of blood was slowing.

Reluctantly, Dirk set his fingers to Heinrich's neck.

There was no pulse.

"Dammit!" Dirk clenched his fists so tight the knuckles went pale. "Why didn't you stay behind me, you idiot?"

Heinrich's words came back to him. About Dirk proving he was better. About putting the other man in his debt. Heinrich must have thought Dirk would use it to stop the butler reporting him. But was that worth dying for?

Then Dirk thought about the things he'd put his life at risk for - everything from freeing slaves to finding old books. Stopping a burglar preying on a guest wasn't as important a reason as some, but maybe it wasn't as dumb as the rest.

Voices were coming, drawn by the sounds of fighting. Blaze-Simms, Noriko, and Isabelle appeared at the end of the corridor, all armed. They stared in shock at Dirk and the body beside him.

"Wasn't me," he said, pointing at Heinrich.

"Nobody thought it was, old chap," Blaze-Simms said.

Heinrich hadn't wanted to be rescued. But then, neither had Isabelle. As Dirk looked at her, he finally fitted the pieces together. Her logic was a lot like Heinrich's. Or to look at it the other way, Dirk's actions were the same with both. However well-intentioned, keeping coming to the rescue meant keeping on proving that he was better than them, that they needed him. For a woman like Isabelle McNair - hell, maybe for any woman worth knowing - that wasn't a way they wanted to be.

Weighed down with more kinds of sorrow than he knew what to do with, Dirk reached out for the hand Noriko was offering and let her help him up. He was shirtless, blood-soaked and bruised. A good man lay dead next to him and a wounded monster was roaming the castle.

It was a hell of a moment for sudden bursts of self-reflection.

Chapter 6: Thief, Hunter, Soldier

Dirk hovered hesitantly in the stairwell, peering into the corridor outside Isabelle's room. Ingrid and another servant had finished cleaning up the blood half an hour before. Isabelle was with Beatrix in one of the parlours, consoling her on the loss of Heinrich, who had apparently been with the family since she was young. If ever there was a time to act, it was now. The thought left Dirk feeling dirty, but that didn't stop it being true.

The door was solid pine, painted white like those of the castle's other well-appointed rooms. An ornate silver-plated handle gleamed above the keyhole. None of what he saw told him anything he didn't already know. Yet still he waited.

He tried to tell himself that the bright lighting was the problem. More lanterns had been lit throughout the castle following the attack, to prevent anyone else being taken by surprise. That meant he was more likely to be spotted breaking into Isabelle's room. It was a reason to be cautious.

But it wasn't a great reason. Not with everything else that was going on. It was needless hesitation at a time when every moment mattered. So why hadn't he stepped out into the light and gotten to work?

The answer, as so often, was Isabelle's anger. He knew that she had reasons for it, even if he didn't consider them much better than his reasons for hesitating. Wouldn't doing this just reinforce her anger by proving that he couldn't be trusted?

Except that it was her treachery that had gotten them into this place. All he'd done was try to help. Why should he feel guilty for doing what needed to be done?

His eyes were drawn to a row of dark spots near the bottom of the door. Heinrich's blood had soaked through a flaw in the paint, staining the pristine surface so deeply that it wouldn't wash away. Tomorrow someone would paint over it. Today, it was a reminder of what Dirk had witnessed here. A shocking death, and a close brush with his own mortality.

Death could come at any moment. Life was too short to waste.

He peered up and down the stairs one last time. Seeing no-one, hearing no-one, he let his excuses go with a deep breath and crept out into the hallway.

As before, he started by trying the door handle. As before, the door was locked. Sinking into a crouch, he peered into the keyhole.

There was darkness beyond - a good sign, given what he was about to do. But that meant he could see nothing of the mechanisms. It barely mattered. He understood the bare basics of the locksmith's art - any private investigator picked up a little - but not enough to pick this. He would have to rely on the skill of others instead.

He drew a slender metal cylinder from his pocket, something no wider than a pencil and only as long as his little finger. Following Blaze-Simms's instruction, he inserted it in the lock and twisted a narrow band on its surface. Tiny rubber-ended grips shot out, locking the device in place.

Then he turned the tiny winding key until it wouldn't turn any more.

The device whirred and clicked. To Dirk, crouched alone in the silence of the corridor, it sounded like the loudest noise in the world. Then a Prussian gun opened fire outside, and he stopped worrying about any sounds he might make. At last there was a thunk from inside the door and the device fell silent.

Dirk turned the handle and pushed the door back just enough for him to slip into the darkness beyond, retrieving Blaze-Simms's device on the way. A bandage trailing from his forearm caught on the latch. He winced as his wound was pulled open and fresh blood dribbled down the edge of the door. Quickly shutting it behind him, he re-tied the bandage in the gloom, then pulled a box of matches from his pocket and lit a candle.

That small, flickering light danced across a room fit for a royal palace. As Dirk lit more candles in a silver stand on the dresser, their glow reflected off a floor-length mirror in a golden frame, another mirror at head height above a pristine porcelain basin, and a suit of plate armour standing guard in the corner. Silk sheets, velvet curtains, embossed floral wallpaper, a marble fireplace with an enamelled cigarette box on the mantle...

It was the sort of opulence whose beauty took Dirk's breath away and whose cost sickened him. There were folks living in slums in New York, Manchester, and Berlin who could have lived for a year off the price of just one of those mirrors. He didn't hold it against someone like Beatrix personally - most folks just went along with the values they were taught - but it was a reminder of what dark and twisted things let the Red Castle exist.

Amid such wealth, there were plenty of hiding places for the stones. If he wasn't to miss one then he needed to be systematic.

Starting to the left of the door, he worked his way around, opening cupboards and drawers, lifting boxes and peering under chairs, putting everything back where he found it.

As one drawer slid out, he found himself staring at a pile of Isabelle's underwear. He flushed, slammed it shut, then cursed himself for an irrational jackass. A stone could be hiding here as easily as anywhere else, and he'd seen more than just Isabelle's underwear.

Still, he felt like the intruder he was, and it was only slowly that he opened the drawer again.

Caught up in his own conflicting thoughts, he barely registered the sound of footsteps in the corridor or the way they stopped outside the door.

"Hello?" Ingrid called out.

Quiet as he could, Dirk slid the drawer shut and stepped over to the candlestick.

"Hello?" Ingrid said uncertainly.

Dirk blew out the candles and scrambled under the bed, just as the door handle turned and the door swung open.

From his position under the bed, Dirk could see Ingrid's shoes, her ankles, and the bottom of her skirts illuminated by a candle in her hand and the light from the corridor. She paused in the doorway, turning as if to peer at the edge of the door. Then she sniffed, sniffed again, and walked over to the table holding the candlestick. There was a rustle as she leaned forward for a closer look.

If he'd still been working for the Pinkerton detectives, Dirk would have hired her on the spot. Warm wicks, molten wax, lingering trails of smoke - she'd spotted the tell-tale signs. Ingrid might have made quite the detective if she hadn't been born to a life of service. Maybe she could yet.

That wasn't a good thing for Dirk.

His fingers dug into the rug as he watched her feet cross to the dresser, where she could inspect the lamp. There was a scraping sound as she pushed a drawer in an extra inch. He could see her tension in the stiffness of her movements. With monsters and Prussians both threatening the castle, it showed great courage not to run straight off for help. It also showed smarts, knowing that might give an intruder the chance to get away.

The wardrobe door swung open at her touch, then swung closed again. At last came the moment Dirk had been dreading as she approached the bed.

He lay still. There was always a chance she might get distracted, might not see him in the gloom, might-

She bent over, lifted up the valance and stared straight at him. Her expression went from surprise to relief to an angry scowl.

"Herr Dynamo," she said.

"Hi." Dirk rolled out the other side of the bed then stood, staring across the sheets at her. It could have been worse, the girl was clearly fond of him. He could talk his way out of this. "Listen, I know this doesn't look good, but I've got reasons for being here. I'm sure you don't need to tell Mrs McNair."

"You," Ingrid said. "I think you good man. You not. You bad man. Thief."

"No!" Dirk said. "Least, not the bad part. Just give me a chance to-"

"I tell Gräfin," Ingrid said, waving a finger at him. "You bad thief man."

She strode towards the door. Dirk leapt to intercept her. As his hand closed around her arm, a look of terrible alarm filled her face. Immediately, Dirk let go.

"I'm sorry," he said, hanging his head in shame. "You go tell the Gräfin."

#

Dirk's bowie knife lay next to a pile of bullets on his bed, the only possessions worth a damn that he hadn't left back in Paris. For all he knew his bag was here - after all, they'd loaded their luggage into the balloon Isabelle and Noriko took. But it wasn't until now that he'd thought to ask, and it really didn't seem the time.

A knocking on the door made him look up from cleaning and reloading his gun.

"Who is it?" he called out.

"It's me," Blaze-Simms said. "That is to say, it's Sir Timothy. I mean, you can't see me through the door, and I don't know how well you can hear, so saying 'it's me' might not have been the best thing I could-"

"Come in, Tim," Dirk said.

The door opened and Blaze-Simms came in. He was smeared with dust and oil, his tailcoat was unbuttoned and his cravat was askew. Usually these were signs that he'd been inventing, but his expression was one of concern rather than excitement.

"I say, old chap," he said, "what are you up to?"

"Getting ready for trouble," Dirk replied, slamming the chamber of his Gravemaker closed. He holstered the pistol, drew a whetstone from his pocket and set to work sharpening the knife. Candles cast shadows into the corners of the room and across its high beamed ceiling.

"I'm really not sure these are appropriate for dealing with ladies," Blaze-Simms said, looking at the weapons. "Even angry ones."

"This ain't for them." Dirk paused in his work. He wasn't any more comfortable with this conversation than with the things he'd been feeling, but he couldn't avoid either of them forever. He put the knife and the whetstone down, then looked Blaze-Simms in the eye. "Word's gotten around, huh?"

"I'm afraid so. Beatrix is terribly cross."

"And Isabelle?"

"Strangely quiet. A little smug maybe?"

"Could be worse," Dirk said, unsure what the worse might be.

"So, this..." Blaze-Simms waved towards the knife.

"I've been trying to do everything at once, and getting all of it wrong," Dirk said. "Getting obsessed with getting the stones, when we're in real danger. It's like... I don't know what it's like."

"Like that time in Moscow?"

Just the name of the city conjured vivid memories. Blaze-Simms pausing to admire Vladimir Petrovsky's laboratory. Angry Cossacks poured in through the ceiling. The Englishman gathering samples while Dirk fought off Tsarist agents. In the here and now, Blaze-Simms had the decency to look sheepish at the memory.

"Just like that," Dirk said, not mentioning the hundred other times his friend had acted that way.

"Is it really about the stones?" Blaze-Simms asked.

"Does it really matter?" Dirk snatched up the knife and slid it into its sheath. "What's important is that there are real threats. From now on I'm dealing with them in order of how likely they are to get us all killed. First the monsters, then the Prussians, then back to dealing with Mrs McNair and the stones."

"I really don't think there's any risk Isabelle will kill you."

"Maybe not, but she's damn close to driving me insane."

"Did you say monsters?"

He'd never wanted to tell anyone what was going on in his head. It was awkward to even think about and talking about feelings wasn't something he'd ever felt right with. But suddenly the urge was overwhelming. Like the first trickle of water that presaged the bursting of a damn, the acknowledgement of his frustration left the rest bursting to get out. If he was going to talk with anyone, it ought to be his best friend.

"Listen, Tim," he began. "This ain't my usual way of dealing with stuff, but I want to-"

"Dirk Dynamo!" His name was a screech echoing down the hallway and through the door, losing none of its ear-splitting force along the way. Dirk took a step back as angry strides and furiously rustling skirts announced Gräfin Beatrix's imminent arrival. She stormed into the room, her face a picture of fury, and planted her hands on her hips as she glared at him.

"I should throw you out of my castle this instant," she declared.

"You'd be well within your rights," Dirk said.

"And then I should sue you," she said.

"Can't say I disagree."

"And then I should... Then I should..." She pointed at him. "You're meant to be arguing. How can there be any passion in life if you won't argue?"

Dirk shrugged.

"Passion ain't exactly my thing," he said.

"That's not what I hear." Beatrix smiled and raised an eyebrow, then seemed to remember that she wanted to be furious. "Do you have anything to say in your defence?"

"Nothing that ain't been said already. I tried to rob a guest in your house. I got caught up in that when there were real threats to face. You want me to leave, I'll head off now. Try to sneak out through the Prussian lines. Fight if I have to. Pick up chasing Mrs McNair and the stones later, if I can ever find her again."

"No." The voice came as if from nowhere, cool and calm. Without pausing for thought, Dirk drew his gun and spun around, looking for the source. Beatrix backed up against the wall, clutching a hand to her chest, while Blaze-Simms glanced around in curiosity.

A shadow detached from the ceiling beams. With a sound no louder than the dropping of a handkerchief, Noriko landed on the floor by the window.

"How long have you been here?" Dirk asked. Part of him felt outraged that she had been spying on him, but a smarter part knew he was in no place to complain. She wasn't the first of them to violate someone's privacy.

"Dynamo is the second most capable fighter here," Noriko said. "He must stay."

"Excuse me?" Now the Gräfin looked indignant, lips pursed and hands once more on hips. "This is my home. It is not for any guest to tell me what to do."

"We face an army," Noriko said. "And monsters."

"Well, perhaps..." The Gräfin looked away, apparently embarrassed. "Though I don't think we need to worry about-"

"Once we have dealt with these, then we deal with the rest." Noriko prowled forwards until she stood inches from Beatrix. "Yes?"

The Gräfin took a deep breath and squared her shoulders as if preparing for another dramatic outburst. Then a colder look crossed her eyes and she let out a long sigh.

"Fine," she said. "Perhaps it's time we worked out a plan."

#

As dawn broke, there were three of them left sitting in the grand hall - Dirk, Blaze-Simms, and Noriko. The rest of the castle's inhabitants had finally gone to bed, leaving empty coffee cups and plans of the building scattered across the table. The servants had looked uncomfortable leaving that mess. Almost as uncomfortable as when Dirk invited them all to sit and join the planning. They'd play their part when the fighting came, but none of them were going to throw off the shackles of oppression any time soon.

"You sure you can't come monster hunting with us?" Dirk asked. "You're one hell of a fighter."

"You are a hunter," Noriko said. "I am a warrior and a commander. We cannot leave these people without a leader against the Prussians. We cannot ignore the monsters. Each of us must do what they do best."

"I wish we had the rest of your ninjas here," Blaze-Simms said. "This plan feels terribly weak. A dozen servants and a handful of adventurers against an entire Prussian army."

"We may lose," Noriko said. "But we will not surrender."

A grandfather clock chimed in the corner of the room. As if on queue, artillery began to fire outside, the same roar that had greeted each morning since their arrival.

"Wish I'd had time to sleep before doing this." Dirk downed his last cold cup of coffee. "Guess that'll have to do instead. You ready, Tim?"

"Absolutely!" Blaze-Simms scooped up the loose gears scattered in front of them, dropped them into his pocket and reached for his rifle. "I can't wait to get hold of some of these things and have a look at how they're put together.

Working out the genus will be the first priority, but there are many other questions."

"You understand we're going to kill them, not study them, right?" Dirk asked.

"Can't I do both?"

"Let's see how it goes." Dirk stretched ready for action. Grabbing a last cigar from the box on the mantle, he lit it on a candle and took a deep, satisfying drag. If he was going to risk death at the hands of those deadly creatures, he deserved one small indulgence first. "Plan's come together. Let's get to work."

Chapter 7: Down in a Hole

Corridors weren't great places to go hunting. Ones with stone floors were the worst. You might not get many tracks on wooden boards, but at least there was a chance that something would scratch or snag, leaving a mark of its passing. With carpets and rugs, you got dirt stains and indentations, even if they could be hard to spot. With stone, unless the prey had really filthy feet or there was a lot of dust, there was seldom a trail at all.

But Dirk had spent half his life hunting one quarry or another - animals, treasures, fugitives, enemy agents. He'd found that if you thought real hard, there was always a way to do it.

When that way involved listening for the slightest of sounds, having Timothy Blaze-Simms along wasn't a great help.

"Sorry," the inventor whispered as his pocket watch chimed, once again disturbing the stillness of the corridor. "I thought I'd turned that off."

He pulled the watch out and started fiddling with the dials on its side, while Dirk peered down the four passages running off this junction, their only light the lanterns they carried. A gargoyle cast a shadow across the ceiling, its small stone wings growing huge as a silhouette against the arched stones. A rat skittered to a stop at the edge of the darkness, peered up at Dirk with beady eyes, and scurried away again without even a chitter.

These creatures, whatever they were, had the vermin scared into silence.

"Which way?" Blaze-Simms asked as he put his watch away.

Dirk shook his head. Two hours and not a single clue. A different approach was needed.

"Let's go talk to the Graf," he said.

"You think he might have learnt something about these creatures?" Blaze-Simms asked.

"Reckon so," Dirk said, as they set off up the corridor. He still hadn't got this place straight in his head - every time he thought he'd learnt the layout, he rounded a corner and a door wasn't where he'd expected. But he knew roughly which way they needed to go, and that was better than nothing. "If I lived down here, and those things were running around, I'd have taken an interest in them."

"He seems like a man of science," Blaze-Simms said. "Did you see the equipment in his room? Chemicals, glassware, burners, scales, all sorts. At the very least, he's a keen chemist. His curiosity must have been peaked."

"I just figured he was cooking his own drugs," Dirk said. "Keeping himself entertained while he's locked up."

"He wouldn't be the first chemist to go down that path," Blaze-Simms said. "And being locked in those rooms, unable to get out into the world, it must be maddening for a man with an agile mind."

"That should help with the other thing I want to discuss," Dirk said.

"What's that, old chap?"

"Getting his help with Isabelle and the stones. I figure we get him out of that cell, he might help us out. After all, he's the lord around here."

"I say, what a splendid idea!" Blaze-Simms hesitated. "Although, wasn't he locked up for a reason?"

"And I'm gonna let him out for a reason."

They reached a fork in the corridor. One way led up a flight of steps, the other down a slope.

"Reckon we're heading up," Dirk said.

The stairs twisted and turned, ascending in a way no sane architect would have chosen. At times the walls were carved blocks, at other points the bare stone of the mountainside, its rough surface the same red that made the castle so distinctive.

"I wonder what minerals give it that colour," Blaze-Simms said, pausing to scrape at the rock with a pen-knife. He brushed the resulting dust into a glass bottle no larger than his little finger.

"You can ponder that later," Dirk said. "Once we've dealt with all the strangeness we already know about.

A sound caught his attention and he stopped, hand out to hold back his companion. The tunnel widened up ahead and from there came the scratching of claws against the ground. Larger claws than any rat could have.

A breeze blew down the tunnel and Dirk caught a whiff of something putrid.

"Back," he said softly. "And get your gun ready."

Blaze-Simms obeyed, heals clicking against the stones. Taking a cautious step forward, Dirk reached beneath his arm for the Gravemaker pistol. The hairs on the back of his neck stood up as if his skin had been brushed by an icy cold wind.

No, not as if he had felt that breeze against his neck. Because he had.

He looked up at the uneven and shadowy stone of the ceiling. A pool of darkness hung above him, a tunnel that emerged directly over his head. Staring out of it were a pair of glittering green eyes.

As Dirk flung himself forwards the creature dropped, landing in the space where he had been. Claws caught his boot, threatening to drag him back, and he kicked out. There was a crunch as he hit something, followed by a screech.

Two more creatures had descended behind the first. Scaled snouts snapped. Scales shimmered. Muscles rippled in the darkness.

There was a whir of strange machinery and a sound of footsteps as Blaze-Simms retreated while trying to bring his gun to bear. The two of them were separated by the monsters. The best Dirk could do for his friend was to keep the creatures occupied.

One hand still grasping his lantern, he used the other to push himself up. Claws slashed at him again, ripping his pants but missing flesh. Like a sprinter at the blocks, Dirk dashed away. His footsteps echoed as he emerged from the widening tunnel into a cave, the lantern light illuminating a dead end twenty feet away.

Another of the creatures was in front of him. It wasn't like the one he had fought before. Its head was short and split by a wide jaw, its back hunched, its scales large and glittering blue-green. Rather than slash with its claws it swung a huge fist at him.

Dirk ran forward, ducking under the fist. As he did so he pulled out his knife. A second later he collided with the creature's chest, ramming the knife in up to the hilt. It scraped across scales and bones and became caught between the ribs.

The creature punched Dirk in the back, crushing him against its body and driving the blade deeper. Blood spurted across Dirk's hand and the handle became slippery, but he managed to twist it, levering ribs apart. With a sucking sound the blade came free and fresh blood poured down between them.

The creature seemed weaker as it grabbed Dirk by the upper arm, but not so weak that it couldn't fling him across the cave. He hit the ground hard, inches from a hole that disappeared down into darkness. The lantern smashed against the ground, burning oil spreading across the pink rocks and brightening the cave.

The large creature leaned against the wall, staring down at itself as it clutched its chest. The original three were closing on Dirk now, claws raised. He had just enough time to notice all were different in some way from each other - longer arms, smoother tails, smaller eyes - before they leapt at him.

Lashing out with his knife, he caught one across the arm and it screeched in pain. Another slammed into him, claws sinking into his shoulder. The pain was agonising as a claw jammed in between the bones. Momentarily weakened, he felt his heel cross the edge of the pit behind him.

The creature leaned forward, snapping at him with razor teeth, and Dirk was forced to lean back. They swayed for a moment on the brink of oblivion, as the burning oil consumed itself and the flames sank to almost nothing. Then Dirk lost his footing, the creature pressed forwards, and the two of them fell.

The creature writhed. There was a crack as Dirk's head hit the wall, a momentary flash of searing pain, and then blackness.

#

After being knocked out, the first of Dirk's senses to recover was always taste, closely followed by smell. He'd suffered more blows to the head than he cared to remember, and been left unconscious everywhere from seconds to hours. Each time, it was taste that came back first, then smell.

That was seldom a good thing.

His mouth was full of blood. Before he was aware enough to know what he was doing, he opened his lips to spit it out. Something else trickled in. Something that tasted as rotten as this place stank. His stomach lurched and he rolled onto his hands and knees just in time to avoid puking down himself. As he did so, he felt the thick layer of waste beneath him and the flies buzzing across his skin.

Opening his eyes, he saw only blackness. A moment of terror struck. Was he blind? His head was throbbing, the back warm and sticky with blood. He'd met veterans who had lost their sight to a blow to the head - was he now one of them?

Then he remembered lantern oil burning out on the floor above. The reason he couldn't see was that he was in a dark pit, with no light to guide him.

That memory was followed by another - the monster falling with him. He leapt to his feet, almost slipping over in the filth, and held his hands out ready to fend off an attack.

When nothing came, he crouched and felt around on the ground. There it was - the body of one of those creatures, still a little warm to the touch. Against the odds, it seemed that Dirk had come off better in the fall.

Standing up had been too much for his battered head. A wave of nauseating dizziness overcame him and he vomited again, this time all over the dead creature at his feet. The one advantage of the dreadful stench down here was that he couldn't smell his own puke. As sources of comfort went, that one was pretty cold.

Stretching his hands out, he turned until he found a wall. It was smooth and slimy, impossible to grip. With tentative footsteps, he worked his way around the pit, feeling the walls as he went. His hands became covered in a thick, oily mess, without finding anything that might help him climb up.

For a while, he tried rummaging around in the filth, hoping that his knife had fallen down with him. With that, he might have been able to make some gaps between stones, even if it ruined the blade in the process. But the rotten goop was too thick for him to find anything.

As his hands touched the dead creature once more, a terrible sense of familiarity swept over him. He had been trapped in a hole like this once before, down in the darkness with a rotting corpse. It had been one of the worst experiences of his life.

Twelve years old, already a veteran of the pits, he had been sent down a neglected shaft off the main mine works. The hope was that he might find something others hadn't, with his sharp eyes and his ability to clamber where adults couldn't. He wandered around those tunnels for over an hour, enjoying the freedom of having no-one hovering nearby, waiting to tell him what to do and beat him when he got it wrong. No-one putting explosives in his hands and sending him to plant them.

But as he'd wandered through those tunnels, a row of old boards had given way beneath him. His lantern had flown from his hand as he plunged into the darkness of a pit.

Gritting his teeth, the adult Dirk tried not to think about the rest. The body of the sheep that had somehow gotten down there, and into whose rotting remains he had fallen. The stink of putrescence in the all-consuming blackness. The terror that he might die down there all alone.

This wasn't like that. He could find a way out.

Tipping back his head, Dirk shouted as loud as he could for help.

He had done that back then, as well. His voice hadn't been as deep, and it had been filled with fear, a fear that rose the longer he waited there in the darkness, half-certain that no-one would come for him.

That same panic gripped Dirk now. His breath came fast, his pulse racing.

Taking deep breaths, he fought back the memory. That was in the past. It was his brain playing tricks on him, his mind addled by the blow to his head. He didn't need to think about it. He could get through this. Even if no-one could hear him, he could get out.

With increasingly frantic movements, he rummaged around in the filth, trying to find something to help him. His knife. His gun. A rock. Anything.

His fingers closed around something hard, and for a moment he felt relief. Then he realised that it was just the leg of the rotting sheep, and he flung it away from him in horror.

No, not the sheep. The sheep was far in the past. It was the leg of the monster. The monster was dead. It would be OK. He could get out.

Except that he couldn't. There was no way to climb, no way to dig, nothing he could fight to get out. Trapped and helpless in the pitch darkness, he could hold back the memory no longer. It swept over him, as real as if it were happening there and then. The feeling of being totally, utterly and helplessly alone. The certainty that no-one was coming for him. The emotions of a child, alone and helpless, believing that he was going to die.

It was as if a single blow hit his whole body at once, knocking the energy from him. He sank to the ground, tears running down his face, lost in the confusion of past and present, his head hot and throbbing with pain.

At first he didn't recognise Isabelle's voice for what it was. He thought she was just one more fragment of memory, torturing him with past hurts. But then he heard her again, cutting through the darkness.

"Dirk?" she called in the distance. "Dirk, are you there?"

"Here!" he shouted, as loud and desperate as he had ever been. "Over here! Down in the pit!"

A distant circle of glowing ceiling appeared above him, growing brighter as the light source approached the pit. Then a lantern appeared and Isabelle's face beside it.

Dirk laughed with relief. But as the sound left him the feeling was replaced by sadness. He slumped sobbing to the ground.

"Dirk?" Isabelle said. "Dirk, are you alright?"

The lantern disappeared from view and there was a clunk as she set it down. Dirk couldn't understand the noises that followed. He was too caught up in fighting back the tears and the terror to work it out. Even if he was rescued, his father would beat him for this.

Except that his father was dead, and Dirk had been out of his grasp long before that.

Rope tumbled over the edge of the pit, dangling down the wall in front of Dirk. Isabelle reappeared.

"Hurry up," she said. "We need to get out of here. Timothy distracted those creatures, but they'll be back."

Forcing himself to his feet, Dirk took hold of the rope. He pushed everything else from his mind and just focused on putting one hand above the other, hauling himself up the wall with tired fingers and slippery feet. It was exhausting, but at last he heaved himself over the edge of the pit and lay staring at the ceiling.

"Come on," Isabelle said sharply. "We have to go."

She coiled the rope and turned to look at him as he sat up. Then her expression softened.

"Dirk, are you alright?" she asked.

"The mine," he whispered, intensely glad that she was there - the only person he had ever explained that place to. "While I was down there, I felt like I was back in the mine. The very worst part of it."

"Oh, Dirk." She wrapped her arms around him, the filth in which he was covered smearing her lace-fringed dress. "I'm so sorry."

"It doesn't matter," he said. He felt that he should shrug it all off - the memories, his emotions, her sympathy. This wasn't how a man behaved. But he didn't want to shrug it off, and then and there he hadn't the strength to battle his own desires. "It ain't real any more."

"It looks like it was real enough to you." She stood and offered him a hand, helping him to his feet.

"You rescued me this time," he said, as they started off down the corridor, back towards the heart of the castle.

Isabelle laughed. "I suppose I did. And how do you feel about that?"

"Erm..." Dirk didn't want to say embarrassed, but he had to admit there was some of that. He knew that he shouldn't feel this way. If anyone had said they felt embarrassed at being rescued by him, he would have told them not to sweat it. But this was different.

Wasn't it?

"Now imagine how you would feel if it was always this way around," Isabelle said, an edge of steel beneath her soft tone.

"Yeah, I'm starting to get it," Dirk said. "I ain't entirely sure, but I reckon I might feel sorry about all that later."

"Well, that's a start," Isabelle said with a smile.

Between them, they found their way through the tangled tunnels back to the main staircase, laughing together at the dead ends they took along the way. The throbbing in Dirk's head was fading, though he still felt an unsettling mix of fear, desperation, and embarrassment just beneath the surface of his thoughts.

As they trudged wearily up the stairs, sounds of fighting drifted down to them. They picked up the pace, Isabelle drawing a small pistol from the back of her dress.

Emerging into a hallway, they saw bodies on the ground and smelled gun smoke. As they looked around, trying to grasp what was happening, Noriko raced out of a corridor, blood dripping from her side and a shuriken star in each hand. She ran towards the main doorway at the far end of the hall.

A Prussian soldier appeared in that doorway, gun raised. There was a sharp crack and blood spurted from Noriko's left shoulder. Her arm fell limp and a shuriken clattered to the floor. Her other arm swept around, there was a flash of steel through the air, and the soldier let go of his gun, hands going to the blood spurting from his throat.

Noriko leapt, kicking the dying man back through the doorway, and grabbed hold of the heavy oak door. Dirk and Isabelle rushed over. Bullets whistled down the corridor towards them, chips of stone flying as they hit the doorway or the floor. The three of them swung the door shut, and Dirk slammed the solid bar into place.

Noriko turned to looked at them, her face pale and her breath ragged.

"The outer rooms have fallen," she said, slumping against the wall. "The rest is only a matter of time."

Chapter 8: Talking Things Through

The grip of Dirk's pistol felt calmingly familiar beneath his hand. His fingers tightened around it as the thudding beyond the barricade grew. So far, the Prussian attacks on the distant door had been ineffective, just making a lot of noise. Dirk didn't reckon that would last.

"I should be back there," he said, nodding across the dining hall and down the corridor. "Taking them on."

"Stop moving your head." Isabelle grabbed his jaw and turned his face towards her. "Now follow my finger with your eyes."

Doing as he was told seemed the easiest way out of this and back to the fight, so Dirk watched as Isabelle moved her finger slowly back and forth. Beyond her, he could see Gräfin Beatrix tending to a scowling and heavily bandaged Noriko.

"I didn't know you knew medicine," he said.

"I'm a woman of mystery," Isabelle replied playfully , but her smile quickly faded. "Sometimes playing nurse is the only option left to a woman."

Apparently satisfied, she took a final look at the bandages holding a compress to the back of his head, then the ones wrapping his other wounds.

"Put this on." She handed him a dress shirt that looked like it would just about fit. "Your old one is absolutely filthy."

"So are my pants," Dirk said. "So am I."

"If there was time for a bath I would insist that you take one."

A sharp bang reached them through a high window. It was followed by a crash and loud Germanic cursing.

"Take that, you blighters!" Blaze-Simms yelled somewhere in the distance.

"He ain't fighting them single-handed, is he?" Dirk said with concern. Blaze-Simms was smart and inventive, but the Englishman's situational awareness wasn't great and that could be disastrous if he was caught out on his own.

"He's laying traps," Isabelle said. "He'll be fine."

"We should be fighting," Noriko said. Her patience as a patient apparently spent, she pushed herself up from her chair, paused, and leaned against the table. Her hand settled on the handle of her katana.

"I'm with you." Dirk stood, ready to brush Isabelle aside and get to the action. But she stood firm in front of him, arms folded.

"Neither of you are going anywhere," she said. "Noriko, you've lost too much blood, and you can barely use that arm. Dirk, I don't think your concussion has cleared."

"If things were peaceful we'd rest and recover," Dirk said. "But they ain't, so we need to fight."

"No." Isabelle placed her hand against his chest and pushed. To his surprise, Dirk wobbled and his vision blurred as he sank back into his seat.

"Even if you could fight, you shouldn't," Isabelle continued. "There is an entire army out there. Their artillery has reduced the outer defences to rubble. Their soldiers have taken the south wing. Judging by our lack of monsters, they're also drawing attention in the tunnels. Against them, we have four adventurers, a dozen distinctly un-military servants, and Beatie, who is a cracking shot with a bow but prone to dramatic fainting at the sight of blood."

"It's just all so overwhelming at times," the Gräfin said, pressing a hand against her forehead. "The blood, the horror, those poor young men, their lives torn away."

"You're right, ma'am," Dirk said, remembering fields littered with bodies in blue and grey, the sight of friends torn apart by bullets, bayonets and shrapnel. "War is hell."

"You must tell me about it sometime, Mister Dynamo," the Gräfin said. "Release the pain within you and find a shoulder to-"

"Not now, Beatie," Isabelle said sharply. "We need to focus on getting out of this hell, and that means negotiating."

The Gräfin pouted until Isabelle turned to look at her. Faced with the seriousness of her friend's expression, Beatrix rolled her eyes.

"Fine," she said. "But how will we get those thugs to talk with us?"

"They're soldiers," Isabelle said. "They spend their whole time around other men. I'm sure that Colonel Wulff will treasure the chance to talk with a woman."

"Of course!" Beatrix clapped her hands. "Let's see... You should let down your hair, maybe undo a button or two. Ooh, or I have a dress that-"

"Please, Beatie." Isabelle looked down at herself. "I don't need such cheap tricks."

Looking the same way, Dirk couldn't help but agree. What man was going to say no to Isabelle McNair? But this would put her in danger, and he didn't think he could face that.

As he was about to protest, offering himself as negotiator or bodyguard, memories of their arguments flashed into his mind. All the times he'd assumed that she needed protection, that the woman with a sword in her parasol and a gun in her handbag couldn't take care of herself.

He forced himself to stay quiet, and was surprised to see Isabelle shoot him a quizzical look.

"No comments?" she asked.

Dirk shook his head. "Reckon you know negotiating better than I do."

As Isabelle set out with a white flag and a shout of "Truce!", the guns fell silent and the pounding at the doors ceased. She vanished from view, then there was a thud as the door opened, and the castle went quiet.

For the next two hours, Dirk sat perched in agitation on the edge of his seat. He should have been sleeping - he needed the rest - but he was too preoccupied, too many thoughts dancing through his brain. Instead he exercised, using a stone shaken from the ceiling as an improvised dumbbell. When he tired of that, he got up and went in search of reading matter in the drawing room. Most of the books there were in German, but there were also French, English, Russian, and Italian volumes. He flicked through a dozen books on anatomy, full of vivid illustrations of sliced open bodies, but none of them had text in English. As last he found a copy of Gibbon's Decline and Fall of the Roman Empire and returned with it to the hall. If he couldn't act to improve their situation, he might as well learn.

But hard as he tried, he couldn't get the histories of the Caesars to stick in his brain. Battles and truces, plots and schemes, they danced through his mind and out the far side. The spine of the book buckled beneath the pressure of his fingers as frustration took hold. No amount of deep breathing helped.

Noriko, lying on a pile of blankets across the stone hall, appeared to be sleeping. Judging by her wounds, that was more about inevitability than choice. Blaze-Simms spread wires, glass tubes, and gears across the dining table as he assembled some sort of gadget inside a wooden box. Across the table from the inventor, the Gräfin drank wine, read a gothic novel, and made conversation with anyone who would listen. Periodically, a servant would bring tea, coffee, and sandwiches for all, and more wine for their mistress.

After his third cup of tea, Blaze-Simms held a teaspoon over his box, flipped a switch, and smiled in delight as sparks danced across the silverware.

"That should put the wind up them, eh?" he said.

"Sure, buddy," Dirk replied. "Whatever you say."

At last came the sound of a distant door thudding, followed by the scraping of a bar into place. Dirk bolted to his feet, then sat back down, embarrassed at both his eagerness and his inability to affect events. Footsteps clacked up the corridor to the hall and Isabelle came in frowning.

"I have to say, I expected better of German hospitality," she said, crossing to the table and pouring herself a cup of over-stewed tea. "What sort of colonel keeps a lady waiting and then doesn't even offer her a drink?"

She added milk and sugar to the cup, then sat down, straightened her skirts, and took a sip.

"Well?" Beatrix asked. "Are they utterly intent on ruining me and my beautiful castle?"

Sighing, Isabelle put her cup down.

"They will only accept a surrender if you agree to join their newly unified Germany," she said.

"Outrageous!" Beatrix exclaimed, flinging her glass against the wall. It shattered, leaving wine dribbling down the stones. "The House of Klingemann bows to no poxy Prussian."

"It could save your castle," Blaze-Simms said. "Isn't that worth something?"

"Well, perhaps," she said, blinking. "But it is a heavy price to pay in lost dignity."

A servant appeared at her elbow and poured another glass of wine. In the quiet, Dirk got up, poured himself a cup of coffee, and sat down opposite Isabelle. She looked at him with a forced smile.

"What else did they demand?" Noriko's lips were the only part of her that moved. To all intents and purposes, she still appeared to be asleep.

"There was more?" Dirk asked.

"You know me too well," Isabelle said, looking at Noriko.

"I know Europeans too well," the ninja replied.

Isabelle pushed her cup away across the table.

"They demand that all the castle's guests hand themselves over as prisoners," she said. "Wulff is intent upon punishing us for what happened in Paris, and for our resistance here."

It would have been the perfect moment for a dramatic declaration from Beatrix, stating her intent to defend her guests. Instead, she sat in thoughtful silence.

"We have six hours to decide," Isabelle said. "I suggest that we pack our bags. One way or another, the Gräfin may need us to leave her castle."

The adventurers, Noriko included, rose and headed out of the room. As they walked down the corridor towards the guest rooms, Isabelle held up a hand and ushered them into a small parlour. The fireplace here was filled with cold ashes and only a single candle lit the room.

"This doesn't look good," she whispered once the four of them were gathered close. "Beatie doesn't want to surrender, she's far too proud, but she doesn't have the status to force concessions from the Prussians."

"The Graf," Noriko said. "You want him?"

Dirk exchanged a look with Blaze-Simms. He had been hoping to free the Graf for his own purposes. This could work out well.

"You're hoping he might take your side against me," Isabelle said, looking directly at him.

After a moment's hesitation, Dirk nodded. "I'd thought of that, yeah."

"I'm willing to risk it," Isabelle said. Dirk didn't know whether to be disappointed or relieved. It made things easier - did it make them too easy? "We can't all go. Noriko is too badly hurt, and I'll do best at keeping Beatie distracted. It's up to you boys."

"Come on, Tim." Picking up the poker from beside the fireplace, Dirk headed for the door. "Bring your gun - there's still monsters out there."

"Dirk," Isabelle called after him.

He turned around, uncertain what to expect, and they stood staring at each other.

Isabelle hesitated.

"Don't take too long," she said at last. "The Prussians won't give us all day."

#

Weapons at the ready, lanterns held high, Dirk and Blaze-Simms made their way back into the tunnels. That meandering mess of corridors and caves, of stone both carved and bare, was increasingly cold and creepily quiet.

Down the spiral staircase, down two tunnels and into a third, they stalked through the darkness beneath the Red Castle. Though he tried not to let it show, Dirk felt unsettled by the tunnels in a way he hadn't before. The vivid memories that had come back in the pit still haunted him. However hard he pushed them from his mind, old terror still clawed at his heart.

The deeper they went, the more certain Dirk became that something was watching them. The hissing of scales across rough stone followed them around each bend in the corridor. The hissing of strange breath echoed out of darkened rooms to left and right. Raising his lantern, Dirk caught a momentary glimpse of a glittering eye before it scurried away. Their earlier encounter had made the creatures cautious but not so fearful that they fled the adventurers.

Dirk had learnt enough to avoid the labyrinthine confusion of the deeper tunnels. That knowledge led him straight to the door of the Graf's chambers, sweat clammy on his skin and heart hammering, watching over his shoulder every step of the way.

At last, to his relief, he slid back the hatch in the solid metal door.

"Graf Victor?" Dirk said. "Graf, we've come to get you out of here."

The aristocrat looked up from his workbench in the centre of the room. Some sort of body was laid out there, the parts spread around as if for an anatomical diagram. The sparking box at the end of the table could have been a camera, though one unlike anything Dirk had seen before. It roused his curiosity, but that was nothing next to the urgency with which he wanted to leave the tunnels.

"Herr Dynamo!" Graf Victor put a spool of cotton down next to the exposed muscles of what might have been a leg. "Have you really brought my wife to her senses?"

"Not exactly," Dirk said. "Stand back. And maybe duck beneath your table."

Beside him, Blaze-Simms attached a small package wrapped in greased paper to each of the door's hinges. He stuck fuses in and was about to cut them to length when Dirk grabbed his wrist.

"We'll need more than that." Dirk took Blaze-Simms's small knife and cut twice as far down the fuses. "Trust me, I've got experience with this."

"Alright then." Blaze-Simms lit a match against the rough stone wall and touched it the fuses. They sparked down towards the explosives as the two adventurers retreated around a corner.

"We shouldn't really need this," Blaze-Simms said. "I've been improving the mix in my explosives, but I still don't think-"

A colossal roar filled the corridor. Dust scoured Dirk's skin as it blasted around the corner on a hot wind.

"I say!" Blaze-Simms said. "I've out done myself."

With a clang like Hell's gate slamming shut, the door fell to the ground. Graf Victor Klingemann emerged through the smoke, brushing at the lapels of his black jacket and smiling a narrow, mischievous smile.

"Splendid work," he said. "Shall we?"

Without waiting for a response, he strode off down the corridor. Dirk hurried after him, Blaze-Simms at his side. The Graf had a swift, stalking pace that carried him so fast they almost had to run.

"Wait!" Dirk called out. "It's not safe. You should stay with us."

Rounding a corner, he saw the Graf stop abruptly in the middle of a corridor, and beyond him exactly what Dirk had feared - five beasts with long snouts, razor claws and gleaming scales, all staring hungrily at the Graf.

Heart hammering, Dirk set down his lamp, raised the poker and drew his gun. He had almost died when they faced three before, and he hadn't had time to recover from that. He'd just have to hope that he'd learnt enough to deal with all these.

This place just got better and better.

There was a chugging sound and a hiss of escaping steam as Blaze-Simms primed Eloise, readying the experimental firearm for action.

"Ready?" Dirk asked.

"Never," Blaze-Simms replied. "But that's what makes it all so exciting, don't you think?"

"Step back slowly, Graf," Dirk said. "We're covering you."

The nobleman didn't seem to hear him. Instead, he held out his hand, palm upward, reaching towards the creatures.

"My beauties," Graf Victor said. "They thought I was mad. First that you were impossible. Then that you were too dangerous. But I showed them. Life can rise from the anatomist's table, as deadly and beautiful as any of God's creations."

A shiver ran up Dirk's spine as the creatures stepped forward and, one by one, laid their heads down before the Graf.

"My darlings," the Graf said. "My greatest creations. No more need for terror. I am free."

Chapter 9: United at Last

"You made those things?" Dirk struggled to keep the incredulity from his voice.

It made a terrible sort of sense. He'd seen beasts transformed by science before - a mutated bear on Hakon, giant rats below London, horse breeds developed through centuries of slow selection. If humanity could transform life, why not create it from parts as well? The evidence had been there in front of him - the Graf's laboratory equipment, his imprisonment for mad acts, the presence of the beasts here and only here. But there had been so much else going on, he'd never even come close to putting the pieces together.

Could he have worked it out? Should he have? He didn't know. But he did know that he'd let this man out, to continue creating murderous monsters like the ones that killed Heinrich. The ones glaring at Dirk with angry eyes and bared teeth.

"Remarkable!" Blaze-Simms said excitedly. "How did you do it?"

"It was simple enough for a man of my gifts," Graf Victor said. "Tanks of nutrients with galvanic currents to encourage super-charged growth, in which I immersed samples of tissue immediately after dissection, before they could deteriorate. Careful selection and alignment of the component parts - easiest with lizards, though I managed to incorporate mammalian elements. Chemicals from the Far East and west Africa to encourage growth in the joined parts. Applying the right energies for resuscitation. Most of the equipment and all my notes are still in my cell, if you would care to look over them."

"I say!" Blaze-Simms said, his grin so wide he risked the top of his head falling off. "That's terribly decent of you."

"Yeah, decent," Dirk said, remembering the carnage the beasts had caused, to him as well as others in the castle.

"What is the point of genius if you do not share it with the world?" the Graf asked. His smile turned into a scowl. "A point my wife never understood."

His gaze grew unfocused and he stood, silently staring at the floor.

Dirk considered what had happened when the Graf shared that genius. Servants living their lives in terror. Poor old Heinrich, shredded by beasts his own master had let loose. He figured that the Gräfin had understood all too well, that her mistake hadn't been locking this man up, it had been letting him keep hold of the tools of his so-called science.

"But how do the creatures get out?" Blaze-Simms asked, pulling a notebook from his pocket. "You're locked in there."

"My bathroom is little more than a cave," the Graf said, shaking his head. "The plumbing a tunnel running into an underground stream. The climb down is too difficult for me, the water too fast, and frankly I would rather be a prisoner than swim through my own sewer to freedom. But my babies..." He stroked the head of one of the monsters. "My babies are not so constrained."

An hour ago, Dirk had wanted nothing more than to get this guy on his side, to use him to negotiate with the

Prussians. Now the thought made he feel sick. He'd rather face everything the Prussians could throw his way than let this madness continue.

"Come on," he said, grabbing Blaze-Simms by the elbow and dragging him down the tunnels the way they had come. His lantern seemed dimmer than before, the darkness closing in more tightly around them. A smell of rot brought back the tingling of nausea and fear.

But he was determined. He knew what he had to do.

"Isn't this splendid," Blaze-Simms said.

"Splendid?" Dirk repeated, glancing back to make sure they had left the Graf far behind. "Are you insane? The man's a damn killer."

"No, the creatures are killers, he just made them."

"Made them and let them loose down here." Dirk was seething. People had got hurt and killed for nothing more than a madman's experiments. If he'd taken a minute to think it through maybe he could have stopped this. He could have saved them.

There it was again, he realised. The instinct that had caused so much strife between him and Isabelle. The desire to rescue others from their plight, to be their saviour instead of the man who helped them save themselves.

The corridor leading to the cell still smelled of explosives and rock dust. They stepped over the fallen door and into Graf Victor's prison.

It wasn't a prison in any way most prisoners would recognise. With a laboratory table in the centre, a vast four-poster bed in one corner, and a velvet cushioned chair surrounded by book shelves, it felt more like a scientific hobbyist's drawing room. A door next to the bookshelves - this one without a lock - led to a room full of scientific tools, jars of chemicals, and preserved specimens of animal and human body parts. Dirk hoped the humans had been sourced through anatomists and executioners, though he wouldn't put anything past the Graf right now.

Returning to the main room, he found Blaze-Simms in the armchair, a pile of papers on the coffee table next to him. He was leafing through them in high excitement.

"This is extraordinary, Dirk," he said. "The things the Graf has achieved... I don't even know where to begin."

"With a match," Dirk said.

"What?" Blaze-Simms looked up in confusion.

"This ain't a good kind of science," Dirk said. "Taking the bodies of the dead and making them into monsters. Sending beasts into the darkness just to see what they'll do."

"We don't know that's why they were out there."

"Really?" Dirk asked. "You saw the look on his face. Do you think it was an accident that they were roaming the tunnels?"

"Well, no." Blaze-Simms admitted. "But you can't possibly mean what I think you mean."

"I do," Dirk said. "We smash this place up and burn it down. We're deep enough into the rock that it won't spread through the castle."

"But all this progress..."

"Do you really want instructions for those things getting into the world?"

Blaze-Simms gaze shifted from the papers in front of him to Dirk's bandaged head, then finally over to the workbench.

"I suppose not." He sighed and reached inside his jacket. "Here."

He threw a small brass box to Dirk, who caught it and looked at it in uncertainty. He pressed its only button and a foot-long flame leapt out, almost igniting his shirt.

Together they pulled the books and papers from the shelves, piling them up in the storage cupboard and on the worktable. Blaze-Simms added bedsheets to the pile of paper kindling, while Dirk pulled down bookshelves and smashed them up, adding them to the heaps. They weren't well-constructed fires, but they would do the job.

Returning one last time to the storage room, he looked at the rows of preserved body parts.

"Sorry it ain't a proper burial," he said, in case the spirits of the dead still lingered around the jars. He might not believe in God, but he'd seen that ghosts could be real enough. "Guess a cremation will have to do."

Then he lit the edge of the papers.

The flames took hold swiftly, turning documents to ash, igniting the sheets and setting the broken shelves ablaze. As the heat took hold, one of the jars of liquid bubbled and then shattered, its contents igniting in a burst of green flames.

"We'd better get out of here," he said as he lit the other fire.

They hurried back up through the tunnels, acrid smoke billowing after them.

#

"There you are!" the Graf exclaimed as they emerged into the main hall. "I feared that I had lost my rescuers in our little maze."

Part of the barricade at the far end of the hallway had been pulled down. Through that gap came snarls and hisses of bestial rage, the crack of gunfire and panicked shouting in German.

"My pretties are helping solve our problems," the Graf explained.

"I can see that," Dirk said coldly, looking at the other end of the room. The castle's remaining servants were gathered there, including Ingrid. They carried the weapons with which they had been manning the barricade, but none dared to raise them. Instead they were backed up into a corner, while one of the Graf's beasts prowled in front of them, tale swishing from side to side, drool running from its forked tongue as it eyed them hungrily.

Soft footsteps announced the arrival of Isabelle, Noriko and Gräfin Beatrix. Isabelle was holding the ninja up with one arm, but both of them carried blades - Isabelle her elegant parasol swordstick and Noriko her katana. Beatrix carried a gun.

"I see you haven't lost your flair for the absurd, Victor," she said, wide skirts sweeping across the floor as she approached her husband.

"And that you retain your taste for the melodramatic," he replied. "You never could resist an audience."

"What on earth do you mean?" she said, jutting out her chin.

"I mean that you would not be using English if these people all spoke German," he replied before shifting language.

Dirk didn't need to understand the words to know that the conversation was turning ugly. The Graf waved his hands as he gestured around the room and snapped angrily at his wife. Beatrix placed her hands on her hips as she gave as good back, her tone shifting through fierce exclamations to angry growls. Hot words flew back and forth as the two grew closer and more red-faced.

Suddenly, the Graf turned to look at Dirk.

"What have you done?" the nobleman asked, his nose twitching.

Taking a deep breath, Dirk caught the stink of burning chemicals. Smoke from the dungeon trickled in an oily stream out of the doorway behind him.

"Keeping folks safe," he said. "You got a problem with that?"

"How dare you?" the Graf shouted. "This is an outrage."

Beatrix grabbed his arm, turning him towards her, and they returned to talking loudly in German.

As Dirk looked away, Isabelle caught his eye. She raised a single enquiring eyebrow. Despite all the chaos around him, despite the childlike fear still gripping the depths of his mind, despite the sounds of violence that underlay everything around him, Dirk smiled.

Isabelle smiled back. They both laughed.

"Are you alright, old chap?" Blaze-Simms whispered from beside him. "Not taken another knock on the head, have you?"

"Nothing like that," Dirk said. "I just realised that there are more important things than who's right or wrong about Paris. That maybe, just maybe, I've let my hurt feelings get in the way of what makes me happy."

"Which is?"

"Us and our friends working together against a common threat."

"I was hoping that you would say learning." Blaze-Simms sounded a little hurt. "After all, we are still looking for the Great Library."

"Don't worry," Dirk said. "That's on the list too. But there's something else I need to deal with first."

Across the room, the beast snarled and licked its lips. The servants cringed back, one man whimpering from behind Ingrid, who held a poker out in front of her, trying but failing to hide her terror.

Drawing his gun, Dirk strode towards them, his footsteps heavy on the tiles. The creature turned when he was just three feet away, its face twisting towards him at the perfect moment. He squeezed the trigger, sending a bullet through its brain, followed by two more for good measure as it hit the ground. Blood, brains, and shards of skull spattered across the wall next to the servants, whose looks of shock turned quickly to gratitude and relief. They came out of their corner, some prodding at the twisted body to make sure it was dead.

"Thank you," Ingrid said. Stepping up on tiptoes, she planted a kiss on Dirk's lips.

They both blushed as she stepped back and hurried to join her colleagues. Fearing Isabelle's reaction, Dirk looked over to see that she was laughing again. He blushed even more deeply.

"Outrage upon outrage!" Graf Victor strode up to Dirk and slapped him across the face. "You defile my laboratory. You kill my creations. You court my wife. This cannot stand!"

"Court your wife?" Dirk said in amazement. "I never even tried to-"

"I told you he would deny it," Beatrix said, coming to stand beside her husband. "But you should have seen the way he looked at me. He was like a beast driven mad with passion."

She flung a hand to her forehead and made as if to swoon. In a move so smooth it could only come from frequent practice, the Graf caught his wife so that she leaned back in his arms, eyes closed, bosom protruding, a perfectly posed vignette from a romantic oil painting.

"Really, Beatie," Isabelle said, her tone sharp. "More dramatics? More leaning on men to get things done? This is exactly the sort of behaviour the network was created to avoid."

"You are no fun, Isabelle," Beatrix said, straightening up. "I don't think I want you here any more. Or your friends who have so rudely killed my husband's pets."

"The pets you hated," Isabelle said.

"That is behind us now," the Graf said. "My wife and I have had enough of your rudeness."

"Rudeness?" Dirk exclaimed. "We've been defending your damn castle."

"And destroying it." The Graf pointed towards the smoke still drifting into the room. "I hear that you blew up half of the southern entrance."

"That was a mistake," Blaze-Simms said.

"So was having you here. You should leave now."

"Gladly," Isabelle snapped.

Dirk and Isabelle supporting Noriko between them, the four adventurers headed towards their rooms. Behind them, servants edged nervously towards the barricade. There were fewer sounds of snarling, hissing, and screams now. Most of the combat noise was gunfire, accompanied by excited German shouting.

"That network you mentioned," Dirk said. "That's the women you want to share the findings from the Great Library with?"

"That's right," Isabelle replied. "And I have no intention of swerving from that course."

"That's what I figured. How about if we worked together, and I helped ensure that your folks got to read those books?"

"What about the Epiphany Club's claim on them?"

Dirk hesitated. What about the Club? He'd worked with them for a long time. He believed in their mission to learn about the world. But Isabelle had opened his eyes to another perspective, to people who weren't served by gentlemen's scholarly societies.

"We can share the books," he said. "Make copies maybe. I'll sort something out."

"That sounds splendid in principle, but how can I be sure that is what will happen?"

"I'm trusting you despite what happened in Paris. Could you maybe trust me despite the other men you've met?"

"I can try."

Blaze-Simms headed off towards his room and its inevitable litter of half-made inventions. Dirk hoped that their previous getaways had taught him to pack quickly. He'd had enough practice.

Behind them, the sound of gunfire had faded away. He didn't reckon that was just a matter of distance. The last of the monsters was dead at last. That left the Prussians and the few servants still defending the castle. He didn't feel great about that, and he hoped the servants all got through it in one piece, but it was the Graf and Gräfin's problem to deal with now.

"Reckon I should apologise," Dirk said. "I've gotten to understanding a bit more about what I was doing. About being rescued and taking care of yourself. About how I ain't always been helping in the best way."

"I know that your heart is in the right place," Isabelle said. "I could perhaps have been a little kinder in our dealings. Trusted that there could be a better sort of man."

"It ain't always easy to-"

"Now?" Noriko said, her words little more than a hiss of pain. "Now you have this conversation?"

They had reached her room. Pushing herself away from the others, Noriko opened her door and leaned against the frame, breathing hard.

"We need to be gone," she said. "Don't take longer than Timothy with your baggage."

Chapter 10: Getaway

Dirk looked at the carpet bag on the bed. Last time he'd seen it, he'd been putting it into the balloon they were leaving Paris in. The balloon Isabelle and Noriko had taken. That explained how it had got to the castle. It seemed that thawing tensions had finally led to its return.

He opened it up, and there they were - the possessions that made up his life. Three shirts, repeatedly repaired. Two pairs of pants, carefully patched. Underwear. Spare boots. A few toiletries. Needle and thread and other odds and ends. Nothing he wasn't willing to leave behind if he had to.

Except that, as he shut the bag, he realised that he'd missed it. For all that he talked a practical talk, some attachments had been creeping up on him lately. Things he cared about as much as becoming the toughest, smartest guy he could.

Of course, that didn't mean smarts didn't matter any more. He was back on track to get hold of the lost Great Library of Alexandria, as long as he, his friends, and the tablets they'd gathered could get out of here intact.

He grabbed the bag, dashed down the corridor, and banged on Blaze-Simms's door.

"Come on, Tim," he called out. "We ain't got time to dawdle."

"Coming!" Blaze-Simms flung the door open and emerged, top hat askew. He had a large case in one hand, clothing sticking out around the edges. In his other hand was a sack that clinked, full of whatever inventions he'd been working on here. Over his shoulder was slung his gun. Half-wound springs protruded from the pockets of his tail-coat.

"You're getting better at getting going," Dirk said.

"Learning from the best." Blaze-Simms smiled excitedly. "Shall we?"

The next stop was Noriko's room. Like Dirk, she had only one small bag, and beside it a roll of black cloth.

"I'll take those," Dirk said, picking them up. The weight of the cloth spoke to the range of weapons wrapped up in there, a matching set with the two blades at her side. "You focus on staying upright."

Noriko nodded. Dirk liked that about her - she was proud but not stupid about it. Seemed like someone he should start learning from.

A stairwell carried them to the all too familiar corridor outside Isabelle's room. For a moment Dirk paused, remembering Heinrich lying there, blood pouring from him. Justice had been done against those monsters, even if it hadn't worked out how Dirk had expected. He wondered if Heinrich had known that his master was behind it all. Had he suspected but stayed loyal like a good servant? It didn't seem like they'd ever know.

Isabelle emerged from her room. She had turned a curtain tie into an improvised belt, with her parasol sword-stick hanging like a scabbard at one hip and her small pistol thrust into the front. They went with her dress as neatly as if the whole outfit were planned.

"It saddens me to leave the hat boxes behind," she said, shouldering her bag. "But I am sure that Cairo can provide."

"What's the plan?" Blaze-Simms asked.

"There's a small stable by the south gate," Isabelle said. "The carriage there is a little on the small side, but will do in a pinch. We can pick up something more substantial when we reach a town."

"Maybe there will be a train," Blaze-Simms said. "I hear that the Prussians are mad for them. I'd love to get a look at one of their engines."

They headed along the corridor, down another flight of stairs, and towards the entrance hall. The castle was strangely quiet, only their footsteps and Noriko's ragged breathing filling the void. It was as if everyone - Prussian soldiers, servants, even the birds and bats that circled the castle - was waiting for them to get out of the way.

As they came into the entrance hall, Dirk saw why so many of the castle's inhabitants had gone quiet.

The siege was over.

Three plushly upholstered chairs sat in the centre of the hall, facing the visitors as they hurried into view. The room was still littered with the remnants of battle - bloodstains, shell casings, strips of stained bandage. But there in the centre, around those three chairs and the coffee table in front of them, was a small circle of civilised calm.

Gräfin Beatrix occupied the middle seat, a glass of red wine in her hand and a smile on her face. From her expression, it would have been impossible to tell that her life and home were in terrible danger an hour before.

To her right sat Graf Victor, one narrow leg crossed over the other. He swirled the wine around the inside of his glass and raised it to sniff the bouquet. There was a sinister twinkle in his eyes, but it was nothing compared with the expression of the man seated in the third chair.

Colonel Wulff had shed the bandages that swathed his face on their previous meeting. What this revealed was every bit as ugly as Dirk expected. Most of the skin was the raw red of a deep and painful burn. Skin peeled at the edges, as if the colonel's flesh were retreating from the wounds. Only small patches of hair remained on his head and both of his eyebrows were gone. One eye was swollen almost shut.

As he drank his wine, a trickle ran out of the slumped side of his mouth, dribbling off his medal and leaving a dark stain on his blue uniform jacket.

Advancing cautiously down the wide steps, Dirk descended to the tiled floor of the hall, facing their hosts and the man whose face he had destroyed.

"I would invite you to join us," Beatrix said. "But as you can see, the seats are all taken."

Prussian soldiers stood in every doorway, guns at the ready.

"That is most considerate of you," Isabelle said, her voice as casually pleasant as if they were meeting at a church picnic. "Might I say what a pleasure it is to see you all one last time. In particular to see Graf Victor - we've felt your absence during our visit."

"Things have been difficult," the Graf said. "But Beatrix and I have reconciled our differences."

He ran his fingers lightly across the back of her hand. She turned the hand over and clasped his, fingers interlaced.

"You provided us with the inspiration," Beatrix said. "Finding that we had a common foe gave us a reason to see past our arguments and to make our differences work together. I will run the castle, Victor will continue with his experiments, and together we will make our mark as part of the new Germany.

"Some people run from their differences." She glanced meaningfully from Isabelle to Dirk. "We have chosen to embrace them."

"What some folks do ain't for you to-" Dirk began, but Isabelle silenced him with a touch on the arm.

"I thought that you didn't want to be part of this new Germany," she said.

"What use is a mind that cannot change?" Beatrix asked. "If we have learnt one thing from your visit, it is that we Germans are stronger when we work together. Especially when faced with an outside threat."

"Is that what you have labelled me now?" Isabelle asked, and for the first time an edge of anxiety crept into her voice. "An outsider? A threat?"

"You made yourself that way," Beatrix replied, her grip on her husband's hand tightening. "I chose to act on it."

"You choose your nation over your whole gender?"

"I choose myself. Unlike your life, mine contains more than an ideological crusade."

Icy silence filled the hall as the two women stared at each other.

"We'll be leaving now," Dirk said.

"No, Herr Dynamo." Wulff raised a hand and his men raised their guns. "You will be surrendering."

"Ain't my style," Dirk said, looking around the room. At this range, at least one bullet was likely to hit. Then there'd be another volley before they reached the door. Even if no-one died, they'd be slowed down by wounds, with the Prussians pursuing them.

So they had to fight. Except that the Prussians had their guns aimed while his was still holstered. And beyond this handful of soldiers there were dozens more.

Blaze-Simms's sack of half-made inventions crashed to the ground. In his hands he held one last piece of machinery - a wooden box covered in wires and chunks of esoteric glassware. Before anyone could ask what it was he flicked a switch.

Dirk's skin tingled. All over his body, hairs stood on end. Sparks crackled around the handle of his pistol, the Gräfin's jewellery, the fittings of the chairs, the suits of armour lining the walls, and every other piece of metal in the room. So much electricity danced around the guns of the soldiers that the barrels seemed to glow before their alarmed eyes.

"If anybody pulls a trigger their gun will explode," Blaze-Simms said. "Now please excuse us, but it's time to leave."

Face blank, he started back up the stairs. The others followed.

"You will regret this, Sir Timothy," Colonel Wulff growled.

"I fear that you're right," Blaze-Simms said.

As they reached the landing above, out of sight of the great hall, the inventor leaned against the wall, his whole body shaking. The box rattled in his hands.

"Tim, you OK?" Dirk said in alarm.

"Oh, yes." Blaze-Simms smiled then stifled a burst of laughter. "But we should move quickly before they call my bluff."

"It won't stop the guns firing?"

"My dear chap, if I could do that don't you think I would have used it days ago? This is just cheap static trickery, and it's already running out."

The sparks were fading around Dirk's gun.

"How do we get to the carriage now?" Noriko asked.

"We don't," Dirk said.

"The balloon," Isabelle said, echoing his thoughts. "It's still on the roof."

Turning on her heel, she strode purposefully down the corridor and into a stairwell. Dirk and the others hurried after her, Noriko wincing as she went.

There was a dull thud and smoke poured from Blaze-Simms's box. He dropped it with a crash of smashing glass.

"There goes my bluff," he said as footsteps followed them through the castle.

#

The hot air balloon inflated with excruciating slowness, rising from the battlements so slowly that Dirk could barely see it move.

"Can't you speed that up?" he asked, raising his voice to be heard over the wind. Icy rain stung his face and darkened the stones on which he stood.

"I have." Blaze-Simms pointed at a bundle of pipes he'd attached to the burner. "But it will still take time."

"That ain't something we've got a whole lot of," Dirk said.

Racing footsteps emerged from the stairwell in the corner of the tower. Isabelle appeared, skirts hitched up to let her run.

"Get ready," she said. "They're almost through that last barricade."

Straining at the weight, Dirk picked up a gargoyle he'd removed from the battlements. Its sneering, pointy-nosed face pressed into his chest and a red stone wing blocked his view as he walked over to the top of the stairs.

There was a crash of splintering wood somewhere below, followed by triumphant shouts and the clatter of sturdy boots on old stone. At they came closer, Dirk heaved the gargoyle down the spiral staircase. One wing snapped off as it hit the wall, but the rest of it kept going, crashing from one stair to the next, gaining speed as it hurtled around the corner and out of sight. A moment later there were shouts of alarm, screams of pain, and a huge thud as the gargoyle hit something sturdier than itself.

"One left," Dirk said, shifting the other gargoyle to the top of the stairs. Behind him, the balloon was starting to lift off the ground, though it still only seemed half inflated. Blaze-Simms tried to help Noriko into the basket, but even injured she was agile enough by herself.

"Does this remind you of old times?" Isabelle asked. "The sounds of guns, the rush of action, the challenge of fighting off an army?"

"It reminds me of why I left those times behind," Dirk said. "War has its place, but peace gives you more time to read."

Footsteps emerged from the stairwell again, slower this time and quieter.

"They're trying to creep up on us," Isabelle said, drawing her sword. "How precious."

This time Dirk waited until he saw the muzzle of a gun appear around the corner. Then he gave the gargoyle an almighty shove. Tumbling head over tail, it bounced down the steps, chips of stone flying, and hit the men around the corner. There were shouts of alarm, the sound of a gun as someone pulled their trigger in panic, and the "thud thud thud" of the gargoyle descending deeper into the castle.

Dirk drew his pistol and a katana that he'd borrowed off Noriko. The blade shone even in the grey light of a storm-shrouded day. Raindrops exploded as they hit its edge.

"I suppose there are some parts I miss about war," Dirk said. "Camaraderie grows stronger in the face of danger. There ain't a lot of other places you find that bond."

"Nothing in this world is entirely good or entirely bad," Isabelle said. She took a shot down the stairwell, than backed up as a dozen guns fired back.

"Is that a quote?"

"Does it matter? Words don't grow any smarter with age."

"Then it's a good thing people do." Dirk grinned at her, then grew flustered as he realised he might have made the wrong implication. "I mean. I ain't always been too smart, and now I'm-"

"Adorable as your blundering is, I think it's time." Isabelle raised her pistol. There was a bang, a flash, and the first Prussian around the corner tumbled back, leaving a bloody smear halfway up the wall.

Nervously at first, and then with the grim bravery of men who feared their superiors as much as their opponents, the Prussians began their attack. Men poked their heads and guns around long enough to fire at Dirk and Isabelle, or to be shot at. As shootouts went it was slow and drawn out, the soldiers slow to muster their courage or drag away wounded comrades.

But slow wasn't slow enough, with the balloon only limply rising. Bullets chipped away the stone of the door frame, splinters of pink rock scything past Dirk's cheek. He emptied his revolver once, reloaded, emptied it again. Isabelle did the same. Still the soldiers kept coming. Soon Dirk and Isabelle were out of bullets and looking for loose stones to throw, while the Prussians kept firing.

"What now?" Isabelle asked, ducking behind the door frame as another volley hit. "Should we go down to face them or wait for them to come to us?"

"We fight here," Dirk said. "If we can keep them in the stairwell while we're up top then we'll have room to manoeuvre while they're still crammed in together. Don't let them use their numbers."

"Maybe they won't notice that we're out of ammunition."

"Wulff will," Dirk said with certainty.

Sure enough, there was a moment's lull filled with the click of bayonets being fixed. Then the Prussians came storming up the stairs.

There were a hell of a lot Prussians, more than Dirk could have imagined would fit into that stairwell. One fell back when Dirk knocked aside his rifle and punched him in the face. Another went down to a sword blow to the leg. A third stumbled on his comrades and smacked his head on the wall. But every time more came, like the heads of a gun-wielding hydra.

Soon the fight became a blur of blood, movement, and moments of pain. Dirk and Isabelle hacked and slashed, punched and kicked, while the rain poured down and lightning flashed across the sky. A puddle formed around their feet and ran down the steps, washing away the blood, making men slip and slide in their ascent.

Still the Prussians kept coming, as Dirk's arm began to ache and a bayonet thrust drew blood from his shin. After everything that had happened over the past few days, he couldn't keep this up. Beside him, Isabelle's movements became slower, her expression grim.

Dirk dodged another thrust towards his leg. He slipped on the wet flagstones, pain shooting from his knee as it slammed into the ground. Swinging his sword, he was just in time to parry the blow that followed.

A Prussian towered over him, rifle raised.

There was a chugging sound, a brief green glow, and the Prussian toppled sideways, blood gushing from his shoulder.

"Ready to go!" Blaze-Simms yelled from the basket of the balloon. He was frantically cranking the handle that charged his strange gun.

Isabelle swiped at the soldier in front of her. As he took a step back she kneed him in the groin and he fell back with a grunt. Raising his good leg, Dirk kicked as hard as he could, sending another man sailing back down the stairwell. The Prussians crashed into the colleagues behind them, tumbling back in a jumble of arms and legs. Dirk scrambled to his feet and the two adventurers ran.

The balloon was straining at its moorings, the basket hanging six inches off the ground. Wincing at the pressure on his injured leg, Dirk flung himself headfirst over the edge of the basket. Isabelle vaulted in beside him in a flurry of damp skirts.

"Tally-ho!" Blaze-Simms exclaimed.

He let off another shot, then released the ropes holding them in place. Slowly at first, then faster with each passing moment, the balloon lifted into the air.

Dirk heard a scrabbling of fingers against the basket as the Prussians tried to grab them, then a bark of gunfire as they soared out of reach. A bullet punctured the basketwork next to his face, but nothing hit any of the passengers.

"This is going to be an exciting ride," Blaze-Simms said as the storm roared around them.

"After that castle, this place seems pretty calm," Dirk said.

Between the adventurers and their baggage, the basket was pretty much full. In the centre, the top of a bag hung open, revealing the precious carved stones that would guide them to their destination.

"Next stop Egypt!" Blaze-Simms said.

Isabelle caught Dirk's gaze.

"He does know how far away that is, doesn't he?" she said quietly.

Dirk shrugged.

"It ain't always easy," he said, "but sometimes you've just got to trust folks to get things right enough."

They smiled at each other. Dirk's leg was bleeding, his muscles ached, and he was soaked to the bone.

He couldn't remember the last time he'd felt so good. Their group was together. They had all the stones. Between them, they had the smarts to follow those clues.

The Great Library of Alexandria was almost in sight.

Book 5: Dead Men and Dynamite

Chapter 1: Dressed to Impress

Dirk Dynamo jutted out his square jaw, trying to get a better look at his bow tie in the mirror. He'd tried to tie the damn thing a dozen times now and however he did it the bow came out crooked.

This shouldn't have been hard. Give him a decent length of rope and he could tie everything from a horse hitch to a hangman's noose. Yet here he was, stuffed into an over-starched shirt, unable to manage one lousy scrap of silk.

A knocking drew his attention away from the mirror.

"Come in," he said.

The door of the guest room opened and Sir Timothy Blaze-Simms appeared in a gangle of thin limbs and rattling pockets. His tie was annoyingly straight, his tailcoat a perfect fit, and gold cufflinks gleamed at his wrists. Behind a pair of wire-rimmed glasses, he was grinning like a child.

"Isn't this place splendid?" he said as he shut the door a little too loudly and flung himself down in the only chair. "They have the latest telegraph machines and one of those dumb waiters with the clever counterweights."

"I'm sure it's swell," Dirk said. "But do I really have to go to this party?"

"We're guests in the British embassy," Blaze-Simms said. "Not attending the reception for the French delegation would be terribly rude."

"I thought you folks and the French liked offending to each other?"

"Yes, but it's good manners to turn up and be rude in person."

The tie still wasn't straight but Dirk had had enough. It would have to do. He slid his holster over his shoulders, a far more comfortable fit.

"Allow me." Blaze-Simms got out of his seat. With darting movements of his slim fingers he unfastened and re-tied the bow-tie. The result was a work of impeccable symmetry.

"Thanks, Tim," Dirk said.

He picked his Gravemaker revolver up off the nightstand and slid it into the holster.

"You're not taking that, are you?" Blaze-Simms asked with a frown.

"There might be trouble," Dirk said, hearing defensiveness creep into his voice.

"It's not a meeting with street gangs," Blaze-Simms said. "Besides, it'll ruin the line of your jacket."

Dirk didn't give a damn about the line of his jacket and he was about to say as much. Then he remembered who else would be at the party.

"Alright," he said, reluctantly removing the holster and pulling on his tailcoat. "But if we get into a fight-"

"Then we'll improvise," Blaze-Simms said. "After all these years, I think we've got rather good at it, don't you?"

Dirk grinned. "Reckon we have."

#

The British embassy in Cairo was more elegant, more extensive, and far more cramped than the one Dirk had visited on the island of Hakon. That small African outpost had held a single diplomat and his serving staff. This was full of delegates from every sector of British government, from the ambassador to the naval attaché to a score of civil servants of unclear rank and constant activity. Each of them came with a wife, a secretary, and a translator. Then there were the valets, maids, assistants, guards, accountants, chefs... It went on and on. Membership of the scholarly Epiphany Club had earned Dirk and his companions guest rooms but not anyone's time or attention.

Dirk and Blaze-Simms strode down the broad staircase into the ballroom. Hundreds of guests in sharp suits and ball gowns were being served by dozens of waiters in black tailcoats and ties.

At the bottom of the staircase, a broad man with an equally broad grin held out a hand to Blaze-Simms.

"I say, Blaze-Simms Minor, isn't it?" the man said. "I'm Noiseby. Used to row with your brother at Oxford."

"I say!" Blaze-Simms said. "How splendid to see you, old chap."

Noiseby snatched two glasses of champagne from a passing waiter and the two men fell to talking excitedly about "the old days". Everybody they mentioned had a nickname that would have embarrassed the family dog and clearly relished the sort of trouble that would have got Dirk locked up in his youth, but that among British aristocrats was labelled as "fun japes". Not knowing any of the people mentioned, or much liking the sound of them, Dirk headed off in search of a stiffer drink to get him through the night.

A bar of rich, dark wood stretched along the back wall. Dirk ordered the largest whiskey they could give him and took up residence at one end, next to a floor-length mirror.

"How do, lad," said a deep voice behind him.

Dirk turned to see the enormous form of George Braithwaite. The Yorkshireman was one of the few people as tall and tough as Dirk. His bushy beard completed an intimidating image the gruff man seemed to relish.

"Good to see someone sane," Dirk said, raising his glass. "What happened to Paris?"

"Weren't much point selling tinned beef to the Frenchies any more," Braithwaite said. "They were too busy licking their wounds after that kicking from the Prussians. Besides, I got a better offer."

"Selling guano again?" Dirk asked.

"Even better," Braithwaite said with a smile. "I'm here at the embassy. Part of the trade delegation."

He winked and Dirk returned the gesture. If he hadn't already known that Braithwaite was a spy, he would have done now. If a government didn't want to explain a man's job, they usually stuck him in a trade delegation. He'd been in one himself once, back in his Pinkerton days, and he'd done no trade and very little delegating.

Dirk's spirits rose. It was good to have another friendly face around the place, especially one whose influence might help them cut through some red tape.

"How are your local contacts?" he asked.

"Depends on the sort of contacts you want," Braithwaite said.

"The sort who could help us find something in the desert," Dirk said. "We're on what you might call an academic adventure, and we're going to need local knowledge and skills."

What knowledge and skills remained to be seen. Somewhere out in the desert lay the hidden remains of the Great Library of Alexandria, concealed beneath the sands for thousands of years. Through scrutinising ancient tablets, Blaze-Simms had worked out a lot about the library's location, but Egypt in the 1870s wasn't the same as Egypt two thousand years before. They might need local learning to bridge that gap. They might need folks to help dig up the remains. They'd certainly need someone to advise them on surviving in the desert.

"I'm sure I can help," Braithwaite said. "I know some lads who-"

He stopped mid-sentence. A woman was walking toward them, diamonds gleaming against the grey silk of her dress. She toyed with a champagne flute as she smiled up at him.

"Monsieur Braithwaite, are you going to introduce me to your friend?" she asked.

"Madame Cluny, this is Dirk Dynamo, scholar and adventurer," Braithwaite said. "Mister Dynamo, this is Madame Marie Cluny."

"A pleasure to meet you," Madame Cluny said. She held out her gloved hand to be kissed. Dirk responded by giving her a hearty handshake.

"Mighty fine to meet you, ma'am," he said.

As Braithwaite and Cluny began a polite conversation about local affairs, Dirk found his attention torn away by another woman moving through the crowd.

Isabelle McNair was always a figure of poise and beauty. But in a crowd like this, she truly shone. She circled the room, a glass in her hand and an expression of delight on her face, both of them sparkling as brightly as the simple silver necklace at her throat. She laughed and smiled, and those around her did the same, her evident pleasure in their company spreading like a ripple of joy through the reception.

For the briefest moment, she glanced at Dirk. Was it just his hopeful imagination, or did her smile flash even brighter then?

He dragged his attention back to the conversation in hand. Something about the opening of the Suez Canal a year and a half before.

"Must have been a proud moment for you," he said, trying to hide his distraction. "Seeing that first French ship sail through."

"It would have been," Madame Cluny said, her expression growing cold, "if Mister Braithwaite's friend Captain

Nares had not broken with protocol and sailed through in front of us."

For a long moment they stood in awkward silence while Cluny glared at her drink.

"So what brings you to Egypt?" Dirk asked, dipping into the polite conversational topics Isabelle had primed him with.

"My husband is with the trade delegation," she said.

The sight of Isabelle moving closer caught Dirk's attention.

"That's nice," he said distractedly. "Him and Braithwaite being in the same line of..."

The words trailed off as he saw the stiff expressions on his companions' faces. Husband to a trade delegate was as good a cover as being a trade delegate. The British and French were competing out here and these two clearly new each other well.

Maybe "nice" wasn't the right word for their connection. And maybe drawing attention to it didn't come under the heading of polite conversation.

"Trade, politics, stuff like this, it ain't really my thing," Dirk said.

"Really," Cluny said flatly. "What a surprise."

"I might just go find my friends," Dirk said. "Nice to meet you though."

"It has been... pleasant," Cluny replied.

Dirk hurried away. He washed away the bitter taste of self-recrimination with whiskey, then grabbed another from the bar. If he was this distracted then he shouldn't be doing the delicate work of making friends and influencing people. Maybe he could just focus on Isabelle instead.

He worked his way across the room, peering over people's heads as he tried to spot her distinctive blue dress. Every way he turned, he seemed to bump into someone, drawing glares and muttered complaints. The fuss these folks made, he'd have thought they'd never had an elbow jogged in their lives.

Some folks tried to draw him into conversation as he passed. He did his best to join in, but it was tough going. He'd never much cared for cricket, knew nothing about the spice trade running through the canal, and had never met any of the folks who cropped up in local gossip. Even when the conversation was steered towards him and his life, it was clear that he was an object of novelty, both as an American and as a scholarly adventurer. Whether they meant to or not, they all left him feeling condescended to.

"Dynamo." A slender hand took his elbow. Miura Noriko had appeared as if from nowhere at his side. Her lace-fringed dress didn't suit her as well as her usual ninja garb, but it was at least black.

"How you doing?" Dirk asked.

"Better than you," she replied. "Come dance, before you tread on more toes."

She drew him into the open space in the centre of the room. A string quartet were playing waltzes on a balcony above. Noriko placed one hand on his shoulder and took his hand with the other.

Dirk looked uneasily at the couples around them. All were moving in time to the music, drifting past each other with effortless grace.

"You know this dance?" he asked.

"Dancing is easy," Noriko replied.

They stood for a moment as she watched him expectantly. Then she shrugged and started moving him around the floor.

Dirk had been taught to dance from time to time. It was one of those things you had to do to blend in, whether you were at a harvest party in the deep south or a high society gathering at a European court. But he'd never felt confident in it. Now he found the feeling even worse. Under the judging eyes of half the ballroom, he stumbled over his own feet as he tried not to crash into the other dancers.

"Not enough space," he grumbled. "And why's everybody watching us? What's so damn funny?"

"The man is meant to lead," Noriko said.

"Oh." Dirk blushed. "I can do that."

He tried to take control of the dance, pulling Noriko across the floor. There was a flash of alarm in her eyes as they wheeled, collided with another couple, and stumbled toward the wall.

Now people were laughing out loud. Not that they had the decency to do it to Dirk's face - the minute he looked at them they turned away, leaving him with no-one to shout at, no excuse to turn to his fists and vent his frustration.

"Calm yourself," Noriko said.

"You calm yourself." Dirk let her go. Turning away from the dance floor, he grabbed a glass from a passing waiter and stomped toward the corner of the room. This time, he didn't bump into anyone. They were all getting out of his way.

He didn't dare look around. If Isabelle was watching, he didn't want to know.

He flung himself down in a chair and emptied the glass. Sparkling wine tickled his throat and left an unpleasant aftertaste, half sharp and half sweet. But at least it dulled some of the buzzing in his brain.

Why did he feel so damn embarrassed? Who cared what a bunch of snooty aristocrats thought of him? They're weren't any better than he was. They'd all be in the same boat if Marx was right and revolution finally came.

But he did feel embarrassed. He cared how he looked in front of these people. Isabelle's people.

Whatever had gotten into him, it was turning him into an idiot.

Somebody put two glasses of whiskey down on the table beside him. Then came an ashtray, a box of matches, and a pair of cigars.

"Thanks," Dirk said, drawing his eyes up to his benefactor.

Isabelle smiled down at him. He sat up straight, his cheeks burning.

"May I?" she asked, pointing to the seat beside him.

"Of course. But shouldn't you be..." He waved towards the assembled mass of Cairo high society, none of which was paying attention to him any more.

"I needed a break," she said. "And I couldn't think of better company to take it in."

She picked up the cigars, lit one, passed it to Dirk, and then lit the other for herself. It was a strange thing to see a society lady do. He looked around, expecting people to be staring their way. But Braithwaite and Noriko stood between their sheltered corner and the rest of the room, diverting folks with conversation about the lively dance just starting.

Dirk took a deep drag on the cigar. Warm, sweet smoke soothed his mind.

"I'm sorry," he said. "This sort of place just ain't me."

"You must have been to places like this before," Isabelle said. "Between your work for the Pinkerton agency and for the Epiphany Club, you've been all over."

"My heart just ain't in it," Dirk admitted. "I'm distracted. Want to get out there and find the library."

"And we will. We've got all the stones now. Timothy has deciphered the symbols on them and drawn out the geographical references. He's pieced nearly all of it together. We're closer than we've ever been."

"I guess," Dirk said, pausing to sip from his whiskey. "Still, not acting on it, that's frustrating."

"I've seen you stake places out. I know you can wait."

"Like I say, I'm distracted."

"By me?"

The words struck him dumb. Sure, he'd been thinking about this. Thinking about it a hell of a lot. But he hadn't expected to have to talk.

"Yep," he said at last.

"You feel uncertain?" she asked softly. "Not knowing where you stand? Not knowing where this is going?"

"Yep," he managed.

"I'll tell you a secret."

She leaned in close. He could smell cigar smoke, champagne, and her skin. His heart leapt.

"I feel the same way." She placed a hand on his. "I don't know how we can make this work. I don't know if it even will in the end. But I want to try, if that's alright with you."

On the very last word, her voice trembled and she squeezed his hand harder.

Dirk looked at her. A smile broke out across his face and she smiled back. He'd never wanted to kiss anyone more in his life, but he knew that would be far beyond even the faux pas he'd made so far.

"That's more than alright," he said.

"Good." She dropped her cigar into the ashtray and rose to her feet, her hand still wrapped around his. "I'm done circulating for the evening and you've done more than enough on that front."

"So what now?" he asked, standing and following her out into the room.

"Now I'm going to teach you to dance properly," she said. "And after that, we're going to go treasure hunting."

Dirk eyed the dance floor with trepidation.

"Won't folks be watching and laughing?" he asked.

"I won't mind if you don't," Isabelle said.

As Dirk wrapped an arm around her waist, he realised that this time he really didn't. He had the most beautiful woman in the world in his arms. A week from now, he'd have his hands on the greatest store of lost knowledge the world had ever seen. Compared with that, who cared about a little laughter?

Chapter 2: Shopping for Knives

The streets of Cairo were noisy and crowded, jammed full of locals and of travellers from every corner of the globe. The smells of sweat and spices filled the air. Wherever Dirk looked, there was something to distract the eye, from acrobats performing on a corner to swathes of brightly coloured cloth hanging outside a merchant's shop. With so much going on, it was almost impossible for anyone to keep their attention on what was in front of them.

It was perfect for the work Dirk was about.

"Dash it all, I thought she'd be here by now." Blaze-Simms sat up straight, craning his neck as he peered through the crowds.

"Hold your horses," Dirk said. He enjoyed a sip of his strong black coffee and leaned back in his seat, the pavement cafe's rickety furniture creaking beneath him. "This sort of work's all about patience, remember."

"I suppose so." Blaze-Simms pulled out a notebook and started scribbling.. "It's just that we're so close, I want to be up and at it."

Dirk smiled and shook his head. He was in too good a mood for Tim's impatience to bother him.

"Hey, this was your idea," he said.

"More like Braithwaite's," Blaze-Simms said.

"OK, but helping Braithwaite out was your idea."

"True..."

Blaze-Simms's voice trailed off, distracted by whatever he was making notes about. Dirk figured he could leave him be for a while. A shop across the street had caught his eye, reminding him of an absence in his life, and now seemed as good a time as any to fill the gap.

Leaving Blaze-Simms and the coffee behind, he crossed the street, weaving through the bustling crowd. In most American cities, folks got out of his way, not wanting to block the way of someone bigger and tougher looking than themselves. Here though, they seemed indifferent to his looming bulk. Women and men hurried into his path as if he weren't there, forcing him to pause, twist, and sidestep through the throng.

At last he reached the iron monger's shop. Carefully positioning himself to keep an eye on a particular building down the street, he began perusing the knives laid out on a well worn trestle.

"Can I help you, sir?" The shop's owner appeared, smiling benignly through a beard flecked with grey. His English was good though heavily accented. "Something exotic to hang over the mantlepiece, yes? A souvenir of our exotic land?"

Dirk crouched, pulled up one trouser leg, and unstrapped his ankle sheath. He held it out for the iron monger to see.

"Something to fit this, if you have it," he said.

The man ran an appraising eye over the leatherwork.

"A practical man," he said. "I have just the thing."

He picked a knife out of the pile. It was heavy looking, with a curved tip and a plain handle. Bowing his head, he held it out for Dirk to examine.

"No," said a quiet voice beside Dirk.

He turned to see a woman, dressed from head to toe in the all-concealing black robes some of the locals seemed to like. Only a pair of eyes showed, glinting with steady strength.

"Noriko?" he asked, surprised.

She gave a tiny nod. The iron monger glanced between them, his smile fixed.

"This metal is weak." Noriko tapped the blade with her finger. "Bring something of real value."

Dirk could almost see the iron monger's thoughts play out across his face. Surprise at being challenged by a woman, confusion about these two strangers, and then the moment of decision, that sometimes it was best just to go with the flow.

"You have a good eye," he said. "I will be back."

He put the knife down and headed into the shadows of his shop.

Hard as he peered at the knife, Dirk couldn't work out what Noriko had spotted. He found himself intrigued.

"How did you know?" he asked.

"My grandfather was a katana maker," she said. "I grew up by the light of his forge."

Was it Dirk's imagination, or was there a wistfulness in her voice he'd never heard before? He was about to ask more, but a figure caught his eye.

"It's time," he said, moving to hide his face behind a stand of pots and pans.

Down the street, Marie Cluny was approaching a shop crowded with curios and antiquities, from statues of dog-headed gods to chairs with hieroglyphs carved up the sides.

She didn't rush, but her course was direct, her interest in other shops cursory.

Braithwaite had been right. This place was important to the French. That being the case, Braithwaite was probably right about why. An antiquities shop was a natural stopping off point for wanderers and foreigners, from acquisitive low-lives to high-society ladies. In other words, the perfect cover for a covert message drop.

He waited until Cluny had gone inside, then got ready to make their move.

"You go wait out front," he murmured to Noriko. "She'll never recognise you in that."

The ninja slid into the crowd, just one more Egyptian woman in an Egyptian street.

Dirk wove his way back across the road, to find Blaze-Simms still at his table, papers spread out in front of him.

"You know about explosives, don't you?" the inventor asked.

"All too well," Dirk said, remembering a youth spent down mines. "But now ain't the time. She's here."

"I say!" Blaze-Simms snatched up the papers and shoved them into a pocket, the bundle spoiling the line of his previously impeccable jacket. In the time since Dirk left, he'd also managed to dribble coffee down his pristine white shirt.

Dirk approached the antiquities dealer as inconspicuously as he could with Blaze-Simms in tow. He'd considered leaving his colleague back at the embassy, but this job had been Blaze-Simms's idea and he could come in surprisingly useful when things took an unexpected turn. Sometimes spycraft was all about unexpected turns.

As they'd planned, Blaze-Simms stopped at a spice stall next to their target, while Dirk passed the doorway and stopped in an alley mouth opposite. He leaned casually against the mud brick wall, its shadow offering welcome relief from the midday sun, watching the shop front out of the corner of his eye.

Across the way, a westerner in a striped suit and straw hat was drinking tea from a tall glass in a cafe. His eyes spent as much time on the street as on the newspaper spread in front of him. Two doors down, another European had taken off his hat and was patting the sweat from his brow with a yellow handkerchief. That made two French agents here to back up Cluny, with a woman browsing a silk stall a potential third.

An explosive sneeze burst through the sounds of the crowd. Blaze-Simms, a bag of pepper in his hands and half its content down his front, began apologising profusely to the spice seller, only for another, even louder sneeze to interrupt his flow.

Dirk watched the Englishman from the corner of his eye, while carefully not looking at the French agents. The man with the yellow handkerchief was watching Blaze-Simms with a suspicious eye.

Blaze-Simms looked up and down the street in what Dirk assumed was meant to be a subtle appraisal. The furtive movement of his head, followed by another sneeze, only encouraged the French agent's attention. The man shoved his handkerchief into a pocket and started walking across the street.

Dirk shifted his weight, ready to head out into the crowd. He was loath to lose his vantage point and to draw attention to himself into the bargain, but if the Frenchman reached Blaze-Simms there was a good chance that he would let something slip, blowing their plan. Dirk didn't care much who won in this pissing contest between the Brits and the French, but it galled him to think that he and his companions might fail over something so trivial as a bag of pepper.

Halfway across the street, a woman dressed from head to toe in black bumped into the Frenchman. As she moved on, he patted at his jacket, then reached inside. Something was clearly amiss, as his face widened in alarm.

"Hey!" he called out, turning to pursue the woman. "My wallet!"

Dirk stifled a grin as the French agent disappeared up the street, pursuing Noriko in her all-concealing black robes. Even if there weren't a hundred other women dressed like that with whom to confuse her, there was no way he would catch up. She was far too nimble for that.

From the opposite direction, another figure caught Dirk's eye. Wearing a pale blue dress and sheltered by a parasol, Isabelle passed through the crowd with refined ease. Dirk knew he wouldn't be the only man there watching her, espionage or no espionage. But that wasn't a problem. Her part in this didn't need her to blend in.

As she passed by, she treated him to a subtle wink, the gesture hidden from most of the world by her parasol. Dirk couldn't help but grin a little. He hoped that anyone watching would put it down to the natural reaction of a red-blooded man watching a fine lady walk by.

They'd timed it perfectly. As Isabelle entered the antiques shop, the shopkeeper was holding out a small statue of a jackal-headed dog for Madame Cluny to examine. To the rest of the world, it would look like nothing more than a seller offering his customer wares. But Dirk would have bet the house on that statue being what Cluny was here for, with a message hidden somewhere inside. He'd used the same technique himself more than once and so he knew the way this dance played out.

Isabelle's exclamation of excitement was so loud that Dirk heard it across the street. The shopkeeper turned, offering her his best salesman grin, as she stared as if enraptured at the statue. She pulled out her purse and reached for the jackal-headed god.

In credit to the shopkeeper, he mostly managed to hide his alarm. His expression barely faltered as he smoothly drew the statue out of reach and directed Isabelle's attention to his other wares, even as Cluny took a step back, trying to stay out of the way until this was dealt with. Dirk wished he could hear the conversation - the shopkeeper making increasingly frantic attempts to divert Isabelle from the statue while trying to maintain his facade as a man only interested in making a quick buck. How long before Cluny was forced to step in and start a bidding war for the piece? Or would the shopkeeper find an excuse to flat out refuse Isabelle?

"She is good at this." The voice from behind Dirk made him jump even though he recognised it. There was almost no-one who could creep up without him noticing.

"You're pretty damn good too," he said, keeping his eyes on the shop rather than turning to look at Noriko. "That was smooth work with the guy's wallet."

"It was easy," Noriko said. "These men are barely worth the title of spies."

They watched as the conversation in the shop became increasingly animated. Isabelle's charming and reasonable demeanour were making it hard for the shopkeeper to do his job of saying no. Dirk stifle a laugh as he watched the drama play out in front of Madame Cluny, who clutched her purse and shifted from foot to foot in mounting frustration.

He was so focused on the scene that it took him a moment to realise that Noriko had spoken again.

"Sorry, what was that?" he asked, turning to look at her.

"I said that you make her happy," Noriko said. "And that I am pleased to see that."

"I..." Dirk didn't know what to say. He might have expected a line like that out of a lady's father if he was asking for permission to propose. Even then, he'd have felt uncomfortable discussing his romance with a third party, and he and Noriko hadn't exactly had a lot of heart to hearts.

"What I do, it does not allow me many friends," Noriko said. "I think that Isabelle is my friend now."

"Reckon we all are," Dirk said. "If you'll have us."

"Thank you." Most of Noriko's face was still hidden but he could have sworn he saw something soften around her eyes. "I will miss you, when the time comes to move on. As I am sure you will miss each other."

"I'm sure it won't come to that. I mean..."

He hesitated. What did he mean? After all, they were close to finding the treasure they had been seeking. Once that was done, he and Blaze-Simms would go back to the Club, Noriko would return to Japan, and Isabelle... He had assumed that the two of them would be together, but he'd given no thought to how that would actually work. She had a life beyond this adventure and so did he. The odds of those two lives taking them to the same place were pretty slim. How could they build anything together without giving up what made them who they were?

"We have a problem," Noriko said.

"Yeah, I'm starting to realise that," Dirk said.

"An immediate problem," Noriko said, pointing into the street.

The French watchers had clearly decided that Madame Cluny needed help in the shop. The woman who had been browsing for silks was heading there, as was the man from the café.

Cursing himself for getting distracted, Dirk stepped out of the alley.

"You take the woman," he said to Noriko. "I'm on the guy."

He didn't know how much the French agents could do to spoil their scheme - that depended on Braithwaite and how soon he played his part. But he didn't want to risk them complicating matters. Complications were what made things go wrong.

"Excuse me." He tapped the man from the café on the shoulder. With his other hand, he snatched up a hat from a nearby stall. "I think you dropped something."

The man turned to face him.

"What exactly did I drop?" said snapped, his French accent confirming what Dirk already knew.

"This."

Dirk waved the hat in the man's face. As the man prepared to protest, Dirk's fist hit him through the hat. He dropped like a stone.

Dirk tossed the hat back onto the stall, then grabbed the man by his ankles and dragged him back into the alleyway.

"Heat stroke," he said to the few people who looked like they might care. It seemed to be enough of an explanation, as everyone got back to whatever they'd been doing.

Having deposited the unconscious French agent in a doorway, Dirk turned to look back into the street. The conversation in the shop was becoming increasingly heated. Isabelle had laid a hand on the statue but the shopkeeper was refusing to let go.

"Why ever not?" Isabelle voice rose loud enough to be heard above the crowd. "I have the money, I can't see any honest reason why you won't sell it to me."

The shopkeeper said something through a fixed grin. Cluny glanced around, then stepped closer, her shoulders tensing as she prepared to intervene.

At the far end of the street, a distinctive figure appeared. Tall, broad, and with a beard like half a hedgerow, Braithwaite would have stood out in any crowd, never mind one where Europeans were in the minority. With him were men in the uniforms of the local police. He handed something to one of them, winked broadly, and then disappeared from view.

The policemen headed down the street, trying hard to look like this was just an ordinary patrol. They made Sir Timothy Blaze-Simms look like masters of subtlety but no-one could challenge their right to be here.

Right on queue, Isabelle raised her voice again.

"This is outrageous!" she exclaimed. "I don't know what sort of scam you're running, but I won't be taken in."

As she strode out into the street, the shopkeeper followed her, making placatory gestures with one hand while the other clutched the statue.

"I say!" Isabelle waved at the passing policemen. "Something is wrong with this shop. This man won't sell me a statue, and he keeps changing his story over whether it's real or not."

The shopkeeper's face went pale as the uniformed men closed in. Behind him, Madame Cluny slipped out of the shop and away.

Heavy footfalls echoed down the alley as Braithwaite arrived in Dirk's hiding place.

"How's it looking?" Braithwaite asked.

"That handoff definitely ain't happening," Dirk said. "Can they make the forgery charges stick?"

"Oh aye," Braithwaite said. "Everyone knows that Ali's emporium is full of fakes. Even after Isabelle takes that statue, they'll have plenty of proof. And with mummies disappearing from archaeological digs, the police are interested in antiquities right now."

"Will this make a big difference to the French?" Dirk asked. "Seems kind of small fry for all this effort."

Braithwaite shrugged.

"Depends what the message in the statue is," he said. "Cutting off one of their communication lines will cause some troubles. But mostly, I just wanted to remind Cluny of who's in charge."

He hauled the unconscious French agent from the ground and slung him over his shoulder.

"I'll make sure this lad gets home in one piece," he said. "There have to be some limits to how we do this."

"Guess I'll see you at the embassy," Dirk said.

He headed back down the street to the iron monger where he'd been browsing earlier. As he approached, the man grinned and waved a knife.

"How about this, my friend?" he said. "One of my finest."

Dirk took the knife and weighed it in his hand. The edge was sharp, the back solid, and though the tip had a curve to it, he reckoned it might fit in the sheath from his old Bowie knife.

"Perfect," he said.

As he reached into his pocket for cash, a familiar figure passed by. As he looked up, Madame Cluny fixed him with a brief but pointed glare. Then she was gone.

Dirk sighed. The knife sat well in his hand. It had a good weight to it and the price wasn't too extortionate. This was a good buy.

He wished he felt half as comfortable about what else he'd done today. Because fun as it had been, he just knew this day would come back to bite him in the ass.

Chapter 3: Local Problems

The sounds of clattering gears and creaking levers drifted in through the window of Dirk's guest room in the British embassy. Whatever device Blaze-Simms had been distracted by, it seemed he'd finished building it, scratching the itch that was his constant desire to invent. Maybe now he'd be back on task. It seemed as good a time as any for Dirk to check in on him.

Setting aside a newspaper and a flat iron that he'd been using as an improvised dumbbell, Dirk got up from his seat and headed out through the floor-length windows. Beyond his room, a broad balcony ran around the exterior of the embassy, connecting together many of the rooms. The angle of the sun meant that the balcony was currently flooded with bright sunlight, along with the noises and smells of the city below. The shouts of shopkeepers, the rumble of waggon wheels, the protests of indignant camels, accompanied by the scents of sweat, spices, and dung. Dirk loved the way that sensory assault brought a city to life, making it more than just bricks and mortar, turning the work of architects into something as flawed and magnificent as humans could be.

Blaze-Simms sat in a rocking chair on the balcony. He'd rigged the chair with a complex system of levers, pulleys, and fan belts, so that the motion as he rocked back and forth caused a fan to waft through the air, cooling him.

"Clever contraption," Dirk said, trying to work out how all the parts fitted together. "Is it a Blaze-Simms original?"

"Partly," Blaze-Simms said, looking up from a handful of papers. "I know a chap called Davy who's working on something similar, but you have to take a different approach when you're not building the chair from scratch."

"How's the library hunt going?"

"Excellent!" Blaze-Simms gestured at a portable card table next to his seat. Assorted papers were spread out upon it, weighed down with teacups, gears, and ornaments he'd borrowed from his room. On the floor lay the stone tablets that they'd gone to such lengths to obtain. One brought by Isabelle and later retrieved from Noriko's ninjas. One fetched from the bottom of the ocean, where it had been guarded by angry ghosts. One from the sewers beneath Paris, snatched out of a secret civil war.

"You said that you'd figured out how it all connects together?" Dirk peered at the stones. He couldn't even read the letters on parts of them, never mind the words they made up. And Blaze-Simms had told him gleefully that there were all sorts of codes and riddles mixed in with the ancient languages. The folks who'd hidden the Great Library of Alexandria had meant for it to stay well hidden.

"Oh yes!" Blaze-Simms waved his papers. "I have to admit, I was a trifle stuck before we got here. But then Isabelle arranged access to some local archives. Did you know that there are private collectors with documents reaching back to the earliest dynasties? A proper examination and comparison of the texts could transform our understanding of history back into the depths of the Old Testament. For example, there are references to the Battle of Megiddo that-"

"The Library, Tim?"

"Oh, yes!"

Blaze-Simms rustled through his papers, set half of them on the table, weighted them down with a half-dismantled clock, and then held out the rest for Dirk to see.

"This is the directions," he said, waving a page of short paragraphs and isolated sentences. He had clearly changed his mind about some of it, as it was littered with annotations and corrections. "The problem is working out where to start."

"That's the problem?" Dirk asked, taking the page so that he could better examine it. Even after years of dealing with Blaze-Simms's handwriting, he still struggled to decipher some parts. There was talk about valleys, roads, directions relative to sun and moon, and descriptions of landmarks such as rock formations and oases. Given how many changes Blaze-Simms had already made, Dirk couldn't help wondering if these directions were really all that reliable, or if, given another day of study, Blaze-Simms would change them some more.

"Oh, yes," Blaze-Simms said, his fan contraption creaking as he leaned forwards. "You see, that tells us the route to take but not where to start taking it from."

Dirk leaned against the balustrade that encircled the balcony. The sun blazed against the back of his neck but he didn't mind - he'd dealt with the heat when working out west. His friend, on the other hand, was reddening and starting to peel from his brief exposure to the Egyptian sun.

If they were heading out into the desert, he'd need to make sure that Blaze-Simms and Isabelle had suitable clothes, not their usual European city styles. Then there would be water, transportation, tools for a likely dig at the end of it all...

"So how do we work out where to start?" Dirk asked.

"We're looking for something like this." Blaze-Simms handed him another sheet of paper. This was a list of points describing a monument. Tall, carved with pictures of battles and of gods, set on a broad pedestal, made of black stone...

That last point was instantly familiar.

Dirk ducked into his room, grabbed the newspaper, and headed out onto the balcony again. He flicked through the pages until he found the article he wanted.

"Reckon we're in luck," he said, feeling pleased. "This says that a large monument of black stone was recently found at a dig south of the city. They're still working on the site. Whole thing's being led by some guy called Maurice Pelletier."

"How splendid!"

Blaze-Simms leapt to his feet. Papers scattered in the breeze from the automated fan. The two of them frantically snatched at the papers before they could get away.

"So how do we get to the dig?" Blaze-Simms asked.

"We should find a native guide," Dirk replied, grabbing a sketch of a pyramid as it went drifting out into the air.

"I already found one," said a voice from inside Dirk's room.

He turned with a smile as Isabelle emerged onto the balcony. She caught the last of the floating sheets and handed it to Blaze-Simms.

"I hope you don't mind," she said, casting a swift, playful look from the room to Dirk while Blaze-Simms wasn't looking.

"Not at all," Dirk replied. "It's mighty fine to see you."

"Why would I mind you finding a guide?" Blaze-Simms asked, placing the papers under the clock. "That's marvellous news."

"Not just any guide," she said. "The best in town. I thought that we would need her sooner or later."

"So when can we leave?" Blaze-Simms asked eagerly.

"If we're going to nose around someone's archaeological dig?" Isabelle asked. "Once we have their permission."

#

"Absolutely not," Maurice Pelletier said, folding his arms across the front of his off-white suit. "There is no place for trouble makers at my dig."

The news that the archaeologist was in town had sounded like a stroke of luck. That was until it turned out that he was not only French but a guest at the French embassy, staying there courtesy of Monsieur and Madame Cluny. Madame Cluny herself sat in an armchair across the lobby of the embassy, smiling as she put up a pretence of not listening to their conversation.

"I assure you, Monsieur Pelletier, we won't be any trouble at all," Isabelle said. "It's a simple matter of academic interest. We won't touch anything. You can have somebody supervise us if you want. And in return we can-"

"No." Pelletier shook his head firmly. "I have heard about you. Friends who have encountered you before. There will be none of your so-called adventures on my site. Good day, madame."

He turned and stormed away, leaving Dirk, Isabelle, and Blaze-Simms to see themselves out. Cluny gave them a small wave as they left, a look of triumph on her face.

Dirk fumed as they strode through the crowded streets. He should have listened to his instincts and kept them out of the Anglo-French spy games. But he hadn't been able to pin down why he thought it was a bad idea, and he knew that instincts couldn't always be trusted. Now the answer was obvious. Every enemy you made was a potentially useful contact that you lost.

"Could you please slow down a little," Isabelle said, taking hold of his arm. "It's far too hot for us to be running to keep up."

"Rather," Blaze-Simms said. "And what beastly luck, that the person running the dig should turn against us like that."

"It ain't about luck," Dirk said. "It's about you getting us caught up in Braithwaite's goddamn spy games. Now Cluny's gonna be turning every Frenchman in Egypt against us. That's half the scholars and explorers in this country."

"Well, we could hardly have said no," Blaze-Simms said.

"That's exactly what we could have said." Dirk stopped and turned to face the Englishman. "We're not some branch of the British government. We don't have to jump when they say so."

"One has a patriotic duty to-"

"My ancestors said no to British patriotism a hundred years ago. I don't need it biting me in the ass now."

"So you're happy to accept British hospitality, but not to return the favour?"

"Not when it means-"

"Enough," Isabelle snapped. "If you two must squabble like schoolboys, at least wait until we're off the streets."

"Sorry," the two men said in unison.

"But I ain't doin' any more favours for Braithwaite," Dirk said.

"Let's cross that bridge when we come to it," Isabelle said. "For now, we need an excuse to get onto that site. Whatever Pelletier's objections, that's where our trail starts."

#

The answer, as it turned out, was once again in the newspaper.

"Mummy smuggling," Noriko said into the silence of the embassy's drawing room.

Dirk, Isabelle, and Blaze-Simms had been enjoying a post-dinner cigar in a set of over-stuffed armchairs. They all looked up, surprised to see that Noriko had appeared among them, carrying a selection of neatly trimmed press cuttings which she now spread across a nearby table. She was wearing a dress of elaborately embroidered oriental silk, as she had been when Dirk first met her on the island of Hakon. But while she might not be dressed like a ninja, her movements were no less silent and efficient.

The newspaper stories told a sorry tale of priceless artefacts disappearing from archaeological sites. Most of them were mummies, the bodies of ancient nobles whisked away before they could even be properly studied. No-one had caught a whiff of the perpetrators yet, but the assumption running through all the articles was that they were being smuggled to Europe and sold to private collectors. Comments by the colonial authorities were full of disappointment at these losses. Those by local sources were filled with a deep outrage at the plundering of their heritage.

"How does this help us?" Dirk asked.

"There is an investigation into the thefts," Noriko said. "If a European archaeologist were to refuse to cooperate with the investigators, it would cast suspicion upon him."

Dirk grinned.

"I like it," he said. "If we're part of the investigating team, even Pelletier will have to let us onto his site. How do we sign up?"

"We already have." Noriko handed them each a document marked with an official seal.

"How did you talk your way onto this?" Dirk asked.

"By not being white," Noriko said. "The locals suspect European meddling, but they cannot find the culprits and so are keen for outside assistance."

"But we're all white," Blaze-Simms said. "Well, I'm a sort of red right now..."

He gingerly touched the back of his neck, making himself wince.

"And that is why I did this without you," Noriko said. "Dynamo, how ready are we to go?"

Dirk quickly ran through the list of equipment he'd been assembling in his head. Then he considered the sources of supplies he'd already found and what remained outstanding.

"Reckon I'll need two days," he said. "Call it three, in case I run into any more problems. Might have to find alternatives if any of the major suppliers are French."

He shot a pointed look at Blaze-Simms, but the Englishman was fiddling with the insides of a nearby grandfather clock, apparently oblivious to the rest of the conversation.

"Three days from tomorrow, then," Noriko said. A hint of a smile crept up her normally placid features. "Soon the library will be ours."

#

Dirk sat on a crate of ration biscuits, his feet up on another box, a book on Egyptian wildlife in one hand while with the other he lifted and lowered his flat iron dumbbell. He didn't mind having the supplies for the expedition in his room. The place was bigger than he was used to and it made it easy to keep an eye on the supplies. But the fact that the British hadn't been able to find them a better storage space, especially after their help with Cluny, was a source of annoyance.

There was a knock at the door.

"Come in," Dirk called out. "It ain't locked."

Isabelle entered and closed the door softly behind her. Dirk dropped the book and the iron, which hit the floor with a clang, and bolted to his feet. He could feel the idiot grin spreading across his face and he was delighted to see Isabelle smile back.

"Hi," he said. "How you doing?"

"Very well, thank you," she said. "And you?"

"I'm great." He gestured at the items that littered his room. Boxes and bags of food. A heap of water skins. Shovels and picks. Spare camel tack in case the reins and saddles they were given proved poor quality. A pile of books he'd been using to educate himself ready for the trip. "All done a day ahead of schedule."

He took a step closer to Isabelle. He wanted to kiss her. It wasn't like they hadn't done that before. Hadn't done a whole lot more, for that matter. But was that where they were at now? How did he even work these things out?

Isabelle frowned.

"There's something we need to talk about," she said.

Dirk's heart sank.

"About the expedition," she continued. "May I take a seat?"

Dirk sighed with relief and pointed her toward the room's only available chair, while he settled back down on his crate.

"What's on your mind?" he asked.

"We've lost our guide."

"What happened?"

"She does a lot of work for the French. She's been told that if she helps us then that ends. Cluny has more influence in this town than we realised."

"Then we'll find a different guide."

"Dirk, England and France are the two big foreign powers out here, the two big sources of income for anyone working with scholars or tourists. No-one even halfway good at their job can afford to risk a big chunk of that."

Dirk looked around the room. The piles of boxes represented something far larger than just buying supplies. They represented the effort it had taken him and his colleagues to get this far. He wasn't going to let that go to waste because Braithwaite had drawn them into a colonial pissing match.

"Come on," he said, getting up and heading for the door. "We're gonna sort this out."

Isabelle in tow, he stomped along the corridor and down a flight of stairs to the door labelled "Head of Trade Delegation". He hammered on the polished wood.

"Braithwaite, you in there?" he called out.

"Aye, lad," came the reply. "No need to break it down. Just come on in."

Dirk flung the door open and strode inside. The room looked for all the world like a perfectly innocent office. Sunlight from the windows illuminating a couple of desks and Braithwaite sitting behind one of them. There were piles of papers, rows of books, and a collection of cloth samples in one corner. But Dirk would have bet his last cent that the maps on the wall and the documents on the shelves held information that was about far more than trade.

"We need you to get us a guide," Dirk said.

"A please would be nice," Braithwaite said, leaning back in his chair.

"Please," Dirk began again, his voice strained, "given that we lost our guide through working for you, can you get us a new one."

"Sorry, lad," Braithwaite said, stroking his beard. "I can't help."

"You said you know people with local knowledge."

"Aye, that I do. But I'm busy right now, and I can't afford to go running around, burning favours to help you go sightseeing."

"Did I mention the part where you got us into this mess?"

Braithwaite sighed and smiled.

"Look lad, I'm genuinely sorry to have caused you trouble," he said. "But Her Majesty's Government has higher priorities than helping you on whatever fanciful mission you're on. Give me a couple of weeks and then I'll see what I can do."

"We've hired camels," Dirk said. "We've bought perishable supplies. We ain't waiting a week."

"Then you aren't getting my help." Braithwaite leaned forward, his expression becoming more serious. "And unless you've gained some manners and a way to make yourself useful, please bugger off out of my office."

Dirk's blood boiled. After everything they'd done, to be treated like this? It was outrageous.

But mad as he was, he couldn't see any way that arguing would help. He suppressed an angry response and strode out of the room, slamming the door behind him. The noise echoed through the corridors of the embassy. A couple of clerks peered out of doorways to see what was happening, then hurriedly retreated when they saw Dirk's face.

"We can wait," Isabelle said, laying a calming hand on Dirk's arm. "We'll lose some money, but it's not the end of the world. Timothy has enough that he won't mind."

"No," Dirk said. "I'm not letting that guy get in my way. I'm not leaving the library out there for someone else to find because of this. What if others are still hunting for it? What if the Dane decides he's interested again?"

"They don't have the stones."

"We don't know what they have. And it ain't like those stones haven't been stolen before."

"Well then what do you suggest?"

Dirk thought back to the pile of books in his room. He'd been reading all about Egypt. About its geography, its wildlife, its weather. He wasn't fool enough to think that book learning was enough to make someone into a local guide. But he'd dealt with plenty of other wildernesses. He reckoned he knew enough to apply that learning here.

"I'll be our guide," he said. "Let's get the hell out of this town."

Chapter 4: Tombs

The journey to the dig site was a satisfying one for Dirk. Few of his recent adventures had given him a chance to flex his skills outdoors. Cities and sewers, castles and caves, it had been a very different experience from his days out west, roaming the wide open plains. He'd been half hoping that Blaze-Simms would learn about a clue hidden in a jungle or some highland wilderness, just so he could spend some solid time in the fresh air.

He took delight in their journey out into the desert. A few days of trail finding and living under canvas restored his energy like nothing else could. By the time they reached the dig, he was ready to take on the world.

They emerged between two low, rocky hills. Suddenly, the land in front of them opened up, revealing a low, dry valley swarming with activity. Porters in native Egyptian garb bustled back and forth amid rows of tents, carrying out the menial tasks that kept any encampment running smoothly - cooking, cleaning, repairing, digging latrine pits. Further down the hillside, the ground was crisscrossed with a network of intersecting trenches. A mixture of locals and Europeans wielded everything from shovels to trowels to tiny brushes as they unveiled the wonders buried beneath the sands of time. Off to the left, a cluster of youths were trying to herd horses and camels back into an enclosure, with decidedly mixed results. The swirl of snorting animals and swearing young men created a storm of noise.

As Dirk and his companions rode down the slope towards the tents, more of the dig site became visible. It was a stunning place. The heads and shoulders of statues emerged from the packed ground, ghosts of an ancient era rising from their desert crypts. On the far side of the valley, a stone gate had been revealed in the hillside, its lintel carved with elaborate hieroglyphics. A couple of hundred yards from that portal, three cylinders of shining black stone lay across the ground while men with shovels worked to unearth a fourth.

"I say, that must be the pillar!" Blaze-Simms practically fell off his camel in his hurry to get down and go explore.

"Tim," Dirk snapped, "keep hold of the reins. We need to find somewhere to tether up and unload."

Blaze-Simms sighed and glared at the camel.

"And I thought I was rid of you, you foul beast," he said.

"I too look forward to not riding these creatures," Noriko said. "They are bad tempered and uncomfortable."

"Don't reckon they think highly of us either," Dirk said, laughing. "Stupid two-legged critters sitting on their backs and giving them hassle all day."

A man emerged from amid the tents and walked toward them, waving his hat in the air. Dirk descended to greet him.

"Salaam," the man said as he approached. He looked to be of Arab descent, with a neatly trimmed beard and a warm smile. His clothes were western - heavy cotton trousers and a shirt covered with the dust of the dig.

"Salaam," Dirk replied. "Can we talk to someone in charge?"

"You already are." The man stuck out his hand. "Asim Waked, site foreman. And you are?"

"Dirk Dynamo." Dirk returned Asim's firm handshake. "This here's Mrs Isabelle McNair, Miss Miura Noriko, and Sir Timothy Blaze-Simms."

"And what brings you to our corner of Egypt, Mr Dynamo?" Asim asked.

Dirk presented the official document Noriko had acquired in Cairo.

"We're here to investigate the disappearance of historical artefacts," he explained.

"Ah, the missing mummies!" Asim said. "Given the value of our site, I am glad to have you here."

He waved a hand and more men emerged from between the tents. Asim rattled off what sounded like a string of instructions in Arabic, then turned back to Dirk.

"They will unload and set up your tents," he said, walking over to Isabelle's camel.

"I'm sure we can manage," Dirk said.

"Nonsense." Asim held out a hand to help Isabelle down. "I cannot have such charming guests left to labour for themselves in the middle of the day."

"That's very kind of you, Mr Waked," Isabelle said, smiling at him as she reached the ground.

"Please, call me Asim," he said, kissing the back of her hand.

Dirk frowned. He knew that Isabelle wasn't really married, but this guy didn't and he was laying the charm on pretty thick.

"Careful with that!" Blaze-Simms exclaimed as the labourers started unloading a crate from Dirk's camel. "There are explosives in there."

Trying to keep his calm, Dirk turned to face Blaze-Simms.

"Explosives?" he asked.

"Not just any old explosives," Blaze-Simms said, smiling excitedly. "The latest thing out of Sweden. It's far safer than using blasting powder or nitroglycerin."

"Why do we have explosives?" Dirk asked.

"In case we have to get into somewhere in a hurry. Explosives are often the most efficient way of digging a hole."

"I know," Dirk said stiffly. "I used to work with them. But didn't you think I might want to know that my baggage could blow me to pieces?"

"That was never likely to happen."

"Likely?"

"What I mean is..." Blaze-Simms's voice trailed off. It seemed that he'd finally thought it through. "Sorry."

"That's OK," Dirk said. He found it hard to stay mad at Blaze-Simms. The guy might do the most ludicrous things at the most inappropriate moments, but his heart was in the right place. Years of putting their lives in danger together had forged a bond it was hard to shake.

He turned to see Asim deep in conversation with Isabelle and Noriko. The foreman looked up and smiled at him.

"You must all be parched," Asim said. "Please, come with me. I will arrange refreshments and then you can have a tour of the site."

The tent he led them to seemed to be an office for running the dig. It was larger than most of the others, a canvas marquee with enough vertical walls for its inhabitants to hang up maps and diagrams of the site. In the centre, a table was littered with sketches and artefacts. While Blaze-Simms began rummaging eagerly through the evidence, Asim led the others to a set of folding seats near the entrance.

Moments later, a woman appeared. She wore a long, simple dress and a headscarf that concealed her hair. Her movements had the abrupt efficiency of an experienced and no-nonsense servant. She placed a stand next to Asim's chair, laid a tray of cups and saucers on it, and then disappeared again.

"You are professional archaeologists?" Asim asked, looking eagerly around the group.

"We dabble," Isabelle replied.

"Police then?" Asim asked, raising an eyebrow.

"More like freelance investigators," Isabelle said, smiling at him.

Asim, whose seat lay between Dirk and Isabelle, flashed her another smile.

"Fascinating," he said. "So how do you come to be hunting our mummy smugglers?"

"Noriko arranged it," Dirk said hastily, trying to draw Asim's attention away from Isabelle. He could feel himself flushing. It was ridiculous, getting all wound up just because Isabelle was giving this guy her best smile. After all, charming people was part of how she worked. But there was no certainty over their relationship. If Isabelle took a liking to this guy, who was to say that she wouldn't choose him over Dirk?

Even inside Dirk's head, it sounded ridiculous. But the thought just wouldn't go away.

In the time it took Dirk to finish stewing on his thoughts, the servant had brought a pot of tea and the conversation had moved on. He realised that Asim was smiling at him now.

"Sorry, what was that?" Dirk asked.

"I said that America has always fascinated me, Mr Dynamo," Asim said. "You must tell me about your wild west."

"It ain't all like in the penny dreadfuls," Dirk said.

"So you haven't been in a shootout?"

"Well, technically, one or two."

"But no Indian raids?"

"I've been on both sides."

"Lynchings?"

"Wish I'd seen less."

Asim threw his head back in laughter.

"Not like the penny dreadfuls indeed." He prodded at Dirk's arm. "Yet here I am, sat next to a living breathing cowboy."

He looked around at Noriko and Isabelle, who laughed along with him. Dirk just found himself blushing more deeply as he saw Isabelle's smile widen. He felt like the butt of a joke and it was a feeling that stung.

"We should go look around," he said, lurching to his feet.

"Oh yes!" Blaze-Simms, still standing by the main table, waved his notebook wildly. "This place is fascinating. So many unusual constructions and carvings to explore. They've just opened up a string of tombs along the south side of the valley, which I suspect may be the resting places of royal officials. Then there are the monuments, the remains of the workers' camp, the ceremonial routes..."

"Tim, focus," Dirk said. "Remember why we're here."

"Oh yes, the lib-"

"The mummy smuggling. We need to look for clues."

"Right. Yes."

Blaze-Simms winked. Dirk tried hard not to roll his eyes.

"You coming?" Dirk said, looking at Isabelle and Noriko.

"Absolutely." Isabelle set aside a teacup and rose to her feet.

"Would you like a guided tour?" Asim asked.

"That's quite alright," Isabelle said. "If you're happy to let us wander then we're happy to leave you to your work."

"Of course," Asim said. "I'm sure I can trust such reputable investigators. Just please, don't move anything without talking to me first."

They headed out of the tent and down toward the excavations. Though parts of the site were bustling with activity, others were quiet, trenches or areas of statuary roped off and left alone while other stretches were exposed.

"I should look at the pillar," Blaze-Simms said. "The carvings on it will be vital in orienting us and setting out the first steps in our route."

"OK then," Dirk said. "While you're doing that, I'll go look at the tombs, keep up the pretence that we're here to investigate the mummy thefts. Someone should keep Tim company."

"I will do that," Noriko said. The brief look she gave Dirk reassured him that she understood her real purpose - not to keep Blaze-Simms company, which he wouldn't notice once he got going looking at the remains, but to keep him out of trouble.

"Then I get to go look at the tombs," Isabelle said. "We can meet back at the main tent in time for supper."

From the centre of the site, the row of tombs looked like little more than a set of cave mouths in the valley side half a mile away. As Dirk and Isabelle approached, their nature became clearer, pale stone doorways emerging from the surroundings. A few local labourers sat nearby, carrying sticks rather than spades - guards set to protect the tombs. With them was the woman who had served tea at Asim's tent and who was now serving water to the guards. Given their inattentiveness, Dirk wasn't surprised that there was a problem with thefts.

"It was good of Asim to give us such a warm reception," Isabelle said as they approached the tombs.

"Yep," Dirk said. "Seems like a nice guy."

"I'm sure he would be pleased to hear you say that."

Dirk fought down his opinions on what would and wouldn't please Asim.

"Let's start with this one," he said, pointing at the nearest tomb.

The guards watched them idly as they approached the doorway, its stones carved with the worn remnants of ancient hieroglyphics. An oil lamp sat near the entrance and Dirk lit it before leading the way into the darkness.

They followed a short passage carved through the hillside, wooden pit props holding up the ceiling where the ancient ground had started to give way. At the end, a short flight of steps led to a round chamber carved out of ancient rock.

It wasn't an elaborate tomb, like the engravings in newspaper reports. A few coloured stains showed where the walls had once been painted, but the ages had destroyed whatever art once lay there. A row of dusty pots and crumbling boxes lined the base of one wall, possessions for the tomb's inhabitant to take into the next life. In the centre of the room was the main attraction - a block of stone eight feet long and half that deep, only just narrow enough to have fitted down the passage into this place. On the top sat a separate slab.

"Hell of an effort for someone who's dead," Dirk said.

"I suppose it was reassuring for others," Isabelle said, laying a hand on the ancient stone. "Knowing that they would be cared for after they were gone."

"As far as I'm concerned, when you're gone you're gone," Dirk said. "All of this is effort that could have gone into caring for the living."

"So if I outlive you I should just throw you on the rubbish heap?" Isabelle asked.

"Do what makes you feel good. That's the part I care about."

"Promise you won't come back to haunt me?"

"I can hope."

Dirk peered more closely at the tomb. The lid was out of line with the rest. It looked like the archaeologists had opened it already and not quite put it back straight.

But why put the lid back at all once they'd removed the contents?

"Stand back," he said, placing his hands against the edge of the lid.

"Dirk," Isabelle said, a hard edge of warning in her voice. "Do I look like a princess?"

"Sorry." Dirk gave her a sheepish look. "Could you give me a hand with this?"

"Of course." She joined him in pushing at the lid, their muscles straining as the weight started to shift.

"Beautiful as a princess, maybe," he said as the stone slid back with a grinding roar.

"Thank you." Isabelle smiled. "I knew there was some charm under all that rugged manliness."

The slab teetered and then fell off the far side of the tomb, landing with a thud that raised a cloud of dust. By the light of the lone oil lamp, they peered into the ancient tomb.

It was empty.

"Well," Isabelle said. "Maybe we really are on the trail of the thieves."

Footsteps approached down the passageway. They turned to see the light of another lamp coming down the stairs. Maurice Pelletier came into view, followed by three of his guards and the woman who had been serving them water.

"I heard that you were here." Pelletier glared at them. "Apparently I am no longer in control of my own dig."

His eyes settled on the tomb.

"You opened it?" he snarled. He walked over and peered down into the tomb. When he turned his attention back to Dirk and Isabelle, his expression was hard as the rock around them. "Caught red handed."

"What?" Dirk frowned.

"These two have robbed the tomb!" Pelletier exclaimed.

"We found it like this," Isabelle said. "We're here to help find the thieves."

"A perfect cover," Pelletier said, turning to his guards. "One of you, go fetch help. We need to restrain these felons before they escape."

Frustrated, Dirk grabbed hold of Pelletier and shoved him up against the wall. The guards made as if to rush at Dirk, but then he flexed his muscles, the seams of his shirt popped, and they stopped in their tracks.

"Don't be a damn idiot," he said. "How the hell could we have robbed this tomb? We only just got here. If we'd been robbing this tomb we'd still be holding the loot."

"You arrived on site hours ago," Pelletier said. "You could have robbed this place, taken your ill-gotten gains, and then returned to see what you missed. I've heard about you and your nefarious tactics."

Two of the guards were circling the room, cautiously approaching Dirk with sticks raised. The third had run off back up the tunnel, calling for help.

Dirk took deep breaths, fighting to suppress his rising temper. Seeing things fall apart so stupidly was making him mad. But venting that at Pelletier wouldn't help. They needed the archaeologist to tolerate them long enough for Blaze-Simms to finish his work. If they got kicked out now, things were going to get damn complicated.

Slowly, he let go of Pelletier and backed off.

"We only just came to this tomb," he said. "We haven't had a chance to rob it."

"Prove it," Pelletier said.

Dirk looked around. Even if the guards were honest men, they clearly hadn't been paying attention to their work. For all they knew, he might be guilty.

"Madam." Isabelle addressed the servant standing in the tunnel mouth. "You served us tea after we arrived. You know that we were at the main tent all that time and you saw when we arrived here. We could not have robbed this tomb, could we?"

The woman hesitated. Dirk stiffened. If she stitched them up for some reason, or equivocated enough to give Pelletier's prejudices breathing room, then he might need to be ready for action.

"No." The woman shook her head. "Monsieur, they have not had a chance to rob you."

Pelletier scowled even more deeply than he had before. But it seemed that the servant's word was enough for him.

"Thank you, Soad," he said, with little trace of real gratitude. "Mr Dynamo, I may not have caught you red handed but your presence here is beyond suspicious. I don't know what part you have played in this theft, but I will find out what it is and you will be punished."

He stormed out, the servant Soad and the guards following him.

Dirk breathed a sigh of relief.

"Let's get out of here," he said. "Hopefully Tim will be done and we can move on."

Just as they were leaving the chamber, something caught his eye. Snagged on a jagged edge of the rough stone were shreds of some old and dirty cloth. Whatever it had been soaked in had left it stiff, almost brittle, and with a lingering smell of spices.

"Mummy wrappings?" Isabelle asked, looking at it. "Perhaps it snagged when they were carrying it out."

"Could be," Dirk said. "But wouldn't the mummy have been in a wooden sarcophagus?"

They headed up the tunnel, Dirk carefully cupping the scrap of cloth in his hand. As they emerged into daylight, Noriko and Blaze-Simms were approaching from the direction of the black stones.

"How'd it go?" Dirk asked. "You sorted our directions?"

Blaze-Simms shook his head.

"Sorry," he said. "I need to examine the whole pillar to finish putting the instructions together."

"They still digging up the last part?" Dirk asked.

"The last part or two," Blaze-Simms said. "Or maybe three. I'm afraid we're going to be here for a while."

Dirk looked across the dig site, to where Pelletier was shouting at his labourers, then gesticulating wildly toward Dirk and his friends.

It was going to be a long and difficult while.

Chapter 5: Strife Amid the Sands

As Dirk headed back to the tent he shared with Blaze-Simms, he saw the Englishman sat in the entrance, playing around with a collection of strings, sticks, and small gear-wheels. In front of him, a candle with pins through its centre was suspended between two blocks of stone. Blaze-Simms was literally burning his candle at both ends and as wax dribbled off the candle swayed back and forth, tugging at the strings and so driving whatever the contraption he was assembling.

"Shouldn't you be down by the pillar?" Dirk asked, sitting down on a rock outside the tent.

"I'm afraid there's no point," Blaze-Simms said. "Pelletier realised that I was taking an interest in it. Now he's diverted all the work to other areas of the site."

"Won't that mess with his research?" Dirk asked.

Blaze-Sims shrugged. "That depends on what else there is to find. This whole site is rich with potential."

Dirk looked down the slope from the encampment to where the digging was taking place. Dust clouded the air as labourers cleared the ground around the ruins Pelletier was interested in today. Even as he'd wandered around the site, getting a casual understanding of what was where, Dirk had found it fascinating. Asim had shown him pieces of jewellery and shards of pottery that revealed connections between this place and other parts of the world. Similarities between its layout and that of other sites seemed to confirm theories about ceremonial life in ancient Egypt.

They even found what might have been an embalmer's workshop, though that had yet to be confirmed. A thousand fascinated facts were unearthed with each day here, but instead of getting to enjoy that, Dirk was distracted dealing with their obstructive host.

Isabelle and Noriko headed up the slope towards them. The Englishwoman was sheltering from the desert heat beneath a parasol. As she walked, she twisted the handle, making the parasol spin above her head. The two adventurers were deep in conversation.

"...if we became more useful," Noriko said as they approached.

"Perhaps," Isabelle said. "But could anything we do make us useful enough to win Pelletier around? I've never encountered such a mule-headed example of humanity, and I've spent time around British peers."

"You're not having any luck either?" Dirk asked as he retrieved camping stools from inside the tent. He set them out for Isabelle and Noriko, then went to fetch another for himself.

"Thank you," Isabelle said. "And no, no luck at all. I talked Asim into diverting some workers to the pillar stones, but Pelletier noticed and sent them back. Now he'll be on the watch for that sort of thing."

Dirk gritted his teeth at Isabelle's mention of the foreman. He had to admit that Asim was one of the friendliest, most helpful guys he'd ever encountered. But the way that friendliness sometimes focused on Isabelle still made him uncomfortable.

He knew better than to get drawn into his own jealousy. The best he could do with that feeling was use it as fuel to motivate him, driving him to do better and so prove himself to Isabelle. Be the best man he could.

"How about if we investigate the mummy thefts?" he said. "I mean really dig into them, not just use it as a cover story."

"This seems like a distraction," Noriko said. "We have enough of those."

"But imagine if we find that lost mummy for Pelletier," Dirk said. "Prove ourselves useful to him. Maybe he'll be grateful enough to help us out."

"He may say that we found it because we stole it," Noriko said.

"Then we make sure to catch the criminals too. That way we've got proof it isn't us."

"I knew you weren't just a pretty face," Isabelle said with a smile.

"It is a good plan," Noriko said. "Where do we start?"

"Asim confirmed that there was a wooden sarcophagus in that tomb," Dirk said. "The scrap of bandages means they took the mummy out separately. Two trips carrying bulky objects. Odds are good that they left tracks somewhere around those caves. Maybe they're still there."

"You and I can look for them," Noriko said. "What can the others do?"

"I'll talk with the archaeologists," Isabelle said. "See if I can coax out anything odd they've seen. What about you, Timothy?"

Blaze-Simms set aside a tangle of string and sticks. He'd connected a selection of spoons to his candle-driven device and now they were digging a small trench in the dirt.

"Actually, I have an alternative idea for how to get help," he said.

"You planning on impressing him with an automated digging machine?" Dirk asked, pointing at the spoons and their steadily increasing hole.

"It is a good idea, isn't it?" Blaze-Simms said brightly. "And I'm very pleased with my progress so far. But that's not what I'm talking about." He looked nervously at Dirk. "My plan involves Braithwaite."

"Like he's going to help us," Dirk said.

"He might if we help him find oil," Blaze-Simms replied. "The French and the British are both looking for it out here in the desert. That's why they're at such loggerheads in Cairo. Braithwaite thinks this dig might even be cover for looking for sources out here. If we can help the British find the oil first then he'll have to help us out."

"No more favours for Braithwaite," Dirk said. "The last one was nothing but trouble."

"But it's a chance to put one over on the French. Isn't that worth a shot?"

"I'm not here to help the British," Dirk said. "You want to do your patriotic duty, do it some other way."

"But what about when we-"

"How many ways do you want me to say no?" Dirk asked, getting to his feet. "I don't work for my own government any more. I'm not working for somebody else's. Especially not when they brought trouble on our heads."

"There's no need to start shouting."

"Maybe if you'd been listening."

"Me? You're the one who kept interrupting!"

"Only because-"

"Enough," Noriko snapped.

For a long moment they sat in silence, Dirk and Blaze-Simms glaring at each other. Dirk knew that the inventor could be woolly headed, but he'd never taken him for blindly patriotic. Getting tangled in the colonial rivalries between Britain and France could only cause them more grief. How hard was it to see that?

"I'm going to go hunt the thieves," he said. "You should all do the same."

#

Dirk had heard the phrase "you don't know what you've got until it's gone" plenty of times, but he'd seldom felt its effects. He'd spent years working by himself, a lone investigator for the Pinkertons or for whoever hired him. Sure, he'd worked with others from time to time, and it had been a constant since he started working with the Epiphany Club. But he hadn't realised how much he'd come to rely upon that.

He crouched by the footprints over the ridge from the tombs. They were a day or two old, the result of at least half a dozen people, most of them wearing flat-soled sandals. They'd been carrying something heavy, just as he'd expected. So far, so good.

The problem came when they left the loose dirt of the land around the valley and got onto rocky ground. Here there were no footprints and no signs of scrapes like the bandages on the tomb wall. They'd been more careful with the casket.

Perhaps if he'd waited and brought Noriko with him she might have spotted something he hadn't. Maybe if he'd brought Blaze-Simms then the Englishman's knowledge of geology and geography might have told him something about where thieves would find a hiding spot. But he wasn't in the mood to go back and see Blaze-Simms, never mind ask him for help.

He knew that this was stubbornness. But he also knew that he'd always found ways to succeed on his own. If the physical evidence wasn't there, he could start looking at suspects instead.

Dusk was falling as he headed back to the dig site. He skirted around the edge of the encampment, watching people return to their tents, until he caught sight of the figure he was after. Dressed in European clothes but with the skin and beard of an Egyptian.

Asim Waked.

Asim was the obvious suspect to start with. As a dig foreman, he would have been to plenty of the sites objects had gone missing from. He'd have the contacts to find a market for them. Here and now, he knew the routines of the camp well enough to sneak something substantial past the guards. Hell, he arranged those routines and those guards. He could just have made sure friends of his were on duty, then used them for the theft.

Dirk watched from the lengthening shadows around the camp. Asim's tent was at the edge, conveniently placed for someone who wanted to sneak in and out. He did a quick round of the camp, checking on the needs of the men working for him, then returned to that tent. Patiently, quietly, not moving so as to not draw attention, Dirk watched him make dinner, offer evening prayers, and wash his dishes.

Just as Dirk was beginning to think that he was wasting his time, Asim looked around as if checking that no-one was watching. Then, quietly and carefully, though not as carefully as Dirk, he walked out of the camp and into the night.

Asim wasn't bad at sneaking, but Dirk had once been a professional and he had no trouble bringing those skills to bear now. He trailed the foreman on a long curve around the outside of the camp, across part of the dig, and towards the tombs.

Dirk almost laughed out loud. He could barely believe how right he'd been. Here was the first suspect he'd come up with heading straight to the loot. If only every case was this easy.

It seemed that he'd been right about Asim scheduling things too. As he approached the tombs, the foreman waved to the guards stationed there and they followed him into one of those darkened tunnel mouths.

As soon as their lamp was out of sight, Dirk followed them into the tomb, feeling his way through the darkness. He ran his fingers across the rough stone of the wall to guide his way and took small, careful steps in case the ground was uneven. By the time he reached a set of stairs, he could see lamplight at the bottom of them and here voices echoing around a chamber. He crept as far down the stairs as he could without revealing himself.

Everything had been going so smoothly, but now Dirk found the obvious flaw in his plan. The men were talking in Arabic and Dirk didn't speak a word of it.

It looked like he'd just have to wait for them to do something incriminating, then raise the alarm.

A sound behind him made him turn. He looked back up the stairs just in time to see the faint light of a candle appearing and behind it another of the dig's labourers. The man took one look at Dirk and gave a shout of alarm.

Dirk cursed his rookie mistake. Even as he rose from a crouch, the man pulled out a pistol and pointed it at him. At the bottom of the stairs, Asim appeared, also with a pistol in his hand.

Dirk reached under his arm and ended up cursing himself again. He'd been so caught up in getting away from the argument with Blaze-Simms that he'd forgotten his gun. He had his boot knife strapped to his shin, and if things got up close and personal he could use that. But right now, it didn't look like going that way.

"Mr Dynamo?" Asim asked, looking extremely surprised.

"That's me," Dirk said.

"I think you'd better come down here," Asim said. "And raise your hands on the way."

Dirk did as he was told. He found himself in a tomb much like the other one he'd been in. There was a stone sarcophagus in the middle and a pile of broken pots in one corner. The walls had been carved instead of just painted and he could make out an image of animal headed gods weighing a man's heart on a set of scales. The Egyptian afterlife stretched out in front of him, not half as appealing as staying alive.

"Who sent you?" Asim asked, his gun still pointed at Dirk. "The British or the French?"

"Like I told you when I got here," Dirk said. "We were sent by the authorities in Cairo."

"As if they object to our activities here," Asim said, shaking his head. "Try another story, Mr Dynamo. Preferably a convincing one."

"I don't really see the British objecting to you stealing from a French find," Dirk said. "And you've seen what the French think of us."

"Stealing?" Asim asked. "What are you talking about?"

"Really?" Dirk asked. "You're going to try to play innocent while standing in a tomb at night?"

"Do I look like I'm playing innocent?" Asim said, waving his gun.

Dirk looked around him again. These men were armed but none of them were carrying picks, shovels, ropes, or any other equipment that would help a tomb robber. They didn't even have sacks to carry whatever they might find in here. And if they were trying to get at a mummy in the sarcophagus then they were being mighty slow about it. During the whole time he'd lurked outside their conversation, they'd made no effort to open the lid.

Realisation dawned.

"You're not the robbers, are you?" Dirk asked.

"What?" Asim looked around, then laughed. "Alright, I see why you might think it. But no."

"Let me guess. You're some sort of band of rebels, intent on driving out the influence of the colonial oppressors."

"How did you know?" Asim asked. His eyes went wide, then narrowed with suspicion. "You are working for them!"

"No," Dirk said. "I've just been through this sort of thing before."

One of the men asked something in Arabic and Asim replied. A conversation broke out, each man talking over the others, several of them waving their hands in what could have been excitement or consternation.

Dirk let out a long breath and lowered his hands.

"Hey!" one of the men shouted, waving a gun at Dirk.

"No need for that," Dirk said. "I'm not with the British or the French."

Asim, his gun still pointing vaguely in Dirk's direction, translated his words.

"You really are just here looking for thieves?" the foreman asked.

"Yep," Dirk replied. "Well, no, I'm looking for..."

He hesitated. Telling a bunch of anti-colonial Egyptians that he, an American, was here to look for the lost Library of Alexandria didn't seem like the best of ideas. They might decide that was the sort of disrespect to their culture that earned a man a bullet in the brain. They might decide he was another colonial oppressor they needed out of the way.

"We came out here to see the sites," he said. "Me and my friends. We're from a club for scholars and explorers. We're looking for the thieves now, but that's just so that we can get back in everybody's good books. What we're really after is a closer look at the remains.

"The last thing I want to do is help someone oppress you folks. Hell, my people had a revolution just to stop that sort of thing. I helped fight to free the slaves and I've got the scars to prove it."

He waited while Asim finished translating. Most of the men had lowered their weapons now. The youngest of them - Dirk reckoned he might still be in his teens - asked an excited question.

"He wants to see your battle scars," Asim said, looking a little embarrassed. "I have to admit, I'm curious to see them too. We don't have many tales of heroism and glory between us."

Dirk laughed.

"There ain't a lot of glory in war," he said. "But sure, I'll show you the scars, maybe tell you a war story or two. And then maybe we can talk about helping each other out. Seems like we've got some enemies in common."

Chapter 6: Thieves in the Night

Dirk woke at first light and lay staring up at the canvas of his tent. He was in the best mood he'd been in since they arrived at the dig. He had allies. He had plans. He had all the skills he needed to carry them out.

He was ready to take on the world.

As often happened, he was up before his companions. He made the most of the opportunity. After warming up his body and brain with morning exercises and a history book, he got cleaned up and headed around to the catering tent. Here, some of the dig's staff were already up and about, boiling water and baking bread ready to feed the archaeologists and their crew. The smell of cooking made Dirk's mouth water.

Dirk looked around for Soad, who supervised the domestic side of life on site. He'd expected to see her at the heart of things, but when he finally spotted her she was stood by the camel enclosure, talking with a young woman who Dirk didn't recognise. When Soad saw him watching, she waved away the young woman and hurried over.

"Salam, Mr Dynamo," she said, bowing her head. "How can I help you?"

"Came to see if I could get a head start on breakfast," Dirk said. "And this might be a long shot, but you don't know where I could find any flowers, do you?"

#

Isabelle was standing outside the tents as Dirk approached, a large tray in his hands. A thoughtful expression filled her face as she brushed her hair and watched the camp come to life.

"Morning," Dirk said, setting the tray down on a flat rock. "I brought you these."

He held out a milk jug. A dozen large daisies peaked out over the rim, along with a couple of poppies. It looked a lot less impressive than he'd hoped for when he'd come up with the idea. Not many flowers grew in the desert and even the best he'd found were on the weary side, their outer petals drooping and dusty. But he'd been told that it was the thought that counted.

"What brought this on?" Isabelle asked, taking the offering with a smile that made his heart thud.

"I never..." Dirk began. "That is to say..."

How could he explain the thought behind it? This sense in the back of his head that they'd been missing out on a traditional courtship and that maybe that was what he needed to do. That she deserved a proper gentleman with flowers and dinners and suchlike, and that he hoped he could be that guy. Or at least something approximating that guy. He'd never done what most folks considered proper romance before, but he wanted to get it right.

Fundamentally, he had very little idea what he was doing, but he was determined to do it as well as he could.

"I'd never brought you flowers," he said. "I figured I should."

Isabelle leaned forward and kissed him on the cheek.

"That's very sweet," she said. "I would go so far as to say charmingly unconventional, given the circumstances."

Dirk beamed. Charmingly unconventional sounded good.

"And what's all this?" she asked, looking at the food piled high on the tray. Tea, coffee, bread, eggs, half a pot of jam. "I hope you don't expect me to eat it all."

"This is for the whole gang," Dirk said. "I figured we could eat breakfast together and plan our next move."

The tent flap opened behind Isabelle and Noriko emerged, blinking, into the sunlight. Within seconds, a razor sharp knife had appeared from her sleeve and she had two slices of fresh bread in her hand. She spread butter evenly across each slice with a single deft flick of the wrist.

"The jam is an unexpected treat," Isabelle said as she poured tea. "Where did that come from?"

"Soad dug it out of Pelletier's private stock," Dirk said. "She was very eager to help."

"Were you charming to her too?" Isabelle asked.

"What? No!" Dirk found himself getting tongue tied again, as happened whenever Isabelle got that mischievous look. "I just... I think she was covering for something."

The flap of the other tent opened and Blaze-Simms emerged. He rubbed a bleary eye and sauntered over to join them.

"I say." He took the tea Isabelle was offering. "How splendid."

Dirk smiled as he reached for the coffee. He had fences to mend as well as plans to set in motion. So far, he seemed to be off to a good start on both.

He took a sip of coffee. It was good and strong, invigoratingly bitter in the way he liked. The only thing he'd still needed to get him ready for the day.

He started explaining about the previous night. About the trails he'd found near the tombs. About his encounter with Asim and his friends. He skirted around some of the details of what they were up to and what he had agreed. After all, he'd allied himself with guys opposed to the British influence in Egypt, and there was an argument there he didn't want to reopen. By the time he got to the end, everybody was looking well fed and ready for action.

"So if Asim isn't the leader of the robbers, then who?" Isabelle asked. "Has he seen anything that might give them away?"

"Not really," Dirk said. "Between running the dig and plotting a little light revolution, he's been too busy to look out for that."

"Should we be looking at Soad?" Isabelle asked. "She's the only other person I've met here who has real influence among the locals."

"Not Pelletier?" Blaze-Simms asked.

"I don't see him robbing himself," Dirk said. "Sure, there might be a profit if he does it the right way, but he's too pompous and full of outrage.

"No, I reckon Isabelle might be right. Soad's got a lot of influence around here and she was mighty keen to distract me after I saw her meeting with some guy at the edge of camp."

"You have a plan to deal with her?" Noriko asked.

"Sure," Dirk said. "The beginnings of one, at least."

#

By mid-afternoon, Dirk suspected that Soad knew they were watching her.

They'd been as discreet as they could, given the circumstances. Covertly watching someone was always harder when they knew who you were, as they'd recognise you following them around. That was why the members of the Epiphany Club had split the duty between them. As long as Soad was in among the tents, Isabelle kept close by, ostensibly making enquiries about supplies for a future expedition into the desert. Down by the tombs sat Blaze-Simms, apparently sketching and making notes about the dig, an excellent excuse for him to constantly keep looking around, and so a good way to cover for his lack of subtlety. Dirk was at the main dig site, wielding a shovel alongside the labourers, happy to get some exercise and maybe win a little favour with Pelletier. And in the hills above the camp, invisible to all, Noriko sat in the shadows, watching and waiting in case their target left.

The speed with which Soad responded only went to prove what Dirk already suspected - that she was more than she seemed. If he wasn't so experienced at his work, he might have missed the moment when she paused by a mirror hanging outside a tent, using it to see if Isabelle was still behind her. He might never have noticed the way she changed her path across the site when she saw Blaze-Simms surveying the ruins, or when she spotted a dust-coated Dirk in the labouring crew.

This was a woman well versed in moving unobserved, and not just in the quiet, stiff way of a professional servant. But Dirk and his companions had a system in place, signalling each other when she moved from one person's territory to another. Their experience working together served them well.

It was the middle of the afternoon before Dirk realised that something was wrong. He hadn't seen Soad for hours. Isabelle was sitting in front of the office tent, drinking tea and looking towards where Blaze-Simms sat. Noriko had left a rock out as a sign she was in her hiding place, meaning that she hadn't had to follow their target across the hillside into the desert. And Blaze-Simms still sat at his post, engrossed in a growing heap of notes.

Making an excuse about the need for water, Dirk set his spade aside and headed over to Isabelle. He was coated in dust and nothing he did could shake the taste of dirt from his mouth. There was a satisfying ache in his muscles, but a twinge of concern tugging at his mind. As he crossed the site, he kept casting his gaze around, in case the missing servant was around and he'd just missed her. But the more he looked, the more certain he became that she wasn't there.

He sat on a stool beside Isabelle and took a swig of water from a canteen. He really had needed that.

"Where'd you see her last?" he asked quietly.

"Heading towards the pillar stones," Isabelle said. "That was an hour ago."

"Let's go have a look around."

They got up and strolled through the camp. Isabelle looped her arm through Dirk's, ignoring the dirt as it spread from his clothes onto her dress. She kept up a flow of conversation, covering their real purpose with the appearance of two friends exploring the fascinating site. But Dirk's gaze was drawn to Blaze-Simms and how little attention he was paying to his surroundings.

"Hey, Tim," he called out as they approached.

"Oh, hello!" Blaze-Simms looked up as if caught by surprise. "How's the digging?"

"When did you last see Soad?" Dirk asked.

"Um, just after lunch," Blaze-Simms said. "She was..."

He looked around.

"Ah." He looked down, embarrassed, at the papers in his hands. There were pictures of the ruins, lines of written notes, and the inevitable design for yet another curious contraption. "I seem to have become distracted."

Dirk took a deep breath, fighting back his frustration. He didn't want to make things any more awkward than they already were between him and the Englishman. If he said what he was really thinking now, awkward would be the least of it.

Besides, what good would venting his anger do? It wouldn't change the fact that, somewhere amid this mess of rocky outcrops and abandoned trenches, Soad had given Blaze-Simms the slip.

"Never mind," he said. "Let's regroup and work out what to do next."

#

Stars twinkled in the clear, black sky of the desert night. The temperature had dropped dramatically since the sun went down and Dirk was glad that he'd retrieved his jacket as well as his pistol before he came out here to keep watch. He wouldn't have minded the chance to light a cigar for the extra comfort, but there was too much risk that would show someone where they were.

"Do you really need those?" he asked Blaze-Simms, who was lying next to him, peering down from their hill-side hiding place towards the entrance to the tombs. The Englishman was wearing a strange contraption built around a bowler hat. A selection of mirrors, crystals, and lenses hung beneath the hat's brim, just in front of the wearer's eyes.

"How else would I see in the dark?" Blaze-Simms asked.

"Night vision," Dirk replied. "The stars. The moon."

"But this magnifies all of that. It-"

"OK, I get it." Dirk shook his head. He didn't want Blaze-Simms to get over-excited and ruin another plan by giving away their location. Best to keep him quiet until their watch ended and Isabelle and Noriko took over.

On the far side of the valley, the camp lay quiet and still. After a hard day of digging, the labourers had fallen into an exhausted sleep, while their archaeologist overseers settled down, content with another day of discovery. The flicker of a single candle showed that Asim was still up, but everybody else was soundly asleep. Even the guards supposedly watching the tombs had started to doze off, weary from a day of watching.

Movement caught Dirk's attention. He looked back toward the entrances to the tombs. Someone was emerging.

"Got them," he hissed.

He didn't know how the robbers had got into the tombs without his noticing. Perhaps they'd hidden in there at the end of the day and were only now emerging. Perhaps they'd snuck in while he watched the guards argue over who would stay awake. Regardless, a figure in pale clothing was stepping out into the night.

"I say," Blaze-Simms whispered. "Dirk, you're not going to believe this."

"Yeah, I see them." Dirk got up into a crouch and started making his way down the hillside, trying to stay as stealthy as he could while moving crabwise across broken ground.

"No, you don't understand," Blaze-Simms said, dislodging stones as he hurried after him. "That's not one of the diggers."

"So she's meeting her gang here," Dirk said. "Makes sense."

"No, that isn't a tomb robber," Blaze-Simms said. "It's a mummy."

Dirk froze, staring in amazement. He was closer now, better able to make out the details of the figure, even though it was still a couple of hundred yards away. Insane as the idea was, Blaze-Simms was right.

The mummy moved with slow, lurching steps as it turned from its tomb and towards the track down the valley. A strip of bandage trailed out in its wake. Its hands were stretched out before it. The places where its eyes should have been glowed with an uncanny blue light.

Of all the things Dirk had imagined seeing tonight, this wasn't one of them. He stared in amazement at the sight.

They'd had it all wrong. They were chasing tomb robbers who didn't exist. He could see his plans crumbling again.

One of the guards strode up behind the mummy, slammed his club against the back of its head, and knocked it to the ground. A moment later, the other two guards were with him. They wrestled with the mummy, pressing its arms against its sides as it struggled to break free. It managed to knock one of them over and rose to its knees, fighting to get back onto its feet. Then one of the men pulled a rope from inside his robes and wrapped it around the creature. The mummy continued its silent struggle, but events were turning against it. Soon its arms were tied and it was reduced to kicking blindly at its assailants. Then they bound the legs too.

As Dirk stared in bewilderment, more men appeared, hurrying down the valley towards them. Dark shapes in the night, moving swiftly and certainly.

One group joined the guards, hefted the mummy above their shoulders, and carried it away, still twitching. Their path took them up the valley side, not past Dirk but towards where he'd found tracks before. Others ran into the tomb, only to emerge a few minutes later, carrying a decorated wooden coffin above their heads. Moving more slowly than the men with the mummy, they too headed up the hillside.

It all took long enough for Dirk to reassemble his scrambled thoughts. Sure, there was a walking corpse out there in the world. And sure, he'd just seen some people kidnap a dead man. But there were still tomb robbers and this was his chance to track them down.

"Come on," he hissed. "Time for action."

He drew his pistol and hurried across the hillside. He wanted to make sure that he didn't lose track of these men. They would know the desert better than him, know the secret ways and the hiding places, know where they were going. He needed to keep them in sight.

Blaze-Simms scurried along beside Dirk, his night vision hat bouncing up and down, held in place by an elasticated strap beneath his chin. He clutched Elloise, his custom built chemically powered rifle, and as he went along he cranked the handle on the side, building up power in the chamber.

As they reached the crest of hill, one of the thieves looked back. Dirk froze and held out a hand, stopping Blaze-Simms in his tracks. They'd dressed darkly, the better to blend in with the night. If they stayed still then with any luck the thieves wouldn't see them.

If the man had spotted his pursuers then he didn't show it. He turned around and followed the rest out of sight.

Moments later, Dirk reached the hilltop. To his relief, the thieves were still in sight, heading across the stony ground where the tracks had stopped. Again, he and Blaze-

Simms hurried after them, as swiftly as they could manage without giving the game away. It reminded him of so many other adventures they'd had together, running through darkened sewers, ancient tunnels, or the starlit jungle of west Africa. The thrill of the chase was hard to beat.

Once again, the coffin bearers disappeared from view, this time around a bend in the track. The hills became more rugged as they moved away from the camp, rocky outcroppings creating a world of deep shadows and starlit angles.

He rounded the bend and came to a halt. The thieves were still there but they had put down the coffin and turned to face their pursuers. Most of them held heavy sticks. A few had pistols.

"This is unfortunate," Soad said, appearing from the shadows behind them. She too was carrying a revolver. "I like to steal corpses, not make them. But as I'm sure you'll understand, we can hardly let you live."

Chapter 7: Negotiations

It wasn't that Dirk would choose fighting as a way to settle things. Not as such. When getting through an issue came down to hurting others and being hurt in return, he figured you were probably scraping the bottom of the human barrel. But he had to admit, there was something satisfying about a fight. The clarity of it all. The simplicity of using his body more than his brain. The clear cut dynamic of two sides clashing and one of them coming out on top.

There was the excitement as well. Going in fists swinging, adrenaline pumping, letting his body do the talking. That exhilaration held a dark joy.

So as Dirk saw the gang of robbers facing him, as he counted his opponents and judged the quality of his weapons, he wasn't half as unhappy as most folks would have been.

"Can't say I'm surprised," he said. "A little disappointed maybe, but I guess that's the way life goes."

He cocked his revolver. Blaze-Simms raised his rifle. Time stretched out as the two sides faced each other, waiting for someone to make the first move.

Dirk made it. He lowered his revolver just a little and shot the nearest gun-wielding thief in the shin. The man collapsed with a cry of pain.

Suddenly, the air was full of the crack of gunfire and of bullets bouncing off rocks. Dirk flung himself sideways, into the shelter provided by an outcrop. On the other side of the path, Blaze-Simms did the same, snapping off a shot with Elloise as he went.

Soad shouted something in Arabic. Dirk didn't know the words, but based on the tone he would have bet on "Don't just stand there, get them!"

Two figures rushed at him, both carrying crude wooden clubs. He couldn't make out their faces in the darkness and that would make it easier to shoot them both down. But Dirk didn't like to kill unless he had to.

As the men got near, Dirk kicked out, sweeping the legs from under one of them. The man fell with a crunch and a yelp. His companion almost tripped over him but managed to turn it into an attack, sticking out his fist and letting his momentum carry him forwards.

Dirk twisted on the spot, letting the fist pass by an inch from his face, and shoved with his free hand. The man staggered but again kept his footing. He swung the club at Dirk, missed, and swung again. Dirk darted forward and punched him in the face.

This time the man fell, hitting the ground with a thud.

His companion was pushing himself up onto his knees. Dirk kicked him in the gut and then, as the man curled up in pain, did it again for good measure. Some folks didn't have the sense to know when they were beaten. When that happened, you had to make sure that they stayed down.

A bullet clipped the rocks to Dirk's left. Another whistled past his face. He raised his gun and fired.

This time he didn't worry about leaving the other fellow alive. They'd tried to kill him and if he didn't do for them then they might succeed. He hit his target squarely in the shoulder and a woman fell back, screaming in pain.

There were still more of the robbers than there were of Dirk and Blaze-Simms. He didn't even see the figure in the shadows to his left until it was too late. A heavy blow hit him across the back of the head and he staggered, the world spinning around him, stars flashing before his eyes. He lurched to the right, avoiding a second blow as much by luck as by design, and backed away from his opponent. But others were closing in now, pressing him into a narrow ravine beside Blaze-Simms.

"Don't suppose you've got any gadgets that would be handy now?" Dirk asked. He waved his gun in the general direction of the attackers, who backed off. They didn't know that he was seeing double or that any shot he took was likely to hit empty air.

"Not really," Blaze-Simms said, cranking the handle of his gun. "Not unless you count a couple of sticks of dynamite."

Questions raced across Dirk's mind. How long had his friend been wandering around with dynamite in his tailcoat? What was he expecting to use it for? Did he realise how dangerous that was? But one particular question was more important than all the rest - could they use the dynamite to get out of this?

It was certainly an option, but it was a messy one. It would be hard to be precise in who and what they hit, with a real risk of hurting themselves in this confined space. Not to mention the presence of a priceless historical artefact in the form of the wooden sarcophagus, an artefact that would be smashed to splinters if it was caught in the blast.

Besides, help should be coming at any moment.

"Just keep shooting," Dirk said, slowly backing off. "Keep them busy."

He and Blaze-Simms retreated along the dirt trail. Dirk was starting to get worried. He'd known that the robbers would outnumber him and Blaze-Simms. He'd arranged for help to be nearby. But he hadn't anticipated getting caught in a fight so far from camp. If that help had lost track of them then things could get mighty tricky.

Noises came from the far side of the gang of thieves. Shouting turned into yelps of pain and the sounds of a scuffle.

"Sounds like the cavalry's arrived," Dirk said, relieved.

The thieves in front of him turned to see what the commotion was about. Dirk seized the opportunity. He leapt forward, grabbed both men, and knocked their heads together. There was a hollow thud and then they both slumped in Dirk's grasp. He was still holding them when a familiar face appeared.

"There you are!" Asim smiled. "I had begun to fear that we might be too late."

"You're just in time," Dirk said. "But it ain't over yet."

Emerging from the narrow ravine, he found Asim standing with the rest of the rebels he had met in the tomb. They carried shovel handles as improvised clubs. Several of them were out of breath and one had blood trickling from a wound on his forehead. Around them, the thwarted thieves lay scattered across the ground.

"Let's get this lot tied up," Dirk said. "Keep an eye out for Soad - she seemed to be in charge."

The rebels lit lanterns and set to work clearing up the field of battle. Soon, they had a row of trussed up men and women sitting on rocks beside the looted coffin. Unsurprisingly, they looked distinctly downcast. To Dirk's disappointment, none of them was the woman he was looking for.

"Alright," he said, looking up and down the line. "Who wants to tell me where you've stashed the loot?"

Asim translated his words into Arabic. Nobody responded. They all just kept staring at their feet.

"Let's try this again." Dirk strode up and down in front of them, swinging a club he'd picked up out of the dirt. He waved it back and forth then slapped it against the palm of his hand, but let the threat it presented remain unspoken. There was another one to be said out loud. "Who doesn't want to be here when the authorities arrive? I hear they take a mighty firm stance on folks looting national history. They ain't exactly kind to the thieves they catch."

That had the gang's attention. They glanced at each other, weighing up their options while Dirk stood in front of them, counting off the moments with the swaying of his club.

At last, someone spoke up, a nervous voice saying something in Arabic.

"He says he can show you," Asim said.

A woman joined in.

"Her too," Asim said with a grin.

Now they were all talking at once, jabbering over each other in a rush to be heard.

"It seems that you have won them all around," Asim said. "Take your pick."

Minutes later, they were on the move again. Dirk, Blaze-Simms, Asim and a couple of his men, and the thief they had chosen as a guide. Soon, the mouth of a cave came into view, lamplight spilling out into the darkness. Sounds of frantic activity emerged - hurried voices and the clatter of things being thrown together, the distinctive signs of people preparing a getaway.

Dirk raised his gun as he stepped into the cave. Beside him, Blaze-Simms did the same.

Soad and two other robbers turned to face them. She had a gun stuffed through her belt and for a moment she glanced down towards it. But she seemed to think better of that idea, instead raising her hands into the air. Her companions did the same.

"Ain't this something," Dirk said, looking around the cave.

Boxes and bags were piled up along one side. Some of them hung open, revealing small stone ornaments, ancient pots, and the glimmer of metal statues. Each of the robbers also held a sack, the familiar gleam of the contents indicating that they had been collecting the most obviously precious artefacts. A necklace hung from Soad's hand, delicate blue gems sparkling in the lamplight.

The most spectacular items were at the back of the cave. There stood a pair of wooden coffins, each in the distinct shape common to Egyptian noble tombs. At the top, each one was carved into the shape of a calm and noble face, with arms folded underneath. Their bodies were painted in white, blue, red, and black, a myriad of tiny pictures decorating boxes designed never to be seen.

Beside them, three mummies were also leaning against the cave wall. The closest one was rocking back and forth as it tried to break free of the ropes binding it.

"Perhaps we could make a deal?" Soad said. "We have far more than this."

"I'm sure you do," Dirk said. "But I'm not interested in bargaining with tomb raiders."

"You think that you will get as good a reward when you hand us in to the government?"

"We won't be the ones handing you in," Dirk said. "I'm planning on leaving that honour to Monsieur Pelletier. In return for a favour or two."

He handed his gun to Asim. Leaving the foreman and Blaze-Simms to manage the prisoners, he pulled out his boot knife, the new one that he'd bought in Cairo. This seemed like a fitting first use for it.

With a couple of quick slashes, he severed the ropes binding the first mummy in place. It tottered for a moment, then headed towards the exit with slow, shambling steps. Dirk didn't know what spirit animated the carefully preserved corpse. He didn't know whether it still counted as a living thing. But somehow it felt right, letting the monster go free.

How many times, he wondered, had he gazed upon mummies in museums? He felt awful, thinking that they had been trapped, bound there against their will.

He cut the cords binding the other two, then stood back.

Neither of them moved.

"What, you thought they all did that?" Soad asked. "That it would have gone unnoticed so long if they did?"

"But what causes it?" Blaze-Simms asked.

Soad shrugged. "All I know is that it makes them harder to sell."

#

They had to fetch camels to bring the tomb robbers' loot back to camp, loading the beasts up with all the wealth that Soad and her people had taken from the site. By the time they were done, it was the middle of the next day and Dirk was utterly exhausted. But he couldn't relax yet. For all this work to have been worthwhile, he needed to cash it in.

Maurice Pelletier watched as their strange caravan entered camp. Camels loaded with caskets, sacks, and bandaged bodies trooped up to the front of the administrative tent. Behind them came a string of captives, their hands bound. And bringing up the rear were Dirk and Blaze-Simms, bruised, dirty, and carrying guns.

"Monsieur Pelletier," Dirk said as they reached the tent. "We thought you might want to see all this."

The archaeologist's eyes widened as they unloaded the camels. Aside from the mummies and their coffins there were canoptic jars, statues, tablets, even jewellery. A crowd gathered to watch, growing with each passing moment, until it seemed like the whole camp had stopped work to see what this was all about. Dirk and Blaze-Simms brought chairs out of the tent and took the chance to rest their weary legs.

"We wondered when you would be back," Isabelle said as she took a seat next to Dirk. "When you didn't wake us for our turn on watch, we thought that you must have found the robbers."

"Sorry you missed out on it," Dirk said.

"I'm just glad that you're both in one piece."

At last, Pelletier finishing overseeing the unpacking and came to talk to them. His face was stern, arms folded in front of him.

"Where is the rest?" he asked.

"In England we say thank you," Blaze-Simms said.

"In England, do you also keep part of any stolen goods you find?" Pelletier asked, his tone cold.

"Hey, we're helping you here," Dirk said.

"And helping yourselves," Pelletier said. "What you have brought includes items taken from this site, but many are still missing. Urns. Tablets. A necklace. A whole mummy."

"Well we didn't take them," Blaze-Simms said. "Did we Dirk?"

"Nope," Dirk said, stifling a small, traitorous feeling of guilt.

"Oh, so you're going to tell me that another mummy just got up and walked away?"

Guilt kicked at Dirk again. After all, he had let the mummy go, and he had no idea what those things did in the wild, or what might have been learnt from studying it.

Then something in what Pelletier had said caught his attention.

"I need a coffee," he said, getting to his feet. "Think I saw some in the back of the tent. Why don't you join me, Monsieur Pelletier?"

"I don't want coffee, I want answers!"

"Then let's see if we can find both."

Pelletier frowned but followed Dirk as he headed into the tent, away from the blazing sunshine and the people crowding around the recovered treasures.

At the back of the tent, a pot of coffee and some small cups sat on a folding table. The pot was lukewarm to the touch, but Dirk figured that cool coffee was far better than no coffee. He poured himself a cup and took a sip before he spoke.

"You said 'another mummy,'" he said.

"Excuse me?" Pelletier replied.

"'Another mummy got up and walked away', like you'd seen it happen before."

"Unbelievable!" Pelletier threw his hands up in the air. "You English make up the most ridiculous things."

"You didn't say no." Dirk studied the man carefully, watching the movements of his face. "Because you're a bad liar and you know it. You're one of those guys who wears his emotions for the world to see. That's why I believed you weren't the one behind the thefts. And it's why I don't believe all this bluster now."

"Fine." Pelletier folded his arms again, clearly making an effort to compose himself. "There have been stories of mummies walking away from tombs."

"Not just stories. You've seen it. And I bet you blamed it on the thieves rather than risk sounding crazy by telling people the truth."

Pelletier blushed. Dirk knew he had him.

"Tell you what," Dirk said, pouring himself another cup of lukewarm coffee. "You get your people digging up that black monument again. You let Tim poke around it all he wants. You stop making any fuss about what's missing, because we both know most of it ain't ever coming back. You do that, and I won't go looking into that mummy you lost. How does that sound?"

"Fine," Pelletier said with a sigh. "You get your way."

"And Monsieur Pelletier?" Dirk said. "Don't ever call me English again."

#

That evening, digging around the pillar continued well past dinner and into the evening. Fired up with the excitement of the day and with Blaze-Simms's wild enthusiasm, the archaeologists set to work unearthing the great black stones, cleaning the dirt from their engravings, and piecing together the separate sculpted chunks. As the sun hit the horizon, Dirk could still hear cries of "I say!" and "How marvellous" as new information was revealed to Blaze-Simms.

The valley was beautiful in the dusk light. A rich orange glow lit up the hilltops, fading into soft pink as it slid down the slopes. As he sat with Isabelle, their chairs drawn up together outside their tents, arms resting gently against each other, he was as contented as he'd been in a good long time.

He didn't want to break the magic of the moment, but he did have something else he wanted to do.

"I got you something," he said.

"More flowers?" she asked. "Because I'm afraid the last lot wilted in the heat. You might want to think again about what makes a romantic gesture."

"I have."

Reaching over the back of the chair, Dirk rummaged inside his jacket. He pulled out a slender necklace of burnished bronze, set with pieces of blue quartz.

"I know a fellow's meant to buy jewellery for the lady he's courting," he said, holding it out for her to see. "There ain't a lot of jeweller's stores out here, so I figured I'd take the chances I had."

Isabelle stared.

"Dirk, is that from the tombs?" she asked.

"It was just going to go into some French aristocrat's private collection," he said. "Better that you get something nice."

Isabelle opened her mouth as if to speak, closed it, then opened it again. He couldn't remember ever seeing her lost for words before.

"Don't you like it?" he asked. "Damn, you think I shouldn't have taken it. That's fine. I can say I found it in one of the bags. No-one ever needs to-"

"Ssh," she said, laying a hand on his. "Dirk, you should know me well enough by now to know that I have no objection to well-intentioned dishonesty. And it is a lovely necklace. It's just that what we have isn't like those romances. It isn't about flowers and dinners and jewellery. And if you try to force it into that mould, I'm afraid that you might break it."

His heart sank.

"But without that stuff, all we have is sharing this adventure," he said. "And that's getting near the end."

"We'll worry about that later," she said, leaning forward to kiss him on the lips. "For now, just enjoy what we have."

She stood and tugged at his hand until he too got out of his seat, uncertain but excited.

"Timothy is going to be busy for a while yet," she said. "Let's make the most of your tent while you have it to yourself."

Across the valley, the sun slipped below the horizon, disappearing in a final flash of orange and gold.

Chapter 8: In the Desert

In all their years working together, this was the most excited that Dirk had ever seen Blaze-Simms. He barely seemed to have slept for three days straight, too busy peering over the carvings on the pillar, overseeing the men digging up new pieces, and comparing it all with his notes. Even Pelletier had become caught up in the excitement, the Englishman and the Frenchman poring over old documents late into the night, comparing codes, symbols, and translations, drawn together by a bond that only academics could share.

While they did that, Dirk had two tasks - preparing for their expedition and making the most of his time with Isabelle.

The future still hung above them like a great weight of uncertainty. His life and her life, these two separate things, waiting to drag them apart. But for now they took tea on the hillside, went for strolls around the tombs, and enjoyed quiet time alone while Blaze-Simms was away from the tent.

In truth, nearly all of Dirk's time was taken up that way. The bulk of preparation for their expedition fell upon Noriko, who didn't seem to mind. As she said, there wasn't much use for the art of the ninja on an archaeological dig, and so she brought her leadership skills to bear instead, ordering around the men that Asim had provided to help them prepare.

At last, Blaze-Simms pieced together the last bits of the puzzle. He knew where they needed to start from. He knew which way to go from there. He had the directions provided by the stone tablets. And he had the confidence of a man who seldom had to face the consequences of his failures.

They spent one last night on Pelletier's site, then rose before dawn, ready to head out into the desert.

Asim helped to bring their camels around. As Noriko loaded the last boxes, Dirk took the foreman aside.

"Here," he said quietly, handing over a few pages of handwritten notes. "Like I promised, that's everything I saw of British and French intelligence in Egypt. Hope it's helpful to you and your people. And if I learn any more, I'll be in touch."

"Thank you, my friend," Asim said. He clung onto Dirk's hand as they shook. "You are a great help to us."

"Just doing my bit to set the world to rights."

Dirk returned to the camels. Noriko and Isabelle had already mounted, but Blaze-Simms was struggling, his stick limbs flailing as he tried to get into the saddle.

"I thought aristocrats were natural riders," Dirk said, helping him up with a steadying hand.

"There aren't a lot of camels in the home counties," Blaze-Simms replied. "Though I have some ideas on how one might make a mechanical engine that mimics their movement, to help with transportation in inhospitable climes."

Dirk smiled. His friend's enthusiasm really was infectious.

"Let's find this library first, huh?" he said.

As the sun rose, they set out down the trail leading into the desert. Despite the early hour, most of the camp were up to see them off. They were the heroes who had stopped the tomb robbers, the mysterious strangers who had managed to put Pelletier into a good mood. Truly, they were a sight worth celebrating.

The only exception lay around a new group of tents at the back of the camp. A group of French and Egyptian officials who had arrived the previous night, summoned to question and carry away the relic robbers. Dirk and his companions had decided to avoid extra complications with the French, and so steered clear of them. But as Dirk looked over, he saw the familiar face of Madame Cluny watching them go.

A small reminder of their past troubles wasn't enough to bring him down. The desert stretched out before him, holding out the promise of strange sites and long lost learning. The Library of Alexandria, so long hidden from humanity, was about to be theirs.

As the first day passed, rocky outcrops gave way to open sand, sculpted into the smooth arcs of dunes by the blowing of the wind. They followed these south and west, away from the dig and deeper into the wilderness.

By the third day, they had entered the sort of desert that featured in children's imaginations and picture books. A place that seemed vast and featureless in its expanse, an ocean of gleaming golden grains.

There must have been enough features for Blaze-Simms to navigate by, as he kept them going, following the course set out in his notes. From time to time he would point out something as they passed. An unusual rock formation, a place where ancient trade routes met, the way the sinking sun touched a feature on the distant horizon. At first, Dirk assumed that these were all markers on their route, but he soon suspected that most were just things that had caught his friend's attention, the wonders of the world providing an endless distraction for Sir Timothy Blaze-Simms.

On the fourth day, a fierce wind blew across the desert. They took shelter in their tents, waiting out the storm.

The day after that was when the problems began.

"What do you mean, you don't know?" Dirk asked, staring at Blaze-Simms across a tin cup full of coffee. Every cup he made tasted a little like mud, thanks to the sand that now permeated their equipment. But the others weren't giving up on their tea and he certainly wasn't giving up on his coffee.

"I'm not sure how else I can explain it," Blaze-Simms said, looking annoyed. "I don't entirely know which way we should be setting out today."

"Don't entirely know, meaning it's kind of that way and we'll work out the details later, or don't entirely know, meaning you've got no clue which way we even start?"

"I mean that the marker we should have found by now is gone." Blaze-Simms pointed at something in his notes, but all Dirk could see was a mass of scribbles. "This is the problem with a trail laid out two thousand years ago. There was always a risk that parts would have gone missing over time."

"And you decided that now was the time to say this?" Dirk said. "Not, say, back at the start of this mess?"

"I rather assumed that we would muddle through." Blaze-Simms smiled sheepishly. "After all, we have so far."

"I..." Dirk shook his head. There was no benefit in losing his temper. He had to keep reminding himself of that. "Why don't you explain what's gone wrong, and we'll do our best to fix it."

"There was supposed to have been a marker by now," Blaze-Simms said. "A stone pillar with a top that looks like a lightning bolt. That lightning bolt would point us towards the next point on the route. But we've come past the point where we should have seen the pillar. I can only conclude that it fell down or was destroyed. Some pagans used it for ceremonial purposes, so perhaps the early church tore it down. It's a fascinating possibility, an insight into the minds of the time."

"Fascinating," Dirk agreed, "but not helpful right now. So how do we go about finding the next clue?"

"Doubling back and heading west would be the best option," Blaze-Simms said. "But the sand storm blew away our tracks. So now..." He shrugged. "I'm afraid that your guess is as good as mine."

"We have another problem." Noriko had appeared silently around the side of the tents. She was holding up a handful of water skins. They were all empty. "One of the camels got loose during the storm. He trampled on these. The water is gone."

Dirk looked down guiltily at his cup. Would he have wasted precious water on coffee if he'd known about this?

"How much do we still have?" he asked.

"Not enough."

The phrase "it never rains but it pours" crossed Dirk's mind. Of course, if it did rain then that would solve one of their problems. It seemed unlikely.

The water was clearly the higher priority. It wasn't the first time he'd had to find water in difficult circumstances, but even as a proud American, he had to admit that this would be tougher than what he'd faced out west.

"Pack everything up," he said. "Then we head for high ground and see what we can find."

"Splendid idea!" Blaze-Simms exclaimed. "We'll be looking for a statue of a cow-headed god next to a-"

"Not yet we won't," Dirk said, determined to keep them focused. If he was going to die, it wouldn't be because of the Englishman's dithering.

With the camels packed, he took the lead, taking them up the dunes until they could see for miles around.

"You still got that seeing-in-the-dark hat, Tim?" he asked.

"Have you taken a knock on the head?" Blaze-Simms asked, looking concerned. "It's bright daylight."

"Just give me the hat."

Blaze-Simms rummaged in his bags until he found the bowler. Feeling utterly absurd, Dirk placed the contraption on his head. Dozens of mirrors, crystals, and lenses crowded around his face. One by one, he yanked them off and stuffed them in his pocket, while Blaze-Simms protested with ever-growing volume. At last, all that remained were the two most powerful lenses. Dirk manoeuvred them until they were both over one eye, cupped his hands around them, and drew one back and forth in its mounting until the distant scenery came into view, magnified hundreds of times over.

"Best telescope you've ever made," he said.

"Oh." Blaze-Simms's tone shifted to one of pleasure. "Thank you. Have I made many?"

Dirk turned his head slowly, scouring the horizon. As last, he caught sight of what he was after - a cluster of greenery amid the golden sands.

"That way," he said. "And better make it quick - none of us will last without water in this heat."

#

They reached the oasis late in the afternoon. It was a small patch of verdant life amid an expanse mostly occupied by death, a place of safety, shelter, and above all water.

They weren't the first ones there. By the small pool at the centre of the oasis, someone had set up a pair of tents. Camels nibbled at the nearest plants. In front of the little encampment, someone had lit a fire and put out a tea pot.

"Well I never!" George Braithwaite exclaimed as he rose to meet them. "If it isn't our friends from the Epiphany Club."

Braithwaite's two companions, pale faced men in straw hats and off-white suits, waved a greeting. Dirk recognised one as Noiseby, the muscular public school buffoon Blaze-Simms had recognised at the embassy party. The other was weaselly looking, with narrow eyes and a limp moustache.

"Mr Braithwaite." Isabelle greeted him with all the warmth and refinement she brought to a society party. "How delightful to see you. What brings you out here?"

"Oh, same as you, I bet," he said. "Out touring the sites."

Beside their tents, the Englishmen had a pile of boxes, blankets, and bags. Thinking back to what Asim had said about oil, Dirk wondered where in that pile the surveying equipment was and whether they already had a likely spot mapped out.

Dirk and his companions unloaded the tents and started setting up camp. There was only so much space around the oasis, and they could hardly ignore the folks who'd given them a home in Cairo, so Dirk swallowed his annoyance and started pitching the tents next to the English group.

"I say!" Blaze-Simms called out as they were preparing the camp. He let go of the rope he was holding and rushed off around the oasis, leaving Dirk to catch the half-assembled canvas as it fell. With a weary sigh, he set it aside and went to see what Blaze-Simms had found.

On the far side of the pool, half-hidden by a cluster of bushes, a statue protruded from the ground. Its face had been worn away by the steady caress of time, but its overall shape was unmistakable.

"A cow-headed god," Dirk said, surprised. "Just like you were looking for."

"It makes sense," Blaze-Simms said. "Oases are important places on any journey and we've kept heading in roughly the same direction. Statistically speaking the odds were in our favour. Probably."

"So we're back on course?" Dirk felt his weary spirits lifting.

"We're back on course. Hoorah!"

"Good work, Tim." Dirk patted his friend on the shoulder. "Now let's put up that tent."

As evening fell, the two groups of travellers sat around a single fire and shared their dinner. Braithwaite dug a bottle of port out of his pack and poured everybody a glass. Dirk returned the favour by sharing out the last of his cigars.

By the light of the fire, Blaze-Simms read over his notes, comparing the direction the cow god was pointing with the needle of a compass.

"We'll need to head west-southwest," he said as he folded the papers away.

"Well there's a coincidence," Braithwaite said. "We're heading that way too. We should travel together."

"What a splendid idea!" Blaze-Simms said.

Dirk looked to Isabelle and Noriko, hoping someone could produce an excuse not to travel with these guys. If they did, they were keeping it to themselves.

A sound of hooves made them look around toward the edge of the oasis. A group of camel riders were approaching from the north.

Something about the way they rode set Dirk on edge. These weren't weary travellers looking for rest at the end of the day. They were alert and purposeful, riding high in the saddle.

He looked around. Two more groups were approaching from the south and east.

"Friends of yours?" he asked Braithwaite.

The Yorkshireman shook his head and reached for something behind him.

The first group of riders reached the encampment, their camels snorting and stamping as they drew near.

"Salam, friends," the lead rider said through the scarf that covered his face. Just like his companions, the only parts of him showing were his hands and his eyes. Those eyes carried the cold, hard look of a man without mercy.

Dirk set aside his tin cup and checked that his gun was in its holster.

All three groups had reached their little encampment now. They spread out in a circle, surrounding the travellers.

"Salam," Isabelle said, her tone all sweetness and reason. "Would you care to join us?"

"I am afraid we cannot stay for long," the leader said. "But perhaps you could share your refreshments with us?" He drew a pistol from his sleeve and pointed it at Isabelle. "Your refreshments and your wealth."

With the slow, well-practised movements of people used to armed confrontations, everyone around the circle rose to their feet. Hands hovered expectantly, ready to grab for weapons.

"There's no need for violence," Isabelle said, reaching into the small bag hanging from her shoulder. "I have some cash that I can spare. Perhaps you could be content with that, rather than risk a confrontation?"

"I don't see much risk," the man said. His companions had also drawn firearms. They held them with the lazy disdain of professional outlaws facing what they took for ordinary citizens.

"Are you sure?" Isabelle asked. Her purse jingled as she drew something out, the shape blurred by the grey of twilight. "But it's such a lovely night."

Dirk tensed, ready for action. Survival in the desert was a difficult enough business. It would become immeasurably more so if robbers took the equipment they needed for their journey. He didn't need secret signs or code words to know that the others would be thinking the same.

There was a bang and a muzzle flash as Isabelle fired her small pistol. As the lead bandit jerked back, his own gun went off.

Dirk dived to the right, rolling as he landed, coming up into a crouch with his revolver drawn. Even as one of the bandits turned towards him, he opened fire.

The peace of the oasis vanished in a chaotic mess of noise and movement. Guns roared. Camels grunted. Men and woman yelled as they leapt for cover or charged at each other. Dirk caught a glimpse of Blaze-Simms raising his rifle, of Isabelle ducking behind a rock, of Noriko leaping and whirling as her blades flashed in the firelight.

He fired until the gun was empty, then drew his knife and charged at the nearest bandit. The man had come down off his camel to take cover behind a tree. He saw Dirk coming too late to get his rifle into position, so used it as a club instead. Dirk ducked beneath the blow and came up swinging, knocking the man flat with an upper cut.

He felt a jab of pain in his leg but ignored it, turning to deal with another assailant. The man swung a punch but

Dirk caught his fist, twisted his arm around until something crunched, and then kicked him away.

Guns were still blazing, but the intensity of the fight was dying down. The bandits had started to retreat. None of them were dead, though several were limping or being supported by friends. As they mounted their camels and disappeared into the night, quiet fell once more across the oasis.

"Is everyone OK?" Dirk asked.

"I don't think you are," Isabelle said, hurrying over to him.

"What?" Dirk looked down. Blood soaked his pants from the thigh down. Now the adrenaline was wearing off, he could feel a deep pain there. "Oh."

His leg gave way beneath him and he sank to the ground.

The others gathered around. Isabelle hastily cut the pants legs open and examined the wound.

"The bullet's gone straight through," she said. "Timothy, fetch a needle and thread. Mr Braithwaite, get some bandages."

While Braithwaite's companions stood watch for more trouble, Isabelle set to work cleaning, sewing up, and bandaging the wound. It hurt like hell, but Dirk had been through this sort of thing enough times that he'd learnt to bite back the pain. In a few months, it would just be one more scar, a story to share with those who liked his sort of tales.

He gritted his teeth as the needle slid through his flesh, a brief blaze of pain.

"What an unfortunate coincidence," Blaze-Simms said. "All this way out in the desert and we run into bandits."

"Coincidence my arse," Braithwaite said. "Those lads knew we were here. This is Cluny sending proxies to get in our way." He laughed. "That woman's not the most subtle."

"I just got shot," Dirk growled, "because of your god-damn spy games?"

"Hazards of the profession," Braithwaite said with a shrug.

"Not my profession," Dirk said. "Yours. I'm not some stooge of the British Empire."

Braithwaite laughed out loud.

"Course not," he said. "It's not like hosting the Epiphany Club brings Britain prestige or influence. It's not like we use all that lovely information you lot gather."

"Not this time."

Despite the pain in his leg, Dirk felt a sense of satisfaction. They were about to find the century's greatest haul of lost knowledge. Who knew what discoveries they would make? Who knew what advancements it might support? And he had the opportunity to keep that out of the hands of the likes of Braithwaite. Better than that, he had already agreed to share it with Isabelle's circle of scholarly women. He was helping the disempowered and stopping the powerful from adding to their strength.

The righteous part of his heart that believed in democracy, equality, and socialism filled with joy.

"Don't be absurd, Dirk," Blaze-Simms said. "Of course we'll be sharing with the British government."

"What?" Dirk turned to look at him, surprised and disappointed.

"We always do," Blaze-Simms said. "I mean, why wouldn't we?"

"Because of the trouble they've caused us?"

"It's still my country."

"Then because of what they might do with it?"

"Still my country."

"This isn't about patriotism. What if we find a recipe for Greek fire? Or guides to the art of war? Why add to their arsenal when we can help change the world?"

Blaze-Simms rubbed his forehead like he was trying to drive some ache away.

"Dirk, I'm not a revolutionary like you," he said. "I don't do politics. I just want to find the Great Library, take it home, and share my learning with the same people I always do."

"The same people that build empires and get innocent people shot!" Dirk yelled, his temper ragged from the ache in his leg. "That is political."

"I'm going to bed." Blaze-Simms turned away with a frown. "Maybe you'll be more rational in the morning."

Dirk sat fuming as Isabelle finished wrapping the bandage around his leg.

"I'm sure this will blow over," she said at last. "You two can get back to being friends."

Dirk frowned. He wasn't so sure. This was a side of Blaze-Simms he had never noticed before, or that maybe he had blinded himself to. Now he looked, he didn't like what he saw.

Chapter 9: Journey's End

"This is it," Blaze-Simms said as the reached a gap between two rocky outcrops. "The last marker on the trail before the library itself."

The rocks stood at the mouth of a pass. Ahead, broken, stony ground led into a valley hidden from view by the sweep of the surrounding land. There had probably been a river here, once upon a time, but it was long gone. All that remained was rock and dirt.

"What now?" Dirk asked. Beneath him, his camel stood still and silent, waiting for his command. He patted its rough neck and it snorted then pawed at the ground. It seemed that the camel, like Dirk, was eager to keep moving.

"Down the valley," Blaze-Simms said. "The entrance will be hidden by two piles of boulders, one dark and one light."

Dirk looked back to where Braithwaite and his companions stood, their camels gathered around them. They had a map out and Noiseby was making a great display of operating some instrument, a box so covered in valves, gears, and random levers that it could have been Blaze-Simms's work.

"Looks like this is where we part ways," Dirk called out.

"Is that so?" Braithwaite asked, looking up from the map. "Where are you lot heading then?"

"Down the valley," Dirk replied, nodding at the gap between the outcrops.

Overhead, a vulture wheeled, soaring on the thermals as it watched for signs of death below, of a predator it could follow to a feast.

"What a coincidence," Braithwaite said. "That's where we're going too."

Dirk held back a suspicious frown. If this was coincidence then he was a camel's ass. The whole time they'd been together, Braithwaite and his companions had taken their lead from Dirk's party. They'd never expressed a plan to go any direction that the adventurers hadn't said first. If that box really did tell them where to go, then its instructions were as near a perfect match for Blaze-Simms's as they could be.

Maybe there really was oil out here in the desert. Maybe the British were even looking for it. But they were definitely interested in what Dirk was doing too.

Not for the first time, Dirk considered calling Braithwaite out on it. The resentment he felt at their treatment by the British was like a stone in his boot, something hard and unpleasant that pressed at him every step of the way. It was one thing to get in the way of enemies, it was quite another to cause trouble for the folks who were meant to be on your side, as Braithwaite had done for them. But even as the resentment ate at Dirk, he knew there was no sense in venting it. What could he do? Short of fighting the British party, nothing would force them to stop following, or even to admit what they were up to.

He pressed his heels into the flanks of his camel and rode it down the valley path.

Isabelle rode beside him, her parasol open to protect her from the desert sun.

"I've been trying to think of a way to shake them off," she said quietly. "But no luck. And now it's going to be even harder."

As the trail descended, the sides of the valley rose around them. The party were squeezed in together, the only choices of direction forward or back.

"I've been thinking the same," Dirk said. "Let's just hope we can leave them at the door."

As expected, the valley was deserted. Not so much as a desert fox moved. But there was still a surprise to be had - camel trails in the dirt.

Dirk halted and Isabelle, taking her queue from him, did the same.

"Is something the matter?" she asked.

Even from up in the saddle, Dirk could see that more than one rider had passed this way. How recently depended on whether the wind got down here to disrupt such dusty prints, but he reckoned the tracks had to be fairly fresh.

Glancing back, he saw that both Noriko and Braithwaite had got down from their camels and were approaching through their small desert caravan. In different circumstances, Dirk would have been glad of Braithwaite's opinion - the man had proved his skills as a tracker and hunter. As things stood, he'd have been happier just to draw on Noriko's knowledge.

"What do you reckon?" Dirk said, gesturing at the tracks.

"Four riders," Braithwaite said. "Maybe five. Riding decent beasts, judging by their gait."

"The ones who have been following us," Noriko said.

They all turned to look at her, expressions as surprised as Dirk felt.

"We've been followed?" Isabelle asked.

"Since the oasis," Noriko said. "When we did not see pursuers this morning, I thought we had lost them. Perhaps they got ahead."

"Why didn't you tell us, lass?" Braithwaite asked.

"Because I do not trust you," she said, her voice cold and flat as the face of a sword. "They could have been yours. I wanted to keep what advantage I had."

Dirk felt a flash of anger at her for hiding the information, only for the anger to vanish as he saw Braithwaite's discomfort.

"Any idea who they are?" he asked.

"Bloody Frogs," Braithwaite said, his face red. "Cluny's got ahead of us."

"How could she do that?" Dirk asked.

"Maybe she has some of the same clues you do," Braithwaite shrugged. "Followed us as far as needed and then got ahead."

"I thought you were all out here looking for oil?" Dirk said, keeping his tone neutral even as he settled one hand on his gun.

Braithwaite gave a bitter laugh.

"Let's stop acting like tits, shall we?" he said. "I'm here to get inside that library, same as Cluny. You lads and lasses have done a lot of good finding the place. Your struggles have provided a nice distraction for the other side. But who gets in there first matters, and I can't risk that being the French."

"Who says you're invited to join us?" Dirk asked.

"Who's going to stop me?"

Dirk drew the gun and laid it across his lap. He was sick of this. Sick of the games. Sick of the intrigues. Sick of governments trying to feed off his hard work.

"I might," he said. "I'm mighty tempted."

"Dirk!" Blaze-Simms exclaimed, riding up next to him. "What are you doing?"

"Threatening me is what he's doing," Braithwaite replied, drawing a shocked gasp from Blaze-Simms. "But he needn't bother. I know you're bluffing, Dynamo. I'm not a threat. I'm not doing you or yours harm. You won't shoot me just for this."

Dirk hated that the man was right, that his own intentions were so easy to read. But it was true.

"Fine," he said, though he didn't put away the gun. "What now?"

"They can't be far ahead of us," Noriko said. "We might catch them outside."

"Then we have to hurry!" Blaze-Simms said. "Before they work out the puzzle on the door."

At his signal, his camel jerked into action, rushing down the valley while the Englishman bounced along on its back, one hand clinging to the reins, the other clutching his top hat to his head.

"A puzzle door." Dirk shook his head and hurried after Blaze-Simms. "Of course there's a damn puzzle door."

#

In the end, it was obvious where they needed to stop. The valley ended in a cliff of broken stone. As promised, piles of contrasting rocks flanked a crevice that disappeared into the cliff, its shadows impenetrably dark compared with the brightness of the Egyptian day.

Four camels were tethered in the open area in front of the stones. In the shade by the crevice, four people stood, all dressed in loose, pale clothes suitable for desert travel. Straw hats and holstered pistols completed their ensembles.

As Dirk's party approached, one of the group stepped out to greet the new arrivals.

"Monsieur Dynamo," Madame Cluny said, raising her hat. "It is a genuine pleasure to see you."

"Can't say I feel the same way," he said. "Not after all the trouble you've caused us. Especially those bandits the other night."

"Bandits?" Cluny asked, her expression a mocking imitation of innocence.

"Don't give me that bullshit," Dirk said. "I get enough from him."

He jerked a thumb at Braithwaite, who, like Dirk and the rest of the party, was descending from his mount.

"How very American," Cluny said. "Direct, uncompromising, crude. Though I had expected better of you, George."

"I doubt that," Braithwaite said. "I wasn't exactly planning on being subtle myself."

"Regardless," Cluny said, "perhaps a more sophisticated solution can now be found. After all, Monsieur Dynamo, my party possess the door to what you want, while you doubtless have some way to get inside. It is time for us to work together, no?"

It was tempting, Dirk would give her that. It might have been worth it, just to see the look on Braithwaite's face. But with Blaze-Simms having all the clues, and having revealed a patriotic streak to match his curiosity, it didn't seem like switching sides was really an option.

Besides, Dirk didn't want to help either of these groups. What he needed was a way to lose them both and get into the library.

"So what, you gonna start shooting to keep us out?" he asked.

"Oh no," Cluny said. "That is not how this is done. Not when we meet face to face."

"Aye, lad," Braithwaite said. "Can't have British and French diplomats killing each other. It would take far too much explaining to the locals."

The three remaining Frenchmen emerged from the shadows at the end of the valley. Each of them held a sturdy stick and one threw a spare to Cluny. She wielded it like a woman who knew what she was doing. The men behind her had a bulk that said they were chosen for action over intelligence.

Dirk saw his opening.

"You think one of your goons is going to take him?" He pointed at the towering figure of Braithwaite and laughed. "I bet they can't even do it all at once."

"Thanks," Braithwaite muttered, snatching a walking stick from the baggage on his camel. Both of his men stepped up, Noiseby carrying a shovel, the weaselly man wielding a surveying instrument on a long pole. They didn't look weak by any means, and without him and his companions it would be a fairly even fight.

"This would be funny if it wasn't pathetic," Dirk said, approaching one of the Frenchmen. "I mean, look at you."

He shoved the man in the chest. The man responded by yelling and swinging his stick at Dirk's head. Dirk sidestepped, twisted, and shoved the man so that he stumbled past, straight into the English agents. Braithwaite shouted angrily and the fight began.

It was a rough, scrappy brawl, the two sides swinging at each other with fists and sticks, shoving and shouldering and kicking. It would have been exciting to be part of it, but Dirk had other things on his mind.

He stepped back and looked around. Noriko and Isabelle had understood his intention and were striding around the edge of the combat towards the great heaps of rocks. But Blaze-Simms had drawn his walking stick and was eyeing up the fray.

Dirk grabbed his friend's arm, just as he was about to hit Cluny with his stick. He dragged the Englishman, squirming and flailing, towards the crevice at the end of the valley.

"Let go of me!" Blaze-Simms exclaimed. "I have to help."

"Help us get into the library," Dirk said. "Then you can go help Braithwaite all you want."

"They need me now."

"What they need is to quit treating other folks as tools. And what we need is to get through here."

As they entered the darkness, Dirk's eyes adjusted. Two great slabs of stone blocked their way, both carved with intricate hieroglyphics. At the centre, they were crossed by a stone disk three feet across. Other disks were embedded in it, their edges indented to make crude interlocking gears. All had hieroglyphs on them.

"See," Dirk said, waving at the doors. "Don't you want to see how this works?"

Blaze-Simms stared, open-mouthed, at the towering blocks of stone and the intricate mechanism with which they were locked. Then he turned to glare at Dirk.

"No," he said. "I won't just be distracted. You made me come here, but you can't make me do what you want."

He folded his arms in front of him.

"You pig-headed idiot!" Dirk exclaimed in exasperation. "You've never met a machine you didn't want to disassemble, but now, when we're inches from the greatest discovery in history, you decide you're not interested?"

"I'm not interested in doing what you want when you won't listen to what I want, you fat-headed colonial lump."

Dirk had punched men out for less. He trembled as he held his fists in check, trying to find words to express the frustration and anger he felt. How could Blaze-Simms prioritise Braithwaite over years of friendship? How could he put country before the curiosity that had bound them together for so long?

Someone laughed. They turned to see Isabelle's face crumpled with mirth.

"I'm sorry," she said. "But if I don't laugh then I'll have to cry. I've seen so many good things ruined by macho posturing, but for it to be you two..."

Dirk glared at her, furious that she could take this so lightly. She covered her mouth and looked away.

"I'm not going in without Braithwaite," Blaze-Simms said.

"I'm not going in with him," Dirk replied.

They stood staring at each other, while the sounds of scuffling echoed around the valley outside.

"Isabelle is right," Noriko said, laying one hand on Dirk's shoulder and the other on Blaze-Simms's. It was an unusually intimate gesture from her, and the surprise of it briefly halted the angry in Dirk's mind. "This is absurd. You two are arguing over a friendship that never was."

"What?" Dirk said, baffled.

"We've been friends for years," Blaze-Simms said, looking equally confused.

"But not in the way you are now treating it," Noriko said. "You have always been different. You worked together but were driven by different passions. Now that threatens to change things between you, and you are treating the difference as a betrayal, not the continuation of your friendship that it is.

"Things between you cannot be as they always were. But that does not mean that you cannot be friends."

Embarrassed, Dirk looked down at his feet. He felt like a small boy being told off by a parent.

"I guess," he said.

Reluctantly, he met Blaze-Simms's gaze.

"I'm sorry," the Englishman said, holding out his hand.

"Me too," Dirk replied, holding out his own.

They shook. It felt like a strange, distant gesture. An improvement on what had come before, but still not right.

Outside, the fighting continued. Someone was yelping and a camel was making loud, discontented noises. Dirk had to admit, the British and French agents sure had stamina.

Either that or none of them could land a punch worth shit.

"Timothy," Noriko said. "Are you really more interested in helping George Braithwaite than in being the first man into the Great Library?"

Blaze-Simms hesitated, then grinned. He pulled a notebook from his pocket.

"It's about lining up the symbols to make a sentence," he said. "A part of a prayer to Anubis."

He started rotating the stone gears. When one got stuck, Dirk stepped up and turned it for him. They both smiled in satisfaction as something clicked into place and the world felt brighter to Dirk.

As he stepped back, Isabelle took his hand.

"Well done," she whispered. "And sorry for laughing."

Dirk shrugged, and in doing so let go of a knot of tension he hadn't realised he was holding.

"It was kind of mean," he said. "But then, so was I."

Blaze-Simms set a final cog into place. With Noriko's help, he rotated the great disk that crossed the doors. It turned slowly, dust falling as stone ground against stone. There was a rumble behind the rock face. More dust fell from the ceiling and for a moment Dirk feared that the roof was about to cave in. He pulled Isabelle tight, feeling her heartbeat as she pressed against him.

Then the doors swung open, the shaking stopped, and Dirk prepared to step into the Great Library.

Chapter 10: The Library

Dirk didn't know when Noriko had fetched their equipment. Sometime in the distractions of the fight and of dealing with the door, she must have got back unnoticed to the camels and grabbed a couple of bags. It wasn't the first time that the ninja had surprised him like this, but he had never been more grateful for her swift, silent efficiency.

"Here." She had retrieved and lit several oil lanterns. She passed one to each of them, then handed one bag to Dirk and slung the other over her shoulder. "Now we go."

Blaze-Simms led the way, grinning like a schoolboy who had been let loose in a toyshop. Dirk's feelings matched his friend's expression. As they stepped through the doors, he was giddy with excitement. This was it. The lost Great Library of Alexandria. The thing they had been hunting for so long. Knowledge long lost to humanity, and he would be one of the first people to see it again.

A short corridor led to a flight of steps carved out of the bedrock. Down they went, walking in single file. As Blaze-Simms reached the bottom he stopped, gasped, and stared around, the rest of them backing up behind him.

"It's magnificent," he said.

Isabelle gently steered Blaze-Simms out of the way, letting the rest of them join him at the bottom of the stairs.

Their lanterns illuminated a series of chambers with high domed ceilings. Pillars held up the roof, ancient paint flaking from their smoothly carved stones. Nooks were carved into the walls and shelves filled the space between them, all rammed full of documents. There were rolls of parchment and papyrus, huge books bound in embossed leather, even heaps of tablets in baked clay and carved stone.

This first chamber was clearly a receiving room. There were no documents here, just a pair of tables. Blaze-Simms scurried over to the nearest shelf, pulled out a document, and hurried back to them. He set his lantern down on the table and, by its light, unrolled the document.

"Socrates," he whispered, as if afraid that speaking out loud might dispel the magic of the place. "It's a lost work of Socrates."

Isabelle took out another manuscript. With incredible care, she turned the pages.

"Look at these illustrations," she said. "They're beautiful."

Dirk set his bag down. It fell open, revealing the tools of a rougher occupation than fitted this place - rope, tent pegs, a stick of dynamite. He left it behind and went to wander through the stacks.

Dirk didn't know enough about ancient languages to read the documents, but just being in their presence was a marvel. He ran his fingers along the shelves, looking at the wonders they had uncovered. If even a small fraction of this was previously lost knowledge, the world was about to be awash in new learning. What machines might they find the designs for here? What potions? What works of art? What moments in history, long lost beneath the sands of time, were about to be revealed?

He would be there for all of it. Listening to the scholars of the Epiphany Club as they explained their findings. Reading the translations as they were made. Knowing that he had been a part of bringing this into the light. From a poor kid setting explosives down a mine to the man who made this possible. It was one hell of a journey.

At last, the excitement became overwhelming. He whooped with joy, the sound echoing around the chambers.

"Is that any way to behave in a library?" Isabelle asked.

He turned to see her beside him, smiling mischievously. He was so thrilled he didn't even feel embarrassed at what he had done.

"Seems like the best way to behave," he said, grinning.

She took his hand and led him deeper into the stacks. In the far wall, he saw another doorway and another flight of stairs leading upward. Another way out of this place.

"Listen, Dirk." Isabelle's expression grew serious. "This is it. The end. The adventure is almost over. We'll find a way to take all of this home, and then... Then it's on to the next quest."

"I guess," Dirk said, not sure what she was getting at.

"When that happens, I would like you to come with me." Isabelle looked up into his eyes. "I can't promise what that life will be like, where I'll be going, what I'll be doing. But if you're willing, I would like you there with me."

"You're asking me to give up on the life I have," Dirk said. "On the Club, on my old friends, on my place in England."

He didn't know why he said it like that. He didn't know what he felt. But he knew the worry flickering in Isabelle's eyes, and he wished that his words hadn't put it there.

"I am," she said. "And I'll understand if you say no. But I would hate myself if I didn't ask."

Before Dirk could answer, angry voices echoed around the room. People shouting at each other in English and French.

Dirk and Isabelle ran back between the shelves of ancient documents. When they reached the entrance chamber, it was more crowded than before. Braithwaite was there. Cluny too, and all their followers. They were bruised and dirty, their clothing torn, and blood trickled from Cluny's split lip.

They still held their sticks. Now they had guns out as well.

"Hands up," Braithwaite said. "All of you."

Dirk, Isabelle, Blaze-Simms, and Noriko all did as they were told. Carefully, Dirk moved over to stand beside the table where he'd set down his bag. He didn't want to do anything that might alarm the battered agents, especially not with them looking so angry and aggrieved.

"I will not be made a fool by a bunch of bloody amateurs," Braithwaite snarled. "Kicking off a fight just so you could get past us. Bloody hilarious. But the games stop here."

"We will be taking the documents," Cluny said, her gesture taking in the assembled agents of the two countries. "Their distribution can be decided by responsible people, politicians and diplomats, not some band of wandering scholars."

"All this knowledge could be dangerous," Braithwaite said. "We need to make sure it's in safe hands."

"By safe hands, you mean not shared with ordinary folks?" Dirk asked, his temper rising.

"Depends what we find," Braithwaite said. "But if need be, aye lad, that's the idea."

Dirk leaned forward, planting his fists on the table. In doing so, he knocked the bag. Something rolled out.

"That ain't fair," he said. "We came all this way to share this knowledge with the world. We did all the hard work. You can't just come in and steal it."

"That is exactly what we can do," Cluny said, turning her gun to point directly at Dirk. "If you don't like it, maybe we'll leave you here. Dead adventurers won't cause the problems dead diplomats would."

"Honestly, George," Isabelle said, shaking her head. "Is this really the way you want this to end? With threats and theft?"

"Let's not pretend you're above that," Braithwaite replied. "I've seen how you lot work."

Dirk had to admit, the man had a point. They'd used violence and deception when they'd needed to, but that had been a means to a noble end.

Hadn't it?

"I thought we were on the same side!" Blaze-Simms said.

"We could have been," Braithwaite said. "But it's a bit bloody late now."

With everyone's attention away from him, Dirk took hold of the object that had rolled out of the bag. He touched the end to a lantern sitting on the table.

The fuse on the dynamite hissed and started to burn down.

Everyone stared at him. Even Noriko looked shocked.

"Enough," Dirk said. "Seems to me that no-one can be trusted with what we've found here. Any country gets hold of some new trick, they'll use it to dominate others, like you do here in Egypt. If the Club gets hold of it, it's going to the British anyway. So." He held up the dynamite, its fuse getting shorter by the second, and pulled out his revolver. "Unless you're sure you can get this off me before it blows, you'd better get running."

There were only two sounds in the silence that followed. The hissing of the fuse as it burned down and the click as Dirk drew back the hammer on his pistol.

Cluny was the first to go, her minions scampering after her. Braithwaite followed, his heavy footsteps like thunder on the stairs, the other British agents a step ahead of him.

"You can put it out now," Blaze-Simms said, smiling at Dirk.

"No," Dirk said. "I meant it. And I know where to put this to bring the whole place down."

He tossed the dynamite, along with two more sticks he'd pulled from the bag, to a spot at the base of one of the pillars. His friends stared at him in horror.

"Now go," he said.

Blaze-Simms grabbed his Socrates document and raced up the stairs. Isabelle followed, then Noriko. Dirk brought up the rear, desperately hoping that he'd timed the fuse right.

As he reached the top of the stairs, there was roar from behind him. A blast of hot air flung him from his feet and out the door of the Great Library.

Behind him, there was a crash of falling stone.

He stumbled out into the daylight.

"What have you done?" George Braithwaite yelled, grabbing him by the collar.

"What had to be done," Dirk replied.

Braithwaite swung a punch at Dirk, but Noriko caught the fist before it landed. With a flick of the wrist, she flung the Yorkshireman to the ground.

"It is over," she said, drawing her katana. Her eyes gleamed as deadly as the cold steel. "Go."

The agents, French and British alike, mounted their camels and galloped off out of the valley. As they went, Dirk walked over to Blaze-Simms, who sat in the dirt, his new manuscript spread out in front of him, notebook and pencil in hand.

"Sorry," Dirk said, laying a hand on his friend's shoulder.

"Hm?" Blaze-Simms looked up. "Oh, yes, bad form old chap, destroying the Library like that." A strange expression crossed his face. "It's not what I would have done, but I do understand. And, well..." He gestured at the manuscript with a grin. "I have this."

It was more than Dirk could ever have expected. A burden seemed to lift from off of his shoulders.

He walked over to where Isabelle and Noriko stood by the camels. Noriko's expression was back to its usual careful blank. Isabelle looked stunned.

"How could you?" she asked. "There would have been another way. We could have kept those documents somehow."

Dirk glanced back at Blaze-Simms. The Englishman was lost to the world, immersed in reading his discovery.

"Funny thing about working with explosives," Dirk said quietly. "You don't just learn what will destroy a place. You learn what won't. Where to put your dynamite to bring the whole roof down. Where to put it if you just want to, say, close up one entrance."

Isabelle's eyes widened.

"You didn't destroy it all?" she asked.

"Nope."

"How will we get back in?"

"See the dust falling from that ledge up there?" Dirk said, nodding to a point on the side of the valley. "That wasn't happening before. That'll be where the other staircase comes out."

"Won't the British and French come back to see what they can retrieve?" Isabelle asked.

"Then your network of learned ladies had better act fast," Dirk said. "I promised you they'd get the books and I ain't going back on that. Out of everyone we've met on this crazy journey, you're just about the only ones I trust."

"Could you help, Noriko?" Isabelle asked. "We'll need to send some quick discreet messages, then help people find this place. I can't think of anyone better for the task."

"Of course," Noriko said. "Once we are done, I will return the stone stolen from my people. And then, if your organisation has space for one more learned lady, perhaps I might..."

"Of course!" Isabelle exclaimed. "Why, you're practically one of us already."

Noriko almost smiled. Then she nodded up the valley. "What about Timothy?"

They watched as Blaze-Simms excitedly pored over his manuscript.

"He'll be fine," Dirk said, and he too smiled.

#

"What a terrible shame," Professor Barrow said as Dirk and Blaze-Simms reached the end of their story. The elderly academic smiled a benevolent smile even as he shook his head. "So much learning lost."

They sat by the fire in the library of the Epiphany Club's Manchester headquarters, Dirk drinking coffee, the other two sipping at cups of tea.

"I did what seemed right at the time," Dirk said.

"I understand," Barrow said. "But it's not really the behaviour we expect of a member of the Club. Our goal is to increase human learning, not destroy it."

His tone wasn't harsh, but it held a stern finality. It saddened Dirk to know that he'd lost the professor's good opinion.

"I understand," Dirk said. "Reckon I'll resign my membership before you boot me out."

"We'll be sorry to lose such a valuable member," Barrow said. "But I think that's for the best." He turned to Blaze-Simms. "I have another opportunity for you, Sir Timothy. Something in Russia. I'll let the two of you say your good-byes before we get into details."

The professor set down his teacup, stood, and left the room without saying goodbye.

Dirk and Blaze-Simms sat in silence, both staring at their shoes. A clock ticked away on the mantelpiece while Dirk mustered the nerve to speak.

"So this is it," Blaze-Simms said.

"This is it," Dirk agreed, those three tiny words bearing a weight of regret.

"I'm sorry that we won't get to work together any longer." Blaze-Simms's eyes were downcast, his expression mournful.

"Me too," Dirk said. Saying it was both a hurt and a relief. "It's been a hell of a lot of fun."

"Are you still mad at me about Braithwaite and all that business?"

"That's the past. Reckon I've done as much to hurt your feelings."

"But things seem... I don't know, it's just not the same."

Dirk stood. He held out his hand and Blaze-Simms shook it, looking up uncertainly from his seat.

"Times change," Dirk said. "And sure, things ain't the same between us any more. But that doesn't mean that we ain't still friends. At least, it doesn't mean that to me."

"Nor to me."

The Englishman leapt to his feet and wrapped his arms around Dirk.

"Goodbye, old chap," he said. "I'll miss you, you know."

"I'll miss you too, Tim." Dirk had never seen his friend act like this. Stunned as he was, he managed to hug him back, and in that moment some of the sorrow seemed to pass away. The world was changing, but that didn't mean it had ended. "See you on another adventure."

Epilogue: Mr McNair

"Mr McNair?" The desk clerk at the Hong Kong Imperial Hotel raised his voice to be heard around the lobby. "Is Mr McNair here?"

Dirk sat, newspaper in his lap, reading about events on the other side of the world. The nation of Germany was going from strength to strength, while in Egypt, the French and British were caught up in a diplomatic scuffle. Another article talked about lost art discovered beneath a Russian palace, and he wondered if that was Blaze-Simms's work. It seemed like the Club's style.

"Mr McNair?" the desk clerk called out again. "Do we have a Mr McNair?"

Dirk looked up with a start, suddenly remembering why that name was important.

"That's me," he called out.

The desk clerk hurried over.

"Telegram from America," he said, handing the note to Dirk.

At that moment, Isabelle appeared in the doorway of the hotel. Smiling brightly, she came to sit beside Dirk, while the clerk returned to his post.

"Hello, Mr McNair," she said, leaning over to give him a kiss.

"Hello, Mrs McNair," he replied, returning the favour.

"Are you sure you're alright with this?" she asked. "Becoming someone new."

"It was never my real name anyway," Dirk said. "As for becoming someone new, I've spent a lot of time digging up the past. Mine, yours, humanity's. I reckon it's time to look to the future."

"Good," Isabelle replied. "Because Noriko has a lead on some Chinese alchemical texts, and a man of your talents could be a huge help."

As they stood, Isabelle slid her arm through his. Dirk smiled. He hadn't found everything he'd set out for, but this treasure put all the old books in the world to shame.

"Lead the way," he said.

About the Author

Andrew Knighton lives in northern England, where the grey skies provide an excellent incentive to stay indoors and write. When not working as a freelance writer, he plays board games, builds Lego, and reads comic books. Maybe one of these days someone will force him to grow up, but it hasn't happened yet.

To receive free short stories and updates on Andrew's new releases, visit andrewknighton.com[1], where you can sign up for his mailing list.

If you enjoyed this book then please leave a review wherever you buy books online - it's just about the most helpful thing you can do for an author.

1. http://andrewknighton.com/

Also by Andrew Knighton

Epiphany Club

Guns and Guano

Suits and Sewers

Aristocrats and Artillery

Sieges and Silverware

Dead Men and Dynamite

Standalone

By Sword, Stave or Stylus

A Mosaic of Stars

Beasts Clothed in Beauty

Demons and the Deep

From a Foreign Shore

Honour Among Thieves

Lies We Will Tell Ourselves

Mud and Brass

Ocean Gods, Roman Blades

Riding the Mainspring

Silence on Second Street

Old Odd Ends
The Epiphany Club

Watch for more at andrewknighton.com.

About the Author

Andrew Knighton is a freelance writer and an author of science fiction, fantasy, and steampunk stories. He lives in Yorkshire with his cat, his computer, and a big pile of books.

Read more at andrewknighton.com.

Printed in Great Britain
by Amazon